Praise for Philip Reeve's novels:

"Big, brave, brilliant"
Guardian

"Phenomenal... Violent and romantic, action-packed
and contemplative, funny and frightening"
The Sunday Times

"A marvellous book, utterly captivating in its imaginative scope
and energy. The only flaw I can see is the difficulty of putting it
down between chapters"
Daily Telegraph

"Witty and thrilling, serious and sensitive, the
Mortal Engines quartet is one of the most daring and
imaginative adventures ever written"
Books for Keeps

"Reeve is a terrific writer"
The Times

"A masterpiece"
Sunday Telegraph

"Mind bogglingly well-imagined"
Independent

"If you've never read a Philip Reeve novel before, you're
in for a treat. His storytelling is accomplished and his
use of language most ingenious and irreverent"
Waterstone's Books Quarterly

"Philip Pullman fans will love Mortal Engines...
I didn't want it to end"
Daily Telegraph

"Intelligent, funny and wise"
Literary Review

PHILIP REEVE was born in Brighton in 1966. At school he became interested in illustration, Arthurian legend and making ultra-low-budget films on Super 8mm cine film. He pursued his enjoyment of writing, drawing, history and acting at VI Form College, and completed his education with a diploma at Cambridgeshire College of Arts and Technology. Three years as an art student having rendered him basically unemployable, he returned to Brighton, there to work in a small independent bookshop while pursuing various non-paying sidelines as writer/producer/director of low budget film and comedy projects in his spare time. He co-wrote a musical, *The Ministry of Biscuits*, but was eventually forced by lack of funds to track down some cartooning work and finally became a freelance illustrator in the early 1990s.

It was during this time that he began to write novels and his debut, *Mortal Engines*, was published in 2001. It won the Smarties Gold Award, the Blue Peter Book of the Year Award and the Blue Peter "Book I Couldn't Put Down" Award, a surprise which prompted him to say "Bloody Hell!" in front of millions of viewers. (Small wonder *he* never got a Blue Peter Badge.) Four sequels followed, the last of which, *A Darkling Plain*, won both the Guardian Children's Fiction Prize and the Los Angeles Times Book Award. There has also been a novel set in Dark Age Britain called *Here Lies Arthur*, which won the Carnegie Medal, and a stand-alone novel for younger readers called *No Such Thing As Dragons*. His latest novels, *Fever Crumb* and *A Web of Air*, return to the world of *Mortal Engines*.

Philip and his wife Sarah moved from Brighton to Devon in 1998, and now live on Dartmoor with their son Sam.

By Philip Reeve

Fever Crumb
A Web of Air
Mortal Engines
Predator's Gold
Infernal Devices
A Darkling Plain

Here Lies Arthur

No Such Thing As Dragons

Larklight
Starcross
Mothstorm

For Sarah
as always,

For my editors, Kirsten Stansfield
and Holly Skeet,
with thanks

And for
Sam Reeve, Tom Skeet and
Edward Stansfield,
one day.

INFERNAL DEVICES

PHILIP REEVE

■SCHOLASTIC

First published in the UK by Scholastic Children's Books
An imprint of Scholastic Ltd
Euston House, 24 Eversholt Street
London, NW1 1DB, UK
Registered office: Westfield Road, Southam, Warwickshire, CV47 0RA
SCHOLASTIC and associated logos are trademarks and/or registered
trademarks of Scholastic Inc.

First published by Scholastic Ltd, 2005
This edition published by Scholastic Ltd, 2010

ISBN 9781407117065

Printed by CPI Bookmarque Ltd, Croydon, Surrey
Papers used by Scholastic Children's Books are
made from wood grown in sustainable forests.

1 3 5 7 9 10 8 6 4 2

www.scholastic.co.uk/zone

CONTENTS

PART ONE

PART ONE

1
THE SLEEPER WAKES

At first there was nothing. Then came a spark; a sizzling sound that stirred frayed webs of dream and memory. And then, with a crackle, a roar, a blue-white rush of electricity was surging through him, bursting into the dry passages of his brain like the tide pouring back into a sea-cave. His body jerked so taut that for a moment he was balanced only on his heels and the back of his armoured skull. He screamed, and awoke to a sleet of static, and a falling feeling.

He remembered dying. He remembered a girl's scarred face gazing down at him as he lay in wet grass. She was someone important, someone he cared about more than any Stalker should care about anything, and there had been something he had wanted to tell her, but he couldn't. Now there was only the after-image of her ruined face.

What was her name? His mouth remembered.

"H. . ."

"It's alive!" said a voice.

"HES. . ."

"Again, please. Quickly."

"Charging. . ."

"HESTER. . ."

"Stand clear!"

And then another lash of electricity scoured away even those last strands of memory, and he knew only that he was the Stalker Shrike. One of his eyes started to work again. He saw vague shapes moving through an ice-storm of interference, and watched while they slowly congealed into human figures, torch-lit against a sky full of scurrying, moonlit clouds. It was raining steadily. Once-born, wearing goggles and uniforms and plastic capes, were gathering around his open grave. Some carried quartz-iodine lanterns; others tended machines with rows of glowing valves and gleaming dials. Cables from the machines trailed down into his body. He sensed that his steel skull-piece had been removed and that the top of his head was open, exposing the Stalker-brain nested inside.

"Mr Shrike? Can you hear me?"

A very young woman was looking down at him. He had a faint, tantalizing memory of a girl, and wondered if this might be her. But no: there had been something broken about the face in his dreams, and this face was perfect; an eastern face with high cheekbones and pale skin, the black eyes framed by heavy black spectacles. Her short hair had been dyed green. Beneath her transparent cape she wore a black uniform, with winged skulls embroidered in silver thread on the high, black collar.

She set a hand on the corroded metal of his chest and said, "Don't be afraid, Mr Shrike. I know this must be confusing for you. You've been dead for more than eighteen years."

"DEAD," he said.

The young woman smiled. Her teeth were white and crooked, slightly too big for her small mouth. "Maybe 'dormant' is a better word. Old Stalkers never really die, Mr Shrike. . ."

There was a rumbling sound, too rhythmic to be thunder. Pulses of orange light flickered on the clouds, throwing the crags that towered above Shrike's resting place into silhouette. Some of the soldiers looked up

4

nervously. One said, "Snout guns. They have broken through the marsh-forts. Their amphibious suburbs will be here within the hour."

The woman glanced over her shoulder and said, "Thank you, Captain," then turned her attention to Shrike again, her hands working quickly inside his skull. "You were badly damaged, and you shut down, but we are going to repair you. I am Doctor Oenone Zero of the Resurrection Corps."

"I DON'T REMEMBER ANYTHING," Shrike told her.

"Your memory was damaged," she replied. "I cannot restore it. I'm sorry."

Anger and a sort of panic rose in him. He felt that this woman had stolen something from him, although he no longer knew what it had been. He tried to bare his claws, but he could not move. He might as well have been just an eye, lying there on the wet earth.

"Don't worry," Dr Zero said. "Your past is not important. You will be working for the Green Storm now. You will soon have new memories."

In the sky behind her smiling face something began to explode in silent smears of red and yellow light. One of the soldiers shouted, "They're coming! General Naga's division is counter-attacking with Tumblers, but that won't hold them for long. . ."

Dr Zero nodded and scrambled up out of the grave, brushing mud from her hands. "We must move Mr Shrike out of here at once." She looked down at Shrike again, smiled. "Don't worry, Mr Shrike. An airship is waiting for us. We are taking you to the central Stalker Works at Batmunkh Tsaka. We shall soon have you up and about again. . ."

She stepped aside to let two bulky figures through.

They were Stalkers; their armour stencilled with a green lightning-bolt symbol which Shrike didn't recognize. They had blank steel faces like the blades of shovels, featureless except for narrow eye-slits, which shone green as they heaved Shrike out of the earth and laid him on a stretcher. The men with the machines hurried alongside as the silent Stalkers carried him down a track towards a fortified air-caravanserai where ship after ship was lifting into the wet sky. Dr Zero ran ahead, shouting, "Quickly! Quickly! Be careful! He's an antique."

The path grew steeper, and Shrike understood the reason for her haste and her men's uneasiness. Through gaps in the crags he glimpsed a great body of water glittering under the steady flashes of gunfire. Upon the water, and far off across it on the flat, dark land, giant shapes were moving. By the light of the blazing airships which speckled the sky above them, and the pale, slow-falling glare of parachute-flares, he could see their armoured tracks, their vast jaws and tier upon tier of iron-clad forts and gun-emplacements.

Traction Cities. An army of them, grinding their way across the marshes. The sight of them stirred faint memories in Shrike. He remembered cities like that. At least, he remembered the idea of them. Whether he had ever been aboard one, and what he had done there, he did not recall.

As his rescuers hurried him towards the waiting airship he saw for just an instant a girl's broken face look up trustingly at him, awaiting something he had promised her.

But who she was, and what her face was doing in his mind, he no longer knew.

2

AT ANCHORAGE-IN-VINELAND

Several months later, and half a world away, Wren Natsworthy lay in bed and watched a sliver of moonlight move slowly across the ceiling of her room. It was past midnight, and she could hear nothing but the sounds of her own body and the soft, occasional creaks as the old house settled. She doubted that there was anywhere in the world as quiet as the place she lived in: Anchorage-in-Vineland, a derelict ice city dug into the rocky southern shore of an unknown island, on a lost lake, in a forgotten corner of the Dead Continent.

But quiet as it was, she could not sleep. She turned on her side and tried to get comfortable, the hot sheets tangling round her. She had had another row with Mum at supper time. It had been one of those rows which started with a tiny seed of disagreement (about Wren wanting to go out with Tildy Smew and the Sastrugi boys instead of washing up), and grew quickly into a terrible battle, with tears and accusations, and age-old grudges being dredged up and lobbed about the house like hand-grenades, while poor Dad stood on the sidelines saying helplessly, "Wren, calm down," and "Hester, please!"

Wren had lost in the end, of course. She had done the washing up, and stomped up to bed as loudly as she could. Ever since, her brain had been hard at work, coming up with hurtful comments which she wished she had made earlier. Mum didn't have any idea what it was like being fifteen. Mum was so ugly that she probably never had any friends when she was a girl, and certainly not friends like Nate Sastrugi, whom all the girls in Anchorage fancied, and who had told Tildy that he really liked Wren. Probably no boy had *ever* liked Mum, except for Dad, of course – and what Dad saw in her was one of The Great Unsolved Mysteries of Vineland, in Wren's opinion.

She rolled over again and tried to stop thinking about it, then gave up and scrambled out of bed. Maybe a walk would clear her head. And if her parents woke and found her gone, and worried that she had drowned herself or run away, well, that would teach Mum not to treat her like a child, wouldn't it? She pulled on her clothes, her socks and boots, and crept downstairs through the breathing silence of the house.

Mum and Dad had chosen this house for themselves sixteen years before, when Anchorage had only just crawled ashore and Wren was nothing but a little curl of flesh adrift in Mum's womb. It was family history; a bedtime story Wren remembered from when she was small. Freya Rasmussen had told Mum and Dad that they might take their pick of the empty houses in the upper city. They had chosen this one, a merchant's villa on a street called Dog Star Court, overlooking the airharbour. A good house, snug and well-built, with tiled floors and fat ceramic heating ducts, walls panelled in wood and bronze. Over the years Mum and Dad had filled it with furniture they found among the other empty houses round about, and decorated it with pictures and hangings, with driftwood dragged up from the shore, and with some of the antiques Dad unearthed on his expeditions into the Dead Hills.

Wren padded across the hall to take down her coat from the rack by the front door, and did not spare a glance or a thought for the prints on the walls or the precious bits of ancient food-processors and telephones in the glass-fronted display case. She had grown up with all this stuff, and it bored her. This past year the whole house had begun to feel too small, as if she had outgrown it. The familiar smells of dust and wood-polish and Dad's books were comforting, but somehow stifling too. She was fifteen years old and her life pinched her like an ill-fitting shoe.

She closed the door behind her as quietly as she could, and hurried along Dog Star Court. Mist hung like smoke over the Dead Hills, and Wren's breath came out as mist, too. It was only early September, but she could already smell winter in the night air.

The moon was low, but the stars were bright and overhead the aurora was shimmering. At the heart of the city the rusty spires of the Winter Palace towered black against the glowing sky, shaggy with ivy. The Winter Palace had been home to Anchorage's rulers once, but the only person who lived there now was Miss Freya, who had been the city's last margravine, and was now its schoolteacher. On every winter weekday since her fifth birthday Wren had gone to the schoolroom on the ground floor of the palace to listen to Miss Freya explaining about geography and logarithms and Municipal Darwinism and a lot of other things that would probably never be any use to her at all. It had bored her at the time, but now that she was fifteen, and too old for school, she missed it horribly. She would never sit in the dear old schoolroom again, unless she did as Miss Freya had asked and went back to help teach the younger children.

Miss Freya had made that offer weeks ago, and she would need an answer soon, for once the harvests were in the children of Anchorage would be going back to their lessons. But Wren didn't know if she wanted to be Miss Freya's assistant or not. She didn't even want to think about it. Not tonight.

At the end of Dog Star Court a stairway led down through the deckplates into the engine district. As Wren went clanging down the stairs a summery smell came up at her, and she heard flakes of rust dislodged by her boots falling among the heaped hay below. Once this part of the city would have been full of life and noise as Anchorage's engines sent it skating over the ice at the top of the world in search of trade. But the city's travels had ended before Wren was born, and the engine districts had been turned into stores for hay and root vegetables, and winter quarters for the cattle. Faint shafts of moonlight, slanting through skylights and holes in the deckplates overhead, showed her the bales stacked up between the empty fuel tanks.

When Wren was younger these abandoned levels had been her playground, and she still liked to walk here when she was feeling sad or bored, imagining what fun it must have been to live aboard a city that moved. The grown-ups were always talking about the bad old days, and how frightening it had been to live in constant danger of being swallowed up by some larger, faster city, but Wren would have loved to see the towering Traction Cities, or to fly from one to another aboard an airship, as Mum and Dad had done before she was born. Dad kept a photograph on his desk that showed them standing on a docking pan aboard a city called San Juan De Los Motores, in front of their pretty little red airship *Jenny Haniver*, but they never talked about the adventures they must have had. All she knew was that they had ended up landing on Anchorage, where the villainous Professor

Pennyroyal had stolen the ship from them, and after that they had settled down, content to play their roles in the cosy, dozy life of Vineland.

Just my luck, thought Wren, breathing in the warm, flowery scent of the baled hay. She would have liked to be an air-trader's daughter. It sounded a glamorous sort of life, and much more interesting than the one she had, stuck on this lonely island, among people whose idea of excitement was a rowing-boat race or a good apple harvest.

A door closed somewhere in the darkness ahead, making her jump. She'd grown so used to the quiet and her own company that the idea of someone else moving around down here was almost frightening. Then she remembered where she was. Busy with her thoughts, she'd walked all the way to the heart of the district, where Caul, Anchorage's engineer, lived alone in an old shed between two tier supports. He was the only inhabitant of Anchorage's lower levels, since nobody else would choose to live down here among the rust and shadows when there were pretty mansions standing empty in the sunlight up above. But Caul was an eccentric. He didn't like sunlight, having been brought up in the undersea thief-hole of Grimsby, and he didn't like company either. He'd been friendly once with old Mr Scabious, the city's former engineer, but since the old man died he had kept himself to himself down here in the depths.

So why would he be wandering about in the engine district at this hour? Intrigued, Wren crept up a ladder on to one of the overhead walkways, from where she had a good view across the old engine pits to Caul's shack. Caul was standing outside the door. He had an electric lantern, and he had raised it up so that he could study a scrap of paper which he held in his other hand. After a moment he pocketed the paper and set off towards the city's edge.

Wren scrambled back down the ladder and started following the light. She felt quite excited. When she was younger, working her way steadily through the small stock of children's books in the margravine's library, her favourite stories had been the ones about plucky school-girl detectives who were forever foiling smugglers and unmasking Anti-Tractionist spy rings. She had always regretted that were no criminals to detect in Vineland. But hadn't Caul been a burglar once? Maybe he was reverting to his old ways!

Except, of course, that there was no point stealing any-thing in Anchorage, where everyone took what they liked from the hundreds of abandoned shops and houses. As she picked her way through the heaps of half-dismantled machinery behind Caul's shack she tried to think of a more likely explanation for his night-time wanderings. Maybe he couldn't sleep, like her. Maybe he was worried about something. Wren's friend Tildy had told her that years and years ago, way back when Anchorage first came to Vineland, Caul had been in love with Miss Freya, and Miss Freya had been in love with Caul, too, but noth-ing had come of it because Caul had been so strange, even in those days. Maybe he wandered the streets of the engine district every night, yearning for his lost love? Or maybe he was in love with someone else, and was going to meet her for a moonlit tryst out on the city's edge?

Pleased by the idea that she would have something really juicy to tell Tildy in the morning, Wren quick-ened her pace.

But when he reached the city's edge Caul did not stop, just hurried down a stairway which led on to the bare earth and started up the hill, sweeping the lantern-beam ahead of him. Wren waited a moment, then followed, jumping down into the springy heather and creeping after him up the track which led to the humming dry-stone turbine house of old Mr Scabious's hydro-electricity plant. Caul did not stop there either, but kept going, climbing between the apple orchards and across the high pasture, into the woods.

At the top of the island, where the pines filled the air with the smell of resin, and crags poked up through the thin turf like the spines on a dragon's back, Caul stopped and turned his lantern off and looked around. Fifty feet behind him, Wren crouched among the criss-cross shadows. A faint wind stirred her hair, and overhead the trees moved their small hands against the sky.

Caul looked down at the sleeping city nestled in the curve of the island's southern shore. Then he turned his back on it, raised his lantern, and switched it on and off, three times. *He's gone mad*, thought Wren, and then, *No – he's signalling to someone, just like the wicked headmaster in* Milly Crisp and the Twelfth Tier Mystery*!*

And sure enough, down among the empty, rocky bays of the north shore, another light flashed back an answer.

Caul moved on, and Wren began to follow him again, dropping down the steep northern flank of the island, out of sight of the city. Maybe he and Miss Freya had got back together, and were too afraid of gossip to let anyone know? It was a romantic thought, and it made Wren smile to herself as she tracked Caul down the last precipitous stretch of sheep-track, through a stand of birch trees and out on to a beach between two headlands.

Miss Freya was not waiting for him. But someone was. A man was standing at the water's edge, watching as Caul went crunching towards him down the shingle. Even from a distance, in the faint light of the aurora, Wren could tell that he was someone she had never seen before.

At first she could not believe it. There *were* no strangers in Vineland. The only people here were those who had come here aboard Anchorage, or been born here since, and Wren knew all of them. But the man on the shore was a stranger to her, and his voice when he spoke was a voice she had never heard.

"Caul, my old shipmate! Good to see you again."

"Gargle," said Caul, sounding uneasy, and not taking the hand which the stranger held out for him to shake.

They said more, but Wren was too busy wondering about the newcomer to listen. Who could he be? How had he come here? What did he want?

When the answer hit her, it was one she didn't like. *Lost Boys.* That's what they'd been called, the gang Caul had been part of, who had burgled Anchorage back in its ice-faring days with their strange, spidery machines. Caul had left them to come with Miss Freya and Mr Scabious. Or had he? Had he been secretly in contact with the Lost Boys all these years, waiting until the city was settled and prosperous before he called them in to rob it again?

But the stranger on the beach wasn't a boy. He was a grown man, with long dark hair. He wore high boots, like a pirate in a storybook, and a coat that came down to his knees. He flicked the skirts of the coat back and

14

stuck his thumbs through his belt, and Wren saw a gun in a holster at his side.

She knew that she was out of her depth. She wanted to run home and tell Mum and Dad of the danger. But the two men had wandered closer to her, and if she ran she would be seen. She wriggled deeper into the low gorse-bushes behind the beach, timing each movement to coincide with the rasp of the little waves breaking on the shingle.

The man called Gargle was speaking, sounding as if he were making some kind of joke, but Caul suddenly cut him off. "What have you come here for, Gargle? I thought I'd seen the last of Lost Boys. It was a bit of a shock to find your message under my door. How long have you been creeping around Anchorage?"

"Since yesterday," said Gargle. "We just dropped by to say hello, and see how you were doing, friendly-like."

"Then why not show yourselves? Why not come and talk to me in daylight? Why leave messages and drag me out here in the middle of the night?"

"Honest, Caul, I wanted to. I'd planned to land my limpet on the mooring beach, all open and above-board, but I sent a few crab-cams in first, of course, just to be sure. Good thing I did, ain't it? What's happened, Caul? I thought you were going to be a big man in this place! Look at you; oily overalls and raggedy hair and a week's worth of beard. Is the Mad Tramp look big in Anchorage this season? I thought you were going to marry their margravine, that Freya What's-her-name."

"Rasmussen," said Caul unhappily. He turned away from the other man. "I thought so too. It didn't work out, Gargle. It's complicated. It's not like you think it's going to be when you just watch it through the crab-cameras. I never really fitted in here."

"I should have thought the Drys would welcome you with open arms," said Gargle, sounding shocked. "After you brung them that map and everything."

Caul shrugged. "They were all kind enough. I just don't fit. I don't know how to talk to them, and talking's important to the Drys. When Mr Scabious was alive it was all right. We worked together, and we didn't need to talk, we had the work instead of words. But now he's gone. . . What about you, anyway? And what about Uncle? How is Uncle?"

"Like you care!"

"I do. I think of him often. Is he –?"

"The old man's still there, Caul," said Gargle.

"Last time I spoke to you, you had plans to get rid of him, take over. . ."

"And I have taken over," said Gargle, with a grin that Wren saw as a white blur in the dark. "Uncle's not as sharp as he was. He never really got over that business at Rogues' Roost. So many of his best boys lost, and all his fault. It nearly did him in, that. He relies on me for nearly everything nowadays. The boys look up to me."

"I bet they do," said Caul, and there was some meaning in his words that Wren couldn't understand, as if they were picking up a conversation that they'd started long ago, before she was even born.

"You said you need my help," said Caul.

"Just thought I'd ask," said Gargle. "For old time's sake."

"What's the plan?"

"There's no plan, exactly." Gargle sounded hurt. "Caul, I didn't come here on a burgling mission. I don't

16

want to rob your nice Dry friends. I'm just after one thing, one little thing, a particular small thing that no one will miss. I've looked with the crab-cams, I've sent my best burglar in, but we can't see it. So I thought, 'What we need is a man on the inside.' And here you are. I told my crew, we can rely on Caul."

"Well, you were wrong," said Caul. His voice was trembly. "I may not fit in here, but I'm not a Lost Boy either. Not any more. I'm not going to help you rob Freya. I want you gone. I won't tell anyone you were here, but I'll be keeping my eyes and ears open. If I hear a crab-cam nosing about, or see that something's gone missing, I'll let the Drys know all about you. I'll make sure they're waiting for you next time you come sneaking into Anchorage."

He turned and strode up the beach, crashing through the gorse barely a foot from the place where Wren was hiding. She heard him fall and curse as he started up the hill, and then the sounds of his going growing fainter and fainter as he climbed. "*Caul!*" called Gargle, but not too loud, a sort of whispering cry, with hurt in it, and disappointment. "*Caul!*" Then he gave up and stood still and pensive, running a hand through his hair.

Wren began to move, very carefully and quietly, getting ready for the moment when he would turn his back on her and she could creep away between the trees. But Gargle did not turn. Instead he raised his head and looked straight at her hiding place and said, "My eyes and ears are sharper than old Caul's, my friend. You can come out now."

17

3
THE LIMPET *AUTOLYCUS*

Wren stood up and turned and started running all in the same lurching, panicked movement, but before she had taken three steps a second stranger came out of the dark to her left and seized hold of her, swinging her round, dumping her on the ground. "Caul!" she started to shout, but a cold hand went across her mouth. Her captor looked down at her – another pale face, half hidden by black swags of hair – and the man from the beach came running up. A torch came on, a thin, blue wash of light that made Wren blink.

"Gently," said the man called Gargle. "Gently now. It's a woman. A young woman. I thought as much." He held the torch away so that Wren could see him. She had expected someone Caul's age, but Gargle was younger. He was smiling. "What's your name, young woman?"

"Wr-Wren," Wren managed to stammer out. "Wr-Wren N-N-N-N-Natsworthy." And when Gargle had managed to fillet out all those extra Ns his smile grew broader and warmer.

"Natsworthy? Not Tom Natsworthy's child?"

"You know Dad?" asked Wren. In her confusion, she wondered if her father had also been coming down for secret meetings with the Lost Boys in the coves of North Shore, but of course Gargle was talking about the old days, before she was born.

"I remember him well," said Gargle. "He was our guest for a bit aboard the *Screw Worm*. He's a good man. Your mother would be his girl, the scar-faced one? What was she called. . . ? Yes, Hester Shaw. I always thought that spoke well of Tom Natsworthy, that he could love someone like her. Appearances don't matter to him. He looks deeper. That's rare among the Drys."

"What are we going to do with her, Gar?" asked the stranger who had caught Wren, in an odd, soft voice. "Is she fishfood?"

"Let's bring her aboard," said Gargle. "I'd like to get to know Tom Natsworthy's daughter."

Wren, who had been calming down, grew panicky again. "I have to go home!" she squeaked, trying to edge away, but Gargle slipped his arm through hers.

"Just come aboard a moment," he said, smiling pleasantly. "I'd like to talk. Explain why I'm lurking in your lake like a thief. Well, I *am* a thief, of course, but I think you should hear my side of the story before you make your decision."

"What decision?" asked Wren.

"The decision about whether or not you tell your parents and your friends what you've seen here tonight."

Wren thought she trusted him, but she wasn't sure. She had never had to think about trusting people before. Confused by Gargle's smile, she looked past him down the beach. The water between the headlands was shining blue. She thought at first that it was just the after-image of the torch on her eyes, but then the blue grew brighter, and brighter still, and she saw that it was a light, shining up through the water from below. Something huge broke the surface about thirty feet off shore.

Behind Caul's shack in the engine district, the limpet which had brought him to Anchorage lay rusting. It was called the *Screw Worm*, and Wren and her friends had often played hide-and-seek between its crook-kneed legs when they were children. She had always thought it a comical sort of thing, with its big flat feet and its windows at the front like boggly eyes. She had never imagined how smoothly a limpet would move, how sleek its curved hull would look, moonlight sliding off it with the water as it waded to the beach.

This limpet was smaller than the *Screw Worm*, and its body was flatter, more like a tick than a spider. Wren thought it was painted with jagged camouflage patterns, but it was hard to be sure in the moonlight. Through the bulging windows she could see a small boy working the controls, his face distorted by the water draining down the glass. He brought the machine to a stop at the water's edge and a ramp came down out of its belly with a shush of hydraulics and grated against the shingle there.

"The limpet *Autolycus*," said Gargle, gesturing for Wren to go aboard. "Pride of the Lost Boy fleet. Come aboard, please. Please. I promise we won't submerge until we've put you ashore."

"What if more Drys come?" asked the other Lost Boy, who wasn't a boy, Wren noticed, but a girl, pretty and sullen-looking. "What if Caul raises the alarm?"

"Caul gave us his promise," said Gargle. "That's good enough for me."

The girl glared at Wren, not convinced. The short black jerkin that she wore hung open and there was a gun stuffed through her belt. *I don't have a choice,* thought Wren. *I'll have to trust Gargle.* And once she had decided that, it was an easy thing to walk up the ramp into the cold, blue belly of the limpet. After all, if Gargle wanted to murder her, he could have done it just as easily on the beach.

She was taken aft into what she guessed was Gargle's private cabin, where hangings hid the dull steel walls, and there were books and trinkets laid about. A joss-stick smouldered, masking the mildew-and-metal smell of the limpet with another smell which made Wren think of sophisticated people and far-off places. She sat down in a chair while Gargle settled himself on the bunk. The girl waited at the bulkhead door, still glaring. The little boy Wren had seen through the window stood behind her, watching Wren with wide, astonished eyes until Gargle said, "Back to your post, Fishcake."

"But. . ."

"Now!"

The boy scampered off. Gargle gave Wren a wry smile. "I'm sorry about that. Fishcake's a newbie, ten years old and fresh from the Burglarium. He's never seen a Dry before, except on the crab-cam screens. And you such a pretty one, too."

Wren blushed and looked down at the floor, where her boots were leaking muddy water over Gargle's rich Stamboul rugs. The "Burglarium" was where the Lost Boys were trained, she remembered. They were kidnapped from the underdecks of raft-towns when they were too young to even know it, and taken down to the sunken city of Grimsby, and trained in all the arts of thieving. And "crab-cams" were the robot cameras they used to spy on their victims. Miss Freya had made her pupils do a whole project on the Lost Boys. At the time Wren had thought it a pointless thing to have to learn about.

Gargle turned to the girl at the door. "Remora, our guest looks chilly. Fetch her some hot chocolate, won't you?"

"I didn't know there were any Lost Girls," said Wren, when the girl had gone.

"A lot's changed in Grimsby since Caul was last there," Gargle replied. "Just between the two of us, Wren, I pretty much run the old place now. I managed to get rid of a lot of the rough, bullying boys who surrounded Uncle, and I sort of persuaded him to start bringing girls down as well as boys. It was doing us no good living without girls. They're a civilizing influence."

Wren looked towards the door. She could see the girl called Remora clattering pans about in some sort of kitchen. She didn't look to Wren like a civilizing influence. "So is she your wife?" she asked, and then, not wanting to seem too prim, "Or your girlfriend or something?"

In the kitchen, Remora looked up sharply. Gargle said, "'Mora? No! The fact is, some of the girls have turned out to be better thieves than the boys. Remora's one of the best burglars we've got. Just as young Fishcake is the best mechanic, for all his tender years. I wanted only the best with me on this mission, see, Wren. There's something in Anchorage that I need very badly. I saw it all those years ago, when I was here with Caul aboard the *Screw Worm*, but I didn't steal it then because I didn't think it was of any use."

"What is it?" asked Wren.

Gargle did not answer her at once, but waited, studying her face, as if he wanted to be quite sure that she could be trusted with what he was about to tell her. Wren liked that. He was not treating her as a child, the way most people still did. "A young woman" he'd called her, and that was how he was speaking to her.

"I hate this," he said at last, leaning towards her, looking intently into her eyes. "You have to believe me. I hate coming in secret like this. I would rather be open;

22

steer the *Autolycus* into your harbour and say, 'Here we are, your friends from Grimsby, come to ask your help.' If Caul had prospered here, the way I hoped he would, that might have been possible. But as it is, who'd trust us? We're Lost Boys. Burglars. They'd never believe that all we want from you is one book, one single book from your margravine's library."

Remora came back into the cabin and handed Wren a tin mug, full of hot, delicious chocolate. "Thank you," said Wren, glad of the distraction, because she didn't want Gargle to see how shocked she was by what he had just said. Miss Freya's library was one of Wren's favourite places; a treasure-cave filled with thousands and thousands of wonderful old books. It had been on the upper floors of the Winter Palace once, but nobody lived on those floors now and Miss Freya had said it was a waste heating them just for the books' sake, so the library had been moved downstairs. . .

"That's why you can't find what you want!" she said suddenly. "The books have all been rearranged since you were last here!"

Gargle nodded, smiling at her admiringly. "Quite right," he said. "It could take our crab-cams weeks to find the right one, and we don't have weeks to waste. So I was wondering, Miss Natsworthy, if you'd help us?"

Wren had just taken a slurp of chocolate. Anchorage's supplies of chocolate had run out years ago, and she had forgotten how good it tasted, but when Gargle asked for her help she almost choked on it. "Me?" she spluttered. "I'm not a burglar. . ."

"I wouldn't ask you to become one," said Gargle. "But your father's a clever man. Friendly with the margravine, from what I remember. I bet you could find out from him where the book we want might be. Just find it, and tell me, and I'll send Remora in to do the rest. It's called the Tin Book."

Wren had been about to refuse, but the fact that she had never heard of the book he named made her hesitate. She'd been expecting him to ask about one of Anchorage's treasures; the great, illuminated *Acts of the Ice Gods*, or Wormwold's *Historia Anchoragia*. She said, "Who on earth would want a whole book about tin?"

Gargle laughed, as if she'd made a joke that he liked. "It's not *about* tin," he said. "That's what it's made of. Sheets of metal."

Wren shook her head. She'd never seen anything like that. "Why do you want it?" she asked.

"Because we're burglars, and I've learned that it's valuable," said Gargle.

"It must be! To come all this way. . ."

"There are people who collect such things; old books and things. We can trade it for stuff we need." Gargle hesitated, still watching her, and then said earnestly, "Please, Wren, just ask your father. Always nosing about in museums and libraries, he was, when I knew him. He might know where the Tin Book is."

Wren thought about it as she drank the rest of the chocolate. If he had been asking her for the illuminated *Acts*, or for some treasured classic, she would have said no at once. But a book made of metal, one that she'd never even heard of. . . It couldn't be very important, could it? It would probably never be missed. And Gargle seemed to want it very badly.

"I'll ask," she said doubtfully.

"Thank you!" Gargle took her hands in his. His hands were warm, and his eyes were rather lovely. Wren thought how nice it would be to tell Tildy that she'd spent the small hours of the night drinking cocoa in the cabin of a dashing underwater pirate, and then remembered that she would never be able to tell Tildy or anybody else about Gargle and the *Autolycus*. That made it even nicer somehow. She had never had a proper secret before.

"I'll meet you up in the trees on the hilltop around six tomorrow," Gargle said. "Is that all right? You can get away?"

"That's supper time. I'd be missed. My mum. . ."

"Noon, then. Noon, or just after."

"All right. . ."

"And for now – would you like Remora to walk you home?"

"I'll find my way," said Wren. "I often walk about in the dark."

"We'll make a Lost Girl of you yet," said Gargle, and laughed to show her he was only joking. He stood up, and she stood up too, and they moved through the limpet's passageways towards the exit ramp, the newbie Fishcake peeking out at them from the control cabin. Outside, the night was cold and the moon shone and the water was lapping against the shore as if nothing had happened. Wren waved and said goodbye and waved again and then walked quickly up the beach and through the trees.

Gargle watched until she was out of sight. The girl Remora came and stood beside him, and slipped her hand into his. "You trust her?" she asked.

"Don't know. Maybe. It's worth a try. We haven't time to hang about here searching for the thing ourselves, and we can't do much with the crab-cams in this dump.

These Drys remember us. They'll soon put two and two together if they start hearing the patter of tiny magnetic feet inside their air-ducts. But don't worry – I'll tell Fishcake to set a couple on watch around Wren's house, so we'll know if she squeals to her people about us."

"And what if she does?"

"Then we'll kill them all," said Gargle. "And I'll let you do Wren yourself, with your pretty little knife." And he kissed her, and they turned and went back aboard.

But Wren, knowing none of this, walked home with a giddy tumble of thoughts inside her head, half guilt, half pleasure, feeling as if she'd grown up more in the past few hours than in all the fifteen years that had gone before.

4

THE LEGEND OF THE TIN BOOK

The next day dawned fair, the sky above the lake harebell blue, the water clear as glass, each of the islands of Vineland sitting neat and still upon its own reflection. Wren, exhausted by her adventures in the night, slept late, but outside her window, Anchorage was waking up. Woodsmoke rose from the chimneys of the city's thirty inhabited houses, and fishermen called out good morning to each other as they made their way down the stairways to the mooring beach.

On the north side of the lake rose a brindled mountain, far higher than the Dead Hills to the south. Its lower slopes were green with scrub and stands of pine and steep meadows where wild flowers grew, and in one of these meadows a group of deer was grazing. There were many deer in the woods on the green shore, and a few had even swum across to set up home upon the wilder islands. People had spent a lot of time debating how they had come here; whether they had survived since the fall of the old American Empire, or come down from the frozen country to the north, or made their way here from some larger pocket of green much further west. But all Hester Natsworthy cared about, as she drew back her bow-string in the shelter of the trees down-wind, was how much meat was on them.

The bow made a quick, soft sound. The deer leaped into the air and came down running, bounding uphill into the shelter of the scrub, all except the largest doe, who fell dead with Hester's arrow in her heart and her thin legs kicking and kicking. Hester walked up the hill and pulled the arrow free, cleaning the point on a handful of dry grass before she replaced it in the quiver on her back. The blood was very bright in the sunlight. She dipped her finger in the wound and smeared some on her forehead, muttering her prayer to the Goddess of the Hunt so that the doe's ghost would not come bothering her. Then she heaved the carcass on to her shoulder and started back down the hill to her boat.

Her fellow Vinelanders seldom hunted deer. They said it was because the fish and birds of the lake were meat enough, but Hester suspected it was because the deer's pretty fur coats and big, dark eyes touched their soft hearts and spoiled their aim. Hester's heart was not soft, and hunting was what she was best at. She enjoyed the stillness and solitude that she found in the morning woods, and sometimes she enjoyed being away from Wren.

Wistfully, Hester remembered the little laughing girl that Wren had once been, playing splish-splash on the lake-shore or snuggling on Hester's lap while Hester sang to her. As Wren looked lovingly up at her, and ran her chubby fingers over the old scar that split Hester's face in half, Hester had thought that here at last was someone who could love her for what she was, and not care what she looked like. Because although Tom always said he didn't care, Hester had never shaken off the faint fear that he must, deep down, want someone prettier than her.

But Wren had grown up, and there had come a day, when she was eight or nine, when she started to see Hester the same way everyone else did. She didn't have to say anything; Hester knew that pitying, embarrassed look well enough, and she could sense Wren's awkwardness when they were out together and met her friends.

Her daughter was ashamed of her.

"It's just a phase," said Tom, when she complained of it to him. Tom adored Wren, and it seemed to Hester that he always took Wren's side. "She'll soon be over it. You know what children are like."

But Hester didn't know what children are like. Her own childhood had ended when she was very young, when her mother and the man she thought was her father had both been murdered by her real father, Thaddeus Valentine. She had no idea what it was like to be a normal girl. As Wren grew, and became more wilful, and her grandfather's long, curved nose stuck out of her face like a knife pushed through a portrait, Hester found it harder and harder to be patient with her. Once or twice, guiltily, she had caught herself wishing that Wren had never been born and that it was just her and Tom again, the way it had been in the old days, on the Bird Roads.

When Wren awoke at last, the sun was high. Through her open window came the calls of the fishermen down at the mooring beach, the laughter of children, the steady thud of an axe as Dad chopped wood in the yard outside. There was still a faint taste of chocolate in her mouth. She lay for a moment enjoying the thought that none of the people she could hear, nobody else in all of Vineland, knew the things she knew. Then she scrambled out of bed and ran to the bathroom to wash. Her reflection peered out at her from the speckled mirror above the sink; a long, narrow, clever face. She hated her beaky nose and the scattering of spots around her too-small mouth, but she liked her eyes; large, wide-set eyes, the irises deep grey. *Mariner's eyes*, Dad had called them once, and even though Wren wasn't sure exactly what that meant, she liked the sound of it. She tied back her coppery hair and remembered Gargle calling her pretty. She'd never thought herself pretty before, but she saw now that he was right.

Running downstairs she found the kitchen empty, Mum's shirts hanging white on the line outside the window. Mum was oddly vain about her clothes. She dressed like a man, in outfits she had taken from the abandoned shops on Boreal Arcade, and she was fussy about keeping things washed and ironed and safe from moth, as if wearing good clothes would make people forget her horrible scarred ruin of a face. It was just another example of how sad she was, thought Wren, pouring herself a glass of milk from the jug in the cold-store, smearing honey on one of yesterday's oatcakes. It was all very well, but it made life difficult for Wren, having a mum who looked so weird. Tildy's dad, old Mr Smew, was only about three feet tall, but he was an Anchorage man through and through, so nobody really noticed his height any more. Mum was different. She was unfriendly, so nobody ever forgot that she was hideous, and an outsider, and that sometimes made Wren feel like an outsider, too.

Maybe that was why she felt so drawn to the Lost Boys. Maybe Gargle had seen the outsideriness in her, and that was what had made him confide in her.

She went out into the yard, eating the oatcake, careful not to get honey on Mum's shirts. Dad was setting small logs one by one on the chopping-block and cutting them in half with the wood-axe. He had his old straw hat on, because his brown hair didn't quite cover the top of his head any more, and his bald patch sometimes caught the sun. He stopped work when he saw Wren, and sat down, putting one hand to his chest. Wren thought he looked as if he was glad of an excuse for a rest, and wondered if his old wound was hurting him again, but all he said was, "So you're up at last?"

"No, I'm just sleep-walking," she said, kicking a few cords of wood out of her way and sitting down beside him. She kissed his cheek and rested her head on his shoulder. Bees buzzed around the hives at the end of the yard, and Wren sat and listened to them and wondered how to broach the subject of the Tin Book of Anchorage. Then she decided to ask him something else instead.

"Dad," she said, "you remember the Lost Boys?"

Dad looked uneasy, as he always did when she asked him about the old days. He fiddled with the bracelet on his wrist; the broad, red-gold wedding bracelet on which his initials were entwined with Mum's. "Lost Boys," he said. "Yes, I'm not likely to forget *them*. . ."

"I was wondering about them," she said. "Were they very wicked?"

"Well, you know Caul," said Dad. "He's not wicked, is he?"

"He's a bit weird."

"Well maybe, but he's a good man. If you were in trouble, you could turn to Caul. It's thanks to him we found this place, you know. If he hadn't escaped from Grimsby and brought us Snøri Ulvaeusson's map. . ."

"Oh, I know that story," said Wren. "Anyway, it's not Caul I was wondering about. I was thinking of the others, back in Grimsby. They were pretty bad, weren't they?"

Tom shook his head. "Their leader, Uncle, was a nasty bit of work. He made them do bad things. But I think the Lost Boys themselves were a mix of good and bad, just like you'd find anywhere. There was a little chap called Gargle, I remember. He's the one who saved Caul when Uncle tried to kill him, and gave Caul the map to bring to us."

"So he was as brave as Caul?"

"In a way, yes."

"And you met him? How old was he?"

"Oh, only a youngster, as I say," said her father, thinking back to his brief, frightening time with the Lost Boys. "Nine or ten. Maybe younger."

Wren felt pleased. If Caul had been nine when Dad met him he couldn't be more than twenty-five now, which wasn't so *very* much older than herself. And he was a good person, who had helped save Anchorage.

"Why this sudden interest?" her father asked.

"Oh, no reason," said Wren casually. It felt strange, lying to Dad. He was the person she loved the most in the whole world. He had always treated Wren like a friend, not a child, and she had always told him everything before. She suddenly wanted very much to tell him what had happened on the north shore and ask him what to do. But she couldn't, could she? It would not be fair to Gargle.

Dad was still looking at her in a puzzled way, so she said, "I just got thinking about them, that's all."

"Because they're Lost?" asked Dad. "Or because they're Boys?"

"Guess," said Wren. She finished her oatcake and

planted a sticky kiss on his cheek. "I'm going to see Tildy. Bye!"

She went out through the gate at the side of the yard and off down Dog Star Court with the sunlight shining on her hair, and Tom stood watching her until she turned the corner, feeling proud of his tall, beautiful daughter, and still amazed, even after all these years, that he and Hester had made this new person.

In the shadows beneath the woodpile a wireless crab-cam trained its lens on him. In an underwater cave on one of the smaller islets his image fluttered on a round, blue screen.

"She nearly gave us away!" said the boy called Fishcake. "He'll guess!"

Gargle patted his shoulder. "Don't worry. Natsworthy's as dim as the others. He doesn't suspect a thing."

Wren walked briskly towards the Smew house, but did not turn in through the gate. She knew full well that Tildy and her family would all be up in their orchard this morning, picking apples. She had even promised to go and help. How could she have imagined that she would find something so much more important to do?

She cut through Boreal Arcade, glancing at her reflection in the dusty windows of the old shops, then ran along Rasmussen Prospekt and up the ramp that led to the Winter Palace. The big front doors were always open in summer. Wren ran in and shouted, "Miss Freya?" but the only answers were the echoes of her own voice bouncing back at her from the high ceilings. She went back outside and followed the gravelled path around the foot of the palace, and there was Miss Freya in her garden, picking beans and putting them in a basket.

"Wren!" she said happily.

"Hello, Miss Freya!"

"Oh, just Freya, please," said Miss Freya, stooping to set her basket down. It seemed to be the main purpose of Miss Freya's life to persuade everybody to call her simply "Freya", but she had never had much success with it. The older people all remembered that she was the last of the House of Rasmussen and still liked to call her "Margravine" or "Your Radiance" or "Light of the Ice Fields". The younger ones knew her as their teacher, so to them she was always "Miss Freya".

"After all," she said, smiling at Wren as she dabbed the perspiration from her round face with a handkerchief, "you're not a schoolgirl any more. We might soon be colleagues. Have you thought any more about coming to help me with the little ones, once apple harvest's over?"

Wren tried to look as if she liked the idea, without actually promising she'd do it. She was afraid that if she agreed to come and help run the school she might end up like Miss Freya, large and kindly and unmarried. Changing the subject as swiftly as she could she asked, "Can I have a look in the library?"

"Of course!" said Miss Freya, as Wren had known she would. "You don't need to ask! Was there a particular book. . .?"

"Just something Daddy mentioned once. The Tin Book."

Wren blushed as she said it, for she wasn't used to telling lies, but Miss Freya didn't notice. "That old thing?" she said. "Oh, it's hardly a book, Wren. More of a curio. Another of the House of Rasmussen's many hand-me-downs."

They went together to the library. It was small wonder, Wren thought, that the Lost Boys needed her help. This huge room was crammed with books from floor to ceiling, arranged according to some private system of Miss Freya's. Tatty old paperbacks by Chung-Mai Spofforth and Rifka Boogie sat side-by-side with the wooden caskets containing precious old scrolls and grimoires. The caskets had the names of the books they held written on the back in small, gold letters, but many were too worn or faded to read, and Lost Boys probably weren't very good readers anyway. How would a poor burglar know where to start?

Miss Freya used a set of steps to reach one of the upper shelves. She was really much too plump to go clambering about on spindly ladders, and Wren felt guilty and afraid that she might fall, but Miss Freya knew exactly what she was looking for, and she was soon down again, flushed from her exertions and holding a casket with the arms of the House of Rasmussen inlaid in narwhal-ivory.

"Have a look," she said, unlocking it with a key that she took from a hook on a nearby wall.

Inside, on a lining of silicon-silk, lay the thing which Gargle had described. It was a book about eight inches high by six across, made from twenty sheets of tin bound with a rusty twirl of wire. The sheets were thick and dull and patched with rust, folded over at the edges to stop readers cutting their fingers on the jagged metal. On the topmost sheet someone had scratched a circle with a crudely drawn eagle inside it; there was lettering around the edge of the circle and more below, but all too worn for Wren to make out any words. The other sheets had aged better and the long rows of letters, numbers and symbols which had been laboriously scratched into their surfaces were still faintly legible. What they meant, Wren could not say. The faded paper label on the back cover, stamped with the arms of Anchorage and the words *Ex Libris Rasmussen*, was the only thing that made any sense at all.

"It's not very impressive, is it?" asked Miss Freya. "It's supposed to be very old, though. There's a legend about it, which the historian Wormwold quotes in his *Historia Anchoragia*. Long ago, in the terrible aftermath of the Sixty Minute War, the people of Anchorage were refugees, sailing a fleet of leaky boats across the northern seas in search of an island where they could rebuild their city. Along the way they encountered a wrecked submarine. The plagues and radiation-storms had killed off all her crew, except for one man, who was dying. He gave a document to my ancestor, Dolly Rasmussen, and told her to preserve it at all costs. So she kept it, and it was handed down from mother to daughter through the House of Rasmussen, until the paper crumbled. Then a copy was made, but because paper was scarce in those years, it was written on old food tins, hammered flat. Of course, the people who did the copying probably had no more idea what it all meant than you or I. The mere fact that it came from the lost world before the war was enough to make it sacred."

Wren turned the metal pages, and the wire that bound them scratched and squeaked. She tried to imagine the long-ago scribe who had so painstakingly engraved these symbols, working by the light of a seal-fat lamp in the dark of that centuries-long winter, copying out each wavering column in a desperate attempt to salvage something from the world the war had destroyed. "What was it for?" she wondered. "Why did the submarine man think it was so important?"

"Nobody knows, Wren. Maybe he died before he could say, or maybe it's just been forgotten. The Tin Book is just another of the many mysteries the Ancients left us. All we know is that the name of an old god crops up several times among all those numbers: *Odin*. So maybe it was a religious text. Oh, and the picture on the front is the presidential seal of the American Empire."

Wren looked critically at the eagle. "It looks more like some sort of bird to me."

Miss Freya laughed. She looked beautiful standing there in the wash of afternoon sunlight from the library windows; as big and golden as the Earth Goddess herself, and Wren loved her, and felt ashamed for planning to rob her. She asked a few more questions about the Tin Book, but she wasn't really interested in the answers. She gave the thing back as soon as she could, and left Miss Freya to her gardening, promising to come back soon and talk about becoming a teacher.

The day was passing quickly, the shadow of the Winter Palace sweeping across the city's rusty deckplates as the sun climbed the sky. Soon it would be time for Wren to keep her rendezvous with Gargle. She was starting to feel more and more nervous about it. However dashing and brave and handsome he was, however much she liked the idea of helping the Lost Boys, she could not steal from people she had known all her life. Sooner or later the Tin Book was sure to be missed, and when it was Miss Freya would remember the interest Wren had shown in it, and know who was responsible.

And what *was* the Tin Book anyway? What made Gargle want it so? Wren was not stupid. She knew that documents from the Ancient era sometimes held clues to things that were very dangerous indeed; Dad had told her once that London, the city he grew up in, had been blown entirely to pieces by a machine called MEDUSA. What if the Tin Book contained instructions for building something like that, and Gargle had found a way of reading it?

She wandered to the south side of Anchorage and down the well-worn fishermen's stairs to the mooring beach, where she sat in the shade of an old, rusted-up caterpillar unit and tried to work out what to do. Her huge secret, which had seemed so exciting, was beginning to feel like a bit of a burden. She wished there was someone she could share it with. But who? Certainly not Mum or Dad or Miss Freya; they would be horrified at the thought of Lost Boys in Vineland. Tildy would probably panic, too. She imagined telling Nate Sastrugi, and asking him to help her, but somehow, now that she knew Gargle, Nate Sastrugi seemed not nearly so handsome; just a boy, rather dull and slow, who didn't know much about anything except fishing.

She didn't notice the rowing boat nosing in towards the beach until her mother got out of it and shouted, "Wren? What are you doing? Come and help me with this."

"This" was a poor little deer, stone dead with a hole in its chest, and Mum was dragging it out of the boat and getting ready to take it up to Dog Star Court, where she would butcher it and salt the meat for winter. Wren stood up and went towards her, then noticed how high the sun was. "I can't!" she said.

"What?"

"I've got to meet someone."

Hester put the deer down and stared at her. "Who? That Sastrugi boy, I suppose?"

Wren had been trying not to start another argument, but the tone of Mum's voice was enough to make her temper flare. "Well, why not?" she asked. "Why shouldn't I? I don't have to be as miserable as you all the time. I'm not a child any more. Just because no boys ever liked you when you were my age—"

"When I was your age," Mum said, low and dangerous, "I saw things you wouldn't believe. I know what people are capable of. That's why we've always tried to protect you, and keep you close and safe, your dad and me."

"Oh, I'm safe all right," said Wren bitterly. "What do you think is going to happen to me in Vineland? Nothing *ever* happens to *anybody* here. You're always hinting about what a terrible time you had, and saying how lucky I am compared with you, but I bet your old life was more exciting than this! I bet Dad thinks so! I've seen the way he looks at that picture of your old ship. He loved being out in the world, flying about, and I bet he would be still if he hadn't got himself stuck here with *you*."

Mum hit her. It was a hard, sudden slap, with the flat of Mum's open hand, and as Wren jerked her head backwards away from the blow Mum's wedding-bracelet grazed her cheek. Wren had not been slapped since she

39

was small. She felt her face burning, and when she touched it little bright specks of blood came away on her fingers from where the bracelet had caught her. She tried to speak, but she could only gasp.

"There," said Mum gruffly. She seemed almost as shocked as Wren. She reached out to touch Wren's face, gently this time, but Wren whirled away from her and ran along the beach and into the cool shadows under Anchorage, running beneath the old city and out into the pastures behind, with her mother's voice somewhere behind her shouting furiously, "Wren! Come back! Get back here!" She kept to the woodshore so the pickers in the orchards wouldn't see her, and ran, and ran, barely thinking about where she was running to until she arrived tearful and out of breath among the crags at the top of the island, and there was Gargle waiting for her.

5

NEWS FROM THE SEA

He was all kindness and concern, sitting her down on a mossy stone, taking off his neckerchief to wipe her face, holding her hand until she was calm enough to speak.

"What is it, Wren? What's wrong?"

"Nothing. Nothing really. My mum. That's all. I hate her."

"Now I'm certain that isn't true." Gargle knelt down beside her. She didn't think that he had looked anywhere but at her face since she found him, and his eyes, behind the smoked blue glasses that he wore, were a friend's eyes, kind and worried. "You're lucky to have a mum," he said. "We Lost Boys, we're just kidnapped when we're little. We none of us know who our mums or our dads are, though we dream about them sometimes, and think how sweet it would be if we could meet them. If your mum's hard on you I think it's just a sign that she's worried about you."

"You don't know her," said Wren, and held her breath to stop hiccuping. When she had finished she said, "I saw the book."

"The Tin Book?" Gargle sounded surprised, as if he'd been so worried about Wren that he'd forgotten the thing that brought him to Vineland in the first place. "Thank you!" he said. "You've done in a morning what might have taken a limpet crew a week or more. Where is it?"

"I don't know," said Wren. "I mean, I don't know if I should tell you. Not unless you tell me what it is. Miss Freya told me all about its history, but. . . Why would anybody want it? What's it for?"

Gargle stood up and walked away from her, staring out between the pines. Wren thought he looked angry, and was afraid that she'd offended him, but when he turned to her again he just seemed sad.

"We're in trouble, Wren," he said. "You've heard of Professor Pennyroyal?"

"Of course," said Wren. "He shot my dad. He nearly led Anchorage to ruin. He stole Mum and Dad's airship and flew off in her. . ."

"Well, he wrote a book about it," Gargle said. "It's called *Predator's Gold*, and in it he talks about what he calls 'parasite pirates' who come up from under the ice to burgle cities. It's mostly rubbish, but it sold like hot cakes among the cities we used to live off of; the north Atlantic raft towns and the ice-runners. They all started installing Old-Tech burglar alarms and checking their undersides for parasites once a day, which makes it kind of hard to attach a limpet to them."

Wren thought about Professor Pennyroyal. All her life she'd been hearing stories of that wicked man. She'd seen the long, L-shaped scar on Dad's chest where Mrs Scabious had opened him up to fetch the bullet out. And now it turned out that the Lost Boys were Pennyroyal's victims, too!

"But I still don't see why you need the Tin Book," she said.

"We've had to send our limpets further and further south," Gargle explained. "Right down into the Middle Sea and the Southern Ocean, where the raft cities don't bother to keep watch for us. At least, they never used to. This past summer, we've started losing limpets. Three went south and never returned. No word, no distress

42

signal, nothing. I think maybe one of those cities has got hold of some kind of device that lets them see us coming, and they've been sinking our limpets, or capturing them. And if some of our people are captured, and tortured, and talk. . ."

"They might come looking for Grimsby?"

"Exactly." Gargle looked thoughtfully at her, as if he was glad he had chosen to tell all this to such an intelligent, perceptive girl. He took her hands again. "We need something that will get us ahead of the Drys again, Wren. That's why I need the Tin Book."

"But it's just a load of old numbers," said Wren. "It came off some old American submarine. . ."

"Exactly," said Gargle. "Those Ancients had subs way ahead of anything we've got. Ships the size of cities that could cruise right round the world without once having to come up for air. If we had that kind of technology we'd never have to fear the Drys again. We could set the whole of Grimsby moving, and they'd never find us."

"So you think the Tin Book is a plan for a submarine?"

"Maybe not exactly. But there might be enough clues in there to help us learn how they worked. Please, Wren. Tell us where it is."

Wren shook her head. "Miss Freya and the rest aren't as scary as you think," she promised him. "Come down to the city with me. Introduce yourself. I asked my dad about you. He says you helped save Vineland. And you've been hurt by Pennyroyal, just like us. I expect Miss Freya will be happy to give you the Tin Book as a gift."

Gargle sighed. "I'd like that, Wren. I'd love it. But it

would all take time. There'd be so much explaining to do, so much mistrust to overcome. And all the time we stay here, more limpets might be disappearing, and whoever's taking them may already be zeroing in on Grimsby. I'm sorry, Wren. We have to do it the Lost Boy way. Tell me where the book is and we'll take it tonight and be off. And maybe, when we have it, and Grimsby's safe again, maybe then I'll return, and introduce myself, and there'll be peace and friendship between our two cities."

Wren pulled free of him and hurried away between the trees, almost running, to a place where she could look down upon the rooftops of Anchorage. He didn't mean what he had said about coming back, she was sure of that. He had just said it to make her feel better. Once he left this place, he would never return. Why should he, when he had a whole world to roam in? A world of cities that floated and flew and rolled beneath skies filled with airships. That's what Gargle would be going back to, while she, all she had to look forward to was being Miss Freya's assistant and growing old and bored in Anchorage and one day – if Mum would let her – becoming Mrs Nate Sastrugi and having a lot of bored little children of her own.

"Wren," he said, behind her.

"No," she said. She turned to face him, trying not to let her voice shake too much. "No, I won't tell you where to find the book. I'll take it myself, and bring it to you, tonight. And then I'll come with you." She laughed and made a big gesture with both arms, trying to take in Anchorage, the lake, the hills beyond, the whole Dead Continent. "I hate this place. It's too small for me. I want to go with you when you leave. I want to

44

see Grimsby, and the Hunting Ground and the Traction Cities and the Bird Roads. That's my price. I'll bring you the Tin Book, if you'll take me with you when you leave."

6

WE ARE MAKING A NEW WORLD

D r Zero took her work seriously. Often she carried on late into the night, long after the Stalker Works were quiet and empty, her busy fingers tinkering inside Shrike's chest cavity or in his open brain. And as she worked, she talked to him, filling the old Stalker in on things he'd missed during his years in the grave. She told him of how the hard-line faction called the Green Storm had seized power in the Anti-Tractionist nations of old Asia and the North, and of their long war against the Traction Cities. She told him of their immortal leader, the Stalker Fang.

"A STALKER?" he asked, surprised. He was growing used to the Green Storm's Stalkers; mindless, faceless things who couldn't even recharge themselves, but had to have their batteries laboriously extracted and replaced after a few days of action. They were the sort of creatures who gave the living dead such a bad name. He could not imagine one of them leading armies.

"Oh, the Stalker Fang is nothing like the rest," Dr Zero assured him. "She is beautiful, and brilliant. She has an Old-Tech brain, like yours, and all sorts of special adaptations. And she was built using the body of a famous League agent, Anna Fang. The Storm like people to think that Anna Fang has come back from the dead to lead our glorious war against the barbarians."

The thought of war stirred instincts deep in Shrike's Stalker-brain. He flexed his hands, but the blades which he knew should be housed inside them did not spring out.

Dr Zero said, "I have removed your finger-glaives."

"HOW AM I TO FIGHT IF I AM UNARMED?" he asked.

"Mr Shrike," Doctor Zero told him, "if we just wanted another lumbering battle-Stalker, I could have built one myself. There is no shortage of dead bodies to Resurrect. But you are an antique, more complex than anything we can build. You're not just a thing, you're a person." She touched his harmless hands. "It made a nice change, to work on a Stalker who was not just another soldier."

An airship named *The Sadness of Things* arrived to carry Shrike to a place they called Forward Command. He stood at Dr Zero's side in the observation gondola as they flew west, over high snow-clad mountains, then the plains of the eastern Hunting Ground, which were Green Storm territory now, with here and there the wreck of a destroyed Traction City rusting in the grass.

"This land was all captured in the first weeks of the war, nearly fourteen years ago," said Dr Zero, still keen to educate her patient. "At first the barbarians were taken completely by surprise when our air-fleets came sweeping down on them out of the mountains. We drove west, herding terrified cities ahead of us, smashing any that dared turn and fight. But slowly the cities started to group together and defend themselves. A union of German-speaking industrials called the *Traktionstadtsgesellschaft* stopped our advance westward and pushed us back to the Rustwater Marshes, and a rabble of slavic traction towns attacked our settlements in Khamchatka and the Altai Shan.

"There has been stalemate ever since. Sometimes we

push west and destroy a few more cities, sometimes they push east and devour a few of our forts or farms."

The landscape below was changing; pitted and scarred by recent fighting. Enormous shell-craters shone like mirrors stitched into a blanket of mud. From this height, the vast track-marks of the enemy's fighting suburbs and the complicated entrenchments and fortifications of the Storm looked almost identical.

"They say we are making the world green again," sighed Dr Zero, "but all we are doing is turning it into mud. . ."

Forward Command turned out to be a captured city; a small, four-tiered place standing motionless on the slopes of a hill at the northern end of the Rustwater Marshes. Its tracks lay curled on the mud around it. The wheels and lower tiers were scorched and ruined, but on the upper levels lights showed dimly in the deepening twilight. Warships came and went from makeshift air-harbours, and flocks of birds wheeled above the wrecked rooftops. Shrike was surprised at the intelligent way the flocks veered to avoid the airships, until *The Sadness of Things* passed close to one and he saw that they were not living birds but Stalkers, their eyes glowing with the same eerie green light as his, their beaks and talons replaced with blades. Below, on roadways bulldozed through the mud, more Stalkers marched, some man-shaped, others bulky, crab-like, multi-legged.

"THE GREEN STORM HAS MANY STALKERS," he said.

"The Green Storm has need of many, with so many battles to fight," replied Dr Zero.

The Sadness of Things settled on a landing-field under the walls of the city's town hall. A man was waiting for them there, a small, bald-headed old man in fur-lined robes, flinching at the sporadic rumbles of gunfire rolling from the marshes to the west. He grinned when he saw Shrike come down the *Sadness*'s gangplank. "Shrikey! Good to see you up and stalking again! Remember me? I was one of old Twixie's assistants. Helped examine you, back in poor old London."

Shrike's brain, which used to hold images of ten thousand once-born faces, now remembered only Dr Zero and a few technicians from the Stalker works. He studied the old man's yellowing teeth, the tattoo of a red wheel sunk in the wrinkles between his bushy eyebrows, then turned to Dr Zero like a child looking to its mother for reassurance.

"This is Dr Popjoy," she told him softly. "Founder of the Resurrection Corps, and our leader's personal Surgeon-Mechanic." Then, to the old man, she said, "I am afraid that Mr Shrike has few memories of his former career, Dr Popjoy. That section of his brain was severely damaged; I was unable to unlock it."

"Pity," said Popjoy absent-mindedly. "Might have been nice to have a chin-wag about the old times. Still, maybe it's for the best." He walked all round the Stalker twice, reaching out to pat Shrike's shiny new body-work and tweak the flexes which trailed from his steel skull. "Excellent!" he chuckled. "A right proper job, Treacle! Couldn't have done it better myself!"

"I seek only to please the Stalker Fang," said Dr Zero meekly.

"As do we all, Treacle. Come on now, we'd best go up; she's expecting us."

Hurricane lanterns burned in the long corridors of the building. Uniformed once-born hurried about shouting commands, waving sheets of paper, talking loudly into field-telephones. Many of them had dyed their hair green as a symbol of their loyalty to the Storm. They spoke in clipped battle-codes which Shrike found that he could understand perfectly; Dr Zero's doing, no doubt. As he followed her and Popjoy up the broad stairways he wondered what other adjustments she had made.

At the top of the stairs was a pair of bullet-pecked bronze doors. "Resurrection Corps," said Popjoy, as the sentries slammed to attention. "Delivery for Her Excellency."

The doors swung wide. The room beyond was big and dark. Shrike's new eyes switched automatically to night-vision and he saw that the far wall had been reinforced with armour plate. One long slot of a window, like the slit in a visor, remained open, glassless, gazing towards the west. The figure who stood at it was not entirely human.

"Your Excellency. . ." Popjoy said.

"Wait." A voice from the darkness; a commanding whisper.

Popjoy waited. In the silence, Shrike detected the faint sound of Doctor Zero's teeth chattering and the nervous drumming of her heart.

Suddenly, a huge pulse of light rose from the western marshes, filling the room with an orange glow that fluttered and stabbed as the first great burst of fire separated into the muzzle-flash of countless individual guns and the drifting white pin-points of phosphorus flares. Forward Command shifted slightly, dead metal creaking under Shrike's feet. After a few more seconds the sound reached him, a far-off rumbling and banging, like somebody moving furniture about in a distant room.

Bathed in the light of her war, the Stalker Fang turned from the viewing-slit to greet her visitors. She wore long, grey robes, and her face was a woman's death-mask cast in bronze. She said, "Our artillery has just launched a bombardment on the forward cities of the *Traktionstadtsgesellschaft*. I shall be flying out shortly to lead the ground attack."

"Another glorious victory, I'm sure, Fang," said Popjoy's voice from somewhere near Shrike's ankles, and Shrike noticed that both Popjoy and Dr Zero had fallen to their knees, pressing their faces to the smooth wood of the floor.

"But not a final victory." The Stalker's voice was a winter wind rustling among frozen reeds. "We need more powerful weapons, Popjoy."

"And you shall have them, Your Excellency," Popjoy promised. "I'm always on the lookout for odd bits of Old-Tech that might serve. In the meantime, we've brought you a small token of the Stalker Corps's esteem."

The Stalker Fang's almond-shaped eyes flared green as they focused on Shrike. "You are the Stalker Shrike," she said, gliding closer. "I have seen images of you. I was told that you had ceased to function."

"He is fully repaired, Excellency," said Popjoy

The Stalker stopped a few paces from Shrike, studying him. "What is the meaning of this, Popjoy?" she asked.

"A birthday present, Excellency!" Popjoy raised himself, grunting with the effort. "A little surprise that Doctor Zero here dreamed up. I'm sure you remember Oenone Zero; daughter of old Hiraku Zero, the airship ace. She's a prodigy; already the finest surgeon-mechanic in the corps. (Apart from yours truly, of course.) Well, Oenone had the notion of digging old Shrikey up and repairing him to mark the anniversary of your glorious Resurrection!"

The Stalker Fang stared at Shrike, saying nothing. Dr Zero was shaking so badly that Shrike could feel the vibrations through the floor.

"Don't tell me you'd forgotten?" chirped Popjoy. "It's seventeen years to the day since I restored you to life in the facility at Rogue's Roost! You're sweet seventeen, Fang. Many happy returns!"

The Stalker Fang watched Shrike with her impassive green eyes. "What am I to do with him?"

Dr Zero looked up for the first time. "I thought – thought – you could k-keep him by you, Excellency," she said. "He will serve you well. While you work to cleanse the world of the cancer of mobile cities, Mr Shrike will keep w-w-watch over you."

"Th-th-there," said Popjoy, mocking her frightened stammer. "He'll keep w-w-watch. A bodyguard as strong as yourself, and with the same heightened senses. . ."

"I doubt he is as strong as me," said the new Stalker.

"Of course not!" Popjoy said hastily. "Her Excellency doesn't need bodyguards, Treacle! What are you wittering about?" He simpered towards the waiting Stalker. "I just thought he might amuse you, Fang."

The Stalker Fang tilted her head on one side, still considering Shrike. "Very well. The unit is impressive. Appoint him to my staff."

A tall door opened at the far end of the gallery. A uniformed aide bowed low and announced, "Excellency, your ship is ready to depart for the front."

Without another word to Popjoy the Stalker turned, and walked away.

"Excellent!" said Popjoy, when she had gone. He rose and switched on an argon lamp, then patted Dr Zero's bottom as she stood up, making her blush. "Good work, Treacle. The Fire Flower was pleased. People say you can't tell what she's thinking, but I put her together, remember; I've a pretty good idea what goes on behind that mask." Dabbing sweat from his bald head with a handkerchief he glanced at Shrike. "So what does the Shrikester think of our glorious leader?"

"SHE IS STRONG," said Shrike.

Popjoy nodded. "She's that all right. My greatest work. There's some amazing machinery inside her. Bits of a Stalker-brain even older than yours. Old-Tech stuff so weird that even *I* can't be sure how it works. I never managed to build another like her. But maybe one's enough, eh, Shrikey?"

Shrike turned back to the window, and the distant battle. Sheets of light sprang into the sky, as if coming from some deep fissure in the earth. The night was full of airships. He thought that it would be good to serve this Stalker Fang; good to obey someone as strong as himself and not take orders from soft, squashable once-born. He would be loyal to her, and perhaps, in time, that loyalty might fill up the empty spaces in his mind,

53

and rid him of the nagging sense that he had lost something precious.

That face, that scarred face.

It fluttered in his brain like a moth, and was gone.

7
SHE'S LEAVING HOME

Night, and a fingernail moon lifting from the mist above the Dead Hills. Wren lay fully dressed on her bed in the house in Dogstar Court, listening to her parents' muffled voices drifting through the wall from their bedroom. It did not take long for them to fade into silence. *Asleep.* She waited, just to be sure. The dullness of their lives made her want to shriek sometimes. Asleep, at this hour, on such a lovely, moony night! But it suited her plans. She put on her boots and went softly out of her room and down the stairs, with the Tin Book of Anchorage heavy in the bag on her shoulder.

It had been so easy to steal that it hadn't felt like stealing at all. It *wasn't* stealing, Wren kept assuring herself: Miss Freya didn't need the Tin Book, and no one else in Anchorage would care that it had gone. It wasn't stealing at all.

But even so, as she propped the note she had spent all evening writing against the bread bin and crept out into the star-silvered streets, she could not help feeling sad that her life in Vineland was ending like this.

When she left Gargle she had run straight back down the hill to the Winter Palace. Miss Freya had still been in the garden, chattering away to Mrs Scabious about the play the younger children would be performing at Moon Festival. Wren went to the library and took down the old wooden casket which Miss Freya had showed her earlier. She took out the Tin Book and locked the box again, setting it safely back in its place on the shelf. Through the open window she could hear Miss Freya saying, "Please, Windolene, just call me Freya; we've known each other long enough. . ."

Wren slipped out of the library, out of the palace, and hurried home with the Tin Book nestled safely inside her jacket, trying not to feel like a thief.

The moon was a windblown feather, caught on the spires of the Winter Palace. A lamp burned in Freya Rasmussen's window, and as Wren hurried past, she thought, *Goodbye, Miss Freya*, and felt as if she would cry.

At home it had been worse. All evening she had been close to tears at the thought of leaving Dad, and she had even started to think she would miss Mum. But it was only for a while. She would come back one day, a princess of the Lost Boys, and everything would be all right. She had given Dad a special hug before she went to bed, which had surprised him. He probably thought she was just upset about her latest fight with Mum.

She went down into the engine district and walked quickly towards the city's edge. She had just left the shadow of the upper tier and was walking along a broad street between two derelict warehouses when Caul stepped into her path.

Wren hugged her bag against herself and tried to dodge past him, but he moved to block her way again. His eyes gleamed faintly in the cage of his hair.

"What do you want?" asked Wren, trying to sound cross instead of just scared.

"You mustn't go," said Caul.

"Why not? I can go if I want. Anyway, I don't know what you're talking about."

"Gargle. I watched last night. I looked back when I reached the hilltop, and I saw you come out of that limpet. Did he ask you to help him? Did you agree?"

Wren didn't answer.

"Wren, you can't trust Gargle," Caul told her. "He was just a boy when I worked with him, but he was cunning even then. He knows how to use people. How to hide what he really wants. Whatever he's asked you to do for him, don't."

"And how are you going to stop me?" asked Wren.

"I'll tell Tom and Hester."

"Why not tell Miss Freya too, while you're about it?" Wren teased. "I'm sure she'd love to know. But you won't do it, will you? If you were going to tell Mum and Dad you'd have done it as soon as you saw me come off the *Autolycus*. You wouldn't betray your own people."

"You have *no idea* –" Caul started to say, but while he was still busy hunting for the right words she darted past him and away, her running footsteps ringing down the metal stairs at the end of the street and then falling quiet as she jumped off the last stair and on to the earth. The bag banged against her side, and her heart was thumping. She looked back to see if Caul was chasing her, but he was just standing where she had left him, not moving. She waved, then turned away and started running up the hill.

Hester had fallen asleep quickly that night, but something disturbed Tom just as he was drifting off. Only later would he realize that it had been the sound of the street door closing.

He lay in the dark and listened to his heart beat. Sometimes it seemed to him to falter, and sometimes there was a pain, or not quite a pain, but a sense that something was wrong inside him, where Pennyroyal's bullet had torn into his body all those years ago. Exercise always made it worse. He should not have cut those logs this morning. But the logs had needed cutting, and if he had not cut them he would have had to explain to Hester about the pains around his heart, and she would worry, and make him go and consult Windolene Scabious, who was Anchorage's doctor, and Windolene would want to examine him, and he was afraid of what she might discover. It was better not to think about it. Better just to thank the gods for these good years he'd had with Hester, and with Wren, and worry about the future when it happened.

But his future was already running towards him, down Rasmussen Prospekt, through Boreal Arcade, up Dog Star Court; it was through the front gate and sprinting up the steps; it was pounding hard at his front door.

"Great Quirke!" said Tom, startled, sitting up. Beside him, Hester groaned and rolled over, surfacing slowly. Tom threw the covers off and ran downstairs in his nightshirt. Through the glass panels of the front door a blurred figure loomed like a ghost, fists hammering the woodwork. A voice called Tom's name.

"Caul?" he said. "It's open."

This was not the first time Caul had woken Tom with bad news. Once before, when Anchorage was ice-borne and Hester had taken off alone aboard the *Jenny*, he had appeared out of the night to warn Tom what was happening. He had just been a boy then. Now, with his long hair and his beard and his wide, wild eyes he looked like some maniac prophet. He burst into the hall, knocking over the hat-stand and sweeping Tom's collection of Ancient mobile telephone casings to the floor.

"Caul, calm down!" said Tom. "What's the matter?"

"Wren," said the former Lost Boy. "It's Wren. . ."

"Wren's in her room," said Tom, but he felt suddenly uneasy, recalling the strange way Wren had hugged him when she said goodnight, and that scratch on her cheek which she said she'd done walking into a thorn-bush. He'd sensed that something was wrong. "Wren?" he called up the stairs.

"She's gone!" shouted Caul.

"Gone? Gone where?"

Hester was halfway down the stairs, pulling on her shirt. She ran back up, and Tom heard her kick the door of Wren's bedroom open. "Gods and goddesses!" she shouted, and reappeared at the top of the stairs. "Tom, he's right. She's taken her bag and her coat. . ."

Tom said, "I expect she's out with Tildy Smew on some midnight jaunt. This is Vineland. What harm can come to her?"

"Lost Boys," said Caul. He was pacing to and fro, his hands deep in the pockets of his filthy old coat. The wild animal smell of him filled the hall. "You remember Gargle? He left a note. Wanted me to help him. Stealing something. Don't know what. Wren must have followed me and got caught. He's using her. She's gone to him."

59

Hester went through into the kitchen and came back with a square of paper.

"Tom, look. . ."

It was a note from their daughter.

Dearest Daddy and Mummy, she had written,
I have decided to leave Vineland. Some Lost Boys are here. Don't worry, they mean no harm. They are going to take me with them. I shall see the Raft Cities and the Hunting Ground and the whole wide world, and have adventures, like you did. I'm sorry I couldn't say goodbye but you would only try to stop me going. I will take good care of myself and come home soon with all sorts of tales to tell you.
love Wren xxxxx

Hester dropped to her knees and scrabbled at the hall rug. Beneath it, set into the floor, was the safe where the merchant whose house this had been once stored his valuables. All it held now were a few cardboard boxes of ammunition, and a gun. Hester pulled the gun out, unwrapping it from its oilcloth bindings.

"Where are they, Caul?" she asked.

"Het –" said Tom.

"I should have told you sooner," Caul muttered, "but it's Gargle. *Gargle.* He saved my life once. . ."

"*Where?*"

"A cove on North Shore. Where the trees come down nearly to the water. Please, I don't want anyone hurt."

"Should have thought of that before," said Hester, checking the gun's action. Most of the guns she had taken from the Huntsmen of Arkangel she had thrown off the city's stern while it was still at sea, but this one she had kept, just in case. It wasn't as pretty as the others; no snarling wolf's-head on the butt or silver chasing on the barrel. It was just a heavy, black .38 Schadenfreude; an ugly, reliable tool for killing people. She slipped bullets into its six chambers and snapped it shut, then stuffed it through her belt and pushed past Tom to the door, snatching her coat from the rack. "Wake the others," she told him, and went out into the night.

From the top of the island Wren could see the *Autolycus* squatting like a beached crab in the cove where she had first seen Gargle. The blue light from the limpet's open hatch gleamed on the water. She started down the sheep-track towards it, slithering on loose earth, tripping on roots, the breath cold at the back of her throat as she ran through the trees and the gorse towards the spider-crab silhouette.

Gargle was standing in the shallows, at the foot of the ramp that led up through the open hatch. Remora was with him, and as Wren drew near she saw Fishcake come down the ramp to join them. "Ready to go?" she heard Gargle ask.

"Touch of a button," the boy replied.

The limpet's engines were idling, a thin plume of exhaust smoke rising from sealable vents on its back. A crab-cam glinted as it scurried up one of the legs and home to its port on the hull. Other cameras were creeping quickly down the beach, looking so spider-like that

Wren almost wanted to run away, but she told herself that if she was to travel with the Lost Boys she would have to get used to them, so she made herself walk calmly between them down the shingle.

"It's me," she called softly, as Gargle spun towards the sound of her footsteps. "I've got the Tin Book."

Anchorage-in-Vineland was waking up, indignant and alarmed. As Hester climbed the path to the woods she could hear doors slamming in the city behind her, and people shouting as they prepared to go and do their bit against the Lost Boys. Some of the younger men almost caught up with her as she drew near to the top of the island, but she left them behind on the descent; they stuck to the zigzag path while she just went straight down, crashing through the brush and surfing down screes in a rattle of bouncing stones. She felt excited, and happy that Wren needed her at last. Her father couldn't save her from the Lost Boys. Nobody else in Vineland could. Only Hester had the strength to deal with them, and when she had killed them all Wren would come to her senses and realize what danger she had been in and be grateful, and she and Hester would be friends again.

Hester slithered into a briar-patch at the hill's foot and looked back. There was no sign of the others. She pulled the gun out of her belt and started towards the cove.

*

"Here," said Wren, sliding the heavy bag off her shoulder and holding it out to Gargle. "It's in there. My stuff, too."

Remora said, "Better tell her, Gar. It's time to go."

Gargle had pulled the Tin Book out and was leafing through it, ignoring both of them.

"I'm coming with you, remember?" said Wren, starting to grow uneasy, because this wasn't the welcome she'd expected. "I'm coming with you. That was the deal."

She could hear a childish, whingeing note creeping into her voice, and knew that she wasn't coming across as brave and grown-up and adventurous, which was how she wanted Gargle to see her. It suddenly occurred to her that she was nothing to him; nothing but a way to get hold of the Tin Book.

"That's it," said Gargle to himself. He threw Wren's bag back at her, then handed the Tin Book to Fishcake, who stuffed it into a leather satchel which hung at his side.

"I'm coming with you," Wren reminded Gargle. "I *am* coming with you, aren't I?"

Gargle moved closer to her. There was a mocking tone in his voice when he spoke. "Thing is, Wren, I've been having a think about that, and we haven't got the space, after all."

Wren blinked quickly, trying to stop the tears from coming. Flinging her bag down on the shingle, she shouted, "You promised you'd take me with you!" She could see Remora watching her, whispering something to little Fishcake which made him smirk, too. How stupid they must think her!

"I want to see things!" she shouted. "I want to do

things! I don't want to stay here and marry Nate Sastrugi and be a schoolteacher and get old and die!"

Gargle seemed to be angered by all the noise she was making. "Wren," he hissed, and instantly, like a furious echo, another voice out of the darkness shouted, "Wren!"

"Mum!" gasped Wren.

"Damn!" muttered Remora.

Gargle didn't say anything at all, just dragged the gas-pistol from his belt and fired towards the beach. In the blue flash of the gun Wren saw her mother striding across the shingle, barely flinching as the shot whipped past her. She held her own gun out stiffly in front of her. *Whack*, it went, *whack, whack, whack*; dull, flat sounds like books being snapped shut. The first bullet rebounded from the *Autolycus* with a clang; the next two hissed away over the lake; the fourth hit Gargle between the eyes. Something thick and wet spattered Wren's face and clothes.

"Gargle!" shrieked Fishcake.

Gargle went down on his knees, then flopped forward with his bottom in the air and his face in the chuckling waves.

Fishcake scrambled through the shallows towards him, getting in Remora's way as she pulled out her own gun. "Fishcake, get aboard!" she screamed. "Get back to Grimsby!" Hester put two bullets through her, kicking her backwards and down into the lake.

"Gargle!" Fishcake was wailing.

Hester was reloading her gun, empty shells jinking on the shingle around her feet. She shouted, "Wren, come here!" Shaking with fright, Wren stumbled gladly towards her, but suddenly Fishcake's arm was round her waist, tugging her back. The snout of Gargle's pistol ground against her chin.

"Drop the gun!" Fishcake shouted, "Or I'll, I'll *kill* her, I'll *kill* her!"

"Mummy!" squeaked Wren. She couldn't breathe properly. She knew suddenly that she had had all the adventures she would ever want. She longed to be safe at home. "Mummy! Help!"

Hester edged forward. Her gun was raised, but she dared not pull the trigger, they all knew that; there was too much danger of hitting Wren.

"Let her go!" she ordered.

"What, so you can shoot me?" sobbed Fishcake. Twisting Wren about so that her body was always between him and her mother, he started to drag her with him up the boarding ramp. His gun was still pressed under her chin, pushing her head up. She could feel him shaking, and although she could easily have overpowered him she dared not try, in case the gun went off. He pulled her through the hatch into the limpet, and slammed his elbow against the button that raised the ramp. A ricochet howled off across the lake as Hester shot at the hydraulics and missed. "Mummy!" shouted Wren again, and had a brief glimpse of her mother shouting something back as the hatch closed. Then Fishcake shoved her through a doorway into the complicated electrical clutter of the control cabin. She felt the limpet shiver as he began working the controls with one hand, the other still pointing the gun at her head. "Please," she said. The cabin lurched. Wren saw lights on the hillside behind the beach. "Help!" she shouted. Waves were slapping at the cabin windows, and she glimpsed the moon for a moment, shivery and unreal

65

through the rising water. Then it was gone, and the note of the engines changed, and she thought, *We've submerged, I'll never get home now!* and her stomach turned over and she fainted.

Hester ran down the beach, firing her gun at the limpet until its black hull was lost in a boiling of white water. Then there was nothing to do but shout Wren's name over and over, hoarse, useless, her lonely voice the only sound remaining as the lap and wash of the *Autolycus*'s wake faded into silence.

No; not quite silence. Slowly Hester became aware of other sounds: dogs barking, shouts. Lanterns and torches bobbed on the hillside. Mr Smew came charging through the gorse, waving an antique wolf-rifle twice as tall as him and shouting, "Where are they, the sub-aquatic fiends? Let me at them!"

More people followed him. Hester went to meet them, shrugging aside the hands that reached for her, the questions.

"Are you all right, Mrs Natsworthy?"

"We heard shooting!"

"Was it the Lost Boys?"

The bodies in the shallows stirred gently as the waves broke round them, dragging long smears of red away into the lake. Caul knelt beside one of them and said in a soft, puzzled voice, "Gargle." The air stank of gunsmoke and exhaust fumes.

Tom ran up, looking stupidly about and seeing only his daughter's going-away bag lying forlorn upon the shingle. "Where's Wren?" he asked. "Hester, what happened?"

Hester turned away and would not answer. It was Freya Rasmussen, in the end, who came to him and took his hands in hers and said, "Oh, Tom, they've gone, and I think Wren is with them; I think they've taken Wren."

8
KIDNAPPED

"*Daddy, Mummy's face is all funny.*"

"*I know.*"

"*But why is it all funny?*"

"*Because a bad man cut her when she was just a little girl.*"

"*Did it hurt?*"

"*I think so. I think it hurt a lot, and for a long time. But it's all right now.*"

"*Will the bad man come back?*"

"*No, Wren, he's dead. He's been dead a long time. There are no bad men at Anchorage-in-Vineland. That's why we live here. We're safe here; nobody knows about us, and nobody will try to hurt us, and no hungry cities will come to gobble us up. It's just us, quite safe; Mummy, and Daddy, and Wren.*"

The voices of her childhood whispered in Wren's memory as she slowly returned to her senses. She was lying on the floor of a tiny cabin which held a metal washbasin and a metal toilet. The toilet smelled of chemicals. A dim blue bulb glowed in a cage on the roof. The walls vibrated slightly. She could hear the threshing, churning sound of the *Autolycus*'s motors, and another sound, a creaking and whispering, which she guessed was water pressing against the hull.

Well, bad men have come to Anchorage-in-Vineland now, she thought, *and they've escaped with what they wanted, and I've helped them. Only question left is, what are they going to do with me?*

Dad had been taken by the Lost Boys once, yet he'd survived all right, and returned to Anchorage to marry

Mum. So that must mean that there was hope for Wren, mustn't it? But thinking of Dad made her think of Mum, and that made her remember what Mum had done, and the memory filled her with a sick horror. Inside her head, like an echo that would not fade, she could hear the crack and spatter of the bullet hitting Gargle.

She was not sure how long she lay there, shivering, whimpering, too shocked and miserable to move. At last the hard floor grew so uncomfortable that she forced herself to stand up. *Get a grip, Wren*, she told herself crossly.

The stuff on her clothes had dried brown and crusty, like spilled goulash. She ran some water into the metal handbasin and tried to sponge it off, then washed her face and hair as well as she could.

After a long time a key grated in the lock and the door opened. Fishcake came and looked in at her. The gun was still in his hand. His face looked hard and white in the blue light, as if he'd been carved out of ivory.

"I'm sorry," she said.

"Shut up," said Fishcake. His voice sounded hard, too. "I ought to kill you."

"Me?" Wren wriggled, trying to burrow into the deck. "But I haven't done anything! I got you the Tin Book like Gargle asked. . ."

"And your witch of a mother killed him!" Fishcake shouted. The gun in his hand wobbled as big sobs shook his body. Wren wondered if he was going to shoot her, but he didn't. She felt scared of him and angry at him and somehow responsible for him, all at the same time.

"I'm very sorry," she said. "About Remora, too."

Fishcake sniffed loudly. "'Mora was Gargle's girl," he

said. "Everybody says he's in love with her. He was never really going to take you with him. I heard him and 'Mor talking about you, saying how stupid you were. . ." He started to cry again. "What are the Lost Boys going to do without Gargle?" he asked. "It's all right for him; him and 'Mora are down in the Sunless Country together. What about the rest of us? What about me?"

He looked at Wren again. In this underworld light his eyes looked black; two holes opening on to empty space. "I ought to kill you, just so your Mum would know how it feels to have someone you love took away. But that would make me as bad as her, wouldn't it?"

He stepped back, the door slammed shut, and the key grated in the lock.

"I'm going after her," said Tom.

Everyone politely ignored him. They thought that going after Wren would be impossible, but they were all too kind to say so. They thought that the shock of what had happened was making him talk wildly. And he *had* been shocked; quite numb with it when they first told him she was gone. He had run up and down the beach shouting her name at the waves as if the Lost Boys who had taken her might hear him and relent, until his heart had twisted and kicked so painfully inside him that he thought he was going to die right there and then upon the shingle, without ever seeing Wren again.

But he hadn't died. Kind hands had led him to a boat, and rowed him back to Anchorage, where now he sat with Hester and Freya and a dozen other Vinelanders in one of the smaller rooms of the Winter Palace.

"It's my fault, you see," he explained. "She was asking about the Lost Boys only this morning. I should have guessed something was going on."

"No fault of yours, Tom," said Smew, glaring at Hester, who sat silent and scowling beside her husband. "If *certain people* hadn't gone racing off ahead of the rest of us and started *shooting*. . ."

Several other Vinelanders muttered in agreement. They had always respected Hester, for saving them from the Huntsmen of Arkangel, but they had never liked her. They all remembered the way she had killed Piotr Masgard; killed him when there had been no more need for killing, and hacked and hacked at his body long after he was dead. Small wonder that the gods would send bad luck to a woman who could do such things. It was just a shame they'd waited sixteen years to send it, and that it had fallen on her nice husband and her lovely daughter too.

Hester knew what they were thinking. "I was only defending myself," she said. "I was defending all of us. I promised Freya once I'd look after this dump and guard it from harm, and that's what I was doing. You want somebody to blame, blame him."

She pointed at Caul, who sat awkwardly in a far corner. But nobody seemed to think badly of what Caul had done. His former friends had come asking for his help, and he had refused. You couldn't expect him to betray them. They were his people.

"What were the Lost Boys here for anyway?" asked Mr Aaqiuk.

"Lost Girls, too," said Smew, still glowering at Hester. "One of those kids she shot was just a girl."

"But what brought them back to Anchorage, after all these years?"

Everyone turned to look at Caul. He shrugged. "Don't know. Didn't ask. Thought the less I knew, the better."

"Oh, gods and goddesses!" said Freya suddenly, and went running from the room. When she returned, she was carrying the empty casket that had once held the Tin Book of Anchorage. "Wren came asking about it," she said. "This was what the Lost Boys came here for."

"Why?" asked Tom. "It's not worth anything, is it?"

Freya shrugged. "I didn't think so. But here it is, gone. They must have asked Wren to get it for them and. . ."

"The stupid little—" Hester started to say.

"Be quiet, Het," snapped Tom. He was thinking of Wren as a child, and of how, when she was frightened by thunder or a bad dream, he would hold her tight till she was calm again. He could not bear the thought of her trapped aboard that limpet, alone and afraid, with nobody to make it better. "I'm going after her," he said again.

"Then I'm coming too," Hester agreed, taking his hand. They had been parted once before, when Hester was a prisoner at Rogues' Roost, and they had vowed then that they would never be apart again. She said, "We'll go together."

"But how?" asked Freya.

"I'll help."

Caul had risen to his feet. He circled the room with his back to the wall, lamplight gleaming in his eyes. "It's my fault," he said. "I thought maybe if I didn't help them they'd leave us alone. I didn't think they'd turn to Wren. I'd forgotten how clever Gargle can . . . could be." He put a hand to his throat, to the shiny red scars that the ropes had left where Uncle tried to hang him. He said, "I remember Wren being born. I played with her when she was little. I'll help. The *Screw Worm*'ll take you all the way to Grimsby if needs be."

"That old limpet of yours?" Hester sounded angry, as if she thought Caul was mocking them.

"I thought the *Screw Worm* broke down years ago," said Tom. "That summer that you and Mr Scabious dug out the harbour-mouth. . ."

"I've repaired her," said Caul. "What do you think I've been doing with my time, down in the district? Picking fluff out of my belly-button? I've been repairing the *Worm*. All right, repairing the *Worm and* picking fluff out of my belly button. She's not perfect, but she's seaworthy. No fuel, of course. . ."

"I reckon there might be a drop left in the old air-harbour tanks," said Mr Aakiuq. "And we can recharge her accumulators from the hydro-plant."

"Then she could be ready in a few days," Caul said. "Maybe a week."

"Wren will be miles away by then!" Hester said.

"It doesn't matter," said Tom firmly. Usually it was Hester who was the firm one, and Tom who did as she said, but he was utterly certain about this. He *had* to get Wren back. If Wren were lost, what would be the point of going on living? He took Hester's hand, sure that she felt the same. "We'll find her," he promised. "We've faced worse things than Lost Boys in our time. Even if we have to go all the way to Grimsby, we'll find her."

9

THE MESSAGE

The *Autolycus* made its way south and east along the winding river-systems of the Dead Continent. Fishcake knew his way back to the sea, for he had helped Gargle map these channels on the journey from Grimsby. It was simple enough to retrace the route which had brought the *Autolycus* through the Dead Hills to Vineland, except that all the way Fishcake kept thinking, *The last time we passed through this lake Gargle was here*, or, *Last time we crossed this sand-bar 'Mor made that joke...*

He had to do something. But what could he do? He had loved Gar, and he loved Gar still, but Gar was gone, and crying would not bring him back. What could he do? He had to do *something...*

Always before there had been someone to tell him what to do. He had never acted on his own, or made his own plans, except for that one, panic-driven moment back in Vineland when he grabbed that gun and pointed it at Wren to stop Wren's mum from shooting him, and even that had not worked out as he meant it to, for he had ended up with Wren as a captive, and he didn't know what he should do with her either.

On the third night after the fight at Vineland he cut the limpet's engines and climbed out on to the roof. The dead hills of America rose stark against the shining sky. Certain that Lady Death and all the gods of war and vengeance watched over this land, Fishcake raised his voice so that they would all hear him. "I'll revenge you, Gargle! I'll revenge you, 'Mora! I'll find Hester

Natsworthy again one day, and when I do, I promise you I'll kill her."

Next day the limpet reached the coast, crept across a stretch of dismal saltings and slid gratefully into the grey sea. Safe in the deeps, Fishcake set a course for home, then went aft to see his prisoner. Wren was curled up on the floor of the toilet. Staring at her fragile, sleeping face Fishcake wished he had not had to capture her, for she was pretty, and none of this had been her fault. But it was too late now to let her go.

He prodded her with his foot. "We're at sea now," he told her as she woke. "You don't have to stay in there any more. There's fifty fathoms of cold water above us, so don't even think about trying to escape."

"At sea?" Wren knew that the open sea was a long way from Anchorage-in-Vineland. She bit her lip to stop herself from crying.

"I'm going to take you to Grimsby," said Fishcake. "Uncle or one of the older boys will know what to do with you. You can clean yourself up if you want. You can take some of Remora's old clothes from her locker."

"Thank you," whispered Wren.

"I'm not doing it for your sake," Fishcake said sharply, to show her he wasn't soft. "It's the stink, see? I can't be breathing your reek all the way to Grimsby."

Wren went aft. For four days she had seen nothing but the inside of the toilet cubicle, and after that even the narrow passageways of the *Autolycus* seemed roomy. Remora's locker was decorated with pictures snipped out of stolen magazines; hairstyles and clothes. There were photographs of Remora and Gargle laughing, their arms around each other. There was a bag of make-up, and a teddy bear, and a book on interpreting your dreams. Wren took some clothes and changed, then went and stared at her reflection in the mirror above the sink, which wasn't really a mirror but just a sheet of polished metal bolted to the wall. Already she looked older and thinner, swamped by Remora's shapeless dark clothes. Wren the Lost Girl. When she had stuffed her own filthy clothes into one of the bags the limpet crews used for loot and tied it shut, there was nothing of Vineland left about her but her boots.

She sat in the hold, listening to Fishcake clattering about on the bridge. Her stomach rumbled, but the Lost Boy had offered her no food, and she was afraid to ask for any. It was a bit embarrassing, being held prisoner by someone so much younger than her, but Fishcake's feelings were balanced on such a knife-edge that Wren was still afraid he might kill her if she annoyed him. Better stay quiet. She drank foul-tasting water from the sink faucet and thought about escape. Daring plans formed in her mind, only to burst like bubbles after a few seconds. Even if she somehow overpowered her little captor she would never be able to steer the limpet back to Vineland. She was stuck here, and it was all her own fault. She had been incredibly, dangerously stupid; she could see that now, and it made her ashamed, because she had always thought herself clever. Hadn't Miss Freya always said that Wren had more brains than any of the other young people in Vineland?

"Well, Wren," she said, hugging herself for comfort,

"if you're going to stay alive, and find your way back to Mum and Dad, you'll have to start using them."

The *Autolycus* was a hundred miles from shore when the signal came in. Fishcake thought at first that it must be a message from another limpet, although he didn't know that any others were operating on this side of the ocean. Then he noticed something strange; the signal was being broadcast simultaneously on the limpet-to-limpet frequency *and* on the wavelength which the limpets used to receive pictures from their wireless crab-cams.

He flicked some switches, and the bank of circular screens above his station slowly flooded with light.

Huddled on the floor of the hold, Wren heard voices. She crept to the door of the control cabin and peeked through. Fishcake was staring up at the screens. All six showed the same strange image; a city, seen from above, cruising on a calm sea. It was hard to tell on this grainy, ghosting picture what size of city it was, but it looked pleasant, with many ornate white cupolas and domes, and lots of long pennants streaming in the wind.

"What's that?" asked Wren.

Fishcake glanced round, but if he was surprised to find her standing there, he didn't show it. He turned his face to the screens again. "I don't know," he said. "I've never seen anything like this before. It keeps repeating. Watch."

The picture changed. A kindly looking man and woman sat side-by-side upon a sofa. They seemed to be looking straight at Wren and Fishcake, and although they were strangers, and dressed in the robes and turbans of rich townspeople, something in their sad and gentle smiles made Wren think of her own mum and dad and how they must be missing her.

"Greetings, children of the deep!" said the man. "We are speaking to you on behalf of WOPCART: the World Organization for Parents of Children Abducted from Raft Towns. For half a century boys – and lately girls too – have been vanishing from cities which cross the Atlantic and the Ice Wastes. Only in recent years, thanks to the explorer Nimrod Pennyroyal, have we become aware of the parasite pirates who secretly burgle and infest such cities, and who steal children away to train as thieves and burglars like themselves."

"Pennyroyal again!" said Wren crossly.

"Shush!" said Fishcake. "Listen!"

The woman was speaking now, still smiling, but weeping too, as she leaned towards the viewers. "Now the good people of the raft resort of Brighton have brought us north into your home waters. If you tune your radio equipment to 680 kilocycles, you will pick up the signal of Brighton's homing beacon. We know that you probably have no memories of the mummies and daddies from whom you were stolen when you were so very little, and who have been missing you so very much. But if you come to us, come in your submarines to meet us here in Brighton, we are sure that many of you will recognize your own families, and they you. We do not want to harm you, or take you from your new friends or your exciting new life beneath the waves. We only want a chance to see our dear lost boys again. . ."

Here, the woman's voice grew high and wobbly; she hid her face in her handkerchief while her husband patted her arm and took over.

"WOPCART has many members," he explained, and the picture changed again to show a crowd of people gathered on one of the city's observation platforms. "Every one of us has lost a child, and longs to see him again and learn what has happened to him. Or, indeed, her. Oh, children of the deep, if you can hear this message, we beg you, come to us!"

The image lingered for a moment, while sad music swelled and the members of WOPCART all smiled and waved at the camera and the sea breeze plucked at their coats and robes and hats. Then it was replaced by a printed sign which read, *WOPCART – Summer Expedition. (In Association with the Mayor and Council of Brighton.)* The music faded, there was a moment of blackness, and the transmission began again. "Greetings, children of the deep. . ."

"See?" asked Fishcake, turning to Wren. He had forgotten that she was his hostage, so eager was he to share the astonishing message with somebody. His eyes were shining; his whole face was radiant, and Wren realized for the first time how young he really was; just a small boy, far from home and longing for love and comfort.

"What do you think I should do?" he asked. "I checked for Brighton's homing beacon. They're close. About fifty, sixty miles south-west of us. I never heard of a city coming that near to the Dead Continent. . ."

Wren could feel the sense of yearning building in the cramped cabin as Fishcake imagined that city full of mums and dads floating fifty miles away. What if she could persuade him to rendezvous with Brighton? She was sure that she would be far better off there than down in Grimsby. So would Fishcake, probably, so she need not feel guilty about it.

She came into the cabin and sat down in the swivel chair beside his. "Maybe they've come here because they're searching for Lost Boys," she said. "They could have been zigzagging their way north for weeks, transmitting that message over and over. Gargle told me that limpets had gone missing. He thought something bad had happened to them, but what if they just heard that message and went to find their families. . .?"

"Why haven't they contacted Grimsby, then?" asked Fishcake.

"Maybe they're having too much fun," suggested Wren. "Maybe they were scared that Gargle would punish them for going to Brighton without his orders."

Fishcake gazed up at the screens. "Those people look so rich. The Lost Boys only take kids nobody's going to miss; orphans and urchins from the under-decks who nobody wants. . ."

"That's what Gargle and Uncle told you," said Wren. "What if it isn't true? What if they take children from rich families sometimes, too? Anyway, probably even an orphan would be missed by somebody. Probably even an urchin's mummy and daddy would want to find him, if he got himself stolen away. . ."

Two big tears ran down Fishcake's face, pearly in the light from the screens.

"I'll send a message-fish to Grimsby and ask Uncle what to do," he decided.

"But Fishcake," said Wren, "he might tell you not to go!"

"Uncle Knows Best," said Fishcake, but he didn't sound very certain.

"Anyway, by the time you get a reply, Brighton might have sailed away. Autumn's coming. Storms and high seas. Miss Freya always taught us that raft cities head for sheltered waters in the autumn. So this might be your only chance. . ."

"But it's one of the rules. What they teach us in the Burglarium. Never show yourself. Never give the Drys a chance to find out about the Lost Boys, that's what Gargle says. . ."

"These Drys seem to know all about you already," Wren reminded him.

Fishcake shook his head and smudged the tears away with the heel of his hand. His Burglarium training was fighting against the rising hope that his own mother and father might have been among that crowd of smiling faces on the screens. He did not remember them, but he felt sure that if he met his parents in the flesh he would know them at once.

"All right," he said. "We'll go closer. We'll have a good look at this Brighton place, get crab-cams aboard if we can. Check these WOPCART people are on the level. . ." He looked at Wren, and pitied her; after all, she had no hope of finding *her* parents aboard the waiting city.

"You must be starved," he said.

"Pretty hungry," admitted Wren.

Fishcake smiled shyly at her. "Me too. 'Mora used to do all the cooking. Do you know how to cook?"

10
THE PARENT TRAP

Usually at this time of year the raft resort of Brighton would have been cruising the Middle Sea, anchoring now and then so that visitors from the mobile towns and cities which prowled the shores could come out by balloon and motor-launch to explore its amusement arcades and aquarium, its beaches and boutiques. But business had been poor these past few seasons, and so the council had agreed to venture into the North Atlantic in search of parasite pirates.

Now they were beginning to regret it. There had been much excitement when the first three limpets made contact, east of the Azores. Crowds of visitors had come swarming out by airship from the cities of the Hunting Ground to see the strange new arrivals. But that had been weeks ago. There had been no sign of Lost Boys since, and the long banners which were stretched along the city's bows, declaring *WOPCART Summer Expedition* and *Brighton Welcomes Parasite Pirates* were starting to look tattered and a little bit sad.

Fishcake brought the *Autolycus* up to periscope depth about a mile from Brighton. A night had passed since he first picked up the transmission from WOPCART. The morning sky was the colour of the inside of a cowrie-shell, and big grey waves heaved up and down. When Wren took a turn at the periscope she could not see Brighton at all, just the waves, which now and then allowed her a glimpse of a big island away to windward, ringed by dirty white cliffs, with clouds hugging its summit.

And then she realized that it was not an island at all; what she had taken for cliffs were rows of white buildings, and the clouds were steam and exhaust fumes rising from a dense thicket of smoke-stacks. It was a city, a three-tiered raft city with two outrigger-districts linked to its central hull by spidery gantries, and a bank of huge paddle wheels beating the sea to foam astern. "Oh!" cried Wren, amazed. She'd seen pictures of cities in books, but she had never grasped how big they really were; far bigger than Anchorage-in-Vineland. Airships moved to-and-fro above a jagged skyline of spires and domes and rooftops, and a circular deckplate held up by immense gasbags hung a few hundred feet above the upper tier, anchored to it by thick hawsers. Wren could see green trees on the edge of the deckplate, and a building with unlikely onion domes.

"What's *that*?" she gasped.

"That's called Cloud 9," said Fishcake, who had managed to get a picture of the city from a crab-cam which he had sent up to perch upon the periscope. He had fetched out the *Autolycus*'s tattered old copy of *Cade's Almanac of Traction Towns (Maritime Edition)*, and was comparing Ms Cade's diagram of Brighton with the image on the screen. "It's a sort of airborne park. The big building in the middle is where the Mayor of Brighton lives."

"Gosh!" breathed Wren. "I mean – Gosh!"

"No jaws," said Fishcake, checking the screens to make sure Brighton had not added anything nasty since *Cade's Almanac* went to press. There were a few air-defence cannon mounted on revolving platforms on the promenades, but no more weapons than any town carried in these troubled times. "It's just a pleasure resort."

He lowered the periscope. As he switched off the crab-cam signal the screens filled again with the transmission from Brighton, clearer and stronger now that the limpet was so close. "We only want to see our dear lost boys again," the woman from WOPCART was saying. Fishcake felt a silly, happy hopefulness rising up inside him. What if she was his mummy? *Mums and dads are a chain that binds, a pain, a strain, they stop boys being boys.* That's what he'd been taught to chant down in the Burglarium. Now that he was faced with the prospect of meeting his own mum and dad he found that he'd never really believed it. He'd been missing his parents his whole life long, and he'd not even known it until he heard the message from WOPCART.

He took the *Autolycus* deeper, nearer; down into the shadows beneath Brighton's hull. Trailing cables and a huge, complicated steering-array loomed out of the murk; green forests of weed swirled through the cone of light from the limpet's nose-lamp. Near the city's bows a metallic sphere dangled on cables; Fishcake guessed it was the machine which WOPCART used to transmit their message through the sea.

A metallic ping rang through the cabin. Wren thought that something must have fallen over in the hold, but the sound came again and then again, chiming out a rhythm, as if someone were carefully tapping the outside of the hull with a hammer.

"Oh, gods!" said Fishcake suddenly.

"What?" asked Wren. "What is that noise?"

Fishcake was frantically working the limpet's controls, steering for brighter water beyond the edge of the city. "Gargle told us he ran into something like this once, under a big predator-raft. It's a type of Old-Tech listening device. . . The mummies and daddies know we're here now!" He wasn't sure if he was scared or happy.

With a grinding clang the limpet lurched awkwardly sideways, throwing Wren off her feet. At first she thought it was because of something Fishcake had done. "You might have warned me," she complained, rubbing the elbow she'd banged on a bulkhead. Then she saw that the boy looked just as startled as her.

"What's happening?" she whispered.

"I don't know, I don't *know*!"

No mistaking the next sensation. The *Autolycus* was rising quickly upwards. Water foamed white as it broke the surface, and sunlight burst into the cabin, blindingly bright after so many days in the dark. When Wren could see again the limpet was hanging high above the waves, and being swung sideways over a broad metal deck which jutted out from Brighton's bows. People were running across the deck; not the smiley, well-dressed mums and dads she'd seen on the screens but rough-looking, tough-looking men in rubberized overalls. Wren felt a jolt of fear at the sight of them. Then, looking past them, she relaxed, for overlooking the deck was a pleasant promenade, and the people lining the railings there looked much more like Parents of Children Abducted from Raft Towns; beaming, happy, pointing down excitedly at the limpet as it was dumped on the deck.

Fishcake was already halfway up the ladder which led to the hatch on the roof. As he popped it open the sound of cheering burst into the limpet, and a big, amplified voice began shouting something, the words confused and echoey.

Wren followed him up the ladder. Out on the hull, Fishcake was crouched against the periscope mounting, looking nervously about him, confused by the sunlight and the thundering cheers. The magnetic grapple which had dragged the limpet from the sea had been released, and dangled dripping overhead, attached to the jib of a crane. The people on the promenade were shouting and cheering and waving their arms in the air. Wren touched Fishcake's shoulder to reassure him. The rubber-suited men had formed a loose ring around the limpet and were closing in cautiously. Wren supposed they must be dockers or fishermen hired to pull the limpets aboard. She smiled at them, but they did not smile back. Straining her ears, she began to make out what the booming voice was saying.

". . .and for those of you who have just joined us," it bellowed, through squalls of feedback, "Brighton has captured a fourth pirate submarine! There are the crew, creeping out on to the hull – as desperate-looking a pair of young cut-throats as you could hope to meet! But don't worry, ladies and gentlemen; the world will soon be rid of these parasites for ever!"

"It's a trap!" said Wren. Fishcake, who hadn't understood what the announcer was saying, turned a shocked white face towards her. "It's not real!" she cried, standing up, shouting. "Fishcake! It's a—"

And two men came up the limpet's side, unfurling something between them which turned out to be a net. They dropped it over Fishcake, who kicked and struggled and shouted and reached for Wren's hand. "Does this mean they aren't our mummies and daddies?" he asked her, his voice going squeaky and ready to cry. "You lied! You lied to me!"

Then strong hands grabbed him from behind and tore him away from Wren, and more hands grabbed her, rough hands in rubber gauntlets that stank of fish and oil. A net went over her, and though she wriggled and lashed out with fists and feet she could not stop her captor throwing her over his shoulder, carrying her down the limpet's flank and dumping her heavily on the deck. She heard Fishcake's sobs turn suddenly to a sharp squeal, and a moment later she understood why. A man grabbed her arm and burned the back of her hand with a hot iron stamp, branding her with a sort of logo:

Shkin

"Mummy! Mummy!" Fishcake was howling as they dragged him away, still not wanting to believe that WOPCART and all the smiley parents had been nothing but bait.

"Leave him alone!" screamed Wren, weeping with the pain of her seared hand. "He's only ten! How can you be so beastly? He thought you were his parents!"

"That's the idea, boy." A big, burly man in a waterproof cape stooped over her, belching out a hot fug of whiskey fumes as he peered into her face. "Hang on," Wren heard him say. "Look, Miss Weems – this one's a girl."

A brittle, beautiful woman in black shoved him aside. She had a brand on her hand just like Wren's, but hers was old, and had faded to a raised scar, not much darker than the surrounding skin. "Interesting," she said, looking at Wren. "We've heard rumours of female parasites, but she's the first we've seen."

"I'm not a Lost Girl!" Wren shouted through the tight wet mesh of the net. "I was a prisoner aboard the *Autolycus*, Fishcake took me from my home. . ."

The woman sneered at her. "I don't care who you are, girl. We are slave-dealers You are just merchandise, as far as we're concerned."

"But I'm – you can't make me a slave!"

"*Au contraire*, child; our contract with Mayor Pennyroyal is perfectly clear; anyone we dredge up in one of those parasite machines becomes the property of the Shkin Corporation."

"Mayor Pennyroyal?" cried Wren. "You don't mean. . . Not *Nimrod* Pennyroyal?"

The woman seemed surprised that a Lost Girl should recognize that name. "Yes. Nimrod Pennyroyal has been Mayor of Brighton these past twelve years or more."

"But he can't be! Who'd want Pennyroyal for mayor? He's a fraud! A traitor! An airship thief!"

Miss Weems made some notes upon a clipboard. "Take her to the slave-pens," she told one of her men. "Inform Mr Shkin of the catch. I believe it's a good sign. We may be drawing close to the pirate nest."

11
FOUR AGAINST GRIMSBY

On the morning of their departure, when the *Screw Worm* was ready at last and Hester and Tom were waiting for Caul to run a few final tests on the engines, Freya Rasmussen came down to the mooring beach and announced that she was coming too. Nothing that Tom or Hester could say seemed to change her mind.

"It'll be dangerous."

"Well, *you're* both going."

"You're needed here."

"Oh, Anchorage-in-Vineland runs itself perfectly well without me. Anyway, I told Mrs Aakiuq that she can be Acting Margravine while I'm away, and you don't want to disappoint her, do you? She's made herself a special hat and everything. . ." Beaming, Freya clambered up the *Screw Worm*'s boarding ladder and dumped her bulky going-away bag through the hatch.

"Don't you understand, Snow Queen?" Hester said. "We're not off to Grimsby to pay a social call. We're going to get Wren back, and if I have to kill every Lost Boy who stands in my way. . ."

"You'll only make things worse," said Freya tartly. "There's been too much killing already. That's why you need me along. I can talk to Uncle and make him see reason."

Hester let out an exasperated howl and looked to Caul, sure that he would not want Freya along for the ride, but Caul was saying nothing, staring away across the shining water.

So it was settled, and the voyage began like a picnic trip, with Tom and Freya waving from the *Screw Worm*'s open hatchways as the limpet nosed out into the lake, and all of Anchorage-in-Vineland lining the beach to cheer them on their way.

As the city passed out of sight behind the headland and the *Screw Worm* folded in its legs and prepared to submerge, Freya went down into the cabin, where Caul was hunched over the rusty controls. But Tom stayed out on the hull until the last moment, watching the passing shorelines, the green slopes reflecting in the rippled water. Birds were calling in the reed-beds, their songs echoing the car-alarms and mobile phone trills which their distant ancestors must have heard; sound-fossils of a vanished world. They made Tom think of the Ancient settlements he had begun to excavate in the Dead Hills and the relics of forgotten lives he had unearthed there. Would he ever return with Wren to finish his work?

"We'll come back," promised Tom, as he climbed inside to join Hester. But Hester said nothing. She did not think that she would ever see Anchorage-in-Vineland again.

In the cramped control cabin of the *Screw Worm* there was no way for Caul to avoid talking to Freya Rasmussen. He wondered if that was half the reason for her deciding to come. As the waters closed over the nose windows she sat down beside him and spread Snøri Ulvaeusson's ancient map upon the pilot's console and said, "So, do you remember the way back to Grimsby?"

He nodded.

"I was sure you would," she said. "I'm surprised you haven't made the trip before."

"To Grimsby?" He turned to look at her, but the kind, careful way she was watching him made him uneasy, so he stared at the controls instead. "Why would I want to go back to Grimsby? Have you forgotten what happened the last time I was there? If Gargle hadn't cut me down. . ."

"But you still want to go back," said Freya gently. "Why else did you repair the *Worm*?"

Caul squinted into the silty darkness ahead of the limpet, pretending to be keeping a lookout for sunken rocks. "I thought about it," he admitted. "That's the trouble. I couldn't stop thinking about it. Even in the first weeks at Vineland, when there was so much to do and everybody was so kind and welcoming and you. . ."

He glanced sideways at her and away. She was still watching him. Why was she always so kind to him? Sixteen years ago she had offered him her love, and he'd turned her down, for reasons he still couldn't quite understand. He wouldn't have blamed her if she'd banished him back to the sea.

"That's why I live down in the under-deck," he admitted. "Because it's the bit of Anchorage that's the most like Grimsby. And every night, when I'm dreaming, I hear Uncle's voice. 'Come back to Grimsby, Caul,' it says." He looked at Freya nervously. He'd never told anyone this, and he was afraid she might think he was mad. He thought it himself, sometimes. "Uncle whispers to me, the way he used to whisper out of the speakers on the Burglarium ceiling when I was small. Even the waves on the beach talk with his voice. 'Grimsby's your home, Caul, my boy. You don't belong with the Drys. Come home to Grimsby.'"

Freya reached out to touch him, then thought better

of it. She said, "But when Gargle showed up, asking for you to help him, you turned him down. You could have given him the Tin Book and gone back with him on the *Autolycus*."

"I wanted to," said Caul. "You don't know how much I wanted to."

"But you didn't. You chose Anchorage over Grimsby."

"Only 'cos I was afraid," said Caul. "Only 'cos I was afraid that when I got there I'd find I don't fit in any better with the Lost Boys than I do with you Drys. Maybe I'm not either any more. Maybe I'm nothing at all."

Freya did touch him then. She laid her hand on his shoulder and felt him flinch away from her, quick and shy, like a frightened animal. Sometimes she thought that Caul was as much of a mystery to her now as he had been all those years ago when he first came to her out of the sea. He would have been so much happier if he had just let her love him. And so would she. It hadn't exactly ruined her life, for so many other good things had happened to her, but sometimes she did feel sad that she had no husband and no children of her own. It seemed to her that there were some people – and Caul was one, and Hester Natsworthy another – who just didn't have the knack of being happy.

Or was there more to it than that? She thought of the waves on the beach whispering to Caul with Uncle's voice, and felt spooked and uneasy. If Uncle could speak to him in Vineland, what would it be like for him when they reached Grimsby? And if things went badly there, and it came to a fight, would Caul be on her side, or on Uncle's?

12
BUSINESS IN GREAT WATERS

"That's right, your worship! Hold it! Smile!"

A tray of flash-powder exploded with a soft chuff, and a ball of smoke rose into the sunlit air of Cloud 9 like a party balloon. Nimrod Pennyroyal, explorer, author and mayor, was having his photograph taken for the *Brighton Evening Palimpsest* again, posing this time with Digby Slingback and Sardona Flysch, the actor and actress who played the grieving spokespeople of WOPCART in the messages Brighton was beaming into the Atlantic.

"So, your worship," the *Palimpsest*'s reporter asked, while the photographer loaded a fresh plate into his camera, "can you remind our readers what gave you the idea of this expedition against the parasite pirates?"

"I considered it my duty," said Pennyroyal, beaming, and adjusting his chain-of-office, which twinkled prettily in the sun. "After all, it was I who first alerted the world to the existence of these maritime miscreants; you can read of my encounters with them in my interpolitan best-seller *Predator's Gold* (just twenty-five Brightonian Dolphins from all good bookshops). In recent years, we have had more and more reports of their raids and burglaries and have started to deduce how their organization operates. I considered it my duty to take our city north and capture as many of them as I could."

"Of course, your worship, some of your critics have suggested that it is all a publicity stunt, designed to attract more visitors to Brighton and sell more copies of your books. . ."

Pennyroyal made scoffing noises. "My books sell well

enough without publicity stunts. And if news of our quest to rid the oceans of these parasites brings more tourists to Brighton, what is wrong with that? Brighton is a tourist city, and it's the mayor's job to help boost it. And may I remind you that our little fishing expedition is not costing Brighton's ratepayers a penny. Thanks to the partnership deal I worked out, all the underwater sensing equipment and limpet-traps are paid for by one of our most eminent businessmen, Mr Nabisco Shkin. This fake organization for pirates' parents was all Shkin's idea. I know some people think it's rather cruel, but you must admit it's worked a treat. Shkin understands the psychology of these parentless louts perfectly, you see. He was an orphan himself, you know; an urchin from the underdeck who pulled himself up by his bootstraps, so he knew just how to appeal to them."

"And does your worship think we shall catch more pirates soon?"

"Wait and see!" chuckled Pennyroyal, presenting his best profile to the camera as the photographer lined up another shot. "The boys we took from the first three limpets were hard-nuts who refused to divulge the location of their base. This latest catch includes a younger boy, and a girl too; much easier to crack. I believe the next few days will bring big results!"

In fact, what the next few days brought was a change in the weather. A storm sweeping off the Dead Continent chopped the ocean into steep, white waves and threw Brighton up and down so violently that even the residents felt queasy, and a lot of the visitors who had flown in from the Hunting Ground to watch Pennyroyal's people fishing for pirates took to their airships and sky-yachts and went hurrying home. The Brightonians (those who were not feeling too ill to walk about) glared up through the blustering rain at the underbelly of Cloud 9 hanging in the wet sky and wondered why they had agreed to let Pennyroyal bring them out on to this wild, unfriendly ocean.

Down below the pitching decks, on Brighton's lowest level, Wren lay on the floor of her narrow cage in the Shkin Corporation's holding pens and wished she were dead. Above her head an argon lamp swung to and fro, splashing light across the metal walls and the rows of cages which sat waiting for more Lost Boys to be lured aboard. Fishcake lay in one; the others held the crews of the limpets which had been captured earlier. The burn on Wren's hand hurt terribly. She supposed she would bear that raised weal for the rest of her life – although that might not be very long.

"Are we sinking?" she asked, when the Shkin Corporation's guard came round and flashed his torch at her to check that she was still alive.

The guard chuckled. "Feels like it, don't it? But Brighton's ridden out worse than this. Don't worry; we'll soon be hoovering up the rest of your chums."

"They're not my chums," said Wren bitterly. "I'm not a Lost Boy. . ."

"Change the record, love," the man said wearily. "I heard you telling Monica Weems that same story down on Fishmarket Hard when we first dredged you up. The answer's still the same. Don't matter who you are. You're merchandise now. You'll fetch a good price in Nuevo Maya."

Memories of old geography lessons stirred in Wren's brain; the big globe in the schoolroom at the Winter Palace, and Miss Freya saying, "Here is Nuevo Maya, which used to be called South America before the isthmus which linked it to North America was severed by Slow Bombs in the Sixty Minute War."

Nuevo Maya was thousands of miles away! If they took her there, how could she ever find her way home?

The guard leaned on her cage and leered at her through the bars. "You don't think Mr Shkin'd try and sell a bunch of lairy pirates off as house-slaves and nursemaids, do you? You'll end up as fighters aboard one of them big Nuevo-Mayan ziggurat cities. Lovely shows they have in them arenas. Gangs of slaves pitched in against each other, or fighting souped-up dismantling machines and captured Green Storm Stalkers. Blood and guts all over the shop. But it's all done in honour of their funny Nuevo-Mayan gods, so it's quite spiritual really."

Spiritual or not, Wren didn't think she fancied it. She had to find a way out of this horrible mess. But her brain, about which Miss Freya had said such nice things, was too addled by the pitching of the city to think of anything.

"I hope we do sink!" she shouted weakly after the guard as he went on his way. "That'd serve you right! I hope we sink before you trap any more poor Lost Boys!"

But next day the storm slackened and the waves subsided, and that evening the crews of three more limpets were dragged sheepish and weeping into the slave-pens. There were four more limpets that night, and another three the following day; one of them sensed a trap and fled before the magnetic grapples caught it, but Brighton gave chase and dropped depth-charges until a white plume of water burst from the ocean to drench the cheering spectators on the starboard observation decks, and bits of limpet and Lost Boy came bobbing to the surface.

"Word must have reached Grimsby by now," said Krill, one of the boys who'd been taken earlier, watching white-faced from his cage as the pens around him filled with captives. "Old Uncle will do something. He'll rescue us."

"Word *has* reached Grimsby," said the new arrivals.

"That's where we came from. . ."

"We picked up that message a couple of days ago."

"Uncle said it was a trap and we shouldn't listen, but we sneaked out anyway."

"We thought our mums and dads would be here. . ."

Krill hung his head and started to cry. He had led raiding parties against statics in the Western Archipelago, slaughtering any Dry who stood against him, but here in the Shkin Corporation's warehouse he was just another lost teenager.

Wren reached through the bars and tugged at Fishcake's sleeve. The newbie was curled up on the floor of the neighbouring cage. He had not spoken to Wren since they were brought in, and she guessed he blamed her for what had happened to him. Maybe he was right. If only she hadn't been so keen to persuade him to come to Brighton!

"Fishcake," she asked gently. "How many Lost Boys are there? Altogether, I mean."

Fishcake would not look at her, but after a moment he muttered, "About sixty, I s'pose. That's not counting Uncle, and the newbies too young to ride limpets."

"But there are at least forty of you here!" Wren said. "Grimsby must be nearly empty. . ."

The warehouse door rattled open, letting in another bunch of people. *More prisoners,* Wren thought, and didn't even bother to look at them; it was too depressing. But the sound of tramping feet stopped beside her cage, and she glanced up to see that the newcomers were not Lost Boys, just two Shkin Corporation guards and the odious Miss Weems.

"Fetch her out," Miss Weems commanded. Wren was alarmed. Had Miss Weems finally accepted that she was not a Lost Girl? Perhaps the Shkin Corporation had realized that she would never cut the mustard in those Nuevo-Mayan arenas, and were planning to throw her overboard rather than waste any more food and water keeping her alive?

"The master wishes to see you," said Miss Weems. The captive Lost Boys watched from their cages as Wren was led away.

A door behind the slave-pens opened on to a room no bigger than a cupboard. The guards shoved Wren inside, then crowded in behind her. It was only when Miss Weems pulled a lever on the wall and Wren felt the floor jerk under her that she realized this was an elevator. The elevators of Anchorage had all been out of order for years, but this one was working perfectly; it rose so fast that Wren felt as if her stomach had been left behind.

Having been dragged to the slave-pens in a net, Wren did not really understand the layout of the Shkin Corporation building. It was a tower, whose lower storeys, down in Brighton's depths, held the captive slaves. The middle floors, on the city's second tier, housed a few special cells for luxury goods and the offices of administrators. The higher levels, which poked up through the resort's top tier in a fashionable district called Queen's Park, were the offices of the Corporation's founder, Mr Nabisco Shkin. This topmost part was as white and beautiful as any iceberg, and gave no hint of the dangerous nine-tenths which lurked below. Local people called it the Pepperpot.

The elevator stopped on the top floor, and Wren stepped out into a large, circular room. It was beautifully furnished, with plush black draperies, black carpets, and black pictures in golden frames hanging on the black walls. But what made Wren catch her breath was the view from the windows. She was looking out over the rooftops of Brighton; the sun was shining, bright flags were flying, sky-yachts and air-pedalos were rising from the harbour and legions of gulls were wheeling and soaring around the chimney-pots and far out over the sparkling sea. Spray from the paddle-wheels blew across the city on a gentle breeze, and the sunlight shining through it filled the streets with drifting rainbows.

For a moment Wren almost forgot her misery, her hunger, the pain of her branded hand. Joy bubbled up in her. She was on a raft city; on one of the wonderful cities she had always dreamed about, and it was even more beautiful than she could have hoped.

"The girl, Mr Shkin," announced Miss Weems, with an ingratiating whine in her voice which Wren had not heard before. One of the guards turned Wren around to face a man who sat quietly watching her from a black swivel chair.

Nabisco Shkin sat very still, one leg crossed over the other, one patent-leather shoe blinking with reflected light as his foot tapped ever so slightly up and down, his only movement. A dove-grey suit; grey gloves; grey hair; grey eyes; grey face; grey voice. He said, "I am delighted to meet you, my dear," but he didn't sound delighted. Didn't look it either. Didn't look as if he'd know what delight was. He said, "Monica tells me that you claim to come from Anchorage."

"I do!" cried Wren, grateful that someone was prepared to listen to her at last. "My name is Wren Natsworthy, and I was kidnapped—"

"*Nobody* comes from Anchorage." Shkin stood up and circled her. His eyes were on her all the time. "Anchorage sank years ago, west of Greenland."

"No, it didn't!" blurted Wren. "It—"

Shkin raised one finger and turned to his desk. Turned back with something in his hands. It was the book that Wren had stolen from Miss Freya. She had forgotten all about it until now.

"What is this?" he asked.

"That's the Tin Book," she said. "Just an old curio from the Black Centuries. It's why the *Autolycus* came to Anchorage. I think it's got something to do with submarines. I helped the Lost Boys steal it but it all went wrong and Fishcake ended up taking me hostage, and if you could take me back there, sir, I'm sure my mum and dad and Miss Freya would reward you. . ."

"Anchorage again." Shkin put the book down and studied her. "Why do you persist in this ridiculous story? Anchorage is home to no one but fish. Everyone in Brighton knows that. Our beloved Mayor Pennyroyal made rather a lot of money with his book about its final days. *Predator's Gold* ends with Anchorage sinking to what our ever-original mayor describes as 'a watery grave'."

"Well, Pennyroyal's a liar!" Wren said angrily, thinking how unfair it was that Pennyroyal should have survived at all, let alone grown rich from his fibs. "He's a coward and a liar, and he shot my dad and stole Mum and Dad's airship so he could run away from Anchorage when he thought Arkangel was going to eat it. He can't possibly know what happened after that. Whatever he wrote, he must have made it up."

Nabisco Shkin raised one grey eyebrow about an eighth of an inch, which was his way of showing surprise. At the same instant, Wren had an idea. She was the only person in the whole of the outside world who knew the truth about Anchorage. Surely that must make her valuable? Far too valuable to be auctioned off with the rest of the Lost Boys as an arena slave!

She felt as if a tiny door had opened very far away from her, on the other side of an enormous, darkened room; she could see a way out.

She said, "Anchorage found its way to a green bit on the Dead Continent. It thrived there, and I'm proof of it. Don't you think Pennyroyal would like to know that?"

Nabisco Shkin had been about to silence her again, but when she said that he hesitated, and his eyebrow shot up a full quarter-inch. He settled into his chair again, his eyes still fixed on Wren. "Explain," he said.

"Well, he'll want to know about Anchorage, won't he?' Wren stammered. "I mean, if he's made all that money telling people about us, think how interested he'll be to learn what really happened. He could write a sequel! He could have an expedition to take me home, and write a book about it!" And even if he couldn't, she thought, at least life as a slave in that floaty palace thing would be better than the arenas of Nuevo Maya. She said eagerly, "He'll be dying to talk to me."

Shkin nodded slowly. A smile flickered for a moment

around his thin mouth, then gave up the effort. He had been irritated by the crack that Pennyroyal had made about the underdeck in his interview in the *Palimpsest*, reminding everyone of Shkin's beginnings as a child thief in the dank alleys of Mole's Combe. Maybe this girl was a gift from his gods; a way to get his own back on Brighton's absurd mayor.

"If your story is true," he said, "you might indeed be of interest to Mayor Pennyroyal. But how can you prove it?"

Wren pointed to the Tin Book, which lay on his desk. "That's the proof. It's a famous artefact from the margravine's library. . ."

"I do not recall Pennyroyal mentioning it in his tediously detailed account of Anchorage's treasures," said Shkin. "What if he does not recognize it? That leaves only your word, and who would believe the word of a slave and a Lost Girl?"

"He can ask me stuff," said Wren desperately. "He can ask me things about my mum and dad and Mr Scabious and Miss Freya, stuff that's not in his book, stuff that only somebody who'd lived in Anchorage could know about."

"Interesting." Shkin gave another of his slow-motion nods. "Monica," he said, "this girl is to be transferred to the second tier. Make sure she is treated as a luxury item from now on."

"Don't forget Fishcake," said Wren. "He's been to Anchorage too."

"Indeed," said Shkin, and with a glance at Miss Weems, "Arrange for that boy to be brought to the questioning room. It's time I had a word with him."

13
DR ZERO

As the airship that had carried her from Batmunkh Tsaka swung into the shoals of other ships above Tienjing, Oenone Zero looked down from the gondola windows, delighted by the gaily painted houses balanced on their impossible ledges, the gardens like window-boxes, the sunlight silvering high-level canals, and the bright robes of the citizens thronging on the spidery bridges and the steep, ladder-like streets. This city, high in the central mountains of Shan Guo, had been the birthplace of Anti-Tractionism. Here Lama Batmunkh had founded the Anti-Traction League, and here the League had had its capital ever since.

But the League was gone now, the old High Council overthrown, and the signs of the Green Storm's war were everywhere. As the airship descended towards the military docking pans at the Jade Pagoda, Oenone found it harder and harder to ignore the hideous concrete rocket emplacements which disfigured Tienjing's parks and the armies of ugly windmills flailing and rattling on the mountainsides, generating clean energy for the war-effort. For fourteen years no one had been allowed to do anything that was *not* part of the war effort, and the civilian quarters of the city showed signs of long neglect. Wherever Oenone looked, buildings were falling into disrepair, and the shadows of patrolling dreadnoughts slithered across decaying roofs.

The Jade Pagoda was not made of jade, nor was it a pagoda. The name was just a relic that Tienjing's founders had brought with them when they first fled into these mountains; it had probably belonged once to some pleasant summer palace in the lowlands, long since devoured by hungry cities. It didn't suit the grim stone fortress which loomed over Oenone as she disembarked on the snow-scoured pan. On spikes above the outer gates the heads of anti-war protestors and people who failed to recycle their household waste were turning dry and papery as wasps' nests in the mountain air. Huge slogans had been painted on the walls: *THE WORLD MADE GREEN AGAIN!* and *ONE LAST PUSH WILL SMASH THE PAN-GERMAN TRACTION-WEDGE!*

Soldiers of the Stalker Fang's elite air-legion manned the inner gate, and stepped out to bar the way as Oenone heaved her pack on to her shoulder and started up the steps from the docking pan.

"Papers, young man," barked the sub-officer in charge. It was a mistake which Oenone was used to. In the Storm's lands all surplus food was earmarked for the fighters at the front, and the yearly famines of her childhood had left her as slight and flat-chested as a boy of fourteen. She waited patiently while the sub-officer checked her pass, and saw his face change when he realized who she was. "Let her through! Let her through!" he shouted, lashing at his men with the flat of his sword, punishing them in the hope that Dr Zero would not punish him. "Let her through at once! This is Dr Zero, the leader's new surgeon-mechanic!"

Oenone had been four years old when the Green Storm seized power, and she had no clear memories of the time before the war. Her father, who had been killed in a skirmish with pirates at Rogues' Roost, was just a face in a photograph on the family shrine.

Oenone grew up shy and clever on an airbase in remote Aleutia where her mother worked as a mechanic. At school she sang propaganda songs like "The East Is Green" and "We Thank The Stalker Fang For Our Happy Childhoods". At home her bedtime stories were the tales her aviator brother Eno told, of victories on distant battlefields. Her playthings were broken Stalkers, shipped back from the fighting in Khamchatka and piled up behind the base. She felt so sorry for them that she started trying to make them better, not understanding then that they were dead already, and would best be left in peace. She learned the secrets that lay beneath their armour, the braille of their brains. She grew so good with them that the base commander started calling for the Zero girl instead of his own surgeon-mechanics when one of his Stalkers went wrong. She earned extra rations for her mother and herself that way, until she was sixteen, when the Green Storm heard of her talents and sent her to a training facility, then to a front-line Resurrection unit in the Altai Shan.

In that underground world of trenches and dug-outs she toiled through the long, murderous winter of '22. Dead soldiers were dragged out of the frozen mud by salvage teams and dumped on the Resurrection slabs, where Oenone and her comrades turned them into Stalkers and sent them marching back into the line.

She was surprised at how quickly she stopped feeling horror, and pity. She learned not to look at the faces of the people she worked on. That way they weren't people at all, just broken things that had to be stripped down and repaired as fast as possible. There was a sense of comradeship in the Resurrection room, which Oenone liked. The other surgeon-mechanics joked and teased each other as they worked, but because Oenone was so young they called her "little sister" and took care of her. They were impressed by how quickly and carefully she worked, and the easy way she solved problems that they could not. Sometimes she heard them talking about her, using words like "genius".

Oenone felt proud that she had pleased them, and proud that she was playing a part in the struggle for the Good Earth. Again and again that winter the cities of the enemy tried to advance across the shell-torn stretch of Hell which separated their Hunting Ground from the territories of the Green Storm, and they were so vast and so many that it sometimes seemed to Oenone that nothing would be able to stop them. But Green Storm guns and catapults hurled shells against their tracks, and Green Storm carriers flung Tumblers down upon their upperworks, and Green Storm warships routed their fighter-screens, and brave Green Storm rocket units crept between their huge wheels and blasted holes in their undersides through which squads of Green Storm Stalkers could swarm. And always, in the end, when enough of their people had been killed, the cities gave up and slunk away. Sometimes, when one was badly damaged, the others would turn on it and tear it apart.

At first Oenone was terrified by the howl and crump of the incoming snout-gun rounds, and the whistle of snipers' bullets slicing the cold air above the communications trenches. But weeks went by, and then months, and she slowly grew used to the terror. It was like working on the bodies in the Resurrection room; you learned to stop feeling things. She didn't even feel anything when word came from Aleutia that her mother's airbase had been eaten by amphibious suburbs.

And then, during the spring offensive of '23, she recognized one of the bodies that the salvage teams dumped in front of her. There was a pattern of moles on his chest which she knew as well as the constellations he had taught her when she was little. Even before she peeled aside the bloody rag that someone had draped over his face she knew that he was her brother Eno. Because their letters to each other had been censored, she hadn't even known that he was in her sector.

She stared at him while she mechanically pulled on her rubber gauntlets. She did not want to Resurrect him, but she knew what would happen to her if she refused. Sometimes soldiers on the line tried to stop the Corps taking the bodies of their comrades for Resurrection; the Green Storm denounced them as Crypto-Tractionists, and they were shot and Resurrected with their friends. Oenone did not want to be shot. At the sight of Eno all her feelings had returned, and her fear of death came back so suddenly and so powerfully that she could barely breathe. She did not ever want to be like Eno; cold and helpless on a slab.

"Surgeon-Mechanic?" asked one of her assistants. "Are you unwell?"

Oenone wanted to be sick. She waved him away and tried to control herself. It was wrong to even think of not Resurrecting Eno. She told herself that she should be happy for her brother, because thanks to her his body would be able to go on fighting the barbarians even after death. But she was not happy.

Her assistants were staring at her, so she said, "Scalpel. Bonesaw. Rib-spreaders," and set to work. She opened Eno's body and took out his internal organs, replacing them with engines, battery-housings and preservative pumps. She cut off his hands and replaced them with the steel hands of a Stalker. She cut off his private parts. She took out his eyes. She took off his skin, and wired a mysterious net of electrodes into the fibres of his muscles. She opened his skull and fitted a machine the size of a peach-stone into his brain, then watched him writhe and shudder as it unspooled wire-thin cilia down his spinal cord, connecting to his nervous system and to the other machines she had installed.

"This isn't really you," she told him, whispering to him constantly as she worked. "You are in the Sunless Country, and this is just a thing you've left behind, that we can use, like recycling a bottle or a crate. Doesn't the Green Storm tell us to recycle everything, for the sake of the Good Earth?"

When she had finished she handed him over to a junior surgeon-mechanic who would fit the exoskeleton and finger-glaives. Then she went outside and smoked a cigarette, and watched airships on fire above no-man's land.

It was after that that the dead started talking to her. It seemed strange that they should be so chatty when her own brother had said nothing at all, but when she looked into their faces, which she always made a point of doing after Eno, she could hear them whispering in her mind.

They all asked her same thing. *Who will end this? Who will put an end to this endless war?*

"I'll do it," Oenone Zero promised, her small voice drowning in the thunder of the guns. "At least, I'll try."

*

"Treacle!" cried Popjoy cheerfully, when she finally arrived at his offices, high in the pagoda. He was packing. In the big trunk that sat open on his desk Oenone could see books, files, papers, a framed portrait of the Stalker Fang and an enamel mug with the logo of the Resurrection Corps and the slogan *You Don't Have To Be A Mad Scientist To Work Here – But It Helps!* Popjoy was standing on a chair to unhook a picture of the Rogues' Roost airbase, which he dusted with his cuff before stowing in the trunk. Then he blew Doctor Zero a kiss.

"Congratulations! I've just been to see Fang, and it's official! She's so impressed with your work on old Shrikey that she's decided to let me retire at last! I'm off to my weekend place at Batmunkh Gompa for a well-earned rest. A spot of fishing; tinkering with a few pet projects; I might even write my memoirs. And you, Treacle; you're to be my replacement."

How strange, thought Oenone. This was what she had been working for ever since her epiphany in the trenches; to be the Stalker Fang's personal surgeon-mechanic. For this she had overcome her natural shyness and fought for a transfer to the central Stalker Works. For this she had put up with Dr Popjoy's unpleasant sense of humour and wandering hands. For this she had spent years tracking down the grave of the notorious Stalker Shrike, and months repairing him, proving to everyone that she was at least Popjoy's equal. Yet now that the moment had arrived, she could not even find a smile. Her knees felt weak. She gripped the door-frame to stop herself from falling.

"Cheer up, Treacle!" Popjoy leered. "It's good news! Power! Money! And all you have to do in return is check Her Excellency's oil-levels from time to time, buff up her bodywork, keep a weather-eye open for rust. She's basically indestructible, so you shouldn't have too many problems. If you have any worries, send word to me. Otherwise. . ."

Otherwise, I'm on my own, thought Oenone Zero, climbing the stairs to the highest level of the pagoda, the Stalker Fang's own quarters. It was all wrong, of course; if there were justice in the world a man like Popjoy, who had unleashed so much suffering and evil, would suffer himself. Instead, he was going to end his days in luxury, doing a spot of fishing, tinkering with a few pet projects. But at least by retiring he would allow Oenone Zero a chance to fulfil her promise to the dead.

Sentries clattered to attention as she passed. Flunkeys bowed low before her and swung open the doors that led into the Stalker Fang's conference chamber. Clerks and staff officers looked up from a big map of the Rustwater and did not bother to return Oenone's low bow. Fang looked up too, her green eyes flaring. She had returned from the front line only a few hours before, and her armour was crusted with dried mud and the blood of townie soldiers. "My new Surgeon-Mechanic," she whispered.

"At your service, Excellency," murmured Oenone Zero, and dropped to her knees before the Stalker. When she found the courage to lift her head, everyone had gone back to their war-maps, and the only eyes that lingered on her were those of Mr Shrike.

So everything was in place. She was on the inside; a member of the central staff. Soon she would put in motion the plan she'd thought of in her louse-infested bunk on the Altai Front. She would assassinate the Stalker Fang.

110

14

SOLD!

Later, Wren would sometimes tell people that she knew what it was like to be a slave, but she didn't, not really. The old trade was thriving in those years. Prisoners taken by both sides in the long war were sold wholesale to men like Shkin, who packed them into leaky, under-heated air-freighters and shipped them off along the Bird Roads to work on giant industrial platforms or the endless entrenchments and city-traps of the Storm. Slavery for them meant grinding labour, the ripping apart of families, random cruelty and an early death. The worst Wren had to put up with was Nimrod Pennyroyal's writing.

They had moved her, after that first interview with Shkin, into a comfortable cell in the middle levels of the Pepperpot. She had a soft bed, a basin to wash in, three meals a day and a new linen dress which rather suited her. And she had a copy of *Predator's Gold*, delivered by Miss Weems, "with Mr Shkin's compliments".

For a few hours each day a reflector outside the barred window caught a beam of sunshine falling through a skylight in the deckplates above and filled Wren's cell with light. As she curled up on her bunk and opened the lurid covers of Pennyroyal's book, she could almost imagine herself back in her own bedroom in Dog Star Court, where she had often sat beside the window reading. But she had never read anything like *Predator's Gold*. How strange it was, to find the places and people and stories she had known all her life so changed and twisted!

She had been afraid that reading about Mum and

Dad would make her homesickness worse, but she need not have worried. Dad did not feature at all in Pennyroyal's book. As for Hester Shaw, "a titian-haired Amazon of the air whose divine face was marred only by a livid scar, where some brigand had drawn his stiletto across the damask flesh of her cheek", she was barely recognizable as Mum.

And one night, as Wren lay sleepless, thinking indignantly about all that she had read, it struck her that she had made another terrible mistake. She'd thought herself so clever for persuading Shkin to take her to the mayor, but she'd been assuming that *Predator's Gold* would be mostly true. She had not imagined just how much Pennyroyal had lied about his time in Anchorage. By telling the real story, Wren could destroy his reputation and his career. Pennyroyal might well want to buy her, but not so that he could write books about her. He would want to silence her, quickly and permanently.

Alone in her cell, Wren hid her face in the pillow and whined with fear. What had she done? And how could she undo it? She jumped from her bunk and started towards the door, meaning to shout for a guard. She would tell Shkin that she had lied about Anchorage; she was just a Lost Girl after all, and of no interest to Professor Pennyroyal. But then she would be back where she had started, or worse – Shkin would say she had been wasting his time. She imagined that a man like Shkin would have unpleasant ways of getting even with people who wasted his time.

"Think, Wren, *think*!" she whispered.

And all the while, beneath her feet, Brighton's powerful Mitchell & Nixon engines boomed and pounded, pushing the city steadily northwards.

After his interview with Wren, Shkin had questioned Fishcake. The newbie had proved highly cooperative. He was tired out and terrified, and eager for some new master who would look after him and tell him what to do. After a few kind-sounding words from Nabisco Shkin he confirmed Wren's story about Anchorage. After a few more, he told the slave-dealer where Grimsby lay.

Shkin's people relayed the information to the Mayor and the Council. Brighton adjusted its course, and soon the Old-Tech instruments on the bridge detected the spires of a sunken city in the depths below. Brighton circled for a while, broadcasting its treacherous message, and succeeded in winkling out a last few limpets. When no more appeared, Pennyroyal decided that the expedition was at an end.

The original plan had been to send men down in captured limpets to explore the pirate lair. But the voyage north had taken longer than expected; it was late in the season, more storms were forecast, and the people of Brighton, who had the attention-span of midges, were growing bored. Depth charges were dropped, resulting in a few spectacular underwater explosions and a lot of floating debris, which the city's shopkeepers scooped up in nets and put on sale as souvenirs of Grimsby. Pennyroyal made a speech declaring that the North Atlantic was now safe for decent raft-cities again, and Brighton turned south, setting a course back to the warmer waters of the Middle Sea, where it had promised to rendezvous with a cluster of Traction-Cities to celebrate Moon Festival.

*

The following afternoon, Wren's door was unlocked and a lot of black-clad guards came packing into her cell, followed by Nabisco Shkin himself.

"Well, my dear," he said, glancing at the copy of *Predator's Gold* which lay on her bunk. "Were you gripped by our mayor's adventures? Did you notice any errors in his account?"

Wren barely knew where to start. "It's all rubbish!" she said indignantly. "The people of Anchorage didn't *force* Pennyroyal to guide them across the High Ice; they made him Acting Navigator, which was a great honour, and he made a proper hash of it. And it wasn't him who fought off the Huntsmen, it was my mum, and she didn't get killed by Masgard, like she does in the book; she's still alive. And she'd *never* have sold Anchorage's course to Arkangel. And when she's dying and she says to Pennyroyal, 'Take my airship, save yourself,' that's just poo; Pennyroyal *stole* the ship, and shot Dad so he could take off in her – he doesn't mention Dad, of course. And as for that thing that Miss Freya does on page 81. . ."

She stopped, remembering her predicament. Shkin was watching her, as careful and calculating as ever. Maybe giving her the book had just been a way of testing her, seeing if she would stick to her story about Anchorage in the face of all Pennyroyal's lies.

"Interesting," Shkin said, and snapped his fingers at one of the guards, who stepped smartly forward to clamp a pair of pretty silver manacles on Wren's wrists. "I always suspected that His Worship's tales of adventure were somewhat embroidered. I think it is time we took you up to meet him."

*

Down the stairways of the Pepperpot to a garage where a sleek black bug stood waiting. "What about Fishcake?" Wren asked, as Shkin's men pushed her inside. "What have you done with poor little Fishcake?"

"He will be remaining at the Pepperpot." Shkin settled himself beside her on the bug's back seat and checked his pocket watch. "Cloud 9," he told the driver, and the bug set off, out into the dingy streets of the Laines, a district of antique shops and cheap hotels which filled most of Brighton's middle tier.

In other circumstances Wren would have been fascinated by the passing shop-fronts packed with junk and Old-Tech, the strangely dressed people, the tier-supports plastered with the handbills of hopeless fringe theatre companies. Now, however, she was too busy wondering how she was going to keep herself alive. It would all be a matter of timing, she decided. If she were clever enough, and kept her nerve, she might still be able to get herself out of Shkin's hands without Pennyroyal ever realizing who she really was. . .

The bug climbed a long ramp to the upper tier. Clearing tourists out of the way with blasts of its hooter, it sped along Ocean Boulevard, the oval promenade that ringed Brighton's upper city. It passed hotels and restaurants, palm trees and crazy-golf courses, fairgrounds, floral clocks and bingo parlours. It crossed a bridge that spanned the shallow end of the Sea Pool, a lake of cleaned and filtered sea-water fringed by artifical beaches. At last it arrived in the Old Steine, the circular plaza where the thick steel hawsers which tied Cloud 9 to Brighton were attached.

The floating deckplate hovered about two hundred feet above Wren's head. Looking up, she could see a glass-walled control room jutting from its underbelly like an elaborate, upside-down greenhouse. Men were moving about inside, operating banks of brass levers which adjusted Cloud 9's trim and altitude. Small engine pods were mounted all around the deckplate's edge, and Wren presumed that in rough weather they would be used to keep Cloud 9 on station above the city. On this windless afternoon only a few were switched on, acting as fans to blow Brighton's exhaust smoke away from the mayor's palace.

In the middle of Old Steine, where the Cloud 9 tow-lines were bolted to huge, rusty stanchions, a yellow cable car waited to take visitors up to the Pavilion. As Shkin's bug squeaked to a stop beside it, red-coated soldiers came hurrying to study the papers of Shkin and his men and run Old-Tech metal-detectors over their clothes.

"There was a time when just about anyone was allowed to go up and wander in the Pavilion gardens," said Shkin. "That's all changed since the war started. There's no fighting in our part of the world, of course – the African Anti-Tractionists have no stomach for the Green Storm's crusade – but Pennyroyal is still terrified that saboteurs or terrorists might take a potshot at him."

That was the first Wren heard about the war between the cities and the Storm. It explained why there were all those big, ugly gun batteries on the city's esplanades, and why security was so tight.

"Purpose of your visit to Cloud 9, Mr Shkin?" asked the commander.

"I have an interesting piece of merchandise to show to the mayor."

"I'm not sure His Worship is buying slaves at the moment, sir."

"Oh, he will not want to miss the chance of adding this one to his staff. I suggest you let us up without further delay, unless you wish to spend the rest of your career down on Tier 3, picking pubes out of the Sea Pool filters. . ."

There were no more objections. Shkin and his party were ushered quickly aboard, the cable car shuddered and Wren, looking from its big windows, saw Brighton fall away below her. "Oh look," she murmured, entranced, but Shkin and his men had seen it all before.

Suddenly the howl of super-charged engine-pods filled the cable car and swift shadows came flickering across its windows. Beyond the web of Cloud 9's hawsers a flock of fierce, spiky shapes cut through the afternoon sky. Wren shrieked, imagining that there had been an explosion up on Cloud 9 and that this was the debris raining down, but the shapes veered in formation and hurtled away across Brighton's rooftops, their shadows speeding across the busy streets.

"But they've got no envelopes!" Wren cried. "No gasbags! How do they stay up? Heavier-than-air flight is impossible!"

Some of Shkin's men laughed. The slave-trader himself looked faintly pleased, as if her innocence added credence to her story. "Not impossible," he said. "The secret of heavier-than-air flight was rediscovered a few years ago by cities eager to defend themselves against the Storm's air-fleets. There is nothing like fourteen years of war to encourage technological advances. . ." He raised his voice as the flying machines came swooping back, filling the sky with the bellow of engines and the peevish squeal of air-brakes. "This lot are called the Flying Ferrets. A mercenary air-force, hired by our esteemed mayor to protect his palace. . ."

Wren turned to the window again as the machines sped by. They were fragile-looking contraptions, all string and balsa wood and varnished paper, their cock-pits stripped down to a bucket-seat and a nest of control-sticks. Some had two bat-like wings, others three or four or ten; some flapped along beneath black, creaking things like broken umbrellas. On their massive engine-pods were painted hawks and sharks and naked ladies and raffish, devil-may-care names: *Damn You, Gravity!* and *Bad Hair Day*; *Contents Under Pressure* and *Delayed Gratification Now!* A begoggled aviatrix waved at Wren from the cockpit of something called the *Combat Wombat.* Wren waved back, but the squadron was already pulling away, dwindling to a cluster of specks far off above the sea.

Wren was trembling as the cable car carried her up through the belly of Cloud 9 to its terminus in the Pavilion gardens. She had always believed that Dad and Miss Freya knew everything there was to know about the world outside of Anchorage-in-Vineland, but clearly it had changed a lot in the sixteen years since they crossed the ice. They had known nothing about this terrible war, which was almost as old as she was, and she doubted they could even imagine the bizarre flying machines she had just seen. It made her feel even further away from them.

The pang of homesickness faded as her minders led her out of the upper cable-car terminus and along grav-elled paths towards the hub of Cloud 9, where the sugar-pink minarets and meringue domes of Pennyroyal's

118

palace rose from gardens filled with palm trees and cypresses, follies and fountains. Flocks of gaudy parakeets wheeled overhead, and above them Cloud 9's transparent gasbags shone in the sunlight like enormous bubbles.

"Your business?" asked a house-slave, stepping out to bar Shkin's way.

"Nabisco Shkin," the slave-dealer replied, and that was enough; the man bowed and stammered something and waved the visitors on, up an elegant white staircase to a broad sun-deck. At the heart of the sun-deck was a pool. In the middle of the pool, adrift on his airbed in a gold lamé swimming costume, a cocktail in one hand, a book in the other, his round face tilted to the sun, lounged Nimrod Pennyroyal.

Wren had worked out that Pennyroyal must be at least sixty-five, so she was expecting someone quite frail. But Pennyroyal had aged well. He had lost some weight, and most of his hair, but otherwise he looked not much different from the photographs Wren had seen of him, taken during his brief, unhappy stint as Anchorage's chief navigator. A bevy of attractive slave-girls trod water around his floating bed, clutching fresh drinks, a bookmark, trays of cakes and sweets and other items such as a busy mayor might need. A boy of Wren's age, long and black as an evening shadow, stood on the poolside waving an ostrich-feather fan.

"I see that Green Storm prisoner I sold you has settled in well," said Shkin.

"Ah? Oh!" Pennyroyal opened his eyes and sat up. "Ah! Afternoon, Shkin." He twisted round on his airbed to peer at the youth. "Yes, Mrs Pennyroyal is delighted with him. Makes a very handy fan-bearer. Lovely wafting action. And he goes so well with the dining-room wall-paper." He looked at Shkin again, and Wren had the impression that he wasn't particularly pleased to see the slave-trader. "Anyway, Nabisco, old chap, to what do I owe the um, ah. . ."

Shkin bowed faintly. "This girl was taken from one of the limpets we fished up last week. I thought you might wish to purchase her for the Pavilion." He gestured towards Wren, and his assistants moved her closer to the poolside so that the mayor might have a better view of her.

Pennyroyal peered at her. "Lost Girl, eh? She scrubs up well, I must say. But I thought we agreed we don't want any of her crowd hanging about in Brighton. Weren't you planning to sell them all to Nuevo Maya?"

"Afraid one of them might know a few awkward facts about your past, Pennyroyal?" said Shkin.

"Eh? What are you suggesting?"

"This girl," Shkin announced, "has lately arrived from the Dead Continent. From a city long thought lost, but actually thriving in that blasted land. A city of which I believe Your Worship has fond memories."

Reaching behind him, Shkin took something from one of his lackeys and lobbed it across the pool so that it landed on Pennyroyal's airbed. The Tin Book. Pennyroyal picked it up and studied the cover with a puzzled frown, then turned it over and looked at the paper label on the back.

"Great Gods!" he gasped, spilling his drink into the pool. "Anchorage!"

"This girl," Shkin said, "is none other than the daughter of your old travelling companion Hester Shaw."

"Oh cripes!" yelped Pennyroyal, and with a sudden, spasmodic lurch capsized his air-bed.

"I was concerned to discover that there are certain discrepancies between the story she tells and the version of events in your worship's interpolitan bestseller *Predator's Gold*," explained Nabisco Shkin, looking not the least bit concerned as he stood there on the poolside, leaning on his black steel cane, watching Pennyroyal splash and flounder. "So I decided it might be best if I gave your worship the opportunity to purchase her before her account can become publicly known and . . . *confuse* Your Worship's many readers. Naturally, she is priced at a premium. Shall we say, a thousand gold pieces?"

"Never!" spluttered Pennyroyal, standing up in the shallow end with all the dignity an elderly gentleman in a gold lamé swimming costume can muster. "You're nothing but a gangster, Shkin! I will not be intimidated by your puerile attempt to ah, er. . . It's not true is it? It can't be true! Hester Shaw had no daughter – and anyway, ah, Anchorage sank, didn't it; went down with all hands. . ."

"Ask her," said Shkin brightly, pointing the tip of his cane at Wren. "Ask Miss Natsworthy here."

Pennyroyal gawped at Wren, his eyes so full of fear that for a moment Wren felt almost sorry for him. "Well, girl?" he asked. "What do you say? Do you really claim to be from Anchorage?"

Wren took a deep breath and clenched her fists. Now that she was facing this legendary traitor and villain she felt less certain than ever that her plan would work.

"No," she said.

Shkin turned to stare at her.

121

"Of course it's not true," said Wren, managing a tight little laugh. "Anchorage went down in Arctic waters years and years ago. Everyone who has read your magnificent book knows that, Professor Pennyroyal. I'm just a poor Lost Girl from Grimsby."

Wren had turned her story this way and that in her mind on the way from the Pepperpot, and could not see how it could be disproved. Of course, if anyone asked the other Lost Boys, they would all say that Wren was not one of their tribe, and Fishcake knew who she really was – but why would Pennyroyal believe their word over Wren's? She could say that Shkin had bribed them to back him up.

"I've never been to Anchorage," she said firmly.

Shkin's nostrils flared. "Very well then; the book, the Tin Book, stamped with the seal of Anchorage's rulers – how do you explain that?"

Wren had already worked out an answer to that. "I brought it with me from Grimsby," she said. "It is a present for Your Worship. The Lost Boys stole it years and years ago, like we've stolen all sorts of things from all sorts of cities. Anchorage is a wreck, sunk at the bottom of the sea. Nobody lives there."

"But she told me herself she was Hester Shaw's daughter!" said Shkin. "Why would she lie?"

"Because of your wonderful books, Your Worship," explained Wren, and gazed at the mayor as adoringly as she could. "I have read them all. Whenever my limpet attached itself to a new city I would always burgle the bookshops first, in the hope that there would be a new Nimrod Pennyroyal. I told Mr Shkin I was from Anchorage just so that he would bring me to meet you."

Pennyroyal looked hopeful. He *so* wanted to believe her. "But your name," he said. "Natsworthy. . ."

"Oh, it's not my *real* name," Wren said brightly. "I looked up Hester Shaw in Uncle's records, and it said she used to travel with someone called that."

"Oh, really?" Pennyroyal tried to hide his relief. "Never heard of him."

Wren smiled, pleased at how easy it was to lie, and how good she was turning out to be at it. Her story didn't make a lot of sense, but when you tell someone something that they want to hear, they tend to believe you; WOPCART had taught her that.

She said, "I was planning to keep up the pretence, Professor, in the hope that you would take me into your household. Even if I were only the lowliest of your slaves, at least I would be close to the author of *Predator's Gold* and . . . and all those other books." She lowered her eyes demurely. "But as soon as I saw you, sir, I realized that you would never be taken in by my lies, and so I resolved to tell you the truth."

"Very commendable," said Pennyroyal. "Quite right too. I saw through it in an instant, you know. Although oddly enough you do bear a slight resemblance to poor Hester. That's why I was startled when you first appeared. That young woman was very, very dear to me, and it is the deepest regret of my life that I didn't manage to save her."

Ooh, you rotten liar! thought Wren, but all she said was, "I expect I must go now, sir. I expect Mr Shkin will wish to make what profit of me he can. But I go happily, for at least I have spoken with the finest author of the age."

"Absolutely not!" Pennyroyal heaved himself out of the pool and stood dripping, waving away the girls who came hurrying round him with towels, clothes and a portable changing tent. "I will not hear of it, Shkin! This delightful, intelligent young person has shown pluck, initiative and sound literary judgement. I forbid you to flog her off as a common slave."

"I have my overheads to consider, Your Worship." Shkin was angry now; white with it, and struggling to keep himself under control.

"I'll buy her myself then," said Pennyroyal. He wasn't a sentimental man, but he didn't like to think of this discerning girl being punished for her love of his books – besides, house-slaves were tax-deductible. "My wife can always use a few extra handmaidens about the place," he explained, "especially now, with the preparations for the Moon Festival ball to attend to. Tell you what, I'll give you twenty Dolphins for her. That's more than fair."

"Twenty?" sneered Shkin, as if such a sum were too small to even contemplate.

"Sold!" said Pennyroyal quickly. "My people will pay you. And next time, my dear fellow, try not to be so gullible. Honestly, how could anyone believe that this girl came from America? Quite absurd!"

Shkin bowed slightly. "As you say, Your Worship. Absurd." He held out his hand. "The Tin Book, if you please."

Pennyroyal, who had been leafing through the Tin Book, snapped it shut and clutched it to his chest. "I think not, Shkin. The girl said this was a present for me."

"It is my property!"

"No it's not. Your contract with the council states that any Lost Boys you fished up were yours. This isn't a Lost Boy, not by any stretch of the imagination. It's some sort of Ancient code, possibly valuable. It is my duty as mayor of Brighton to hang on to it for, ah, further study."

Shkin stared for a long moment at the mayor, then at Wren. He manufactured a smile. "No doubt we shall all meet again," he said pleasantly, and turned, snapping his fingers for his men to follow him as he walked briskly away.

Pennyroyal's girls clustered around him, enclosing him within his changing-tent. For a short time Wren was left alone. She grinned, flushed with her own cleverness. She might still be a slave, but she was a posh slave, in the house of the mayor himself! She would get good food and fine clothes, and probably never have to carry anything much heavier than the odd tray of fairy-cakes. And she would meet all kinds of interesting people. Handsome aviators, for instance, who might be persuaded to fly her home to Vineland.

Her only regret was that she hadn't managed to bring Fishcake up here with her. She felt responsible for the boy, and hoped that the slave-dealer wouldn't take out his anger on him. But it would be all right. One way or another, she would escape, and then maybe she'd find a way of helping Fishcake, too.

Nabisco Shkin was not a man who let his emotions show, and by the time the cable car set him down again on Brighton's deckplates he had mastered his temper. At the Pepperpot he greeted Miss Weems with no more than his customary coldness, and told her, "Bring me the little Lost Boy."

Soon afterwards he was sitting calmly in his office, watching Fishcake tuck into a second bowl of chocolate ice cream and listening again to his account of the *Autolycus*'s voyage to Vineland. This boy was telling the truth, Shkin was sure of it. But there was no point in trying to use him to discredit the mayor; he was young, and easily influenced; if it came to a trial, Pennyroyal's lawyers would tear him to shreds. Shkin closed his eyes thoughtfully, and pictured Vineland. "Are you quite certain you can find the place again, boy?"

"Oh yes, Mr Shkin," said Fishcake, with his mouth full.

Shkin smiled at him over the tips of his steepled fingers. "Good. Very good," he said. "You know, boy; every now and then I acquire a slave who proves too useful or too bright to part with; Miss Weems for example. I hope that you will be another."

Fishcake nervously returned the smile. "You mean you ain't going to sell me off to them Nuevo-Mayan devils, sir?"

"No, no, no, no," Shkin assured him, shaking his head. "I want you to serve me, Fishcake. We'll have you trained up as an apprentice. And next summer, when the weather improves, I shall outfit an expedition, and you will lead us to Anchorage-in-Vineland. I imagine those Vinelanders or Anchorites or whatever they call themselves will fetch a good price at the slave-markets."

Fishcake listened wide-eyed, then grinned. "Yes, Mr Shkin! Thank you, Mr Shkin!"

Shkin leaned back in his chair, his temper quite restored. He would revenge himself on Pennyroyal by showing the whole world that Anchorage had survived. As for that treacherous little vixen Wren, let her see how clever she felt when the Shkin Corporation enslaved all her family and friends.

15
CHILDREN OF THE DEEP

The limpet *Screw Worm* had been built long before the Lost Boys started to use wireless crab-cams. Even its radio set had stopped working long ago. It had no way of receiving the broadcasts from Brighton, and so Hester, Tom and Freya never had to find out whether Caul's desire to meet his parents would have outweighed his loyalty to his friends. Deaf to WOPCART's invitations, the *Screw Worm* swam north into the deep, cold waters of the Greenland Trench. On the same late summer afternoon that Wren came face to face with Pennyroyal, its passengers finally sighted Grimsby.

Tom had visited the underwater city once before, but Hester and Freya knew it only from his descriptions. They jostled for a view as Caul steered the limpet closer.

Grimsby had been a giant industrial raft once. Now it was a drowned wreck, resting on the slopes of an undersea mountain. Weed and barnacles and rust were all working hard to camouflage it, blurring the outlines of buildings and paddle-wheels until it was difficult to tell where Grimsby ended and the mountain began.

"Where are the lights?" asked Tom. His strongest memory of the Lost Boys' lair was the surreal glow of lamplight in the windows of Grimsby's sunken Town Hall. Now, the whole city lay in darkness.

"Something's wrong," said Caul.

Something bumped against the *Screw Worm*'s hull. Shards of splintered wood and torn plastic revolved in the splay of light from the nose-lantern. The limpet was swimming through a zone of drifting wreckage.

"The whole place is dead –" Hester said, and then stopped short, because if that were true then Wren was probably dead as well.

"Look at the Burglarium!" Caul whispered, shocked. A big building slid by on the starboard side, a building where he had spent much of his childhood, now lightless and open to the sea, litter swirling around huge, jagged rents in its walls. A boy's body turned slow somersaults as the *Worm*'s wake reached it. Others tumbled in the flooded glastic tunnel which had once linked the Burglarium to the Town Hall. "Power plant's gone, too," he added, as they passed over a domed building which had been smashed like an eggshell. His voice sounded tight and strained. "The Town Hall looks all right. Nobody about, though. I'll see if we can get inside."

It was sixteen years since Caul had fled this place, but he had made the approach to the limpet pens a thousand times in his dreams since then. He swung the *Screw Worm* towards the water-door at the base of the Town Hall. The door stood open. Silvery fish were darting in and out.

"Still no one," he said. "It should be closed. There should be sentry-subs to check us out."

"Maybe they're trying to raise us on the radio and we can't hear them," Tom suggested hopefully.

"What do we do?" asked Freya.

"We go in, of course," said Hester. She checked the gun in her belt, the knife in her boot. If there were any Lost Boys left alive in there, she meant to show them what Valentine's daughter was made of.

The *Screw Worm* slid into the tunnels. Automatic doors opened ahead and closed behind. "The emergency power must be on," said Caul. "That's something. . ."

"It could be a trap," said Hester. "They might be wait-ing for us."

But no one was waiting for the *Screw Worm*. It sur-faced in one of the moon-pools in the floor of the limpet pen and its passengers scrambled out into cold, stale air. The darkness was broken only by a few dim, red emer-gency lights. Air-pumps wheezed asthmatically. The big space, which Tom remembered as being filled with Lost Boys and limpets, was deserted. Docking cranes stood mournfully above the empty moon-pools, like the skele-tons of dinosaurs in an abandoned museum. A fat cargo submarine wallowed in a dock on the far side of the pens, her hatches open. A half-dismantled limpet lay in a repair-yard, but there was no sign of the mechanics who should have been working on her.

Tom fetched an electric lantern from the *Screw Worm*'s hold and went ahead, still trying to hope that he would find Wren here somewhere, alive and safe and running to hug him. He shone the lantern into the inky shadows under the cranes. Once or twice he thought he glimpsed a crab-cam scuttling away from the light. Nothing else moved.

"Where is everybody?" he whispered.

"Well, here's one of them," said Hester.

The big door at the back of the pens stood half open, and on the threshold lay a boy of Wren's age, curled up, staring, dead. Hester pushed past Tom and stepped over the body. In the corridor outside the pens lay a half-dozen more, some killed by sword-thrusts, others by metal spears from harpoon-guns.

"Looks like the Lost Boys have been fighting among themselves," she said. "Nice of them to save us the trouble."

Tom stepped gingerly over the dead boy and looked up. Cold drops of water pattered on his upturned face. "This place is leaking like a rusty tin can," he murmured.

"Uncle will know how to fix it," said Caul. The others turned to look at him, surprised by the confidence in his voice. He felt surprised by it himself. "Uncle built Grimsby," he reminded them. "He made the first few rooms airtight and built the first limpet all on his own, without anyone to help him." He nodded, fingering his neck. The old rope-burns were still there, hard under his fingertips, reminders of how much he had feared and hated Uncle at the end. But before that, for a long time, he had loved him. Now that he was here again, and the Burglarium was a ruin and the Lost Boys gone, he found that the fear and the hate had gone as well and that only love was left. He remembered how safe he used to feel, curled up in his bunk while Uncle's voice whispered from the ceiling-speakers through the long night-shift. The world had been simple then, and he had been happy.

"Uncle Knows Best," he murmured.

A sudden movement in the shadows further down the corridor made Hester swing her gun up. Freya grabbed her arm before she could shoot, and Tom yelled "Het, no!" The echoes of his voice went booming away up staircases and down side-passages, and the face which had been pinned for an instant in his lantern beam vanished as its owner darted backwards into the shadows.

"It's all right," said Freya, moving past Hester, her hands held out in front of her. "We won't hurt you."

The darkness was suddenly full of soft footfalls, rustlings. Eyes glinted in the lantern-light. Out from their hiding places the children of Grimsby came creeping, smudged white faces pale as petals. They were newbies, too young to take their places yet among the Lost Boys. A few were as old as nine or ten; most were much younger. They stared at their visitors with wide, scared eyes. One girl, older and bolder than the rest, came close to Freya and said, "Are you our mummies and daddies?"

Freya knelt down so that her face was level with the children's. "No," she said. "No, I'm sorry, we're not."

"But our mummies and daddies are coming, aren't they?" whispered another child.

"There was a message. . ."

"They said they were near," said a little boy, tugging at Caul's hand and looking up earnestly into his face. "They said we should go to them, and a lot of the big boys wanted to, even though Uncle said not. . ."

"And when the other boys tried stopping them they fought them and killed them dead!"

"And then they went anyway. They took all the limpets."

"We wanted to go with them, but they said there wasn't room and we were only newbies. . ."

"And there were explosions!" said a girl.

"No, that was later, silly," said another. "That was the depth-charges."

"Bang!" shouted the smallest boy, waving his arms about to demonstrate. "Bang!"

"And all the lights went out, and I think some water got in. . ."

All the children were talking at once, crowding into the light from Tom's lantern. Hester held her hand out to one of them, but he backed away and went to snuggle against Freya instead.

131

"Is Wren here?" Hester asked. "We're looking for our daughter, Wren."

"She's lost," Tom explained. "She was aboard the *Autolycus*."

Small faces turned towards him, blank as unwritten pages. The older girl said, "*Autolycus* ain't come back. None of the limpets that went out these last three weeks has come back."

"Then where's Wren?" shouted Tom. He had been terrified that he would find Wren dead. The prospect of not finding her at all was almost as bad. He stared from one bewildered little face to another. "What in Quirke's name has been happening?"

The children backed away from him, frightened.

"Where's Uncle?" asked Caul. Freya smiled at him to let the children see that he was a friend and they should answer his question.

"Maybe he left too," said Hester.

Caul shook his head. "Don't be stupid. Uncle wouldn't leave Grimsby."

"I think he's upstairs," said one of the boys.

"He's very old," said another, doubtfully.

"He doesn't ever leave his chamber now," agreed a third.

Caul nodded. "Good. We'll talk to him. He'll be able to tell us what's happened, and he'll tell us where to find Wren." He could feel the others staring at him. He turned to them and smiled. "It'll be all right. You'll see. Uncle Knows Best."

16

THOSE ARE PEARLS THAT WERE HIS EYES

They made a strange procession, climbing the cluttered stairways of Grimsby, where salt water dripped from hair-line fractures in the high roof and ran in rivulets from step to step. More bodies lay on the landings, forming dams which the dirty water pooled behind. Overhead, crab-cameras clung to ducts and bannisters. Now and then one turned to follow the newcomers with its cyclops eye.

Hester went ahead. Behind her Tom, Caul and Freya were surrounded by children, small hands clutching theirs and reaching out to touch their clothes as if to reassure themselves that these visitors from the world above were real. They were especially drawn to Freya. In shocked, whispery voices they told her all sorts of secrets.

"Whitebait picks his nose."

"I do not!"

"My name's Esbjørn but the big boys at the Burglarium said I had to be called Tuna, only I think Tuna's a stupid name, so can I change back now all the big boys have got killed dead and run away?"

"He sticks his finger right up there. And he eats the bogies."

"I *don't*!"

"Children," asked Freya, "who was it who blew up the Burglarium? How long ago did it happen?"

But the children couldn't answer that; a few days, said some, a week, reckoned others. Their chatter faded as they neared the upper floors. They looked into an enormous chamber, new since Tom and Caul were last in

Grimsby, made by knocking a dozen of the old rooms together. It was stuffed with fine furnishings; plunder from burgled town halls and looted statics. Huge mirrors hung on the walls, and swags of silk and velvet curtained the colossal bed. Clothes and cushions were strewn across the floor, and mobiles made from holed beach-stones and antique seedies hung from the ducts on the ceiling.

"This was Gargle's quarters," explained the children. "Gargle ran things from here."

"Remora made the mobiles," said a little girl. "She's pretty and clever and she's Gargle's favourite."

"I wish Gargle would come back," a boy said. "Gargle would know what to do."

"Gargle's dead," said Hester.

After that the only sounds were the pad of their feet on the wet carpets and a faint voice somewhere ahead, tinny and fizzing as if it were coming through loud-speakers. It said, "We only want to be reunited with our dear, lost children. . ."

Up a final stairway to the chamber of screens, where Grimsby's founder kept watch over his underwater king-dom. Last time Tom had been here it was guarded; this time the guards were gone, and the door was not even locked. Hester kicked it open and went through it with her gun out.

The others crowded in behind. The chamber was large and high-ceilinged, lit blue by the ghostly glow of the screens which covered the walls. They were of every shape and size, from giant public goggle-screens to tiny displays ripped from Old-Tech hospital equip-ment, all linked together by a jungle of flexes and ducts. Up above, in the dark dome of the roof, hung a portable surveillance station; a midget cargo balloon dangling a globe of screens and speakers. And every screen was showing the same picture; a crowd of people on the windswept observation platform of a raft city. "Children of the Deep," the voice from the speakers pleaded, "if you can hear us, we beg you, come to us!"

"Why did they fall for it? Why did they go? Did they prefer a bunch of old Drys to *me*?"

In the middle of the chamber an old man stood with his back to the door, shouting at the recording on the screens. In his hand was a remote-control device; he raised it and pressed a switch that made all the screens go blank and silent, then turned to face Hester and the others.

"Who are you?" he demanded petulantly. "Where's Gargle?"

"Gargle's not coming back," said Tom, as gently as he could. He had bad memories of Uncle, but that did not stop him feeling sorry for the stooped old man who was shuffling towards him in a pair of threadbare bunny-slippers. The tortoise-like head, poking out from layer upon layer of mouldy clothes, blinked short-sightedly at him. Uncle's eyes were clouded with age, and Tom noticed that many of the screens which surrounded him had big magnifying lenses bolted in front of them to make their pictures clearer. He suspected that Uncle was almost blind. No wonder he had come to depend on Gargle.

"Gargle has passed on," he said.

"What, you mean. . .?" Uncle came closer, peering at him. "Dead? Gargle? Little Gargle what gave himself such airs and graces?" His face showed grief, then relief, then anger. "I *told* him! I warned him not to go looking for that rotten book. He wasn't cut out for burgling, Gargle wasn't. More of a planner. He had brains, Gargle did."

"We know," said Hester. "We saw them."

Uncle recoiled from the sound of her voice. "A woman? There's no females allowed in Grimsby. I've always been very strict about that. Gargle always backed me up on that. No girls allowed. Bad luck, that's all they bring. Can't trust them."

"But Uncle. . ." said Freya gently.

"Eugh, there's another one! The whole place is crawling with females!"

"Uncle?" asked Caul.

The old man twitched round, frowning, as if the sound of Caul's voice had tripped a rusty switch inside his head. "Caul, my boy!" he said, and then, with a snarl, "This your doing is it? You got something to do with this? Tell the Drys how to find us, did you? You alone, or are there more?"

He limped away, stabbing at his remote control until the jumbled screens were filled with views of Grimsby, thrusting his parchment face close to the glass to stare at the empty corridors and chambers, the empty limpet pen, the flooded, ruined halls of the Burglarium.

"It's just the four of us, Uncle," said Caul. "We barely know what's happened here. It's nothing to do with us."

"No?" Uncle stared at him, then let out a high-pitched cackle. "Gods, then you've picked a fine time to drop in for a visit!"

"We've come for Tom and Hester's daughter," Caul

said patiently. "Her name's Wren. She was taken from Vineland by the newbie who was with Gargle aboard the *Autolycus*."

"Fishcake? Fishcake, that was his name. . ." Uncle hung his head. When he spoke, he sounded close to tears. "The *Autolycus* is missing. They're all missing, Caul, my boy. The fools got that message about their mums and dads and they went haring straight off to Brighton."

"To Brighton?" Tom had heard of Brighton. A resort town; a bit bohemian, but not a bad sort of place. If Wren were there, she might be all right.

"Why would Brighton want them?" asked Hester suspiciously.

Uncle shrugged and spread his hands and made various other twitchy gestures to show that he had no idea. "I *told* my boys it was a trap. I *told* them. But they wouldn't hear it. Maybe if Gargle had been here. They listen to Gargle. Don't listen to their poor old Uncle any more, what's slaved and worried for them all these years –" Tears of self-pity went creeping down his crumpled old face, and he blew his nose on his sleeve. His gaze slid listlessly over Tom and Hester, then settled on Freya again. "Gods, Caul, is that great fat whale the girl you ran off to Anchorage for? She's let herself go! Come to think of it, you don't look too good yourself. I like my boys to be well turned out, and you. . . Well, you're shabby, that's the truth of it. Gargle told me you'd gone to make something of yourself among the Drys."

Caul felt as if he were a newbie again, being told off for forgetting part of his burgling kit. "Sorry, Uncle," he said.

137

Freya moved to his side, and took his hand in hers. "Caul *has* made something of himself," she said. "We couldn't have built Anchorage-in-Vineland without his help. I'd like to tell you all about it, but first I think we all have to leave this place."

"Leave?" Uncle stared at her as if he'd never heard the word before. "I can't leave! What makes you think I'd want to leave?"

"Sir, this place is finished. You can't keep the children here. . ."

Uncle laughed. "Those lads aren't going anywhere," he said. "They're the future of Grimsby."

The children edged in closer to Freya. She let go Caul's hand to stroke their heads. Everyone could hear the faint groan of stressed metal from the lower floors, the distant splatter of water spilling in.

"But Mr Kael," said Freya. She had remembered something Caul had told her once. Before Uncle became Uncle he had been Stilton Kael, a rich young man from Arkangel. Freya hoped that by using his real name she might be able to get through to him, but it only made him hiss and glare. She pressed on anyway. "Mr Kael, this place is leaking. It's half flooded, and the air smells stale. I don't know much about secret underwater lairs, but I'd say Grimsby's future is going to be pretty short."

Hester snapped off the safety on her Schadenfreude and aimed it in Uncle's general direction. "If you don't want to come," she said, "you don't have to."

Uncle peered at her, then up at his hovering globe of screens, where there was an image of her face far clearer than the one his poor old eyes could provide him with. "You don't understand," he said. "I'm not leaving, and nor are you. We're going to rebuild. Make the place water-tight again. Stronger than ever. Make more limpets, better ones. We are none of us leaving. Tell them, Caul."

Caul flinched, and wondered what to do. He didn't want to betray his friends, but he didn't want to let Uncle down either. The sound of the old man's voice made him shiver with love and pity.

He looked at Freya. "Sorry," he mumbled. Then, with a sudden, quick movement he jerked Hester's gun out of her hand and pointed it at her, then at Tom.

"Caul!" Tom shouted.

Uncle cackled some more. "Good work, boy! I knew you'd come right in the end! I'm quite glad I didn't finish hanging you now. What a shame those others scarpered off before they had a chance to meet you, Caul. You'd be an object lesson. Return of the Prodigal. All these years gone, and you're still loyal to your poor old Uncle." He pulled a key from one of his pockets and held it out towards Caul. "Now get rid of this lot. Lock 'em in Gargle's quarters while we have a proper talk."

Caul kept pointing the gun at Tom, because he knew that Hester was the only one reckless enough to try and overpower him, and that Hester cared more about Tom's safety than her own. He fished the knife out of Hester's boot, then took the key from Uncle and started shooing everyone else backwards towards the open door.

"But Caul—" Freya said.

"Forget it," Hester told her. "I knew we were wrong to trust him. I expect this is the only reason he agreed to bring us here, so he could see his precious Uncle again."

"You won't be hurt," Caul promised. "We'll sort this out. It'll be all right." He didn't know what he was going to do, only that he was glad to be a Lost Boy again.

"Uncle knows best," he said, as he forced his prisoners down the stairs and into Gargle's quarters, locking the doors behind them. "It'll be all right. Uncle always knows best."

17

THE CHAPEL

Nightfall in Tienjing. Above the city the mountains hung huge and pale, a pennant of powder snow flying from each cold summit. Above the mountains, colder yet, the stars were coming out, and the things that were not stars, the dead satellites and orbital platforms of the Ancients, danced their old, slow dance in heaven.

The Stalker Shrike patrolled the silent corridors of the Jade Pagoda, his night-vision eyes probing the shadows, his ears detecting conversations in a distant room, a gust of laughter from the guard-house, the woodworm busy in the panelled walls. He roamed through galleries decorated with ancient carvings of monsters and mountain-demons, none of them as scary as himself. Relishing the grace and power of his re-tuned body, he checked with all his many senses for the faint chemical signature of hidden explosives, or the body-glow of a lurking assassin. He hoped that soon some foolish once-born would try to attack his mistress. He was looking forward to killing again.

A cold breath touched him; a faint change in air-pressure which told him of an outside door being opened and closed, four floors below. He moved quickly to a window and looked down. A forked blob of body-heat was moving through the shadows of the courtyard towards the check-point at the gate. Shrike measured its height and stride against the data he had gathered during his time as bodyguard, and recognized Dr Zero.

Where was she going, on such a cold night, with

curfew due in less than an hour? Shrike pondered the motives of the once-born. Perhaps Dr Zero had a lover in the lower city. But Dr Zero had never seemed interested in love, and anyway, this was not the first time that Shrike had caught her acting strangely. He had noticed the way her heartbeat raced when she was near the Stalker Fang, and smelled the sharp scent that came from her sometimes when Fang glanced her way. He was surprised that his mistress had not noticed these things herself – but then, Fang did not share his interest in the once-born and their ways. Perhaps she did not realize, or did not care, that her surgeon-mechanic was afraid of her.

Shrike's eyes, on maximum magnification, watched Dr Zero show her pass at the check-point and followed her until she was lost to him among the barracks and banners of Tienjing. Why was she so frightened? What scared her so? What was she doing? What was she *planning* to do?

Shrike owed her everything, but he still knew that it was his duty to find out.

Down through the steep, stepped streets Oenone Zero went hurrying in her silicone-silk cloak, hood up, head down. The sky above the city was full of the running lights of carriers and air-destroyers taking off from the military air-harbour, carrying yet more young men and women away to the west, where their deaths were waiting for them on the Rustwater Salient.

Guilt welled up inside Oenone, but she was used to it. Every morning she tended the Stalker Fang's joints and bodywork, and placed her instruments against the Stalker Fang's steel breast to check on the strange Old-Tech power source that nestled where Anna Fang's heart had once been. Every morning she told herself, *I should do it now, today*.

She would not be the first to try. All sorts of fanatical peaceniks and die-hard supporters of the old League had attempted to destroy the Stalker Fang, only to have their knives snap on her armour; or watch her walk unscathed from the ruins of bombed rooms and the wrecks of airships. But Oenone Zero was a scientist, and she had used her scientist's skills to devise a weapon that could destroy even the Stalker Fang.

The trouble was, she hadn't the courage to use it. What if it didn't work? What if it *did* work? Oenone was sure that, without the Stalker to lead it, the Green Storm regime would fall apart – but she doubted it would fall apart so quickly that the Stalker's supporters would not find time to kill her, and she had heard rumours about the things they did to traitors.

Lost in her thoughts, she did not notice that she was being followed as she crossed Double Rainbow Bridge and turned on to the Street of Ten Thousand Deities.

Over the centuries, Anti-Tractionists from all over Europe and Asia had fled into these mountains, and they had brought their own gods with them. Packed side by side, the temples seemed to jostle each other in the dying light. Oenone pushed her way past two wedding processions, a funeral, past shrines decked with lucky money and clattering firecrackers. She passed the temple of the Sky Gods, and the Golden Pagoda of the Gods of the Mountains. She passed the Poskittarium, and the grove

143

of the Apple Goddess. She passed the silent house of Lady Death. At the end of the street, sandwiched between the temples of more popular religions, stood a tiny Christian chapel.

She checked to make sure that no one was watching her before she stepped inside, but she did not think to look up at the rooftops.

Oenone had found the chapel by accident, and was not certain what kept drawing her back to it. She was not a Christian. Few people were any more, except in Africa, and on certain islands of the outermost west. All she knew of Christians was that they worshipped a god nailed to a cross, and what on earth was the use of a god who went around letting himself get nailed to things? It was small wonder that this place had fallen into disuse, its roof gone, weeds growing through the rotting pews. But on nights like this, when she felt that she must get out of the Jade Pagoda or go mad, this was where Oenone came to calm herself.

Snowflakes sifted down on her through a sagging sieve of rafters, settling on her green hair when she threw back her hood. Running her hands over the walls, she read with her fingertips the texts carved in the old stone. Most were illegible, but there was one that she had grown fond of. It was an old fragment, from before the Sixty Minute War, and Oenone was not sure what it meant, but there was something consoling about it.

We die with the dying:
See, they depart, and we go with them.
We are born with the dead:
See, they return, and bring us with them.

The moment of the rose and the moment of the yew-tree
Are of equal duration.

Oenone knelt before the bare stone altar and bowed her head. She didn't believe in him, this ancient god, but she had to talk to someone.

"Help me," she whispered. "If you are there at all, give me strength. Give me courage. I'm so close to her. I could use the weapon now, if only I were brave enough. And it wouldn't be murder, would it, to kill someone who is already dead? I would only be smashing a machine; a dangerous, destructive machine. . ."

She spoke softly, barely moving her lips. No human ear could hear her. But her prayer was heard, just the same. Crouched like a gargoyle on the chapel's ruined steeple, the Stalker Shrike listened carefully to every word.

"Have I the right to do it? It all seemed so clear before, but now I have seen her; how clever she is, and how strong. . . Maybe it *would* be murder. Or am I just making excuses for myself? Am I just looking for a reason not to do it, so that I can live? Send me a sign, God, if you're up there; show me what I should do. . ."

She waited, and Shrike waited with her, but no sign came. The noisy, popular gods of the neighbouring temples seemed to dish out comfort and advice like agony aunts, but the god of this place was less scrutable; maybe he was asleep, or dead. Maybe he was busy with some better world, off at the far end of the universe. Oenone Zero shook her head at her own foolishness and stood up, making ready to leave.

Shrike climbed quickly down the chapel wall and

waited in an alcove by the entrance, where perhaps a statue of the Christians' nailed-up god had once hung. His suspicions had been right. Dr Zero was a traitor, and although he had grown fond of her in his Stalkerish way, he knew that he must eliminate her before she could harm his mistress. His circuitry hummed and tingled at the prospect of a kill. She had taken his claws from him, but he was still strong, and merciless. One blow from his fist would end her easily.

A footstep on the threshold. The young woman stepped out of the chapel, pulling up her hood against the cold wind. She did not see Shrike. She went past him, and walked quickly away along the Street of Ten Thousand Deities, hurrying back to her quarters in the pagoda before the curfew bells were rung.

Shrike lowered his fist, feeling startled and slightly foolish. What had happened to him? He was a Stalker, a killing machine, and yet, when his quarry's eggshell skull had been in reach, he could not strike.

I must warn the Green Storm's secret police, he thought, jumping down from the alcove and following Oenone out into the crowds on the street. He would let the once-born deal with her themselves, down in their white-tiled torture-rooms beneath the Jade Pagoda. But after a few strides he halted. He simply didn't have it in him to betray Oenone Zero.

She has done this to me, he thought, remembering all those lonely night-shifts in the Stalker Works. Somehow, the young surgeon-mechanic had built a barrier in his mind that made it impossible for him to harm her, or tell anyone what she was planning. He had been part of her plans all along. She had given the Stalker Fang a bodyguard who was not capable of guarding her.

He should have hated Dr Zero for using him like that; but he did not have it in him to hate her, either.

He barged through a festival procession outside the shrine of Jomo and climbed homeward through the darkness and the snow. He was not the puppet of Oenone Zero. He could not harm her, but he would keep her from harming his mistress. Somehow he would learn the nature of her plan, and put a stop to it.

18

THE *NAGLFAR*

As soon as he had locked his friends and the children inside Gargle's quarters, Caul sprinted back up the stairs to the chamber of screens. He was shuddering slightly, and half inclined to go back down and unlock the doors again. He kept telling himself that he hadn't chosen Uncle over Freya and the others; he would find a way to stay true to both of them.

"First thing we must do," said Uncle, when Caul rejoined him, "is to get rid of those women. Bad luck, they'll be. You'll see." He had filled his screens with images of the captives in the room below; big, grainy close-ups of Hester and Freya. He said, "They look very pretty, I'm sure, and no doubt you think they're very sweet, but they'll twist round and betray you, like my Anna did me all those years ago. That's why I've always made it the rule that there ain't no girls in Grimsby."

Caul put down Hester's gun. He felt stupid standing there holding it. "But what about the girl who was aboard the *Autolycus* with Gargle?"

"Young Remora?" Uncle snatched the gun and stuffed it away inside his filthy clothes. "I know what you mean. Odd-looking lad. High-pitched voice. Long hair. Too much make-up. I had my doubts when Gargle first introduced me, but Gargle assured me he was a boy. A fine burglar. Poor Remora. I suppose he's dead too?"

"Uncle, there are girls among those poor children we found downstairs. Lots of them are girls."

"Girls? You're sure?" Uncle started thumbing his remote control, hunting for close-ups of the children. Caul saw his friends on the screens look up nervously as crab-cams spidered around on the ceiling above them, jangling Remora's mobiles. Uncle saw only greyish, face-shaped blurs. "Maybe Gargle's kidnapping squads *have* grabbed a few girls by mistake," he muttered grudgingly. "We'll have to get rid of them too, if we're to make a new start. And we will make a new start, Caul, my boy. We'll rebuild Grimsby, stronger and better than it ever was before, and you'll be my right hand. You can move into Gargle's pad, and look after things for me like Gargle used to do."

One of the banks of screens behind him suddenly died, leaving the room even more dimly lit than before. There was a smell of burnt wiring, and when Caul went to investigate he saw that water was flooding down the surfaces of the screens and pooling on the floor below. He touched some to his lips, and tasted brine. *Uncle Knows Best*, he told himself, and he wanted to believe it, because it would have been good to go back to the old days, when he had been so certain about every-thing. Everybody had to believe in something better and greater than themselves. Tom and Freya had their gods, and Hester had Tom, and Caul had Uncle. He would not let Uncle down again, even though he was old, and blind, and confused; even though there was probably nothing that could save Grimsby from the sea.

But he would not let his friends drown with him.

"You look tired, Uncle," he said gently. It was true. How long had the old man been alone in this room, star-ing at the treacherous message from Brighton on his walls of screens? Caul touched his hand. "You should get some rest, now I'm here to keep an eye on things."

Uncle's head jerked round to stare at him, his eyes

149

glittering with something of their old cunning. "You trying to trick me, Caul? That's what Gargle did. 'Have a nap, Uncle, dear,' he'd say. 'Lie down for forty winks, Uncle.' And when I woke up, some of my stuff would be missing, or another boy I'd trusted would be dead, and Gargle telling me it had been an accident. . ."

"Why did you let him get away with it?" asked Caul.

The old man shrugged. "'Cos I was scared of him. And 'cos I was proud of him. He was a sharp one, that Gargle, and it was me who made him that way. He was like a son to me, I s'pose. I like to think that me and Anna might have had sons, if she hadn't tricked me and flown off in that homemade airship of hers. I like to think they'd have been as sharp as Gargle. But I'm glad he's gone, Caul, my boy. I'm glad it's you here now."

Mumbling quietly to himself, Uncle let Caul lead him up the steep stair to his bedchamber. The midget engine-pods of the old cargo balloon whined and clattered as the ball of screens went with them, hanging a few feet above their heads so that Uncle could keep staring up at it, his half-blind eyes flicking nervously from one screen to another. The entrance to his bedroom had been made higher and wider to let the balloon squeeze through. "Gotta keep watching them, Caul," he muttered. "Never know what they'll get up to unwatched. Gotta watch everybody. Everywhere. Always."

The room had been richly furnished once, for the Lost Boys had brought all the finest things they stole here, as tribute to Uncle. But over the years, piece by piece, Gargle must have found excuses to move all the treasures downstairs to his own quarters. All that remained was a bed with a threadbare quilt, some piles of mouldy books and an upturned crate which served as a bedside table; it held an old argon lamp, and a faded photograph of a beautiful young woman in the uniform of an Arkangel slave worker.

"I keep that to remind me," said Uncle, when he saw Caul looking at the picture, and quickly turned it face down. "My Anna Fang. Pretty, weren't she? They've gone and made a Stalker of her now, and put her in charge of the Green Storm, and she rules over half the world, with airships and armies at her command. I've followed her career. Got a book of cuttings, somewhere. Gargle thought he could do a deal with her, but I knew it wouldn't work. Knew it would only lead to trouble. . ."

"What sort of deal?" asked Caul. He had heard Uncle talk about his lost love once before, but he had never heard of the Lost Boys trying to do a deal with the world outside. "Is that why Gargle came to Anchorage? Why he wanted the Tin Book?"

Uncle sat down on the bed, and his moon of surveillance screens dipped until it was hanging just above his head. "Gargle said there was trouble coming. As soon as those first three limpets went missing he said, 'There's trouble coming.' He was right, too, wasn't he? Only he didn't know how soon. He thought if he got hold of that Tin Book he could give it to the Green Storm and ask for their protection in exchange; get them to smash whatever city came hunting for us."

"But why would they want the Tin Book?" asked Caul.

"Who knows?" replied Uncle, with a shrug. "A couple of summers back they sent an expedition to try and find the wreck of Anchorage. They didn't, of course. But Gargle got a crab-cam aboard their ship, and he found out what it was they was hoping to dredge up."

"The Tin Book?"

Uncle nodded. "They weren't ordinary Green Storm, neither. They were special agents, who reported straight to *her*. So Gargle thought, if she's ready to send ships full of herberts halfway round the world in the middle of a war looking for this thing, she must want it pretty bad. And he remembered seeing something like it when he was burgling Anchorage that time, only he didn't think nothing of it then." He shook his head. "I told him it wouldn't work. I told him to stay put. But he was like that, young Gargle; once he got an idea in his head there weren't no stopping him, and off he went, and now he's dead, and that wicked city's stolen all my boys away."

"But what *was* it?" asked Caul. "The Tin Book, I mean? What makes it so valuable?"

Uncle, who had been sniffling miserably, blew his nose on a polka-dot handkerchief and peered at Caul. "Don't know," he said. "We never did find out. Gargle put about the story that it was the plans to some great big Ancient submarine that would save us all, but I think he made that up. What would my poor Anna want with a submarine? No. I reckon it's a weapon. Something big."

He stuffed the handkerchief away and yawned. "Now, my boy. Enough about the past. We should think of the future. We should make plans. Time to start rebuilding. We'll need to nick some stuff. Lucky you brought the *Screw Worm* home with you, that'll come in proper handy, that will. And I've still got the old *Naglfar*. Remember the good old *Naglfar*?"

"Saw her in the pens when we arrived," said Caul. He could see that Uncle was growing sleepy. He helped

152

him lie down, and pulled the tattered quilt over him, tucking it under his chin. "You have a little sleep," he said. "You have a sleep, and when you wake, it'll be time to start."

Uncle smiled up at him, and closed his eyes. The ball of screens hung just above his pillow, and in the cathode-ray glow of the crab-cam pictures his old face looked luminous, a paper mask lit from within by the flickering light of his dreams.

In the chamber below, some of the children had gone to sleep too. The rest sat quietly, watching with large, trusting eyes while Tom told them a story which he used to tell Wren when she was little and woke up scared in the night. They did not seem frightened by the groans and shudders of the dying city, or the dribbles of water creeping down the walls. It had been scary when they were all alone, but now that these kind grown-ups had arrived they felt sure that everything would be all right.

Hester prowled the edges of the room, looking for weapons or ways to pick the heavy locks on the doors, and growing more and more angry as she found none of either.

"What will you do if you do find a way out?" Freya asked her softly. "Sit down. You'll scare the children."

Hester scowled at her. "What will I do? Get down to the limpet pens, of course, and away aboard the *Screw Worm*."

"But we can't all fit aboard the *Screw Worm*. Even if we managed to squeeze all the children into the hold, there wouldn't be air or fuel enough to get us back to Anchorage."

"Who said we were taking the children?" asked Hester. "I came to rescue Wren, not those little savages. Wren's not here, so we'll take the *Worm* to Brighton and try looking there."

"But the children –" cried Freya, and quickly stopped, in case they heard her and guessed what Hester was planning. "Hester, how could you even think such a thing! You have a child of your own!"

"That's right," said Hester. "And if you had, then you'd know how much trouble they bring. And these aren't even ordinary children. It's all very well you coming over all mumsy and nurturing, but these are *Lost Boys*. You can't take them back to Anchorage. What will you do with them there?

"Love them, of course," replied Freya simply.

"Oh, like you did Caul? That really worked, didn't it? They'll rob you blind, and then probably murder you. You've lost your edge, Snow Queen. You asked me once to help you protect Anchorage. Well, I'll protect it by making sure you don't take a gang of burglar-babies home with you as souvenirs of Grimsby."

Freya took a step backwards, as though she didn't like to be so close to Hester. "I don't think Anchorage needs your sort of protection any more," she said. "I was glad of you once. I hoped all those years of peace would bring you peace as well. But you've not changed."

Hester was about to reply when the door behind her opened and Caul came in. She turned on him instead. "Come to gloat over your prisoners?"

Caul would not meet her eye. "You're not prisoners," he said. "I just didn't want anybody to get hurt. And I didn't want you to make Uncle leave. He's an old man. He'd die if he leaves Grimsby."

"He'll die if he stays," said Hester. "Unless he's a really good swimmer."

Caul ignored her, and spoke to Freya and Tom. "He's asleep now. He'll sleep for hours, with luck. That gives you time to get away."

"And what about you?" asked Freya.

Caul shook his head. "I have to stay. I'm all he's got."

"Well, you're more than he deserves," said Tom indignantly. "You do know he'll never really be able to rebuild this place, don't you?"

"You don't understand," said Caul. "Seeing him like this, so old and mad and miserable. . . Of course Grimsby's finished. But Uncle doesn't realize that. I'm the last of his boys, Tom. I've got to stay with him till the end."

Freya was about to try and reason with him, but Hester butted in. "Fine by me. Now, how do you suggest we leave?"

Caul grinned at her, glad of a practical question at last. "The *Naglfar*. She's the cargo submarine we saw in the pens when we first got here. She's old, but she's trusty. She'll take you back to Anchorage all right."

"Then you'll have to come too!" said Freya, relieved. "I can't drive a submarine on my own, or pilot it, or whatever you're supposed to do to them."

"Tom and Hester will help you."

"Tom and Hester are taking the *Screw Worm* and going after Brighton," said Hester.

"No," Caul told her. "You've got to go with Freya. I have to stay with Uncle. I'll help you fuel and provision the *Naglfar*. You can take her back to Anchorage and then, once Freya and the children are safe, then you can carry on to Brighton and find Wren."

And so, for one last time, the limpet pens of Grimsby were filled with the sounds of a submarine being made ready for sea. The *Naglfar* was a rusty, ramshackle old tub, but Caul said that she would swim, and there was room enough in her spacious hold for all the children. He did not tell them what else he knew about her; that she was the submarine which Uncle had stolen years before from Snowmad scavengers, and used to begin his underwater empire. Nor did he mention where her name came from – in the legends of the old north the *Naglfar* was a ship built from dead men's fingernails in which the dark gods would sail to battle at the world's end. He didn't want to give the children nightmares.

So Tom and Caul concentrated on testing the old sub's engines, while Hester filled her tanks with fuel and Freya made some of the older children show her Grimsby's food-stores, where they collected armfuls of provisions to keep them going on the journey back to Vineland.

Everything had to be done quickly. Metallic moans and grumbles kept rolling down the passageways of the building, as hull-plates which had been damaged by Brighton's depth-charges slowly shifted and gave way under the pressure of the sea, and the bulkhead doors slammed shut to seal off the flooded sections. No one had forgotten that Uncle was still up there in his chambers with his mad dreams. But Uncle seemed to be sleeping soundly for the moment; at least, when Tom opened the *Naglfar*'s hatches and looked up at the shadowy roof he could not see any crab-cams on the move.

He leaned against the open hatch-cover for a moment, glad of the cold, for it was growing hot and stuffy in the *Naglfar's* engine room. He had been over-doing it down there, and worrying too much about Wren, and his old wound was hurting him again, sharp, jabbing shards of pain, as if his heart were full of broken glass. He wondered again if he was going to die. He didn't think he was afraid of dying, but he was afraid of dying before he found Wren.

He decided to worry about Caul instead of himself. He climbed out of the submarine and found Hester coming across the dock.

"What are we going to do about Caul?" Tom asked softly, drawing her aside. "He's still set on staying here. Has he forgotten that Uncle tried to have him killed?"

Hester shook her head. "He's not forgotten," she said. "I don't think he *wants* to stay, exactly. It's just that he loves Uncle."

"But Uncle nearly killed him!"

"That doesn't make a difference," said Hester. "Uncle is the nearest thing Caul's got to a mother or a father. Everybody loves their parents. They may not always real-ize that they love them, they may hate them at the same time, but there's always a little bit of love mixed in with the hate, which makes it really . . . complicated."

She stopped, unable to explain herself, thinking of her own complicated feelings for her dead father and her missing child. She wished Wren loved her as much as Caul loved Uncle.

"Freya told me Caul has dreams about this place every night," said Tom. "He dreams about Uncle's voice, whispering to him the way it used to when he was a child. Why would Uncle keep talking to them all, over the speakers, even while they were asleep?"

"Maybe he was sort of brainwashing them," said Hester.

"That's what I think," Tom agreed. "Putting a kind of hook in their minds that would always pull them back to Grimsby, no matter how far they tried to run, or how much they wanted to get away."

"We'll overpower Caul," said Hester. "Knock him on the head and drag him away. He'll come to his senses once we're at sea."

"Maybe," said Tom. "Maybe once this place is gone, and Uncle's dead, he'll be able to forget it."

From the conning tower of the *Naglfar* came a piercing, childish scream. "The cams!" shouted a boy called Eel, whom Freya had told to keep watch because he was too small to do anything else. "The cams are moving!"

Tom and Hester looked up. Above them, crab-cams were scuttling along the rusty jibs of the docking-cranes, clambering over each other as they trained their lenses on the pool where the *Naglfar* wallowed.

"The old man's awake," said Caul, scrambling out of the submarine's forward hatch and climbing down on to the dock with Freya close behind.

"So what?" asked Hester. "He can't stop us leaving now."

"Who said leaving?" asked Uncle's scratchy voice. "Nobody's leaving."

He came limping towards them between the empty moon-pools, Hester's gun looking huge in his papery, quivering hand. Above his head the old balloon hung like a mouldy thought-bubble and the globe of screens beneath it flickered with pictures from the crab-cams. He heaved the gun up and pulled the trigger, sending a bullet clanging into the the metal of the *Naglfar's* conning tower. The sound echoed away between the shadowy docking-cranes, and as if in answer a stressed bulkhead somewhere on the upper levels let out a long groan, like some huge creature dying slowly and painfully of indigestion.

Uncle ignored it. "Uncle Knows Best!" he shouted shrilly. "Stay here and help me rebuild Grimsby, and you will be well rewarded. Try to leave, and you'll be flushed out the water-door to feed the little fishies."

The children twittered. Hester stepped protectively in front of Tom. Caul ran towards the old man. "Uncle," he said, "I think Grimsby is damaged worse than we reckoned."

"Well?" asked Uncle, looking up at a close-up of Caul on one of his screens. "So? It was worse off than this when I first came down here."

"Mr Kael," Freya called softly. "Stilton?"

She walked across the dock, while crab-cameras on the cranes above her frantically zoomed in on her face and hands. Caul tried to stop her, but she shrugged him aside and held out her hand to Uncle. "Caul's right," she said. "Grimsby is coming to an end. It was a bold idea, and I'm glad that I have seen it for myself, but it is time to leave. You can come with us, back to Anchorage. Wouldn't you like to breathe fresh air again, and see the sun?"

"The sun?" asked Uncle, and his eyes suddenly swam with tears. It was a long time since anyone had been kind to him. It was a long time since anyone had called him Stilton. Freya reached out to him and he stared up at his hovering ball of screens, at her gentle white hands hanging huge above him, like wings.

"Leave Grimsby?" he said, but in a wondering way, softly. The crab-cams zoomed until every screen showed Freya, or a part of Freya; her face, her eyes, her mouth, the soft curve of her cheek, her hands; all larger than life, like parts of a self-assembly kit from which a goddess might be constructed. Uncle wanted to hold those kind hands, and go away with her, and see the sun again before he died. He took a half-step towards her, and then remembered Anna Fang, and how she had betrayed him.

"No!" he shouted. "No! I won't! It's all a trick!"

He pointed the gun at her and pulled the trigger, and the huge noise slammed through the pens and made all the children squeal and cover their ears. The bullet went through Freya's smiling face, and her face broke, and there was blackness behind it, and sparks, and as the glass rained down on him Uncle dimly realized that he had not shot Freya but only her image on the largest of his screens. He looked for the real Freya, but Caul pulled her aside and shielded her, and Uncle didn't want to shoot Caul.

From somewhere above him came a long, distracting sigh. The heavy gun drooped in his hands. He looked up. Everyone looked up, even the scared children. The sigh grew louder, and Uncle saw that his shot had opened a hole in the balloon that held his moon of screens aloft. As he watched, it widened swiftly into a long gash like a yawning mouth.

"Uncle!" shouted Caul.

"Caul!" screamed Freya, pulling him back, holding him tight.

"Anna. . ." whispered Uncle.

And the ball of screens came down on him like a boot on a spider. The screens burst, sparks swarming blue and white, shattered glass sleeting across the deck. The collapsing balloon settled over the wreckage like a shroud, and as the smoke from the smashed machines reached the roof a sprinkler system kicked in, filling the limpet pens with cold salt rain.

Tom ran up, and Hester, taking Freya by her shaking shoulders, asking, "Are you all right?"

"I think so," she said, nodding, soaked to the skin and sneezing at the smoke. "Is Uncle –?"

Caul skirted the heap of sparking, smouldering screens. Only Uncle's feet, in their grimy bunny-slippers, poked out from beneath the debris. They twitched a few times, and were still.

"Caul?" asked Freya.

"I'm all right," said Caul. And he was, even though, for some reason, he could not stop crying. He pulled a swag of balloon fabric over the bunny-slippers and turned to face the others. "Come on," he said. "Let's get the *Naglfar* swimming before this place finally falls apart. The *Worm* too. Tom and Hester will need the *Worm* if they're going after Wren."

The work went faster after that. Grimsby was creaking and keening constantly, and sometimes an ominous shudder rippled the water in the moon-pools, as if the unlikely old place somehow knew that its maker was gone, and was dying with him.

The last of the fuel was loaded, and fresh batteries and

kegs of water were rolled aboard the *Screw Worm* and the *Naglfar*. Hester prowled the seeping treasure-hoards of Grimsby, gathering up handfuls of gold coins, for she suspected money might come in useful aboard Brighton. And when nobody was looking she burrowed into the heap of ruined screens until she found her gun, still clutched in Uncle's dead hand. She was certain she would find a use for that.

On the quayside, Tom hugged Freya.

"Good luck," he told her.

"Good luck you," said Freya, holding his face and smiling at him. She hesitated, blushing. She had been meaning to warn Tom, if she could, about his wife. She still didn't think he understood how ruthless Hester could be. She knew that Hester loved him, but she didn't think that Hester cared at all about anybody else, and she was afraid that one day her ruthlessness would bring trouble down on them both.

"Tom," she said, "Watch out for Hester, won't you?"

"We'll watch out for each other, like always," said Tom, misunderstanding.

Freya gave up, and kissed him. "You'll find Wren," she said, "I know it."

Tom nodded. "I know it too. And I'll find the Tin Book as well, if I can. If what Uncle told Caul was true, if the Green Storm are making war on cities.... I saw what they were like at Rogues' Roost, Freya. If that book is the key to something dangerous, we mustn't let them get hold of it..."

"We don't know for sure that it's the key to anything," Freya reminded him. "It would be better to get it back if we can, just to be safe. But Wren is all that really matters. Find her, Tom. And come home safe to Vineland."

Then Tom went with Hester aboard the *Screw Worm*, and Freya watched and waved as the *Worm* submerged, and stood with Caul at the edge of the moonpool till the last ripples faded. The children were waiting for her aboard the *Naglfar*; their high, nervous voices spilling from its open hatches.

"Are we going now?"

"Is it far to Anchorage?"

"Will we really have our own rooms and everything there?"

"Is Uncle really dead?"

"I feel sick!"

Freya took Caul's hand in hers. "Well?" she asked.

"Come on," he said. "Let's go home."

So they went, and Grimsby stood abandoned at last. After a few days even the dim light from its windows faded, and one by one the air-pumps died. Through widening cracks and fissures that there was no one left to repair, the patient sea came creeping in, and the fish made their homes in the halls of the Lost Boys.

Tom would miss the company of Freya, and even Caul, but for Hester it was a relief to be alone with him again. She had never been truly comfortable with anyone but Tom, except for Wren, when Wren was little. She watched lovingly as Tom worked the *Screw Worm*'s strange controls, frowning with concentration as he tried to remember all that Caul had taught him. That night, when the limpet was running smoothly south-by-south-west towards Brighton's cruising grounds and the waters were singing against the hull, she slipped into his bunk and wrapped her long limbs around him and kissed him, remembering how, when they were young and first together in the *Jenny Haniver* they used to kiss for hours. But Tom was too worried about Wren to kiss her back, not properly, and she lay for a long time awake while he slept, and thought bitterly, *He loves her more than ever he loved me.*

19

THE WEDDING WREATH

First frost reached Vineland long before the *Naglfar*. The old submarine, with too many people aboard and her poor old engines grumbling all the way, took several weeks to return to the Dead Continent and nose her way up the winding rivers that the *Screw Worm* had swum down in days. But Caul coaxed her back to Anchorage at last, and she surfaced through a thin covering of ice just off the mooring beach. Freya climbed out waving, and was almost shot again, this time by Mr Smew, who believed the Lost Boys were invading.

And in a way, they were. Anchorage would never be the same again, now that all these boisterous, ill-mannered, sometimes troubled children had come to live there. Freya set about opening the abandoned upper floors of the Winter Palace, and the old building filled with life and noise as the children moved in to their new quarters. Some of them were not quite used to the idea that they were not supposed to steal, and some had nightmares, calling out Uncle's name and Gargle's in their dreams, but Freya was convinced that with patience and love they could be helped to forget their time beneath the sea and grow into happy, healthy Vinelanders.

After all, it had worked with Caul, eventually. Freya wouldn't say what had passed between them on the voyage home, but the former Lost Boy never went back to his shack in the engine district. At the beginning of that October, when the harvests were in and the animals down from the high pastures and the city was preparing for winter, he and the margravine were married.

Freya awoke early on the morning after her wedding; wide awake at five o'clock, the way she used to be when she was young. She climbed out of bed, careful not to wake Caul, and went to the window of her chamber with the floor cold under her bare feet and the tatters of her bridal wreath still hanging in her hair.

When she drew back the curtains she saw that the ice was thick upon the lake, and that a dusting of snow had fallen in the night. She felt glad that her city was back in the domain of the Ice Gods for another six months. The gods of summer, of the lake and the hunt, had all been good to her people, and the gods of the sea and the goddess of love had been very kind to her too, but the Ice Gods were the gods she had grown up with, and she trusted them better than the rest. She breathed on the window and drew their snowflake symbol in the mist and whispered. "Keep Tom safe. And Hester too, though she doesn't deserve it. Lead them to Wren, wherever she may be. And may they all come home again to us, safe and happy and together."

But if the Ice Gods heard her prayer, they sent no sign. The only answer Freya had was the sound of the wind in the spires of the Winter Palace, and her husband's voice, gentle and sleepy, calling her back to her bed.

PART TWO

20

A LIFE ON THE OCEAN WAVE

"Pennyroyal, my dear?"

"Mmmmm?"

Morning in the Pavilion, and the mayor and mayoress sitting at opposite ends of the long table in the breakfast room, screened from the hot sun by muslin blinds. Behind the mayoress's chair her African slave waved an ostrich-feather fan, wafting cool air over her, and rustling the pages of the newspaper which her husband was trying to read.

"Pennyroyal, I am talking to you."

Nimrod Pennyroyal sighed, and put down the paper. "Yes, Boo-Boo, my treasure?"

It is a truth universally acknowledged that a fake explorer in possession of a good fortune must be in search of a wife, and Pennyroyal had got himself lumbered with Boo-Boo Heckmondwyke. Fifteen years earlier, when *Predator's Gold* was topping the best-seller lists aboard every city of the Hunting Ground, she had seemed like a good idea. Her family were old Brighton aristocracy, but poor. Pennyroyal was a mere adventurer, but rich. The marriage allowed the Heckmondwykes to restore their fortunes, and gave Pennyroyal the social clout he needed to get himself elected mayor. Boo-Boo made an excellent wife for a man of ambition; she was good at small-talk and flower arrangements, she planned dinner parties with military precision, and she was expert at opening fêtes, galas and small hospitals.

Yet Pennyroyal had come to regret his marriage. Boo-Boo was such a large, forceful, florid woman that she tired him out just by being in the same room. A keen amateur singer, she had a passion for the operas of the Blue Metal Culture, which went on for days with never a trace of a tune, and usually ended with all the characters dead in a heap. When Pennyroyal annoyed her by questioning the cost of her latest frock or flirting too openly with a councillor's wife over dinner she would practise her scales until the windows rattled, or crank up her gramophone and treat the household to all six hundred verses of the *Harpoon Aria* from *Diana, Princess of Whales*.

"I expect you to *listen* when I talk to you, Pennyroyal," she said now, setting down her croissant in an ominous manner.

"Of course, dear. I was just studying the latest war-reports in the *Palimpsest*. Excellent news from the front. Makes one proud to be a Tractionist, eh?"

"Pennyroyal!"

"Yes, dearest?"

"I have been looking over the arrangements for our Moon Festival Ball," said Boo-Boo, "and I could not help noticing that you have invited the Flying Ferrets."

Pennyroyal made a sort of shrugging motion with his entire body.

"I'm not sure we should be entertaining mercenaries, Nimrod."

"I just happened to invite their leader, Orla Twombley," Pennyroyal protested. "I may have said she could bring a few of her friends if she wanted. Wouldn't want her to feel left out, you know. . . . She's a famous aviatrix. Her flying machine, the *Combat Wombat*, downed three air-dreadnoughts at the Battle of the Bay of Bengal."

As he spoke, a vision of the female air-ace filled

Pennyroyal's mind, sleek and gorgeous in her pink leather flying suit. He had always prided himself on how popular he was with the ladies. Why, in his younger days he had enjoyed passionate romances with exotic and beautiful women. (Minty Bapsnack, Peaches Zanzibar and the Traktiongrad Smolensk Ladies' Croquet Team all sprang to mind.) He'd been rather hoping that the dashing Orla Twombley might soon be added to that list.

"Pretty, isn't she?" said Boo-Boo frostily.

Pennyroyal shifted awkwardly in his chair. "Can't say I've ever really noticed. . ." he mumbled. He hated scenes like this. That nasty, suspicious look in Boo-Boo's eyes was just the sort of thing, he thought, to put a chap right off his breakfast. Luckily he was saved from any further interrogation by one of his house-slaves, who opened the breakfast room door and said, "Mr Plovery to see you, Your Worship."

"Excellent!" cried Pennyroyal, and leaped up gratefully to greet his visitor. "Plovery! My dear fellow! How splendid to see you!"

Walter Plovery, an antique dealer from one of the fouler warrens of the Laines, was the mayor's advisor on Old-Tech, and he had helped Pennyroyal to make himself a tidy little nest-egg by secretly selling off items from the Brighton Museum. He was a small, nervous man with a face which looked as if somebody had moulded it out of dough and then forgotten to bake it. He seemed startled by Pennyroyal's exuberant greeting; people weren't usually so glad to see him – but then, people weren't usually being quizzed about lovely aviatrices by Mrs Pennyroyal when he walked in on them.

"I have been doing some research into that *item* Your

Worship showed me," he said, sidling closer to Pennyroyal. His eyes flicked uncertainly towards Boo-Boo. "You remember, Your Worship? The *item*?"

"Oh, there's no need for secrecy, Plovery," Pennyroyal told him. "Boo-Boo knows all it about it. Don't you, my little upside-down cake? That metal book affair I swiped off of old Shkin last week. I had Plovery take a look at it, just to see what he thought. . ."

Boo-Boo smiled faintly and reached for the newspaper, turning to the gossip page. "Do excuse me, Mr Plovery. I find talk about Old-Tech so dull. . ."

Plovery nodded, bobbed a bow in her general direction and turned back to Pennyroyal. "You still have the item?"

"It's in the safe in my office," said Pennyroyal. "Why? Reckon it might be worth something?"

"Po-o-ossibly," said Plovery, cautiously.

"The Lost Girl who came with it seemed to think it had something to do with submarines."

Mr Plovery allowed himself a chuckle. "Oh no, Your Worship. She clearly knows nothing about the machine-languages of the Ancients."

"A machine language, eh?"

"A code, which would have been used by our ancestors to communicate with one of their computer brains. I can find no example of this particular language anywhere in the historical records. However, it is similar to certain surviving fragments of American military code."

"American, eh?" said Pennyroyal, and then, "Military? That should be worth a bob or two. This war's been dragging on for fourteen years. People are desperate. The R&D departments of the big fighting cities would pay a fortune for a sniff at a super-weapon."

Plovery's face grew ever so slightly pink as he imagined his percentage of a fortune. "Would you like me to try and arrange a sale, Your Worship? I have contacts in the Mobile Free States. . ."

Pennyroyal shook his head. "No, Plovery, I'll handle this. There's no point doing anything until after Moon Festival. I'll pop the book back in my safe until the celebrations are over and then get in touch with a few of my contacts. There's an archaeologist of my aquaintance, a charming young woman named Cruwys Morchard; she often stops in Brighton in the autumn-time, and she always seems to be on the look-out for unusual bits of Old-Tech. Yes, I think I can arrange a sale without troubling you, Plovery."

He shooed the disgruntled Old-Tech dealer away, and sat down to continue his breakfast, only to be confronted with the *Palimpsest*, which his wife was holding up for him to see. There on the front page of the gossip section was a full-length photograph of himself entering a casino in the Laines on the arm of Orla Twombley, who was looking even more goddess-like than Pennyroyal remembered.

"Well," he blustered, "she's not really what I'd call *pretty*. . ."

"Poor Boo-Boo!" said Wren, standing unnoticed on a gallery high above the breakfast room, beside her new friend Cynthia Twite. Pennyroyal's chat with Plovery had been too quiet for her to overhear, but she had listened to every word of the exchange about Orla Twombley. "I don't know how she puts up with it. . ."

173

"Puts up with what?" asked Cynthia innocently.

"Didn't you hear? Boo-Boo thinks he's been having a *liaison* with Orla Twombley!"

"What's a *liaison*?" asked Cynthia, frowning. "Is it a sort of cake?"

Wren sighed. Cynthia was very sweet, very pretty and very dim. She had been a house-slave at the Pavilion for several years, and when Wren arrived Mrs Pennyroyal had asked her to be Wren's friend and explain the workings of the household to her. Wren was glad of the companionship, but she felt she already understood more about the life of the Pavilion than Cynthia had ever known.

"Boo-Boo thinks that Pennyroyal and Ms Twombley are having a fling," she explained patiently.

"Oh!" Cynthia looked scandalized. "Oh, poor Mistress! To think, a man of his age, throwing himself at slinky aviatrixes!"

"I could tell you some things about Pennyroyal that are a lot worse than that," Wren whispered, and then stopped, remembering that she must not tell Cynthia anything. To everyone on Cloud 9, Wren was just a Lost Girl, who knew nothing about Pennyroyal beyond what he'd written in his silly books.

"What?" asked Cynthia, intrigued. "What things?"

"I'll tell you another time," Wren promised, knowing that Cynthia would forget.

To change the subject she said, "Who is that boy behind Boo-Boo's chair? The one with the fan? I saw him at the pool the other day. He always looks so sad."

"Oh, he's another new arrival, like you," said Cynthia excitedly. "He's only been here for a few weeks. His name's Theo Ngoni, and he used to be a Green Storm aviator! He got captured in a big battle somewhere, and Pennyroyal bought him for Boo-Boo as a birthday present. It's meant to be ever so stylish to have a captured Mossie as a slave, but I think it's scary. I mean, we could all be murdered in our beds, couldn't we! Look at him! Don't he look vicious?"

Wren studied the boy. He did not look vicious to her. He was no older than she was, and far too young to be fighting in battles. How terrible it must have been for him, to be defeated and dragged away from his home and sent here to wave a fan at the Pennyroyals all day! No wonder he seemed so miserable. Wren felt sorry for him, and that soon made her feel sorry for herself, too, and reminded her that she should be looking for a way to escape from this place.

For a few days Pennyroyal had taken a special interest in Wren, calling her "my fan from beneath the sea", and lending her his latest book, a history of the war with the Green Storm. But he quickly forgot her, and she became just another of his wife's many slaves.

Her new life was simple. She rose each day at seven, breakfasted, and went with the other girls of Mrs Pennyroyal's household to Mrs Pennyroyal's bedchamber, where they woke Mrs Pennyroyal and helped her dress, and spent an hour working on her hairdo, which was elaborate, expensive and several feet tall. In the mornings, when the mayor went down to the Town Hall, his wife liked to take a long, relaxing wallow in the swimming pool. Sometimes in the afternoons, when Pennyroyal came home tipsy from something he called a "working lunch", Boo-Boo took the cable car down to Brighton and went visiting, or opened things, but she never took any of her pretty young handmaidens with her, just a couple of slave-boys to carry her shopping.

At eight in the evening, dinner was served; usually a big affair, with many guests, and Wren and the other girls running in and out with roast swan, shark steaks, sea-pie and great wobbling desserts. After that, Mrs Pennyroyal had to be helped to bathe, and dress for bed, before the girls were finally allowed to go to their own beds, in a dormitory on the ground floor.

It was hard work sometimes, but when she was not busy attending to the mayoress Wren was allowed to do pretty much what she liked, and what she liked, in those first few weeks, was to wander about the Pavilion and its grounds with Cynthia Twite.

Pennyroyal's palace was a treasure-trove of wonders, and Wren loved the gardens, with their shaded walks and summerhouses, the elaborate topiary maze, the groves of blue-green cypresses and shrines to antique gods. Sometimes, as Brighton steamed south into warmer waters and golden autumn sunshine, she would stand at the handrail at the gardens' edge and look down at the white city below her, at the shining sea, at the circling gulls and the airships and the pennants streaming on the wind, and wonder if it hadn't been worth getting kidnapped and enslaved just to see so much beauty.

But more and more, as the weeks wore by, she missed her mum and dad. She knew she had to get away from Cloud 9. But how? No airships were allowed to land on the airborne deckplate, so the only way off was by cable car, and the cable car was closely guarded by Brighton's red-coated militia. And even if she made it down to Brighton, what good would that do her? She wore the brand of the Shkin Corporation, and if she tried to board an outbound ship she would be taken up as a runaway slave and handed straight back to Shkin.

And all the time she was being carried further and further from her home. Brighton was nosing south down the long coast of the Hunting Ground, while dusty two-tiered traction towns kept pace with it on shore. Everybody was talking about the Moon Festival, Boo-Boo endlessly writing and rewriting the guest-list for the mayor's ball, the cooks in the Pavilion kitchens working overtime to turn out moon-shaped cakes and silver moon-sweets. The rising of the first full moon of autumn was an event sacred to all the most popular religions. There would be parties and processions aboard Brighton, and all over the world the Moon Festival fires would burn in city and static alike. There would even be one lonely bonfire on the Dead Continent, for at Anchorage-in-Vineland Moon Festival was the biggest social event of the year.

Wren imagined her friends piling up driftwood and broken furniture in the meadow behind the city, and maybe wondering where she was, and whether she was safe. How she wished she could be there with them! She couldn't imagine how she had ever thought their lives dull, or why she had argued so with Mummy. Each night, lying in her bed in the slave quarters, she would hug herself and whisper the songs she used to sing when she was little, and pretend that the creaking of the hawsers which attached Cloud 9 to its gas-bags was the murmur of waves against the shores of Vineland.

Wren had almost forgotten Nabisco Shkin, and, to be fair, Nabisco Skin had almost forgotten her. Sometimes as he went about his busy round of meetings he glanced up at Cloud 9 and allowed himself to feel a momentary pleasure at the revenge he would take on the girl who had tricked him, but his plans for a slaving expedition to Vineland were at a very early stage, and he had more pressing business to attend to.

Today, for instance, he had received a very interesting note from a man named Plovery.

Descending to the Pepperpot's mid-level, he exited through a side-door and strode quickly into the maze of the Laines. These narrow streets, lit only by sputtering argon-globes and by shafts of sunlight which poked down through vents and skylights in the deckplates overhead, were the haunt of beggars, thieves and ne'er-do-wells, but Shkin was well enough known to walk them without a bodyguard. Even the most witless of Brighton's lowlifes had a pretty good idea of what would happen to anyone who dared lay a finger on Nabisco Shkin. People stepped out of his way, and turned to watch him when he had gone past. Roistering aviators were tugged out of his path by their friends. Unwary drug-touts and gutter-girls started back as if his glance had burned them. Only one miserable, dread-locked beggar, leading a dog on a length of string, dared to whine, "A few spare dolphins, sir? Just to buy some food?"

"Eat the dog," suggested Shkin, and made a mental note to send a snatch squad to this district once Moon Festival was over. He would be doing his city a favour by sweeping these scum off the streets, and they would all fetch a profit at the autumn markets.

He entered a narrow alleyway behind a fried fish stall, holding a handkerchief to his nose to ward off the stench of pee and batter. In the windows of a scruffy shop at the alley's end mounds of junk and Old-Tech glimmered. PLOVERY, said the faded sign above them, and the jangle of the bell as Shkin opened the door brought the antiquary scurrying from a back room.

"You wished to see me?"

"Why yes, sir, yes. . ." Plovery bowed and beamed, and twined his thin, white fingers into knots. Annoyed at Pennyroyal's decision to find a buyer for the Tin Book without his help, the antiquary had decided to take what he knew about it to another wealthy man. His note had dropped into Shkin's in-tray just an hour ago, and he was impressed and a little startled to find Shkin standing here in person quite so soon. Nervously, he told the slave-dealer all that he had learned.

"Military, eh?" said Shkin, just as Pennyroyal had a few hours earlier. "An ancient weapon?"

"Just a code, sir," Plovery cautioned. "But perhaps a clever man who understood such things might work backwards from the code and reconstruct the machine which it was written for. That could be valuable, sir. And as Pennyroyal told me that he had got the book from you – *I tricked that creep Shkin into handing it over for free* were his exact words, sir, if you'll forgive me – well, I thought you might be interested, sir."

"I have already made arrangements that will repay His Worship for that little episode," said Shkin, annoyed that this wretch knew how Pennyroyal had outwitted him. He was intrigued by Plovery's story, all the same. "You made a copy of the book, of course?"

"No, sir. Pennyroyal will not let it out of his sight. It is in his safe at the Pavilion. But if I had a buyer, sir, I might be able to get my hands on it. I am a frequent visitor to the Pavilion, sir."

Shkin twitched an eyebrow. He was interested, but not interested enough yet to lay down the sort of money that he knew Plovery would want. "I deal in slaves, not Old-Tech."

"Of course, sir. But what if it does turn out to be some ancient weapon? It might tip the balance. End the war. And the war has been so good for business, sir, has it not?"

Shkin pondered for a moment. Then nodded.

"Very well. The thing is mine by rights anyway. 'Finders Keepers', you know. I do not like to think of Pennyroyal profiting from it. I take it you know the combination of his safe?"

Plovery said, "22-09-957. Twenty-second of September, nine-hundred and fifty-seven TE. It's His Worship's birthday."

Shkin smiled. "Very well, Plovery. Fetch me the Tin Book."

21

THE FLIGHT OF A SEAGULL

That afternoon, when luncheon was over and the preparations for dinner not yet begun, Wren wandered through the kitchen garden and out into the grounds behind the Pavilion to watch a wing of the Flying Ferrets take off on patrol. The Ferrets had set up a temporary airfield in a little-used part of the gardens behind the Pavilion. Wren knew most of the strange machines by sight now, and recognized them as they taxied out of their hangars; the *Visible Panty Line* and the *Tumbler Pigeon*, the *Austerity Biscuit* and the *JMW Turner Overdrive*. The ground-crews fitted them into spring-loaded canvas catapults and sent them hurtling over the edge of the deckplate, while the aviators gunned their engines and prayed that their wings would find a purchase on the air before they plunged into the dirty sea off Brighton's stern.

Wren watched from the handrail at the gardens' brink while Ferret after Ferret pulled out of its dive and went zooming off across the rooftops, doing ill-advised aëro-batics and letting off canisters of green and purple smoke. It was a spectacle that she had always enjoyed before, but today it only made her feel more homesick than ever. She would have liked to tell Dad about the Ferrets' machines.

Behind the aërodrome stood a whale-backed hillock of copper, screened by cypress trees. Wren had noticed it from a distance before, but she had never bothered to take a closer look, assuming that it was just another of the abstract sculptures which littered the lawns of Cloud 9, bought by Pennyroyal to keep his supporters in the

Artists' Quarter happy. Today, having nothing better to do, she wandered towards it. As she drew nearer she started to realize that it was a building, with huge, curved doors at one end and a fan-shaped metal pavement outside. The copper curves of its walls and roof were studded with decorative spines, so that it looked like a giant puffer-fish surfacing through the grass. A spindly exterior staircase led up one side, and Wren climbed up it and peeked in through a high window.

In the shady interior sat a sky-yacht so delicate and sleek that even Wren, who knew nothing about airships, could tell that it was ferociously expensive.

"That's the *Peewit*," said a helpful voice behind her. Cynthia was standing at the foot of the stairs. "I've been looking for you *everywhere*, Wren," she added. "I'm going to the household shrine; I simply *must* make a sacrifice to the Goddess of Beauty; I really want to lose weight before Moon Festival. You should come with me. You could ask her to do something about your spots."

Wren was more interested in yachts than spots. She turned back to the window. "The *Peewit*. . . Is she Pennyroyal's?"

"Of course." Cynthia climbed halfway up the stairs. "She's called a Type IV Serapis Moonshadow – very fancy. But the mayor hardly ever takes her up any more. He keeps her polished and full of lifting-gas, but the only time she gets used is when Boo-Boo goes shopping aboard another city."

"Won't the mayor be using her in the MoonFest Regatta?" asked Wren.

"Oh, no; he's got a vintage airship moored down in Brighton. He's going to be flying her, with that Orla Twombley as his co-pilot. She's going to lead a Fly-past of Historic Ships, and there's to be an Air Battle with real rockets, just like in Prof Pennyroyal's books. You wouldn't know it to look at him, but he's had the most amazing adventures on the Bird Roads."

Wren looked again at the yacht, thinking of the airship that Pennyroyal had stolen from her parents all those years before. Might it be possible for her to sneak down here at dead of night, slide open the boathouse doors and take off aboard the *Peewit*? That would be poetic justice, wouldn't it!

A faint drum-beat of hope began to throb deep down inside her. It cheered her up no end as Cynthia took her hand and led her towards the slaves' and servants' shrine behind the Pavilion kitchens. She barely heard her friend's bright chatter about make-up and hairstyles. In her imagination she was already piloting the *Peewit* westward; she was crossing the Dead Hills, the lakes of Vineland were shining blue below her, and her parents were running to greet her as she touched down in the fields of Anchorage.

The only trouble was, Wren had no idea how to fly a Type IV Serapis Moonshadow. Or anything else for that matter. But she knew someone who did.

Boo-Boo Pennyroyal did not like her male and female slaves to mingle. In the operas which she adored, young people brought together in tragic circumstances were forever falling in love with each other and then throwing themselves off things (cliffs, mostly, but sometimes battlements, or rooftops, or the brinks of volcanoes). Boo-Boo was fond of her slaves, and it pained her to

183

think of them plummeting in pairs off the edges of Cloud 9, so she nipped all tragic love affairs firmly in the bud by forbidding the girls and boys to speak to one another. Of course, young people being what they were, girls sometimes fell in love with other girls, or boys with boys, but that *never* happened in the operas, so Boo-Boo didn't notice. The rest were always disobeying her rule and trying to sneak into one another's quarters, which pained Boo-Boo. But at least Theo Ngoni never gave her any cause for concern. Theo Ngoni never spoke to anyone.

Wren, though, was determined to speak to Theo Ngoni, and she found her chance a few days after her discovery of the boathouse. Boo-Boo had gone down to Brighton, and Pennyroyal had collared Wren and Cynthia to act as his towel-holders while he took a dip in the pool. By a lucky chance Theo was on duty at the pool-side too, carrying the mayor's spare swimming goggles on a silver platter. While Pennyroyal dozed on his drifting lilo Wren sidled up to her fellow slave and whispered, "Hello!"

The boy looked at her out of the corners of his eyes, but said nothing. Wren wondered what to do next. She had never been this close to Theo before. He was very handsome, and although Wren was tall, Theo was taller still, which made her feel young and silly as she stood there at his side.

"I'm Wren," she said.

He looked away again, out across the gardens and the blue sea, towards a distant haze on the horizon that Wren had been told was Africa. Maybe he was homesick. She said, "Is that where you come from?"

Theo Ngoni shook his head. "My home was in Zagwa. A static city in the mountains, far to the south."

184

"Oh?" said Wren encouragingly, and, "Is it nice?" but the boy said no more. Determined to keep the conversation going she added, "I didn't know the Green Storm had bases in Africa. That book Prof Pennyroyal lent me said that the African statics didn't approve of the war."

"They don't." Theo turned his head to look at her, but it was a cold look. "I ran away from my family to travel to Shan Guo and join the Storm's youth wing. I thought it would be a glorious thing to fight against the barbarian cities, and sweep them from the earth."

"Gosh, yes," agreed Wren. "I'm an Anti-Tractionist myself, you know."

Theo stared at her. "I thought you were a Lost Girl. From that place under the sea."

"Oh yes, I am," said Wren quickly, annoyed at herself for forgetting. "But Grimsby didn't *move*, it wasn't a *moving* city, so that makes me a Mossie through and through. Did you fight in many battles?"

"Only one," said Theo, looking away again.

"You got captured on your first go? Oh, bad luck!" Wren tried to sound sympathetic, but she was fast losing patience with this sullen, gloomy boy. Maybe all that she'd heard about the Storm and its soldiers was true; they were brainwashed fanatics. Still, she was sure he must want to leave Cloud 9 as badly as she did, and she thought it unlikely that he would betray her to the hated Tractionists, so she decided to take a chance and tell him about her plan.

She glanced round and saw that Pennyroyal was asleep. The other slaves were dozing too, or whispering together on the far side of the pool, while Cynthia, who was closest, was studying her freshly varnished

185

fingernails with a frown of deep concentration. Wren sidled even closer to Theo and whispered, "I know a way we can escape."

Theo said nothing, but he stiffened slightly, which Wren thought was a good sign.

"I know where we can get an airship," she went on. "Cynthia Twite told me you used to be an aviator."

Theo almost smiled at that. "Cynthia Twite is a fool who understands nothing."

"True. But if you can fly an airship. . ."

"I did not fly airships. I flew Tumblers."

"Tumblers?" asked Wren. "What are they? Are they like airships? I mean, if you know the basics. . ." But Theo had clammed up again, narrowing his eyes and staring past her at the horizon. "Oh, come on!" Wren whispered impatiently. "Do you *like* being Pennyroyal's slave? Don't you *want* to escape? I should have thought you'd be itching to get back to the Green Storm. . ."

"I would never go back to the Storm!" Theo said suddenly, angrily, almost dropping the mayoral goggles as he turned to face her. "It is a lie; their great war, the World Made Green Again; my father was right; it is all lies!"

"Oh," said Wren. "Well, what about your home, then? You must want to go back to Zagwa. . ."

Theo stared at the horizon again, but it was not the sea and the sky and the distant shore that he was watching. Even here, in the expensive sunlight of Cloud 9, he could see that last, desperate fight above the Rustwater. The light of guns and rockets and burning ships had glittered in all the little winding waterways below him as he fell. A doomed suburb had been bellowing its distress calls across the marshes and the exultant voices of his comrades had crackled in his headphones, shouting as they began their own drops, "The World Made Green Again!" and "Death to the Pan-German Traction Wedge!" He had thought that those would be the last sounds he would ever hear. But here he was, months later and half a world away, still alive. The gods of war had spared him so that he could stand beside a swimming pool and be talked at by this stupid, skinny white girl who thought herself so clever.

"I can never go home," he said. "Didn't you hear me? I disobeyed my father. I ran away. I can never go home."

Wren shrugged. "All right, suit yourself," she told him, and stomped away before Pennyroyal woke up and saw them talking to each other. She would show Theo Ngoni! She would steal the mayor's yacht on her own, and pilot it back to Vineland herself. It was only a silly airship, after all! How hard could it be?

Dusk settled over Brighton. Along the promenades at the edges of its three tiers strings of coloured bulbs were switched on. Lights blinked and swirled on the fairgrounds and the pleasure-piers. Powerful lamps were lit atop each cabin of the revolving Pharos Wheel, which was mounted near the city's bows and served as both a joyride for the tourists and as a lighthouse to guide night-flying airships to Brighton.

The city was swinging eastward. Soon it would thread itself through the narrow strait which separated Africa from the Great Hunting Ground, and swim proudly into the Middle Sea. Brighton's businessmen were hoping for plenty of visitors when they anchored for Moon Festival. Word of the campaign against the Lost Boys would have spread along the Bird Roads by now, and the captured limpets displayed in the Brighton Aquarium would add a certain educational element to the attractions of the usual MoonFest celebrations. Already sightseers had started arriving from some of the small towns whose lights could be seen on the shore.

Above the coming and going of balloons, the shadows of evening pooled between the cypress groves of Cloud 9, and coloured floodlights made the Pavilion blush pink and gold. A few airships circled it, up from Brighton on an evening pleasure trip. The amplified voices of their pilots were faintly audible on Cloud 9, pointing out features of interest, but new security arrangements prohibited them from coming too close. None of the sightseers noticed a small window swing open in one of the Pavilion's domes, or the bird which flew out of it and up through the web of hawsers to join the cloud of gulls hanging ghostly in the city's wake.

Although it was white like a gull and had a gull's soaring flight, this bird was not a gull; not any more. Its bill had been replaced with a blade, and in the spaces of its skull glowed dim green lights. It rose through the circling flocks and flew away into the deepening twilight.

On and on it flapped, untiring, while days and nights came out of the east to meet it. It crossed the town-torn spine of Italy, and skirted the plumes of erupting volcanoes in Asia Minor. At a Green Storm air-base in the Ziganastra mountains it landed to let the base commander peer at the slip of paper which it carried in a cavity inside its chest. She cursed under her breath when she saw who the coded message was addressed to, and summoned a sleepy surgeon-mechanic to recharge the gull's power-cells.

It went on its way, flying into the haze of smoke above the Rustwater Marshes, where artillery duels were rumbling like autumn storms. A squadron of enormous Traction Cities was crawling eastward, trying to head off a Green Storm counter-attack. On their lower tiers whole buildings had been converted into snout guns. Railways carried huge, high-explosive shells out of the city's innards, and the guns hurled them into the marshy Out-Country ahead, which was said to be crawling with Stalkers and mobile rocket units. Buffeted by passing airships and the fluffy white thistledown of anti-aircraft bursts, the gull let the leading city's slipstream carry it eastward for a while, then rose above the battle and flapped on towards the white mountains that stood on the rim of the world.

The sky grew cold, and the ground rose. The gull flew through zones of high, white silence and over regions where the Storm's troop-movements gave the mountains the busy, scuttling look of ant-hills. At last, on a night of snow and starlight a week after it left Brighton, it landed on a window-sill of the Jade Pagoda, and tapped its bill against the frosty pane.

The window opened. The Stalker Fang took the gull gently in her steel hands and opened its chest. The message she took out had been written by someone called Agent 28. Her green eyes flared slightly brighter. She tore the message into small pieces, and sent for General Naga, commander of her elite air-legion.

"Make ready an assault unit," she told him. "And prepare my ship for battle. We leave for Brighton with the dawn."

22
MURDER ON CLOUD 9

Late October. In Vineland, Wren thought, the grass would be white and stiff with frost until mid-morning; fog would blanket the lake, and perhaps the first snow was already falling. But here on the Middle Sea it was still as warm as midsummer, and the only clouds in the sky were small, white, fluffy ones that looked as if they'd been put there for decoration.

Brighton had cruised slowly along the southern shores of the Hunting Ground for several weeks. Then, with Moon Festival drawing near, it headed south to its appointed rendezvous. Boo-Boo went with her handmaidens to watch from an observation balcony at the edge of Cloud 9 as the land came into view. "Look girls, look!" she cried happily, indicating the coastline with a theatrical sweep of her hand. "Africa!"

Wren, standing at the mayoress's side with an enormous parasol, tried to be impressed, but it was quite difficult. All she could see was a line of low, reddish bluffs rising out of a landscape the colour of biscuits, with a couple of big, ragged mountains lost in the haze beyond. Wren knew from things her father and Miss Freya had told her that Africa had been both the birthplace of mankind and its haven in the centuries of darkness which followed the Sixty Minute War; but the civilizations which once thrived upon those shores had left no traces – or, if they had, they had long since been snaffled up by hungry scavenger towns.

One of the towns that might have done the snaffling came into view soon afterwards. A small, three-tiered place, it was rumbling along on broad, barrel-shaped sand-wheels, trailing a swirl of red dust like a wind-blown cape. Wren glanced at it without very much interest. It felt strange to remember how, two weeks before, she had deserted her post in the middle of Mrs Pennyroyal's hairstyling routine to run and stare in wonderment at a little townlet trundling down on to the shore. She'd seen so many towns and even small cities since then that they seemed quite ordinary now, and certainly not the fabulous things that she had imagined when she lived in Vineland.

And then she looked again, and felt as silly as she had on that long-ago day when she first saw Brighton through the *Autolycus*'s periscope, and mistook it for an island. The things she'd thought were distant mountains were not distant at all. Nor were they mountains. They were Traction Cities so large that, when she first looked at them, her brain had simply not understood what her eyes were showing her. They were lumbering seaward, and through the dust and the drifting exhaust smoke Wren could see that each had nine tiers bristling with chimneys and spires.

"The one on the left is Kom Ombo," the mayoress told her girls. "The other is Benghazi. Mayor Pennyroyal has contracted to meet them here so that their people may taste the delights of Brighton this Moon Festival. They have been hunting sand-towns in the deep desert, poor things, so you can imagine how they will relish good food, fine entertainment and a refreshing dip in the Sea Pool."

To Wren, the approaching cities looked at first just like the pictures she remembered from her dog-eared copy of *A Child's Guide to Municipal Darwinism* back in

Anchorage. Then, as they drew closer, she began to make out differences. These cities were armoured, the exposed buildings on the edge of each tier screened with steel plates and anti-rocket netting. And although the land around their massive tracks was dotted with small, scurrying towns and suburbs and traction villages, these cities were making no attempt to swallow them.

"Moon Festival is a sacred time," said the mayoress, when Wren pointed this out. "A time when, according to tradition, no city hunts or eats another."

"Oh," said Wren, feeling disappointed, for it would have been thrilling to watch a good old-fashioned city chase.

"Of course," Boo-Boo went on, "with the war on and prey so scarce not every mayor abides by tradition nowadays, but if any of those cities tries to eat another, Ms Twombley and her friends will sort them out. It's high time that aëro-floozy made herself useful."

Bang on cue, the Flying Ferrets went tearing through the sky towards the cities, rolling and tumbling and firing off coloured rockets to demonstrate how they would deal with any predator that threatened to break the Moon Festival fast. One peeled off, trailing lilac smoke, to write, WELCOME TO BRIGHTON across the sky. As the thunder of their engines rolled away across the desert, Wren heard the rattle of heavy chains drifting up from Brighton. The city was dropping anchor.

"I have a feeling that this will be a wonderful MoonFest!" said Mrs Pennyroyal brightly, as the girls around her oohed and aahed and applauded the aviators' daring. "Now, come on, all of you; I wish you all to be photographed in your costumes for the mayor's ball."

She turned back towards the Pavilion, and Wren, with

a last glance at the towering cities, hurried after her. All the other girls were busy talking about tomorrow night's ball, and about the charming costumes the house-slaves were to wear. Listening to their excited chatter, Wren found herself feeling almost sorry that she was going to miss the fun. But miss it she must. Tonight, while the household was asleep, Wren meant to creep down to the boathouse and steal the *Peewit*. By the time the sacred moon rose she would be a long, long way from Brighton.

The Pavilion echoed and rang to the sound of preparations for the MoonFest Ball. In the ballroom under the central dome painters and curtain-fitters were hard at work, and musicians were practising, and electricians were covering the ceiling with hundreds of tiny lights. Crates of wine and hampers of food came creaking up from Brighton in the cable car, and the militia drilled in the Pavilion gardens.

It was all costing Pennyroyal a fortune, which he thought rather unfair. The people of Brighton surely wanted their mayor to put on a good show for Moon Festival; it seemed a bit rich that they expected him to pay for it all out of his own pocket. So he felt not the tiniest pang of guilt about inviting Walter Plovery to an informal dinner-party he was holding that night. Between dessert and coffee, while the other guests were discussing their plans for MoonFest and the latest scandals in the Artists' Quarter, Pennyroyal led the antiquary off to take a look at some of the precious antiques in the Pavilion's collection. Together the two men wandered from room to room, studying Stalker's brains and ground-car grilles, fragments of circuit-board like careful embroidery, flattened drinks cans and suits of ancient armour. They made notes of pieces which Plovery thought might fetch a tidy sum from some collectors he knew in Benghazi, and which Pennyroyal reckoned nobody would miss.

Over coffee, Mr Plovery mentally totted up the commission he stood to make on all these sales, and found that he was going to do very nicely. Full of Pennyroyal's food, and charmed by the wit and sophistication of his fellow guests, the antiquary regretted that he had ever made that deal with Shkin about the Tin Book. But Mr Shkin had promised him a very great deal of money, and Plovery, whose aged mother lived in an expensive nursing-home at Black Rock, needed all the money he could get. When the evening ended and the other guests made their way noisily back to the cable car, he doubled back and hid himself in one of the Pavilion's galleries.

The night air made Wren shiver inside her silver lamé nightgown as she stepped out through the servants' entrance into the cold of the garden. She could hear the sea far below, the wind soughing through the rigging, and someone burbling a drunken song down in the streets of Brighton. Clutching the bag of food she had stolen from the kitchens, she hurried across the damp lawn towards the boathouse and the lights of the Flying Ferrets' aërodrome.

The boathouse doors were never locked, and big as

they were they were easy to move, rolling aside on well-oiled casters when Wren leaned her weight against them. The *Peewit*'s sleek envelope gleamed inside the hangar as Wren crept to the gondola. She found that she had been holding her breath, which was silly, because there was nobody about. Over at the aërodrome a gramophone was playing a popular tune. Wren reached for the gondola door, and that was not locked either. She crept inside and used the small electric torch she had pinched from the Pavilion's caretaker to study the dials on the chromium instrument panels, remembering the diagrams in a book she'd looked at in the Pavilion library, *Practical Aviation For Fun And Profit*.

The gas-cells were full, just as Cynthia had told her. The fuel gauge was still on empty, but Wren had thought of a way to deal with that. She took her nightgown off and stashed it behind the instrument panel. Underneath, she was still wearing her day-clothes. She said a quick prayer to the gods of Vineland, then left the airship and walked briskly across the apron in front of the boat-house and through the trees towards the Ferrets' base.

In an old summerhouse which had been commandeered by the mercenary air force, Orla Twombley and a few of her aviators were playing cards. They looked up suspiciously when Wren came tapping at the door.

"Who's that?"

"Looks like one of Boo-Boo's girls."

The aviatrix stood up lazily and opened the door. "Well?"

"I've come with a message from Mrs Pennyroyal," said Wren. Her voice caught a little as she said it, but the aviatrix didn't seem to notice. She looked worried. Maybe she thought Boo-Boo had sent Wren here to tell her off for flirting with the mayor. Wren started to feel more confident. "Mrs Pennyroyal wants the *Peewit* to be fuelled at once," she explained. "She is going across to Benghazi tomorrow morning. Very early tomorrow morning, so she can find lots of bargains at the bazaar. She wonders if your ground-crew would oblige?"

Orla Twombley frowned. "Why ours? Is it not the mayor's men that should be refuelling the old gasbag?"

"Yes," said Wren. "His Worship was supposed to ask them this afternoon, but he forgot, and they've gone off duty now. So if you wouldn't mind getting your people to do it, Mrs Pennyroyal would be ever so grateful."

The aviatrix thought for a moment. She did not want to upset the mayoress. Boo-Boo had powerful relatives who might force Pennyroyal to dispense with the Flying Ferrets' services and hire some other freelance air-force instead. Orla Twombley knew for a fact that the Junkyard Angels and Richard D'Astardley's Flying Circus were both angling to take over the Brighton contract.

She nodded, and turned to her men. "Algy? Ginger? You heard what the young lady said. . ."

Grumpy but obedient, the two aviators set down their cards and their mugs of cocoa and went out with Wren into the night, muttering about what a waste of good fuel it was and wondering why anyone still bothered with airships when heavier-than-air was the way of the future. Wren trailed after them at a distance, and watched as they ran fuel-lines from the big tanks behind their airstrip and linked them to nozzles on the *Peewit*'s underside.

"She'll take a good ten minutes," one of the men said, turning to Wren with a friendly wink. "No need for you to hang about in the cold, kiddo."

Wren thanked him and ran back to the Pavilion. Ten minutes would give her just enough time to fetch Cynthia.

She had decided right from the start that she would not tell Cynthia about her scheme. Cynthia was much too giggly and forgetful to keep a secret, and would probably have blurted out the whole thing to Mrs Pennyroyal. But Wren had no intention of leaving her friend behind. While the *Peewit* was being fuelled she would slip into the dormitory where the girls slept, wake Cynthia as quietly as she could, and bring her down to the boathouse. By the time they got there, the yacht should be ready for take-off.

Mr Plovery used a novel lock-pick which Shkin's people had taken from the Lost Boys to open the door of the mayor's private office. The office was in a tower room, with long windows reaching up towards a shadowy ceiling high above. The blinds were open and the moon shone brightly in, showing the antiquary Pennyroyal's cluttered desk, and the drawing by Walmart Strange behind which Pennyroyal's private safe was hidden.

As he crossed the room, Plovery sensed a movement way up above him in the domed ceiling, and had the oddest feeling that he was being watched. He went cold with panic. What if Pennyroyal had got hold of one of those crab-camera things and was using it to guard his safe?

He almost gave up and ran, but the thought of his mother stopped him. With the money Shkin had promised him for the Tin Book he would be able to move Mum into one of the luxury suites on the top floor of her nursing home, with a view of the parks at the city's stern. He forced himself to stay calm. Pennyroyal wasn't clever enough to set up a surveillance-crab. And if he had, he would certainly have bragged about it to his dinner guests.

Plovery took the picture off the wall and set it down carefully against Pennyroyal's chair. The circular door of the safe confronted him. He reached for the dial and turned it right, then left, then right again. On previous visits to the Pavilion he had often seen Pennyroyal open the safe, and had worked out the combination by listening to the number of clicks the dial made. *Two-two-oh-nine-nine-five-seven*. . . Calmly, carefully, he went through the sequence, and the heavy door swung open.

Inside the safe was a small leather case. Inside the case was the Tin Book of Anchorage. Plovery took it out, holding it reverently, for old things were his love as well as his livelihood. There was something beautiful, he thought, about the way that human handiwork could outlive its makers by so many, many years.

As he reached up to shut the safe he sensed a movement behind him, and turned, and—

Wren was halfway to the dormitory when she heard his horrible, quivering scream. She squeaked and froze, then dived behind a nearby statue. The scream ended in a sort of gargling noise. The echoes faded into silence, and then the Pavilion began to fill with the sounds of doors opening and people shouting to each other. Lights came on. Glancing through the window beside her, Wren saw that light was flooding the gardens too; big security lamps flicking on, and guards running about with wobbling hand-held lanterns.

That's that, she thought, *no chance of escaping now* – and then felt ashamed that she was feeling sorry for herself when she should really have been worrying about whoever it was who had let out that dreadful shriek.

She left her hiding place and ran towards the dormitory. Halfway there she turned a corner and cannoned into Theo Ngoni, coming up a side-passage from the direction of the kitchens. "Oh!" she cried. "What are *you* doing here?"

"I heard someone scream. . ." he said.

"Me too. . ."

"The whole house heard someone scream, my dears." Mrs Pennyroyal was striding towards them in her billowing nightie, like a ship in full sail. Wren jumped away from Theo, wondering if they would be punished for speaking to each other, but the mayoress just looked kindly at them and said, "It seemed to come from my husband's part of the house. Let's see what has happened."

Wren and Theo followed obediently in her wake as she swept toward the larboard wing. Wren thought privately that it had been the sort of scream you hurry *away* from, not *towards*, but Mrs Pennyroyal seemed determined to get to the source of the disturbance. Perhaps she was hoping that her husband had scalded himself on

199

a hot-water bottle or fallen off his balcony, and didn't want to waste good gloating time.

They climbed the winding stairs behind the ballroom and passed the door to a little staircase which led down to the Cloud 9 control room; it was open, with worried-looking crewmen peering out. Lights were burning in the mayor's office, and as they drew closer Wren heard Pennyroyal's voice, shrill and wobbly with alarm, saying, "But the intruder may still be at large!" Slaves and militia were crowded round the open door, but they drew aside respectfully as their Lady Mayoress approached.

Pennyroyal was standing beside his desk, along with two officers of his guard. He looked up as his wife and her retinue entered. "Boo-Boo! Don't look. . ."

Boo-Boo looked, and gasped. Wren looked too, and wished she hadn't. Theo looked, and seemed quite undisturbed, but then he'd been in battle and had probably seen things like this before.

Walter Plovery lay on the floor beneath the open safe. He was clutching the Tin Book of Anchorage, and from the way that it partly hid his face Wren guessed that he had been holding it up to try and protect himself. It had done no good. Something sharp had been driven through the breast of his evening robes into his heart. The smell of the blood reminded Wren very forcefully of her last night in Anchorage and the deaths of Gargle and Remora.

"Must have been a knife," one of the militia officers was saying lamely. "Or maybe a spear. . ."

"A *spear*?" shouted Pennyroyal. "In my Pavilion? On the night before the MoonFest ball?"

The officers swapped sheepish glances. Like most of Brighton's soldiers they had signed up mainly for the uniforms – fetching scarlet numbers, with pink facings and a lot of gold tassels. They had never expected to have to face dead bodies and mysterious intruders, and now that they were they both felt a bit queasy.

"How did he get in?" asked one.

"There's no sign of a break-in," agreed the other.

"Well, I expect he took the spare key from the vase outside," said Pennyroyal. "I always keep a spare key there; Plovery knows that. *Knew* it, rather. . ."

The officers studied the body at their feet and nervously fingered the hilts of their ornamental swords.

"It looks to me as if he was trying to burgle Your Worship's safe," decided the first.

"Yes; what is that thing he's holding?" said the second.

"Nothing!" Pennyroyal snatched the Tin Book from the dead man's hands and thrust it back inside the safe, locking the door behind it. "Nothing of value, and anyway, it isn't here; you didn't see it. . ."

There was a thunder of fleece-lined boots on the stairs, and Orla Twombley burst into the room with half-a-dozen Flying Ferrets at her back. They carried drawn swords, and the aviatrix used hers to point at Wren. "That's the girl!"

"What? I say. . ." Pennyroyal turned to peer at Wren.

"She came asking my lads to ready your sky-yacht," Orla Twombley explained, taking a menacing step towards Wren as if she thought it might be safest to run the girl through where she stood. "Had some cock-and-bull story about the mayoress here wanting the old sack of gas refuelled so she can go shopping in Benghazi. . ."

"Stuff and nonsense!" cried Pennyroyal excitedly.

"The girl was preparing her getaway! Once a burglar, always a burglar, eh?"

Oh, gods! thought Wren. She had never imagined that her careful plan could go as wrong as this. What would they do to her? Send her back to Shkin, probably, and demand a refund. . .

Everybody was talking excitedly, Pennyroyal raising his voice above the rest. "Plovery must have recruited her to help him rob me, only she murdered him for the loot instead! And no doubt this Mossie devil was in it with her!" he added, pointing at Theo. "Well done, Orla, my angel! Without your quick thinking they'd have made off aboard the *Peewit* with the . . . ah . . . contents of my safe."

"Rubbish!" said Boo-Boo, in a voice that made them all fall silent and turn nervously to look at her. She had drawn herself up to her full height, and turned the colour that mayoresses turn when they hear their husbands refer to attractive aviatrices as "my angel" right in front of them. She put her arm around Wren. "What Wren told Miss Twombley was entirely true. I *did* ask for the *Peewit* to be refuelled. I *was* planning to go shopping in Benghazi tomorrow, though I don't suppose I shall feel up to it now. Anyway, Wren and Theo were with me when poor Plovery cried out; neither of them could possibly have done this dreadful deed."

Wren and Theo stared at her, astonished that Boo-Boo would lie to protect them.

"But if it wasn't them," asked Pennyroyal, "who. . .?"

"That is not for me to find out," said Boo-Boo haughtily. "I am returning to my quarters. Please search for your murderer quietly. Come, Wren; come, Theo. We have a busy day tomorrow."

She turned and strode out of the room, past the chastened aviators. Wren curtseyed to Pennyroyal and hurried after Theo and her mistress. "Mrs Pennyroyal," she whispered, as they reached the bottom of the stairs. "Thank you."

Boo-Boo seemed not to hear. "What a dreadful business!" she said. "That poor, poor man. My husband was to blame, I am sure."

"You think the mayor killed him?" asked Theo. He sounded as if he didn't believe it, but Wren knew Professor Pennyroyal was quite capable of murdering someone if it suited him. Look at how he had treated Dad! She could see now how he had fooled everyone in Anchorage for so long, for he was certainly a good actor. How shocked he had looked, standing over Plovery's body. . .

"Old-Tech!" sighed Boo-Boo. "It is never anything but trouble. Oh, I do not say that Pennyroyal wielded the fatal blade himself, but I expect he has set up some nasty booby trap to protect his safe. He would stop at nothing to protect that ridiculous Tin Book. What is so special about it anyway? Do you know, child?"

Wren shook her head. All she knew was that the Tin Book had been the cause of yet another death. She wished she had never taken the horrid thing from Miss Freya's library.

Outside the doors of her bedroom Boo-Boo shooed away the guard and turned to Wren and Theo. She studied them both with a sad smile, taking Wren's hands in hers. "My dear children," she said, "I am so sorry that your attempt to fly away has failed. I'm sure that is what you were doing, Wren? Having my husband's yacht fuelled so that you and Theo could fly away together?"

"I—" said Theo.

"Theo had nothing to do with it!" Wren protested. "I ran into him in the corridor. We were both coming to see what had happened—"

Mrs Pennyroyal raised a hand; she would hear none of it. She had done her best to stop this happening, but now that it had she found that it was all rather thrilling and romantic. "You need not hide the truth from me," she said, and tears came into her eyes. "I hope I am your friend, as well as your mistress. As soon as I saw you together, your tryst interrupted by the death-cry of that unhappy man, I understood everything. How I wish that I had known a burning passion like yours, instead of getting married off to Pennyroyal to please my family. . ."

"But—"

"Ah, but yours is a forbidden love! You remind me of Prince Osmiroid and the beautiful slave-girl Mipsie in Lembit Oriole's wonderful opera *Trodden Weeds*. But you must be patient, my dears. What hope of happiness do you have if you escape? Runaway slaves, penniless and far from home, pursued by bounty hunters wherever you turn. No, you must stay here a while, and meet only in secret. Now that I know how much you long to leave, I shall do all that is in my power to persuade Pennyroyal that he must set you free."

Wren could feel herself blushing. How could anyone imagine that she was in love with Theo Ngoni, of all people? She glanced at him, and was annoyed to see that he looked embarrassed too, as if the very idea that he might be in love with Wren was ridiculous.

"Patience, my lovebirds," the mayoress said, and kissed each of them upon the forehead. She smiled, and opened her bedroom door. "Oh, by the way," she murmured, "not a word to anyone about poor Mr Plovery. I will not allow this terrible event to upset our MoonFest celebrations. . ."

23
BRIGHT, BRIGHTER, BRIGHTON!

Moonfest! A buzz of expectation rose from the raft city as the sun came up. Actors and artists who never usually stirred before noon leaped from their beds at gull-squawk and began putting the finishing touches to decorations and carnival floats, while shopkeepers rolled up their shutters and unfurled their blinds with a gleeful air, dreaming of record takings. Brighton was not a religious city; most of its people thought that religion was at best a fairytale, at worst a con-trick. To them the rising of the first full moon of autumn, which was a solemn, sacred night in other cities, meant only one thing: it was party time!

Actually, it was almost always party time aboard Brighton. When Wren arrived the Aestival Festival, a six-week celebration of the gods of summer, had been petering out in a slew of firework parties and fancy dress parades. Since then there had been the Large Hat Festival, the Cheese Sculpture Biennale, the Festival of Unattended Plays, Poskitt Week, and Mime-Baiting Day (when Brightonians were allowed to get their own back on the city's swarms of irritating street performers). But MoonFest still had a special place in the hearts and wallets of Brightonians, and the growing cluster of towns on shore seemed to promise a bumper harvest of visitors. Even the editor of the *Palimpsest*, who would usually have been delighted to print the rumours he'd been hearing about a mysterious death on Cloud 9 during the night, relegated the story to a small column on page four and filled his front page with Festival news instead.

BOO-BOO'S BEVY OF BEAUTIES BOOSTS BRIGHTON!

Lady Mayoress Boo-Boo Pennyroyal predicted yesterday that this year's MoonFest celebrations will be Brighton's best ever. Mrs Pennyroyal (39) – pictured left, posing for the Palimpsest's photographer along with a bevy of her most beautiful handmaidens – will tonight play hostess to the Middle Sea's richest partygoers when the Pavilion opens its doors and dance-floors for the Mayoral Ball.

"Everybody who is anybody is on their way to Brighton!" said Mrs Pennyroyal. "What better place to celebrate Moon Festival than in this white city, adrift on an azure sea?"

Of course, it wasn't really a white city on an azure sea at all; that was just how it looked from the observation platforms of Cloud 9. Down at deck-level, Brighton was an off-white city, its rooftops streaked with gull droppings, its streets sticky with abandoned snacks, adrift on a slick of its own litter and sewage. But the weather was perfect; a soft onshore breeze to waft the air-taxis across to Benghazi and Kom Ombo and cool their passengers on the journey back; the hot sun baking the metal pavements and releasing complex odours from the puddles of grease and sick which last night's revellers had left behind. As the day wore on the city settled lower in the water, weighed down by the crowds of visitors who filled the streets and artificial beaches, and splashed and shrieked along the fringes of the Sea Pool. By mid-afternoon all the rubbish bins were overflowing, and the gulls fought each other for scavenged scraps of meat and pastry, swooping low over the heads of the long queues that had formed beneath the Pharos Wheel and outside the entrance to the Brighton Aquarium.

Tom Natsworthy, waiting in the line of holidaymakers, ducked as another screaming gull dived past. He had been nervous of large birds ever since he fought with the Green Storm's flying Stalkers at Rogue's Roost. But these greedy gulls were really the least of his worries. He felt sure that the Aquarium's uniformed attendants would be able to tell just by looking at him that he had come aboard Brighton only an hour before, climbing out of a manhole that the *Screw Worm* had bored through the city's hull. He expected at any moment to be dragged out of the queue and denounced as an intruder and a stowaway.

The *Screw Worm* had caught up with Brighton that morning. Tom had approached slowly, frightened of triggering whatever Old-Tech Brighton had used to catch the Lost Boys, but it seemed that the city had turned its sensors off now that its fishing trip was over. Even so, he and Hester had barely dared to breathe as the magnetic clamps engaged and the hull-drill chewed noisily through the resort's deckplates.

Tom had wanted to use the crab-cams to search for signs of Wren, but Hester disagreed. "We're not Lost Boys," she pointed out. "It'd take all sorts of skills we haven't got to steer one of those things through Brighton's plumbing. It could be weeks before we sighted Wren. We'll go up ourselves. We ought to be able to find some sign of all those limpets they fished aboard."

Hester was right. When they emerged from the *Worm* into a deserted alleyway behind Brighton's engine district almost the first thing they saw was a poster pasted to an exhaust duct. It showed a limpet surrounded by savage boys, beneath the words *Parasite Pirates of the Atlantic! Artefacts and captives taken from the Sub-Aquatic Thieves' Den of Grimsby, during Brighton's recent expedition, are on Public Display at the Brighton Aquarium, 11-17 Burchill Square.*

"Captives!" said Tom. "Wren might be there! That's where we've got to go. . ."

Hester, a slower reader than her husband, was still halfway through the text. "What's an Aquiarium?"

"A place for fish. A sort of zoo, or museum."

Hester nodded. "Museums are your department. You go and have a look. I want to go and nose round the air-harbour. I might hear something about Wren there, and I want to see if I can find us a ship; I don't fancy going all the way home in that stinking old limpet."

"We shouldn't split up," said Tom.

"It's only for a while," said Hester. "It'll be quicker." It was just an excuse, of course. The truth was that all the time she'd spent cooped up with Tom beneath the waves had made her irritable. She wanted to be alone for a while; to breathe, and look around this city, without having to listen to him worrying always about Wren. She kissed him quickly and said, "I'll meet you in an hour."

"Back at the *Worm*?"

Hester shook her head. The engine district was getting busy as a new shift clocked on; passers-by might notice them sneaking down their secret manhole. She pointed to another advert, half obscured by the Aquarium poster, for a coffee shop in Old Steine called The Pink Café.

"There. . ."

Luckily, the Aquarium's attendants were only interested in selling tickets and chatting to each other about their plans for the evening. They were not on the lookout for intruders, and even if they had been, there was nothing to distinguish Tom from the other visitors. He was just a youngish, tousled, slightly balding man, perhaps a scholar from the middle tiers of Kom Ombo, and if his clothes were rather rumpled and old-fashioned and he smelled faintly of mildew and brine, well, there was no rule against that. The girl at the turnstile barely glanced at him as she took his money and waved him through.

Inside the Aquarium, bored-looking fish drifted in big, dim tanks and there was such a smell of rust and salt water that Tom could almost have imagined he was back in Grimsby. But nobody was looking at the fish, or the sea horses, or the mangy sea lions. Everyone was heading to the central hall, following the brightly coloured signs to the Parasite Pirates exhibit.

Tom went with them, trying not to look too eager, reminding himself that Wren would probably not be here. He shuffled along among the other visitors, peering at a display of crab-cams and then at a limpet called *Spider Baby* which stood on a dais in the centre of the hall. Whoever had put it there had given it a dramatic pose, rearing back on its four hind legs and waving its front feet in the air, as if it were about to lash out at the visitors. Families posed in front of it to have their photographs taken, the children making scaredy faces, or sticking out their tongues at the looming machine.

Beyond the limpet, in a straw-lined cage, captive Lost Boys squatted and stared at the passing crowds. Sometimes one would fling himself at the bars, shouting abuse, and the visitors would scuttle away, frightened and delighted, while one of the burly attendants poked the savage with an electric prod. Tom felt sorry for the Lost Boys, and almost relieved that Wren was not among them.

Nearby, a pretty young woman in Aquarium livery was pointing out details to a group of children. Tom waited until she had finished, then approached her. "Excuse me," he asked, "could you tell me how many limpets were taken?"

The pretty young woman was really very pretty. Her smile almost dazzled Tom. "Nineteen in total, sir," she said, "and three destroyed at sea."

"And was one of them called the *Autolycus*?"

The smile faded. Flustered, the woman riffled through her exhibition notes. Nobody had ever asked her about a particular limpet before. "Let me see. . . ." she muttered.

"I believe. . . Oh yes! The *Autolycus* was one of the first limpets we caught, way over in the western seas, far from the parasite lair." Her smile returned. "She must have been swimming off on a burgling mission when we snapped her up. . ."

"And the crew?"

The young woman was still smiling, but her eyes were troubled; she was starting to wonder if Tom were some kind of weirdo. "You'd have to ask Mr Shkin, sir. Mr Nabisco Shkin. All the captives are property of the Shkin Corporation."

"And what's the Shkin Corporation?" asked Hester, who had just been told the same thing by a second-hand balloon salesman at the air-harbour.

"Slaves," said the man, spitting a black jet of tobacco juice on to the deckplate at his feet and winking at her. "All them boys and girls they fished up are all slaves now, and serve them right, I say."

A slave, thought Hester, as she strode away through the increasingly busy streets. The shadows of airships and balloon-taxis slid over her as they poured into the air-harbour to offload more cackling crowds of tourists. *A slave.* Hester shouldered a group of language students off the pavement. How was she going to break this to Tom? That his beloved little girl was cooped up in a slave-hold somewhere, or enduring who-knew-what at the hands of cruel owners. . .

To make matters worse, she had learned that her plan of buying an airship would not work. Prices had rocketed since she'd last been aboard a city, and the gold that she had taken from Grimsby wouldn't buy so much as a spare engine pod at the second-hand airship yards.

She spent some of it at a stall behind the harbour instead, buying a pair of jet-black sunglasses to hide her missing eye, and a headdress of silver discs that more or less concealed the scar on her forehead. She bought a new veil, too, and an ankle-length black coat with many buttons to replace the shabby thing she'd worn all the way from Anchorage. Walking on, she found her mood improving. She liked this city. She liked the sunshine and the crowds, the jangle of slot-machines, the tatty frontages of the hotels. She liked being among people who did not know her, and could not guess what lay beneath her veil. She liked the handsome young aviators who smiled at her as she strode past, their eyes drawn to this mysterious woman with her hidden face and long, lean body. And – although she didn't quite admit it to herself – she liked life without Wren. She was almost glad that the girl had got herself kidnapped.

She stopped to study a street-plan and then crossed a footbridge over the Sea Pool and headed aft to Old Steine. There was no sign of Tom at the tables outside The Pink Café. Hester considered having a coffee while she waited for him, then decided that she couldn't afford one at Brighton prices. She wandered around the long curve of the Steine instead, looking at the shop-fronts, until she came to one that stopped her short.

It was a shabby building which had once been a theatre. A cheery pink sign above its door proclaimed *The Nimrod Pennyroyal Experience*, and posters announced: *Re-live Mayor Pennyroyal's Adventures on Five Continents and a Thousand Cities! Educational and Entertaining!* In the window a waxwork of

Pennyroyal, chained to the floor of a cardboard dungeon, raised and lowered its head, peering quizzically at a crescent-shaped blade which swung to and fro above it on a pendulum.

Mayor Pennyroyal? Hester had often wondered what had become of the fake explorer after he shot Tom and stole the *Jenny Haniver*. She had assumed that the gods would have punished him by now for all his lies and tricks; they'd had sixteen years to think of a suitable come-uppance, after all. Instead, they seemed to have rewarded him. Pennyroyal was alive. And Pennyroyal knew what she had done. She had told him herself, in the Aakiuqs' smashed-up kitchen, while she was getting ready to murder Masgard and his huntsmen.

She handed a bronze coin to the man at the ticket booth, and went inside.

It seemed as though Brighton's other visitors had found better ways of educating and entertaining themselves, for the *Nimrod Pennyroyal Experience* was almost deserted. There was a dusty, museum smell, and another smell, tantalizing and out-of-place, which was even more familiar. Hester wandered past unimpressive artefacts in glass cases, past a reconstruction of an Ancient land-fill site which Pennyroyal had once excavated. Paintings and waxwork dioramas showed Pennyroyal battling a bear, escaping from air-pirates, and almost being sacrificed by a cult of Old-Tech-worshipping female warriors – all scenes from Pennyroyal's best-selling books, and all total fibs. Only one of the paintings meant anything to Hester. It showed Pennyroyal, sword in hand, fighting off a horde of savage Huntsmen, while at his side a beautiful young woman expired prettily. It was only after she had stared at the picture for a minute or more that Hester noticed the martyred girl wore an eye-patch and had a fetching little scar on her cheek.

"Gods!" she said aloud. "Is that bimbo supposed to be *me*?"

Her voice sounded loud in the empty, echoey rooms. As it faded Hester heard footsteps and the man from the kiosk put his head round the door and asked, "Everything all right, madam?"

Hester nodded, too angry to speak.

"Magnificent painting, eh?" the curator said. He was a friendly man, middle-aged, with a few strands of sandy hair combed carefully across his bald head. He came and stood next to Hester and beamed proudly at the picture. "It's inspired by the closing chapters of *Predator's Gold*, in which his worship does battle with the Huntsmen of Arkangel."

"Who's the girl?" asked Hester.

"You haven't read *Predator's Gold*?" asked the man, surprised. "That is Hester Shaw, the aviatrix who sells Anchorage to the Huntsmen. She redeems herself, the poor creature, by dying at Pennyroyal's side, cut down by the chief of the Huntsmen, Piotr Masgard."

Hester turned away quickly, climbing a dusty metal staircase towards the upper floor of the museum, barely seeing the displays she passed, her head filled with panicky, racing thoughts. Everything was ruined! Pennyroyal didn't just know what she'd done, he'd written a book about it! There were paintings! Even if Pennyroyal had twisted the facts, the truth was still there, in black and white on the pages of his book. Hester Shaw had sold Anchorage to the Huntsmen. And when Tom found

215

out. . .

Would he still love her, if he knew what she was really like?

She reached the top of the stairs. The familiar smell was stronger up here, and Hester remembered suddenly what it was; a mixture of aviation fuel and lifting gas. She looked up.

The whole upper storey was a single, glass-roofed room, and in its centre, on metal stanchions, sat an airship. It was old and tattered, and the name painted along its flank was *The Arctic Roll,* but Hester would have known that clinker-built gondola and those much-repaired Jeunet-Carot engine pods anywhere. She had lived in those narrow cabins for two years, and flown halfway around the world beneath that old red gasbag. It was the *Jenny Haniver.*

"Ugly old tub, ain't she?"

Hester had not realized that the curator had followed her up the stairs, but here he was, standing just behind her and smiling amiably. "Hester Shaw bequeathed her to Professor Pennyroyal with her dying breath, and he flew her home to Brighton through polar storms and swarms of air-pirates."

A wooden walkway had been built beside the gondola. Half listening to the curator, Hester climbed the steps and peered in through the dusty windows, remembering the ship's real history. There was the stern cabin, with the narrow bunk where she used to sleep with Tom. There was the pilot's seat where she had spent so many long watches. There, on the scuffed planking of the flight-deck floor, Wren had been conceived. . .

She sniffed the air. "She smells ready to fly. . ."

"Yes indeed, madam. Aviatrix, are you?"

Hester looked round at him with a start, wondering if he had guessed who she was, but he was just being friendly. "Yes," she said, and then, because he looked as if he wanted to know more, "I'm Captain Valentine of the *Freya*."

"Ah!" said the curator, satisfied, and nodded to the *Jenny* again. "She'll be leading the fly-past of historic ships tomorrow, Ms Valentine."

Hester touched the cool underside of an engine pod and imagined it roaring into life. She was starting to recover from her shock. After all, Tom knew that Pennyroyal was a liar. Why would he believe anything the old fraud said about her? Beneath her veil she smiled her crooked smile.

"It should be a very fine display," the curator was saying, smiling up at her. "There's going to be a re-enactment of one of Professor Pennyroyal's most desperate adventures; a battle between *The Arctic Roll* and a bunch of old air-tugs dressed up as pirate ships. Real rockets and everything. . ."

Hester looked around the big room. "How do you get her out?"

"Eh?" said the curator. "Oh, the roof opens. Opens right up, like a docking hangar. The mayor will just fly her out."

Hester nodded, and checked the time by her pocket watch. She had forgotten her meeting with Tom, and she was already twenty minutes late. She went back downstairs with the curator hurrying behind her. In the souvenir shop near the exit she helped herself to a copy of *Predator's Gold* and flipped a couple of coins at him to pay for it.

"If I might make so bold, Ms Valentine," said the

curator, rummaging in his cash-box for change, "I was wondering whether you might care to accompany me to the display tomorrow, and perhaps to dinner afterwards?"

But when he looked up, the mysterious aviatrix was gone, and the exit door was swinging softly shut.

Hester walked briskly across the Old Steine towards the café, stuffing Pennyroyal's book into her pocket. The curator's foolish, flattering request made her feel attractive and mysterious again, and the panic she had felt earlier had completely vanished. She knew now that everything would be all right. She would show Tom the book, and they would laugh together at all Pennyroyal's lies about her. Then she would spring Wren from the slave-pens, and they would reclaim the *Jenny Haniver* and fly away together.

The tables outside the café were busy, but there was still no Tom. She turned around, looking for him, annoyed. It was not like Tom to be late, and she wanted to tell him her plans.

"Hester?" asked one of the slave-girls from the café, approaching with a folded piece of paper in her hand. "You are Hester, ain't you? The gentleman said you'd be coming. He asked me to give you this."

The paper was a handbill advertising the Aquarium. On the back, in his neat handwriting, Tom had pencilled, *Dearest Het, I will see you back at the SW. Wren has been taken as a slave; I am going to a place called the Pepperpot to see about buying her back...*

24
THE *REQUIEM VORTEX*

The air-fleet had made good time since leaving Shan Guo. They had crossed the sequinned turquoise waters of the Persian Gulf and were sweeping westward now over the hills of Jabal Hammar. The four destroyers flew in line astern, and around them the air throbbed and tore with the roar of engine pods as an escort of fighter airships – Murasaki Fox Spirits and Zhang Chen Hawkmoths – scoured the sky for townie privateers.

Through a slit in the armoured gondola of the Stalker Fang's flagship *Requiem Vortex* Oenone Zero peered towards the distant ground. Nothing moved down there except the shadows of the ships, but wherever she looked she could see the deep gouges made by the tracks and wheels of passing towns. Jagged bite-marks pitted the hillsides, where mining towns had scooped out gut-fulls of ore-bearing rock.

When she first heard that she was to go with her mistress on this mysterious expedition, Oenone had felt glad. Isolated in the sky, aboard the Stalker's flagship, surely she would find a chance to use her weapon? But the world she had seen on the way, scarred and ruined by Municipal Darwinism, made her wonder afresh if she really had the right. She hated the war, but she hated Traction Cities too. By killing Fang, might she not be handing victory to them? If the Green Storm collapsed, the whole earth might soon look like those wrecked rubble-heaps below her. She did not want that on her conscience.

"Still finding reasons not to do what you came here

for, Oenone," she told herself, in the disappointed tone her mother had used when Oenone was a child, and shirked her schoolwork. "What a coward you are!"

She looked ahead, into a brownish haze that she knew was made partly from the exhaust smoke of cities. Beyond it somewhere lay the Middle Sea, not far off now. Oenone tried to crush her doubts. A battle was coming, and she knew enough about battles to feel sure that there would be moments of such chaos and confusion that she would be able to unleash her device upon the Stalker Fang without anyone understanding what she had done.

She turned from the gun-slit and climbed up into the thundering passageways inside the envelope. As she neared the officers' mess she could hear the voices of some of her comrades, and she paused at the open door, unnoticed, listening.

"She says we are to target only Brighton!" Lieutenant Zhao the gunnery officer was saying, pitching her voice low for fear the Stalker Fang might hear. "Why Brighton? I've read the intelligence reports. Brighton is the least of cities, the merest pleasure-raft."

"She has spies of her own," said Navigator Cheung, staring into his empty cup as though he could divine the Stalker's plans from the tea-leaves there. "She has deep-cover agents who report to nobody but her."

"Yes, but why would she have placed one aboard Brighton?"

"Who knows? There must be something important about the place."

"Such as?" Zhao shook her head. "There are fat predator towns lurking in these hills below us. Why must I save my rockets for Brighton when I could be blowing the tracks off predator towns?"

220

"It is not for us to question her orders, Zhao."

That came from the expedition's second in command, General Naga. Oenone saw the junior officers stiffen and bow their heads at the sound of his voice. Naga had been with the Green Storm since its foundation. There was a famous photograph of him, young and handsome, raising their thunderbolt banner over the wreck of Traktiongrad; Oenone had had a poster of it on her bedroom wall when she was a girl. But Naga was not young any more, and not handsome either; his hair was grey, his long, ochre face seamed and scarred. He was thirty-five; an old man by the standards of the Green Storm military. He had lost an arm at Xanne-Sandansky and the use of his legs at the air-siege of Omsk, and he could only walk and fight because the Resurrection Corps had built him a powered metal exoskeleton.

"I don't like this mission," he admitted, the segments of his mechanical armour scraping as he leaned across the table. "Brighton is no threat to us, and I hear it's spent the summer hammering those parasite brigands up in the north Atlantic. I was a cadet at Rogues' Roost when they attacked our airbase there. I lost good friends to those devils, and I'm glad Brighton's sorted them out. But orders are orders, and orders from the Fire-Flower..."

He stopped suddenly, sensing Oenone standing in the doorway. "Surgeon-Mechanic," he said gruffly, turning towards her. His mechanical hand clamped on his sword-hilt; his exoskeleton clanked and hissed, making a clumsy half-bow. Behind him, Oenone saw fear on the faces of the junior officers as they recognized her. She knew what they were thinking. *How long has she been*

there? How much did she hear? Will she tell the Stalker?
Even Naga was afraid of her.

"Please, forgive me," she said, bowing formally to the
general and again to the officers at the table. She went
into the mess, poured a glass of jasmine tea which she
did not want, and drank it quickly, in silence. Everyone's
eyes lingered on her. They were almost as wary of her as
they were of the Stalker Fang herself, and she felt glad of
that, because it proved that they did not suspect her real
motives.

But someone aboard the *Requiem Vortex* suspected
her. As she left the mess and climbed the companion-
ladders to her cabin high among the reinforced gas-cells,
Shrike watched from the shadows, and waited patiently
for her to make her move.

25
THE PEPPERPOT

Afternoon was turning into evening as Tom walked towards the Pepperpot through streets filled with carnival. A procession was moving slowly along Ocean Boulevard, with pretty girls and boys dressed up as mermaids cavorting on electric floats, giant dancing puppets of the sea-gods, paper lanterns shaped like fish and serpents twirling on long poles, and drag-queens in enormous feathery hats showering down confetti from low-flying cargo balloons. Through gaps between the white buildings Tom kept glimpsing the sea, and once, with a scream of engines, a patrol of those unlikely flying machines came hurtling low over the rooftops. Tom clapped his hands over his ears and turned to watch them pass. He would have been thrilled by them when he was younger, but now they just reminded him of how dangerous the world was, and how much it had altered while he'd been away. The more he saw of it, the more he longed to find Wren and return to the peace of Vineland.

He pushed on through the crowds, heading for the address that the girl at the Aquarium had given him. He knew that Hester would be cross with him later for going without her, but he had been far too anxious to wait any longer for her at The Pink Café. Besides, he kept remembering what she had done to Gargle, and it made him feel uneasy about how she might react when she learned Wren's fate. He wanted to talk calmly to this Shkin fellow. He might turn out to be a reasonable man, who would give Wren back to her parents when he learned the truth. If not, Tom would arrange to buy her back. Either way, there should be no need for violence.

When he saw the Pepperpot he felt even more optimistic. Most slavers' dens were dingy places, tucked away on unmentionable tiers of savage salvage towns, not elegant white towers. Outside the glass front door a guard in smart black livery politely stopped him and ran a metal-detector over him before letting him into a reception area as calm and tasteful as a hotel lobby. There were soft chairs, and hard metallic-green potplants, and a plaque on the wall which read *The Shkin Corporation* and underneath, in smaller letters, *An Investor in People*. The only real clue to what sort of place it was were the angry, muffled shouts and clanging sounds which came up faintly through the sea-grass carpet.

"I'm sorry about the noise," said a well-dressed woman sitting behind a black desk. "It is those filthy Lost Boys. They were very meek when we first brought them aboard, but they are growing more troublesome and contumelious by the day. Never mind. The autumn auctions begin tomorrow, so we shall soon be rid of them."

"Then you have not sold them yet?" cried Tom. "I'm so glad. I'm looking for my daughter. Wren Natsworthy. She was with the Lost Boys, and I think you might have taken her by mistake. . ."

The woman had pencilled-on eyebrows as thin as wire, and she raised them both in surprise. "One moment, please," she said, and leaned across her desk to whisper into a brass and bakelite intercom which Tom thought very futuristic. The intercom whispered back, and after a moment the woman looked up at Tom and smiled and said, "Mr Shkin will see you in person. You may go up."

Tom moved towards the spiral staircase that led up through the ceiling, but the woman pressed a button on her desk, and a narrow door slid open in the wall. Tom realized that it was a lift. It looked nothing like the huge public elevators he remembered from his boyhood in London; just a posh cupboard, panelled in mother-of-pearl, but he tried not to look too surprised, and stepped inside. The door slid shut. He felt his stomach lurch. When the door opened again he was in a quiet, luxurious office where a man was rising to meet him from behind another black steel desk.

"Mr Shkin?" asked Tom, while behind him the door closed softly and the lift went purring down.

Nabisco Shkin bowed low and extended a grey-gloved hand. "My dear Mr Natsworthy," he said softly. "Miss Weems tells me you are interested in one of our slaves. The girl named Wren."

It made Tom angry to hear Wren called a slave so calmly, but he controlled himself and shook Shkin's hand. He said, "Wren is my daughter. She was kidnapped by one of the Lost Boys. I've come to get her back."

"Indeed?" Shkin nodded, watching Tom carefully. "Unfortunately I had no idea of the girl's history. She has already been sold."

"Sold?" cried Tom. "Where is she? Is she still aboard Brighton?"

"I shall have to check my files. We have processed so many slaves this month. . ."

The elevator door opened again, and the room began to fill with men; armed guards in black livery. Tom, taken by surprise, barely realized what was happening before one of the men slammed the handle of a truncheon into his side and two more caught him as he doubled over, breathless and choking.

Nabisco Shkin moved around the room, pulling down canvas blinds to hide the long windows. "A lot of pleasure craft in the sky today," he said conversationally. "Wouldn't want any happy holiday-makers peeking in on us, would we?" The room grew shadowy. He returned to his desk and spoke into the intercom. "Monica, send the boy here. Let's find out if this wretch is really who he claims to be."

Tom's captors twisted his arms painfully behind him and held him tight, but they need not have bothered, for he was in no state to stand, let alone try to overpower four strong guards. He felt his heart flutter and thump, pain twisting through his side. Shkin came closer, pulled up Tom's sleeve with a look of faint distaste and removed his wedding bracelet.

"That's my property!" Tom gasped. "Give it back!"

Shkin tossed the bracelet up in the air and caught it again. "You don't have property any more," he said. "You *are* property. Unless you have papers to prove that you are a free man; but if you are who you say you are, you won't." He held the bracelet up and squinted at it. "HS and TN," he read. "How touching. . ."

The lift bell rang again and another of Shkin's black-clad guards stepped out. This one was just a boy, dressed up like the rest in a black uniform and a peaked black cap with a silver *Shkin* logo on the front.

"Well, Fishcake?" Shkin asked him. "Do you recognize our guest?"

The boy stared at Tom. "That's him all right, Mr

Shkin," he said. "I saw him on the screens when we was at Anchorage. That's Wren's dad."

"How do you. . ." Tom started to ask, and then realized suddenly who this boy must be. Fishcake. That was the lad Uncle had talked about, the newbie who had kidnapped Wren! Tom knew he should feel angry with him, but he didn't. He just felt more angry than ever with Shkin, because he could see the logo branded on the back of the boy's thin hand. What sort of a man would do that to a child? What sort of a city would let a man like that grow rich and prosperous? He said, "Fishcake, please, is Wren all right? Was she hurt at all? Do you know who bought her?"

Fishcake was about to reply, but Shkin said, "Don't answer him, boy." One of the guards hit Tom again, knocking the air out of his lungs in a loud, wordless woof.

"Fishcake has learned obedience," said Shkin. "He knows that if he disobeys me I shall put him back in the holding cells with his friends, and they will rip him to pieces for betraying Grimsby." He tore open Tom's waistcoat, pulled up his shirt and traced with one grey-gloved finger the scars which had been left by Windolene Pye's amateur surgery. There was something like a smile on his face.

"The mayor of this city is a very irritating man, Mr Natsworthy," he said. "I believe that you may be able to help me expose him as a fraud and a liar. But first, your daughter will help me to retrieve something he has stolen from me. Who knows, if you cooperate, I might let you both go free." As he turned to his desk he tossed the bracelet up into the air and caught it again. Leaning down to the brass mouthpiece of the intercom he said,

"Miss Weems, arrange a cell on the mid-levels for Mr Natsworthy, and have a bug ready to take me to Old Steine at seven-thirty. I think I shall be attending His Worship's Ball after all."

Hester had already looked in through the front door of the pretty little tower once, without seeing any sign of Tom. She had looked for him everywhere else that she could think of, hoping that he might have gone back to the *Screw Worm* before attempting to talk to the slavers, or circled back to The Pink Café. Now she was back outside the Pepperpot, feeling angry and faintly scared. She was sure Tom was in there, and that something bad had happened to him. The blinds had been drawn across the windows on one of the upper storeys, and there was a bunch of black-overalled guards in the reception area, chatting to the snooty-looking woman there. Hester wondered if she should barge in and confront them, but she did not want to walk into the same trap as Tom.

The man outside saw her peering in again, and stared, so she walked quickly past as if she were just a curious tourist and went into a coffee shop on the far side of the square, where she drank iced coffee through a straw and had a think. This Shkin character must have decided to take Tom prisoner for some reason. Perhaps he thought Tom was connected with the Lost Boys. Well, that was not so big a problem. She would go and rescue him, just as Tom had come to rescue her, when she had been a prisoner at Rogues' Roost.

But how to get inside that tower? The guard at the door was already wary of her, and with all these carnival crowds about she could not just shoot her way in. Oh, poor Tom! Why had he come here alone? He should have known that he couldn't cope on his own with people like this Nabisco Shkin.

She paid for her iced coffee, and asked the waiter, "Is that Shkin's place? The tower? It looks too small to hold many slaves."

"It's got hidden depths," the waiter replied, glancing happily at the tip she put down on the table. "The cells and stuff are down below. That's where they're keeping all those horrible pirates."

Hester thought again of Rogues' Roost, and of how she had led Tom to safety through the confusion of a Lost Boy raid. Then she left the café, walking quickly, glancing down once to make sure that the gun in her belt didn't spoil the cut of her new coat.

26
WAITING FOR THE MOON

As the sun sank red and fat into the haze above Africa, the breeze stiffened. Brighton began to rock gently on the long, white-capped, shoreward-rolling combers. Undaunted by the heaving pavements, parades of children trooped round Ocean Boulevard with bright banners and huge moon-shaped paper lanterns, and a thousand self-styled artists held private views in one another's houses.

"Keeps 'em busy, I suppose," said Nimrod Pennyroyal, gazing down philosophically at it all from one of Cloud 9's many observation platforms. "There are so many tenth-rate painters and performers on this city, we need a good festival every week or two to make them feel their silly lives are worthwhile." Drifts of bubbles swirled past him, vomited into the evening sky by an art installation in Queen's Park. The breeze brought carnival noises gusting up, too; guitars and cacophoniums jangling in the streets of the historic Muesli Belt, premature fireworks banging and shrieking on the sea-fronts.

On the blue-green evening lawns of the Pavilion Gardens, between the shadows of the cypress groves, the guests were starting to gather. All the men wore formal robes, and the women looked wonderful in ball-gowns of moonlight-silver and midnight blue. Paper lanterns had been strung along all the walks, and between the pillars of the bandstand where some musicians were tuning up. The Flying Ferrets had arrived, looking terribly dashing in their fleece-lined flying suits and white silk scarves, talking loudly about "archie" and "bandits" and "crates" being "ditched in the briny". Orla

Twombley, her hair lacquered into back-swept wings, hung on Pennyroyal's arm.

Drinks and snacks were being served before the dancing began, and Wren was one of the people doing the serving. She felt pretty and conspicuous in her MoonFest costume – baggy trousers and a long tunic made from some floaty, silvery fabric that she could not name – but the guests seemed not to notice her at all; they were only interested in the tray she carried. As she wove her way through the gathering crowds, hands reached out without a thank you or a by-your-leave to snatch at her cargo of drinks and canapés.

Wren didn't mind. She was still tired and uneasy after the events of the night before. All day there had been an odd atmosphere in the Pavilion, with militia men coming and going and security being tightened up. The other slave girls kept coming to ask Wren if she had really seen the body and had there been ever so much blood? To make matters worse, Mrs Pennyroyal smiled knowingly at Wren every time she saw her, and kept finding excuses to send her into rooms where Theo Ngoni was, or Theo into rooms where Wren was, as if she hoped someone would write an opera about them one day, and that there would be a part for a soprano of a certain age as Boo-Boo Pennyroyal, the thoughtful mistress who made their love possible.

Strangely, all this kindness made Wren like Boo-Boo less; it was one thing to keep slaves, but quite another to try and arrange their love affairs. She felt that the mayoress was pairing her and Theo off like a couple of prize poodles.

So she was glad to be invisible for a while, to look and listen. And everywhere she looked, she saw someone she recognized from the society pages of the *Palimpsest*. There were Brighton's leading painters, Robertson Gloom and Ariane Arai. There was the gorgeous Davina Twisty, fresh from her triumph in *Hearts Akimbo* at the Marlborough Theatre. That man in the hat must be the sculptor Gormless, whose ridiculous artworks clogged the city's public spaces like barbed-wire entanglements. And wasn't that the great P. P. Bellman, author of atheistic pop-up books for the trendy toddler? Wren wondered how they would all feel if they knew that a man had been murdered, right here on Cloud 9, less than twenty-four hours ago.

She met Cynthia, and asked her softly, "Is there any news?"

"News?" echoed Cynthia, as bright and brainless as sunshine.

"About poor Mr Plovery? Have they found out who did it yet?"

"Oh!" Cynthia's golden ringlets jiggled as she shook her head. "No. And Mrs Pennyroyal says we ain't to talk about it. But what's all this I hear about you and Theo?"

"It's nothing. Just Boo-Boo's imagination."

"You're blushing, Wren! I knew you fancied him! I saw you talking to him that day at the pool, remember?"

Wren left her giggling and pressed on through the crowd, asking, "Would you care for a drink, Sir? A canapé, Madame?" and gathering up empty glasses and fragments of still emptier conversations.

"Just *look* what La Twisty is wearing!"

"You simply *must* meet Gloom, he's *so* amusing!"

"Have you read Bellman's latest? Quite brilliant! Some of the finest literature of our age is being written for the under-fives. . ."

Dusk deepened. Davina Twisty was persuading some friends and admirers to venture with her into Cloud 9's insanely complicated box-hedge maze. The band played "Golden Echoes" and "The Lunar Lullaby". Soon the moon would rise, and everyone would watch the fireworks before retiring to the pavilion for dancing and more food. Wren, already exhausted, paused in a quiet part of the gardens near the deckplate's edge. It felt nice to be alone at last. She looked across the sea at the armoured cities, and thought how melancholy they looked, crouching there upon the dunes like the temples of a vanished race.

A hand crept on to her shoulder like a grey silk spider. Turning, she looked into the expressionless face of Nabisco Shkin.

"Enjoying the view, my dear?" he asked. "I hope none of His Worship's other guests has noticed you loafing here. The Shkin Corporation has a reputation as a purveyor of only the most hard-working slaves."

Wren pulled away from him and tried to return to the light and laughter of the party, but Shkin barred her way. What did he want with her? He must have been stalking her through the busy gardens, waiting for a moment when he could catch her alone. She felt cold and frightened. Raising her empty tray, she held it in front of her like a shield, but Shkin only laughed. She didn't like his laugh. She'd preferred it when he was silent and icy.

"Why would I harm you, child?" he asked. "I just want you to do a job for me; the simplest and smallest of jobs. Do you know where your new master keeps his private safe?"

Wren nodded.

"Good girl." Shkin held up a neat square of paper

with a number written on it. "This is the combination. I'd like you to fetch me the Tin Book. I sent a friend for it yesterday, but I hear he met with an accident."

Wren lowered her tray, thinking of poor Mr Plovery.

"Don't look so glum!" Shkin told her. "You've stolen it before. Young Fishcake told me all about it."

"I won't do it!" Wren said. "You can't make me!"

"Your poor father," said Shkin. He twirled the square of paper back into an inner pocket of his graphite-coloured evening robe and shrugged faintly. "What a pity, after he came all this way to rescue you!"

Wren couldn't imagine what he meant. Not until he reached into another pocket and brought out a bracelet, which he laid on the tray between them. By the light of lanterns in the nearby trees Wren recognized Dad's wedding bracelet. She had known it all her life; that loop of red gold with the letters HS and TN entwined. But what was it doing on Cloud 9?

"It's a trick!" she said. "Fishcake must have described this to you, and you had a replica made. . ."

"Don't you think it's more likely that your dear daddy has come to Brighton to fetch you home?" asked Shkin. "He is a guest of the Shkin Corporation. If you fail in the task I have set you, he'll die. Rather slowly. So be a good girl, and run up to Pennyroyal's office."

The gardens were falling quiet. Some of the guests were organizing a search-party to look for Davina Twisty, who was lost in the maze. The others shushed them. Moonrise was only a few moments away. The thought of Dad so near made Wren start to cry. How had he come here? How had Shkin found him? And where was Mum? She reached for the bracelet, but Shkin's conjuror's hands whisked it away and set the square of paper in its place.

"Do this little thing for me," he soothed, "and you will be reunited. I'll send you both home to Vineland in one of my own ships."

Wren didn't believe that, but she believed the rest. Dad was in Shkin's power. If she didn't do as Shkin asked, he'd be killed. And the worst of it was, it was all her fault: if she hadn't taken that book in the first place, he would still be safe in Anchorage. So if stealing the book again was the only way to keep him safe a little longer, that was what she would have to do.

"But why me?" she asked. "You must know all sorts of people better at breaking into safes than me. . ."

"You should have more faith in yourself," said Shkin. "You are an accomplished burglar, from what I've heard. Besides, if you are caught, the crime cannot be connected to me; you were the one who brought the Tin Book here; Pennyroyal will believe that you were simply trying to retrieve it for yourself."

Wren picked up the paper. The darkness was growing deeper as her fellow slaves moved between the trees snuffing out the lanterns, but the white square seemed to shine in her hand with a light of its own.

"All right," she said, her voice shrunk down to a whisper. Then, as she put down the tray, "What is it? I ought to know. What is this Tin Book, and why does everybody want it?"

"Not your business," said Shkin, looking past her towards the horizon. "I can make a profit from it. What more reason do I need? Now go; you have work to do."

Wren went, running away between the trees as the sacred moon peeked over the horizon. For a few seconds perfect silence settled over Brighton, for according to the old tradition, wishes made at moonrise on this sacred night were often granted by the Moon Goddess. Pennyroyal's guests were far too sophisticated to believe such fairy-tales, of course, but they bowed their heads regardless, some with shrugs and smiles to show that they were just being ironic, but moved in spite of themselves, remembering the magical MoonFests of their childhood. They wished for love and happiness and yet more wealth, while down in the city Brighton's artists wished for fame and her actors for long runs in successful plays, and on the underdecks their slaves and indentured labourers wished for their freedom. And then the silence was ended by a single firework, then another, then a great broadside of rockets and bangers and a clamouring of gongs and bells and kitchen pans loud enough that the Goddess herself might hear it as she strolled among her porcelain gardens.

Even if the Green Storm fleet had not already picked up the signal of Brighton's wireless beacon they would have been able to home in on the fireworks leaping into the sky above the raft-resort. Feathering their steering vanes the warships swung towards their target, spreading out across the sky, while their crews prepared rocket projectors and machine cannon, Tumbler-bombs and flocks of raptors, and their fighter escorts went prowling ahead.

In the belly of the *Requiem Vortex* Shrike checked on Oenone Zero and found her in her cabin, trying on a steel helmet which made her look even younger and less soldierly than before. Her cowardice perplexed him. He had been sure that she would try and attack the Stalker Fang before the fleet reached its target. Had she given up her plan? Perhaps; he had searched her cabin several times, and found no sign of any weapon.

Sirens were hooting. The ship's companionways and passages were full of frightened once-born and impassive battle-Stalkers hurrying to their posts. Shrike made his way to the forward gondola and found his mistress there, ignoring the crew, staring out instead at the enormous moon.

"WHY ARE WE HERE?" Shrike asked.

The Stalker Fang's bronze death-mask turned to stare at him. She had still told no one the reason for this expedition, and Shrike suspected that if any of the once-born, even Naga, had asked her so bluntly, she would have torn their throat out with her claws for their impertinence. But she only stared at Shrike, and then whispered, "Tell me, Mr Shrike, do you ever remember your former life? Your life as a once-born?"

"I DO NOT EVEN REMEMBER MY LIFE AS A STALKER," said Shrike. (Although a memory flared up as he spoke; a young girl with a bloody face lying on a heap of bladder-wrack and old cork fishing floats. He squashed it quickly, like a man stamping on a flame.) "I REMEMBER NOTHING BEFORE DR ZERO AWAKENED ME ON THE BLACK ISLAND."

Fang turned away, looking out through the glass again, but he could see the reflection of her face, the odd, marsh-gas flaring of her green eyes. "I remembered something once," she said. "Or I almost did. There was a young man I encountered at Rogues' Roost. *Tom*. When I saw him, I felt that I knew him. He was very handsome. Very kind. Anna Fang must have been fond of him. I am not Anna Fang, but when I looked at him I sensed . . . oh, all sorts of intriguing feelings."

"WE ARE THE DEAD," said Shrike, who was starting to grow uncomfortable. "WE DO NOT FEEL. WE DO NOT REMEMBER. WE WERE BUILT TO KILL. WHAT USE ARE MEMORIES?"

"Who knows what the first of our kind were built for, back in the Black Centuries?" asked the other Stalker. "My memories are what have brought us here, Mr Shrike. I made enquiries about this *Tom*. I wished to learn more about him, and perhaps to recapture those strange sensations. I found out that he and his companions had a connection with an ice city called Anchorage, so I sent to the great library of Tienjing for books on Anchorage. They had only one; Wormwold's *Historia Anchoragia*. It told me nothing about Tom, but it was there that I first learned of the Tin Book, and guessed what it contains."

"WHAT IS THE TIN BOOK?" asked Shrike.

"The Tin Book?" The Stalker looked playfully at him, her head on one side, a finger to her lips. "The Tin Book is what we are here for, Mr Shrike."

Hester, too, had been waiting for the moon. Perched on a seat on the lower-tier promenade, she had whiled away the time by glancing through her copy of *Predator's Gold*, and what she had found there cheered her. It seemed to her that Pennyroyal had buried the truth beneath so many lies that nobody would ever be able to unearth it.

At moonrise, as the rowdy crowds flooded out of Brighton's underdecks to watch the fireworks, she shoved her way past them, pushing against the tide into a district of dank slave-barracks and tenements called Mole's Combe. By the time she reached the foot of Shkin's tower the streets around her were deserted except for the seagulls which, startled from their roosts by the racket on the promenades, soared like white phantoms beneath the web of peeling girders overhead.

She had studied the Pepperpot earlier, and decided on a way in. Round on the sternward side, surrounded by bins and fat, snaky ducts, was a small back door, made of rusty metal and studded with rivets like the hatch of a submarine. Above the door a spiffy brass security camera kept watch on visitors, but there were no other defences; the Pepperpot had been designed to keep people in, not out.

Hester approached cautiously, keeping to the shadows. Her heart beat fast. She imagined the blood rushing through her veins and arteries, filling her with her father's cold strength. She felt that both Wren and Tom were very close, and that soon they would all be together again, and happy. Smiling to herself behind her veil, she pulled the Schadenfreude out from inside her coat and waited until the next fusillade of fireworks, then shot the camera off its mountings.

She had just time to stuff the gun away before the door opened and a man came out and stood with his hands on his hips, peering up indignantly at the smouldering wreckage of the camera.

"Happy MoonFest!" called Hester.

The man turned. He looked surprised to see the veiled woman walking towards him, and even more surprised when she shoved her knife between his ribs.

He died very quickly and she heaved his body into the shadows behind the bins and went through the door, closing it softly behind her. She found herself in a corridor. Light and voices came from a small guard-room. She peeked in. There were three more men inside. One was stabbing irritably at the buttons beneath a circular screen which fizzed with static; the others were slumped bored and uncomfortable on office chairs, drinks in their hands, wishing they could be with their wives and their children at the celebrations.

Hester shot the one at the screen first, and killed the others as they sprang up, groping for their guns. She stood quiet for a time in the shadows, waiting for someone to come. No one did. There were so many rockets and maroons being let off in the streets outside the Pepperpot tonight that a few extra bangs made no difference. She reloaded the Schadenfreude, noticing with pride that her hands hardly shook at all.

The Shkin Corporation was well organized, and she was glad of it. A framed plan on the guard-room wall showed her the layout of the place. She took a moment to memorize it, then, silent and sure of herself, she moved towards the slave-pens. Two men stood watch outside a pair of heavy double doors. One lunged at Hester with some sort of electric cattle-prod thing, but she sidestepped and stuck her knife in his back, then cut the throat of the other as he reached for the alarm bell. There was a ring of keys on the second one's belt, and it did not take her long to find the one she needed.

The slave pens were filled with soft breathing and the faint stirrings of caged things. As she grew used to the dark she started to make out the cages ranged around the walls, and the faces staring out at her through the bars.

"Tom?" she called.

All around her people were shifting and whispering. Some of the prisoners in the cages closest to the door could see the dead guards sprawled outside, and were reporting it to their neighbours.

"Who are you?" called a voice from one of the cages.

"Who are *you*?" she asked.

"Name's Krill."

"A Lost Boy?" Hester walked towards the voice. Soon she was close enough to see his eyes shining in the thin spill of light from the door she'd opened. He was watching the keys she held, like a hungry dog watching a forkful of food. She jangled the keys softly, by way of encouragement, as she asked, "Is Wren here? Wren Natsworthy?"

"That Dry girl who was on the *Autolycus*?" asked Krill. "Who's asking?"

"The lady with the keys," said Hester.

She saw Krill's fair head bob in the darkness, nodding. "She was in a cage near me for a while, but they took her away."

"Why?"

"Don't know. Fishcake went too, soon after." (He paused to spit, as if he wanted to clean Fishcake's name out of his mouth. There were murmurs of anger and disgust from the other cages. Fishcake wasn't popular.) "Shkin's men told us he turned nark; betrayed Grimsby. Walks about in a uniform now like he's playing at soldiers. What happened to the girl, I don't know. Sold, I expect."

"What about her father, Tom? He was taken today."

"Never heard of him. There's no Drys in here, lady. Just Lost Boys."

"Could he be in the holding cells on the middle tier?"

"Could be." Krill shifted thoughtfully. Around him, in the other pens, all the other captives were shifting, too, listening, wary as animals. The ones who were close enough to see Hester never took their eyes off the keys. "There'll be more guards up there, though. You'll need something to distract them."

"Did you have anything particular in mind?" asked Hester. Krill grinned, and behind her veil Hester grinned too, because this was exactly what she had planned. She dropped the keys into Krill's cage. "Play nicely," she said. As she ran towards the stairs she could hear him scrabbling through the bunch of keys, trying each one in the lock on the door of his pen, and the voices of the Lost Boys like rising surf, urging him on.

27
THE UNSAFE SAFE

Mayor Pennyroyal had had the Pavilion ballroom specially redecorated for the Festival. The front wall had been replaced with a long row of French windows which opened on to the sun-deck outside and let in the light of the sacred moon. Around the dance-floor swags and cascades of silvery fabric hung from every pillar and cornice, reflecting the Milky Way of tiny bulbs which swirled across the ink-blue ceiling. Spotlights illuminated a podium where a small orchestra played. The walls were covered with priceless works of art; antique masterpieces by Strange and Nias hanging next to the latest snot-paintings by Hoover Daley, master of the Expressionist Sneeze.

In a hive of hexagonal chambers opening off behind the main room were all manner of amusing diversions for the guests. In one was a replica of a "bouncy castle", a strange, inflatable fortification which Pennyroyal claimed had been a key feature of Ancient warfare, but which could also be used as a trampoline. In another, a projector rattled, showing copies of copies of some of the fragments of film which had survived from before the Sixty Minute War. Armoured knights rode through a burning wood, their shadows stretching up the smoke; flying machines lifted into a tropical dawn; a little tramp walked down a dusty road; groundcars chased each other like tiny cities; a man dangled from a broken clock high above some enormous static settlement, and in soft, beautiful close-ups rose the dreaming faces of the screen goddesses.

Wren, running in from the garden on her mission for

Shkin, barely noticed any of it. But as she darted past the film-room towards the spiral staircase which would take her up to Pennyroyal's office, she almost collided with Theo, who was coming in the other direction, clutching his ostrich-feather fan. He wore baggy silver trousers and a pair of silver angel's wings.

"Hello," said Wren. "What's the wing thing about?"

Theo shrugged, and his wings flapped. "All the boys are dressed like this. Boo-Boo's idea. Horrible, isn't it?"

"Vile," agreed Wren, though secretly she thought he looked rather fetching.

"Look," he said, "this idea that Boo-Boo's got about us—"

"It's all right," said Wren. "I don't fancy you either."

"Good."

"Good." She was glad he was there, though, and she didn't want to part from him. She thought how much easier it would be to burgle Pennyroyal's safe if she had an accomplice. Especially an accomplice like Theo, who had been in battles and was probably ten times braver than herself.

"Look," she said, "I've got to do something. . ."

"Another escape attempt?"

"No. I've got to take something from Pennyroyal's safe."

"What? After what happened to that antique-dealer?" Theo stared at her, waiting for her to admit that it was all a joke. When she didn't he said, "It's that book thing, isn't it? That metal book?"

"The Tin Book of Anchorage," Wren said. "Shkin sent Plovery for it, and now Plovery's dead he's sending me."

"Why?" asked Theo. "What's so important about it?"

Wren shrugged. "All I know is everybody seems to want it. . . I think it might be something to do with submarines, but. . ." She paused uneasily. Maybe she shouldn't be telling Theo this. He was Green Storm, after all, or had been once. But she was glad she had. She touched his arm. "He's got my dad at the Pepperpot, and if I don't do what he asks he. . . I don't know what he'll do. Will you help me?"

She did know, of course; she just didn't want to say it. She felt glad that she had Theo to confide in.

"Your dad?' he asked. "I didn't know Lost Girls had fathers. . ."

"I'm not really a Lost Girl," said Wren. "Just mislaid. I told Pennyroyal I came from Grimsby because. . . Oh, Theo, it's too complicated to explain. I just have to save Dad!"

She could tell that he understood. He looked scared and serious. "But if the safe's booby-trapped. . ." he said.

"That's why I want you to keep a lookout. Please, Theo. I don't want to go in there alone."

"I'm supposed to be on duty in the ballroom. Boo-Boo's orders."

"Boo-Boo's having a wonderful time. She won't notice if we sneak off for five minutes."

Theo thought about it, then nodded. "All right. All right."

Gripping his fan like a battleaxe, he followed Wren up some stairs and through a door at the top into an antique-lined corridor. The noise of the party faded as the door swung softly shut behind them, then dipped again as the corridor turned sharply to the left. Creeping past the door to the control-room stairs they heard the faint voices of the crewmen chatting at their stations down below, but there were no other sounds. Everyone else was busy in the ballroom or the kitchens, and this part of the Pavilion was deserted.

They reached the end of the corridor and stopped, staring at Pennyroyal's office door.

"What if he changed the combination of his safe after last night?" whispered Theo. "What if he's changed the locks on the door?"

Wren hadn't thought of that. She prayed that Pennyroyal hadn't either. Her groping fingers quickly found the spare key, still hidden in the vase. At first it didn't seem to fit the lock, but that was only because her hands were trembling so badly. After a few moments of swearing and fumbling the lock snicked and she turned the handle and pushed open the door.

The office looked peaceful and safe. The Walmart Strange drawing was back in its place on the wall. Wren went to it and took it carefully off its hook, laying it down on the desk. Theo followed her into the office and quietly closed the door, then almost knocked a statue off its pedestal with his fan.

"Couldn't you have left that stupid thing outside?" she hissed.

"What, where someone might see it lying about?"

Wren turned to the safe. "Ready?" she asked.

Theo didn't look ready. "You think there's a booby trap inside the safe?" he said.

Wren shook her head. "The safe was open last night, remember, and I didn't see anything booby-trappish in there." All the same, she made sure that she was standing well to one side as she reached for the dial. "Mr Plovery opened the safe and got the book out. That's when something got him. Now hush." She frowned, remembering the combination. *2209957*. . .

As the dial clicked and the tumblers inside the lock chunked and grated, Theo turned slowly around, looking for hidden dangers. There was nowhere much in this small room that a trap could be concealed. The objects on the desk looked innocent enough – a blotter, a few pens, a photograph of Boo-Boo in a heavy black frame. There was a teak filing cabinet against the far wall, a picture hanging above it, and above that just a lot of architectural curlicues and the high, shadowy dome of the ceiling and. . .

Was it just his eyes playing tricks, or was something moving up there?

"Wren –" he said.

Wren had the safe door open. She reached in and drew out a battered black case. "Got it."

"Wren!" Theo shoved her, knocking her sideways. She dropped the case, and had an impression as she fell of something white whirring past her. A blade struck the open door of the safe, hard enough to throw off sparks. Whatever it was scrabbled, turned and came flapping at her as she sprawled on the floor. Wren glimpsed ragged wings, a curved steel beak, a glow of green eyes. Then Theo's fan batted the thing sideways, slamming it hard against the wall. Wren heard something break. The flapping thing fell on the floor and kept on flapping, flailing small clawed feet like bunches of razors. Theo smacked at it with his fan. Whimpering, Wren groped across the desk, found the picture of Boo-Boo and smashed it down hard on the creature's head.

Theo helped Wren up. "All right?' he asked shakily.

"I think so. You?"

247

"Yes."

For a while after that they didn't speak. Theo's arms were still around Wren, and her face was pressed against his shoulder. It was a nice shoulder, warm, with a pleasant smell, and she would have liked to stay like that for longer, but she made herself step away from him, shaking her head hard to clear away all the distracting thoughts that were trying to roost there. Feathers floated about in the moonlight.

"What was it?" she asked, nervously prodding the dead bird-thing with her toe.

"A raptor," said Theo. "A Resurrected bird. I thought only the Storm used them. It must have been set to keep watch on the safe."

"How do you think old Pennyroyal got hold of it?" Wren wondered.

Theo shook his head, puzzled and worried. "Maybe it's not Pennyroyal's."

"That's silly," said Wren. "Who else would want to guard his safe?" She picked up the black case and opened it. Inside, the Tin Book glinted faintly in the firework-light from outside. It looked as dull as ever. It was hard to believe that it had caused so much trouble. She looked at Theo. "You go," she told him. "I'll tidy this place up and then find Shkin."

Theo was staring at the Tin Book. He said, "I'll help."

"No." Wren felt terribly grateful to him, and didn't want to keep him here any longer than she had to. If they were discovered, and Theo was punished for helping her, she would never forgive herself. "Go back downstairs," she said. "I'll follow in a minute or two. I'll find you later."

He started to object again, then seemed to see the

sense in what she said. He nodded, looked thoughtfully at her for a moment, then took up his battered fan and left, while Wren set to work. Gingerly she picked the dead bird up and stuffed it into one of the drawers of the desk, along with all the fallen feathers she could find. It had left a stain of oil or blood or something on the office floor, but there was nothing Wren could do about that. She pulled the Tin Book out of its case, and replaced it with Boo-Boo's broken picture, which was of a similar weight and size.

A sound came from the corridor; someone shouting something. Wren went very still, listening. The shouting sounded angry and scared, but Wren could not make out the words, and after a moment it stopped. "Theo?" said Wren aloud.

The office gave a sudden shudder, as if giant hands had shaken the Pavilion by the shoulders. The faint sound from the ballroom diminished as conversations faltered and the orchestra stopped playing. Wren imagined the musicians looking up from their scores in alarm. Then people laughed, and the music and chatter resumed, climbing quickly back to their former level as if someone were turning up the volume on a recording of party sound-effects.

"Just turbulence," she told herself. Or maybe there had been some sort of problem with the engine pods; now she thought about it, the shouts she had heard might well have been echoing up the little stairway from the control room. Relieved, she went back to work. She put the case back in the safe and closed it, then hung the Walmart Strange in front of it again. Lifting the back of her long tunic, she slipped the Tin Book under the waistband of her trousers. It would be safe there, she thought, but the metal struck cold against her bare back, and the wire binding kept scratching her.

She stepped out into the corridor and locked the door, replacing the key in its hiding place. "Theo?" she hissed. There was no answer. Of course not, he would be back in the ballroom by now, safe.

Then she glimpsed a movement from the corner of her eye. The door to the control-room staircase was open, swinging on its hinges with each faint movement of the building. She stood and stared at it, certain that it had been closed when she passed it with Theo a few minutes earlier. Had one of the men from the control room heard them crashing about in Pennyroyal's office and come up to investigate?

The noise from the ballroom grew suddenly loud and then faded again. Someone had come through the door at the far end of the corridor. Wren heard footsteps approaching quickly along the polished floor. At the place where the corridor bent, a shadow grew on the wall. Panicking, Wren started to move back towards Pennyroyal's office, but there wasn't time to find the key again, so she darted through the open control-room door and pulled it shut behind her.

She found herself in a shadowy little cubicle where iron stairs spiralled down through the floor. She knew that they went through the floor below as well, and through the deckplate beneath it, opening eventually into that little glass bubble which she had seen from the cable car on the day Shkin brought her to Cloud 9. She pressed her ear to the door, and heard the footsteps go past out in the corridor.

She was about to breathe again when a voice from below her called, "Who's there?"

The voice sounded frightened, and oddly familiar.

"Theo?" she said. A dizzy feeling of confusion swept over her. What would Theo be doing down there, in that control room full of Pennyroyal's men? Had he been on Pennyroyal's side all along? Had he gone to tell them about the slave-girl who had just burgled their master's safe?

"Wren," the voice called, "something's happened. I don't know what to do. . ."

He *did* sound frightened. Deciding to trust him, Wren hurried down the tight spiral of stairs with the Tin Book jabbing her in the small of her back at every step. She passed another entrance on the ground floor, and then descended through a shaft of white-painted metal, warty with rivets, which led down through the deckplate. Theo was looking up at her from the foot of the stairs, and stood aside to let her step past him into the control room. Through its glass walls she could see the whole of Brighton beneath her, gaudy with MoonFest illuminations. All around, fireworks were bursting in the clear air, splashing the instrument panels with pink and amber light. It was probably the best view on Cloud 9, but it was wasted on the control room's crew, who were slumped in their seats, dead. One of them still had a knife sticking out of his neck; an ordinary carving knife from the Pavilion kitchens with Pennyroyal's crest on the handle.

"Oh Quirke!" squeaked Wren, wishing she hadn't eaten so many canapés. As she bent over to puke, a rush of thoughts swirled into her head. None of them were pleasant. Hadn't Theo been coming from the direction of the kitchens when she ran into him last night? And now he was standing in a room full of men who'd been killed with a kitchen knife, and she was alone with him.

"It's all right," he said, and she squeaked again as he shyly touched her arm. He didn't understand how scared of him she suddenly was. As she edged away from him he said, "I mean, it's not all right. Look." He tugged at one of the big brass levers on the instrument panel. "Broken. All broken. And here. . ."

On the main control desk was a fat red lever, encased in a glass box and surrounded with exclamation marks and warnings that it should be used only in an emergency. Someone had used it anyway, breaking the glass to get at it.

"What does that do?" asked Wren, but she already knew, because Brighton looked smaller than it had when she entered the control room, and the bangs of the bursting fireworks were growing fainter and fainter.

"Explosive bolts," said Theo. "They're meant to sever the cables in case Brighton sinks or something. Didn't you feel that lurch? Wren, somebody's cut the tow-ropes! We're adrift!"

Wren stared at him, appalled, and in the silence she could clearly hear the sounds of the party continuing upstairs. She and Theo were probably the only people on Cloud 9 who knew what had happened.

"Theo," she said, "you can have the book."

"What?"

She pulled it out of her trousers and held it out to him. Her hands were shaking, making the reflections from the metal cover dance across his puzzled face. "Wren," he said, "you don't think *I* could do this? Even if I could, why would I?"

"Because you're after the book, like everybody else," said Wren. "You're a Green Storm agent, aren't you? I knew there was something strange about you! I bet you

252

got yourself captured deliberately so that you could get into the pavilion and spy on us all. I bet you left that gull to watch over the safe, and now you've set Cloud 9 adrift so that you can murder everybody and make off with the Tin Book! That's why you wouldn't help me steal the *Peewit*, wasn't it? So you could escape in her yourself, once you had the Book!"

"Wren!" shouted Theo. "You're not thinking!" He caught her as she tried to dash past him to the stairs; caught her by both arms and looked earnestly into her face. "If I wanted that damned Tin Book, why would I have let you steal it? I would have let the gull kill you, back in Pennyroyal's office, and taken it for myself. For all I know, *you* could be the Green Storm agent. You're so keen to get this book, and you were sneaking around when Plovery was killed, too. One minute you're a Lost Girl and the next you're not... *You* could be the one who did this!"

"I'm not! I didn't!" Wren gasped.

"Well, nor did I." Theo let her go. She edged backwards, trembling, still clutching the Tin Book.

"I was on my way back to the ballroom when I heard someone shout for help," said Theo. "I opened the door and called down to ask if everything was all right. There was no answer, but I thought I heard someone moving about, so I came down. When I got here they were all dead. I saw that the cable had been cut, and I was going to go and raise the alarm, but I was afraid that you were still upstairs, and someone would find you." He shuddered, and ran his hand over his face.

"There was someone upstairs," said Wren, remembering the footsteps, the shadow. "I heard them go past the door. There's nothing else along that corridor but

Pennyroyal's office. They must have been after the same thing as us. The Tin Book."

Theo stared at her. "That would fit. They came down here first, and did this, but before they could go up the stairs to the office they heard me coming down. They couldn't risk killing me too, in case I was a guest who'd be missed, so they slunk out through the kitchens and then cut back by the ballroom and up to the office that way. . . But why cut us adrift? Why not just take the Book?"

Wren tried to be sick again, but her stomach was empty. "They almost saw me!" she whimpered. "If I hadn't hidden in time they'd have killed me like they did these men. . ."

Theo reached out for her, but wasn't sure if she would want him to touch her. "So you don't still think I did it?" he asked.

Wren shook her head, and went gratefully to him, hiding her face against his chest. "Theo, I'm sorry. . ."

"It's all right," he told her gently. Then he said, "As for last night, I just couldn't sleep. I went to the shrine to say prayers for my mother and father and my sisters. It was a year ago, last Moon Festival, that I left Zagwa. Slipped out of my parents' house while everyone was celebrating, and stowed away on a freighter, off to Shan Guo to join the Green Storm. All the preparations yesterday just made me wonder what they were doing now; whether my parents have forgiven me; whether they miss me. . ."

"I bet they do," said Wren. She turned away and leaned against the window pressing her face to the cool glass. "That's what parents do. They forgive us and miss us, no matter what we've done. Look at my dad, coming all this way to find me. . ."

254

She looked towards Brighton, longing for her father. Fireworks spurted into the sky from somewhere in Montpelier, bursting in bright stars of red and gold. Wren watched them fade as they drifted slantwise down the wind, and then her eye was caught by another movement. She turned her head. There was only the sea; a shifting, sliding pattern of moonlight. But what was that? That long shadow slipping across the wave-tops?

Her view was blotted out by something vast and pale. Huge engine pods slid by, followed by the open gunports of an armoured gondola. Wren saw men wearing goggles and crab-shell helmets standing in gun emplacements that jutted out on gantries, and then tall steering vanes, each emblazoned with a jagged green lightning bolt.

"Theo!" she screamed.

Twenty feet from where they stood, an immense air-destroyer was speeding past Cloud 9.

28
THE AIR ATTACK

In a cell somewhere beneath the Pepperpot's well-appointed reception area Tom lay half-dazed, feeling his face swell where Shkin's heavies had hit him, and fearing for Wren. It had been enough at first just to know that she was alive. He didn't mind too much what happened to him, as long as Wren was safe. But was Wren safe? Shkin's men had told him she'd been sold to *Pennyroyal* of all people! Pennyroyal was not a bad man, he was selfish, and thoughtless, and unscrupulous, and he had once shot Tom in the heart. The old wound hurt Tom again as he lay on the bunk, waiting for something to happen. His chest ached, and he wasn't sure if the ache were real, or just his body's memory of the bullet.

He had quickly lost track of time in this bland, windowless room, where a loop of argon-tube glowed on the beige ceiling like a halo. He had no idea whether it was night or day when the door finally rattled open.

"Brought you something to eat, Mr Natsworthy," said a small voice. "And this."

Tom rolled off the bunk and sat up, rubbing his bruised face. The boy Fishcake stood in the doorway holding a tray with a bowl and a tin cup. A few feet of drab beige corridor were visible behind him. Tom thought vaguely about escape, but his chest hurt too much. He watched as Fishcake advanced towards him and set the tray down on the floor.

"I swapped shifts with someone so I could come and see you," the boy confessed. "It was easy. All the others want the night off, 'cos it's Moon Festival. That's what all the bangs and crashes are about."

Tom listened, and heard faintly the noise of fireworks and gongs from the streets outside.

"I'm sorry you got caught, Mr Natsworthy," Fishcake admitted. "Wren was very nice to me. So I thought you'd want to see this."

He took a crumpled page of newspaper from the pocket of his uniform and held it out for Tom to read. *The Palimpsest*. And there, in the photograph beneath the headline, kneeling among a group of other girls around a large woman with enormous hair. . .

"That's Wren, ain't it?" said Fishcake. "See? I thought you'd want to know she's all right. It's a good life, they say, being a house-slave up on Cloud 9. Look; she's got a fancy frock and a new hairdo and everything."

"Cloud 9? Is that where Wren is?" Tom remembered the floaty palace-thing he had seen hovering above the city. He reached forward, laying a hand on Fishcake's shoulder. "Fishcake, can you find my wife and get a message to her? Tell her where Wren is?"

"That one with the scar?" asked Fishcake, wriggling away. He looked scared, and disgusted. "*She's* not here, is she?"

"She's in Brighton, yes. We came together."

Fishcake had gone a curious colour. His hands shook. "I ain't going near her," he said. "She's evil, that one. She killed Gargle, and Remora, and she'd have killed me too if she could. That's why I had to bring Wren with me. I didn't want to, but she'd have killed me elsewise."

"I'm sure Hester only did what she had to," said Tom, a little uneasily, because he wasn't sure of that at all. "It was tragic, but—"

"She's evil," Fishcake insisted sullenly. "And you're as

bad, even though you think you ain't. Going about with her makes you as bad as she is."

"You still brought me the paper, though," Tom said. "You're a good boy, Fishcake." He smiled at the Lost Boy, who eyed him suspiciously. Tom felt sorry for him. He must have been hurt and betrayed by so many people that he had turned to the first grown-up who showed him any sort of kindness, even though it was only Nabisco Shkin. Tom wished he could take him away from this dreadful city to the safety of Vineland, where he would have the chance of living a normal life, like the children Freya had rescued from Grimsby.

He said, "Fishcake, can you get me out of here?"

"Don't be soft!" said the boy. "Mr Shkin would kill me."

"Mr Shkin would never find you. I'll take you away with me, if you like. We'll find Wren and Hester and we'll go away together."

"Away where? Grimsby's gone. I've got a good job here. Where would I want to go?"

"Anywhere," said Tom. "We could drop you anywhere you liked. Or we could take you back with us to Anchorage-in-Vineland and you could live with us there."

"Live with you?" echoed Fishcake. His eyes seemed to Tom to be as round and bright as the lamp on the ceiling. "What," he said, "like a family?"

"Only if that's what you wanted," said Tom.

Fishcake swallowed loudly. He didn't fancy going anywhere with Hester. Hester deserved to die, and one day he meant to make sure that she did, for he had not forgotten his vow. But he could not help liking Tom. Tom seemed kind, even kinder than Mr Shkin. And Wren had been kind too, even if she hadn't saved him from Brighton's trap. He would have liked to live with Tom and Wren.

"All right," he said. He glanced at the doorway, scared that someone might have overheard. "All right. As long as you promise. . ."

Out in the corridor a nasty, harsh electric bell began to ring, making Tom and Fishcake jump. Doors slammed, and boots pounded on the metal floor. Fishcake snatched the piece of paper from Tom and scampered out of the cell, swinging the door shut behind him. Standing up, Tom ran to peer through the small grille in the top of the door, but he could see nothing. The bell jarred and jangled. Men's voices shouted at the far end of the corridor, and more boots clanged. Then, a sudden, startling bang, and another. Someone screamed. "Fishcake!" shouted Tom. There was another bang, very close, and then Hester's voice, outside in the corridor, shouting, "Tom!"

"Here! In here!" he said, and a moment later her veiled face appeared at the grille.

"I got your note," she said. He ducked away from the door, and her gun punched holes in the lock. She kicked the door open.

"Where's Fishcake?" asked Tom. "You didn't hurt Fishcake? He was here just a minute ago! He had a picture! Wren's on Cloud 9!"

Hester pulled her veil down and kissed him quickly. She smelled of smoke and her dear, ugly face was flushed. "Shut up and run," she said.

He ran, ignoring the warning stabs of pain in his chest. Outside the door of his cell the corridor made a tight turn. Two men lay dead at the corner. Neither of them was Fishcake. Tom clambered gingerly over the corpses and followed his wife up some stairs, past some more bodies. Smoke hung in the air. Shouts and screams came from somewhere under foot.

"What's happening?" he asked. "What's going on down there?"

Hester looked back at him, grinning. "Someone's let the Lost Boys out. Careless, eh? We'd better go out the top way."

The lights went out, all at once. Tom crashed into Hester, who steadied him and said very calmly, "Don't worry."

There was inkish darkness for as long as it took Tom's heart to make five stuttering beats, then dull red lights came on. "Emergency generator," said Hester.

Tom trailed after her, through a series of deserted offices, where the blood-red light shone on the brass handles of filing cabinets and the ivory keys of type-writing machines. He wondered where Hester had found her new coat and what had happened to the old one. He was still wondering when they ran into a bunch of Shkin Corporation men hurrying in the opposite direction. "Get down!" shouted Hester, knocking Tom to the floor. "Not you!" she added, as the guards dived for cover.

The office filled with smoke and stabs of flame and a terrible noise. Not all of the men had guns, and the ones who did fired wildly. Bullets slammed against the walls, smashed the water cooler, and ripped pages from a calendar on the desk. Tom hid behind a filing cabinet and watched as Hester shot the men down one by one. He had not been with her when she fought the Huntsmen, and he had always imagined that she must have been angry and afraid, but there was a terrible calm about her now. When her gun was empty she put it down and killed the last man with a typewriter, the carriage-return bell jingling cheerfully while she smashed in his skull. When she picked up her gun and started to reload it, she was smiling. Tom thought she looked more alive than he had ever seen her before.

"All right?" she asked, pulling him to his feet.

He wasn't, but he was shaking too badly to tell her so, so he just followed her again, up more stairs, and found himself again in the neat reception area where he had spoken to Miss Weems. Her chair was empty now, the sign on the door turned to CLOSED, the guard gone from his post outside. Fireworks boomed and crackled above the rooftops, punching shafts of pink and emerald light through gaps in the blinds. Hester shot the lock off the door and pushed it open, but as Tom crossed the room he heard frightened breathing, then a whimper.

He went down on his knees and peered beneath Miss Weems's desk.

Fishcake's pale, terrified face looked out at him.

"Fishcake, it's all right!" Tom promised, as the boy scrabbled back deeper into the shadows. He waved at Hester to keep her away. "It's only Fishcake," he told her, looking round.

"Leave him, then," said Hester.

"We can't," said Tom. "He's alone, and frightened, and he's been working for Shkin. If the other Lost Boys find him they'll tear him to pieces. Just a figure of speech," he added unconvincingly, as Fishcake moaned with terror.

"That's his fault," said Hester, poised in the doorway, eager to go. "Leave him."

"But he told me where Wren is."

"Fine," said Hester angrily. "He's told you. So we don't need him. Leave him."

"No!" said Tom, more sharply than he meant to. Beneath the desk his hand found Fishcake's, and he hauled the Lost Boy out. "He's coming with us. I promised."

Hester stared at the boy and the boy stared at Hester, and for a moment Tom thought she was going to shoot Fishcake where he stood, but a thunderous howl of defiance and rage came echoing up from the depths of the Pepperpot, the roar of Lost Boys on the war-path, and she stuffed her gun away and slipped through the door, holding it open so that Tom could drag the scared, quaking child with him out of the building and down the steps into the plaza. Huge, reverberating bangs were rebounding from the walls of the surrounding buildings, and dazzling flashes lit up the sky. *Fireworks are so much louder than they were when I was little*, Tom thought, and looking up, saw fierce white airships swooping over the city at rooftop height, raining down rockets from their armoured gondolas.

"Great gods and goddesses!" shouted Hester. "That's all we need!"

"What is it?" whined Fishcake, clinging tight to Tom. "What's happening?"

What was happening was that a squadron of Fox Spirits had been detached from the main body of the Green Storm fleet to silence Brighton's air defences. The MoonFest celebrations were disintegrating into panic as the aviators mistook the firework displays in Queen's

Park and Black Rock for anti-aircraft fire and started strafing them. As carnival processions writhed across Ocean Boulevard like beheaded snakes the *Requiem Vortex* cut through the smoke above them, powering towards Cloud 9. Ahead stood the armoured mountains that were Kom Ombo and Benghazi, smaller towns and suburbs snuggling around their skirts.

"A whole cluster of them!" shouted General Naga, gleeful as a huntsman who has just spied the fox. "That big one ate Palmyra Static a few summers back!" His mechanical armour grated and hissed as it spun him round to face the Stalker Fang, raising his one arm in a jerky salute. "So this is why you brought us west, Excellency! I knew it could not be for that moth-eaten raft resort! Permission to lead the attack. . ."

"Silence," whispered the Stalker Fang. The fires of Brighton shimmered in her bronze face. "The cluster is irrelevant. The other ships will keep those city's batteries and fighters busy, and ensure that the Brightonians do not attempt to help their mayor. Our target is the flying palace. Prepare boarding parties."

Naga had followed the Stalker unquestioningly for sixteen hard years, but this was almost too much for him. As his sub-officers scrambled to relay her orders and fetch sidearms and battle-armour he stood for a moment looking as if he'd been slapped. Then, recalling what became of officers who disputed the Stalker Fang's commands, he hurried to obey.

Wren and Theo ran to the other side of the control room just in time to see the sky between Brighton and the shore blossom with gaudy explosions of flak from Benghazi's air-defence cannon. The crackling, shifting light slid across the envelopes of four big warships and countless fighters.

"A Green Storm Aerial Attack Unit," Theo said.

"Oh, Quirke!" whispered Wren, thinking of her father. "Do you think they'll sink Brighton? My dad's down there! Theo, he'll be killed, and it'll all be my fault!"

"They aren't here for Brighton," said Theo, taking her hand. "They've come for the book! Whoever it was who set the gull on guard and killed these men must have called these ships here, and they've cut us adrift so we can be boarded more easily."

From somewhere outside came the screech of air-raid alarms, like fingernails dragging down the blackboard of the sky.

"We've got to get away," said Wren.

"How?" asked Theo.

"On the *Peewit*, of course. I don't suppose anybody had time to drain her fuel tanks after last night."

Theo shook his head. "Even if we made it to the boat-house, the Storm would shoot us down before we were out of Cloud 9's airspace."

"But the *Peewit*'s a yacht, not a warship!"

"The Storm don't care about details like that."

"But don't you know codes and passwords and things? Couldn't you radio them and tell them you're one of their own people?"

"Wren, I'm *not* one of their people," said Theo. "Not any more. I failed them. If they capture me, they'll have me killed, and sent to Batmunkh Tsaka."

Wren wasn't sure what that meant, but she could see

that he was scared, perhaps as scared as she was. The control room shook as something hit the deckplate overhead, and a rain of sparks and burning wreckage came tumbling down past the windows. She looked up into Theo's face and tried to sound brave. "Theo," she said, "my dad's waiting for me in Brighton, and your mother and father are waiting for you in Zagwa, and they'll all be really miffed if we just hang about up here and let ourselves get killed. Come on. We have to try!"

Still holding hands, they ran up the stairs to the ground-floor entrance, the door the murderer must have left by. It opened into a corridor outside the kitchens. There was no one about. Above them they could hear screams and shouts and the rumble of feet as people fled the ballroom. Explosions in the sky outside splashed skewed diamonds of sour yellow light on the floor under the kitchen windows, and glinted on fallen pans and trays of sweetmeats dropped by slaves who had left in a hurry.

They ran to the nearest exit; and blundered out into the gardens in front of the Pavilion. Crowds of party guests were hurrying across the lawns like frightened sheep. There was no way off Cloud 9, but they wanted to get as far as they could from the Pavilion for fear the Green Storm were about to bomb it. Anyway, they were wealthy, and used to getting everything they needed. Even if the cable car was gone, surely there would be a ship there, or an air-taxi, or some plucky Brightonians organizing a rescue with air-pedaloes and sky-yachts?

Not wanting to be caught up in the stampede, Theo pushed Wren into the shelter of one of Pennyroyal's abstract statues. They huddled together and watched moonlit exhaust-trails billow in the sky around Cloud 9 like skeins of spider-silk as the Flying Ferrets buzzed and tumbled, hurling themselves at the Storm's airships. It was as if each ship had a seed of fire inside of it, and the Flying Ferrets were patiently probing for it with streams of incendiary bullets. When they found it the airship would begin to glow from inside like a MoonFest lantern, then blinding patterns of light would chequer the envelope, and finally the whole thing would become a dazzling pyre, casting eerie shadows from the cypress-groves as the wind carried it past Cloud 9.

But the airships were fighting back, and so were the clouds of Resurrected eagles and condors which flew with them. The birds descended in flapping black clouds upon the Ferrets' flying machines, slashing at the wings and rigging and the unprotected pilots, and as the Ferrets stuggled to evade them they made easy targets for the airships' rockets and machine-cannon. Wings were shredded, fuel-tanks blew apart, rotor-blades came flipping and fluttering across the Pavilion's lawns like bits of an exploding venetian blind. The *Bad Hair Day*, its wings ripped off, plunged burning into the cable-car station. The *Group Captain Mandrake* veered sideways into the *Wrestling Cheese* and both machines crashed together through the flank of a Green Storm destroyer and went down with it, a vast barrel of fire sinking gracefully towards the sea.

Just off the edge of the gardens a larger ship circled, waiting for the fighters to finish off the Ferrets, and beyond it Wren could see the upper tiers of Kom Ombo rising like an armoured island from a sea of smoke. A fat airship was hanging above the city, showering down clouds of tumbling, twirling things that looked like silver seed-pods until they struck a fortress or a gun-emplacement, where they burst with white flashes and flung wreckage high into the night. Wren felt the explosions in her chest, like the beat of a huge drum.

"Tumblers," Theo muttered.

"What, those silver things?" asked Wren. "No, those are bombs. You can tell by the way they go off bang. You told me you used to *fly* Tumblers."

Theo nodded.

"You mean those things have *pilots*? But they'll be blown to bits!"

Another nod.

"Then how come. . .?"

"How come I'm not dead?" Theo shook his head and would not look at her. "Because I'm a coward," he said. "I'm a coward, that's why.

The *Requiem Vortex* prowled through the veils of smoke and ash that hung above the coast. Panic had broken out among the clustered towns and cities there, who all assumed the Green Storm fleet had come for them. Some were running for the shelter of the desert; some inflated buoyancy-sacs and splashed into the sea; some took advantage of the confusion to try and eat their neighbours. Benghazi and Kom Ombo launched clouds of fighter airships, which were torn apart by the faster, fiercer Fox Spirits and by flocks of Stalker-birds.

A gas cell had exploded somewhere near the *Requiem Vortex*'s stern, and spidery Mark IV Stalkers were crawling around on the sheer sides of her envelope, training extinguishers on the blaze. There was damage to the steering vanes, too, and frantic voices echoing from the speaking-tubes claimed that the rear gondola had been destroyed.

The once-born on the bridge were pale and tense; Shrike could see their faces shining with sweat in the hellish light that blazed in through the windows. Beneath her steel helmet Oenone Zero was weeping with fear. The radio crackled out distress calls and damage reports from other ships; the *Sword Flourished In Understandable Pique* had been rammed amidships and was going down in flames; the *Autumn Rain From The Heavenly Mountains* was rudderless and drifting into the flank of Benghazi. Someone aboard a doomed corvette kept screaming and screaming until their signal suddenly cut out.

The Stalker Fang ignored it all. Standing calmly beside the helmsman, she gazed out at Cloud 9 as it drifted slowly away from its parent-city.

"Follow that building," she said.

The ships which had attacked Brighton had quickly veered away to tackle other targets, but the raft resort's troubles were not over. Its engine room was in flames, and half its paddle wheels were wrecked. It had slipped its moorings as the attack began, and was now adrift, trailing black smoke and saffron flame, leaking burning rafts of fuel. Everyone who could have taken charge was either dead or at the mayor's party.

In all the confusion no one paid any heed to the alarms jangling inside the Pepperpot; not until the Lost Boys overpowered the last of their guards and came swarming out to join the fun. From the engine rooms and the sewage farms of the under-tier, and the stinking filter-beds beneath the sea-pool, the slaves of Brighton saw their chance and rushed to join them. Arming themselves with spanners and pool-rakes and meat tenderizers, they swarmed up the city's stairways, looting antique shops and setting fire to art galleries. The good-natured actors and artists of Brighton, who had spent so many dinner parties agreeing with each other about what a terrible life the slaves led and organizing community art projects to show how they shared their pain, fled for their lives, spilling out of the city aboard over-loaded airships and listing motor-launches.

Indeed, so much was happening, and so dense a pall of dirty smoke hung above the battered city, that hardly anyone had noticed Cloud 9 was no longer attached to the rest of Brighton.

29

THE UNEXPLODED BOY

Wren and Theo, waiting for the battle to subside, sat down in the shadow of the big statue, their backs to the plinth which it perched on. A few glasses of punch had been abandoned there earlier in the evening, and Wren drank one. How long had this nightmare been going on? Five minutes? Ten? It seemed a lifetime. Already she had learned to tell the high yammer of the Ferrets' machine-cannon from the throatier stutter of the Storm's guns. The rockets were harder to tell apart, but she always knew when a Tumbler went off, because Theo would jump and hunch his shoulders and squeeze his eyes shut.

"Do you want to tell me about it?" she asked. "These Tumbler things?"

"No."

"You might as well. There's not much else to do."

Theo flinched at the distant sounds of another Tumbler salvo exploding on the skirts of Kom Ombo. Then, in a soft voice that she could barely hear over all the noise, he told her of his brief career as a flying bomb.

"It was back at the start of the Battle of the Rustwater," he said. "Enemy suburbs had broken through all along the line, and the fleet was falling back towards the western borders of Shan Guo. None of us were expecting to go into action. Then the order came in; this place called the Black Island had to be held for a few hours more, because some surgeon-mechanic from the Resurrection Corps was digging up a valuable artefact that mustn't be allowed to fall into townie hands. . ."

Theo could still feel in his belly the sudden, sickening

motion of the carrier going about, and the panic in the companionways as Tumbler pilots scrambled for their ships

"The waiting was worst," he said. "Strapped into our ships, hanging there in the racks in the Tumbler-bay with the doors open under us. You could see the guns going off below. Then the order – 'Tumblers away!' and we went for it."

They went for it; releasing their clamps, and then the long fall, down and down, slaloming between the lovely, deadly blasts of enemy rockets. The earliest Tumblers had been automatic, fitted with Stalker brains, but Stalker brains couldn't zigzag through ground-fire the way a human pilot could, and why waste Stalkers when there were young men like Theo eager for glory and ready to die in the name of a world made green again?

"The target was a city called Jagdstadt Magdeburg," he told Wren. "I hit somewhere on the middle tiers; I thought I was heading for an armoured fort, but it turned out to be just a thin plastic roof over some sort of farming district. I landed in a great deep pile of silage bales. I suppose that's why I wasn't killed, just knocked out for a minute or two. I suppose that's why the Tumbler didn't blow. They're supposed to go off automatically when you hit, but there's a manual override in case of a failure like mine, and I reached for it as soon as I came to, but I couldn't. . . I couldn't bring myself to. . ."

"Of course not," said Wren softly. "You'd missed your target. You couldn't blow up workers. Civilians. It would have been murder."

"It would," said Theo. "But that's not what stopped me. I just didn't want to die."

"Bit late to decide that, wasn't it?"

Theo shrugged. "I just sat there and cried. And after a while they came and defused my Tumbler and dragged me out and took me away. I thought they were going to kill me. I wouldn't have blamed them. But they didn't.

"All my life I'd been hearing stories about the cruelty of the barbarians, the way they tortured prisoners, and maybe some are like that, but these ones tended me like I was one of their own sons. They fed me, and explained how sorry they were that they'd have to sell me as a slave. They couldn't afford to keep Green Storm prisoners aboard, you see, for fear we'd band together and revolt. But I wouldn't have revolted. They'd made me realize how wrong the Storm are. How stupid it all is, this fighting."

He looked up at Wren. "That's why I gave up on the Storm. And now when they catch me, and they find out what I am and what I did, they're going to kill me."

"They won't!" promised Wren. "Because we won't let them catch you! We'll get away somehow. . ."

A growl of engines drowned her out. She stood up cautiously and looked out across the gardens. A huge, battle-scarred white airship was shoving her way in through Cloud 9's rigging.

"Great gods!" said Theo, looking over Wren's shoulder. "That's the *Requiem Vortex*! That's *her* ship!"

Snub-nosed projectors mounted on the airship's engine pods swivelled this way and that, effortlessly blasting any Flying Ferret which came within range. The *Visible Panty Line* and the *Itsy Witsy Teeny Weeny Yellow Polka-Dot Machiney* were smashed apart by rockets, showering shreds of balsa wood and singed canvas over the crowds who cowered on the Pavilion lawns. An ornithopter called *Is That All There Is?*

fluttered around the airship like a gnat pestering a dinosaur, but it could not pierce the reinforced envelope, and after a few seconds a flight of Stalker-birds found it and ripped it into kindling. *Damn You, Gravity!* plunged towards the airship's gondola in a desperate attempt to ram it, but more rockets battered it aside and it went ploughing through the flank of one of Cloud 9's outer gasbags. The Pavilion shuddered, the screaming guests on the lawn began to scream still louder and the whole deckplate tilted steeply as some of the gas which had been supporting it went spewing into the night.

Orla Twombley's *Combat Wombat* and the other surviving Ferrets, realizing that they could do no more, turned tail and sped away.

Wren shielded her face against the dust and smoke as the *Requiem Vortex* swung her engine pods into landing position and touched down on the lawns of Cloud 9. Party-guests who had fled the Pavilion earlier now came fleeing back past Wren and Theo's hiding place, or stood their ground and fashioned flags of surrender out of shirt-fronts and napkins. Redcoats hared through the shrubbery, flinging down their weapons and trying to rid themselves of their fancy uniforms. Machine guns nattered among the ornamental palms. From the open hatches of the warship's gondolas spilled spiky, armoured shapes.

"Stalkers!" yelped Wren. She'd never seen a Stalker, had never really quite believed in Stalkers, but something about the way those armoured figures moved was enough to convince her that they were not human, and that she very much wanted to be far away from them. She started to run, calling out to Theo to follow her. "Come on! We'll cut back through the Pavilion to the boathouse!"

The stairways of the Pavilion were deserted now. Wren and Theo climbed them quickly, stumbling over abandoned party hats and trampled bodies. On the sundeck where Shkin had sold her to Pennyroyal Wren slipped in a fallen trifle and went crashing down. The Tin Book, jammed in her waistband, grazed her spine and dug painfully into her bottom. She thought she could feel blood running down inside her trousers as Theo helped her up. She wondered if she should try to get rid of the book. Or surrender it to the Storm, and beg for mercy. But the Storm had no mercy, did they? She'd seen pamphlets and posters since she'd been in Brighton, headlines in the foreign affairs pages of the *Palimpsest* about *More Mossie Atrocities* and *Further Beastliness by the Green Storm*. If they found that Wren had the Tin Book. . .

From the entrance to the ballroom they looked back across the lawns. The battle was over, and Stalkers were moving about down there, herding crowds of captive guests ahead of them. "I wonder if Shkin's down there?" said Wren.

"And what about Boo-Boo?" said Theo, as they pressed on, crossing the ballroom, where the lights on the walls and ceiling had failed and broken glass crunched underfoot. "What about Pennyroyal?"

"Oh, he'll be all right." said Wren. "I bet it was him who brought them here. Shkin said he was looking for a buyer for the Tin Book. That's just the sort of thing Pennyroyal would do, selling his own city for a profit. . ."

They passed the film room, where the projector was still rattling away. By its light Wren glimpsed a movement on the spiral staircase. "Cynthia!" shouted Theo.

Their fellow slave came running down the stairs, her party costume flickering softly with the reflected colours of the film-loop. What she had been doing up there, Wren could not imagine. Perhaps she had got flustered and run the wrong way when everybody was fleeing from the ballroom. Or maybe Mrs Pennyroyal had sent her back to fetch something; she was carrying something shiny in one hand.

"Cynthia," said Wren, "don't be frightened. We're leaving. We'll take you with us. Won't we, Theo?"

"Where is it, Wren?" snapped Cynthia.

"Where's what?" asked Wren.

"The Tin Book, of course." Cynthia's expression was one that Wren didn't recognize; cold and hard and intelligent, as if her face were under new management. "I've already checked Pennyroyal's safe," she said. "I know it was you who took it. I've known you were up to something ever since you came aboard. Who are you working for? The *Traktionstadtsgesellchaft*? The Africans?"

"I'm not working for anybody," said Wren.

"But *you* are, Cynthia Twite," said Theo. "You're with the Green Storm, aren't you? You killed Plovery and the others. It was you who cut Cloud 9 adrift!"

Cynthia laughed. "Ooh, you catch on fast, African!" She made a polite curtsy. "Agent 28, of the Stalker Fang's private intelligence group. I was rather good, wasn't I? Poor, silly Cynthia. How you all laughed at me, you and Boo-Boo and the rest. And all along, I have been working for a different mistress; for one who will make the world green again." She held her arm out stiffly towards Wren. The shiny thing in her hand was a gun.

Numbly, Wren fetched the Tin Book out from beneath

her tunic and held it up for Cynthia to see. Cynthia snatched it and stepped back. "Thank you," she said, with a trace of her old sweetness. "The Stalker Fang will be delighted."

"She sent you here to find it?" asked Wren, confused. "But how did she know. . ."

Cynthia beamed. "Oh no. She believed it was still in Anchorage. She sent an expedition to the place where Pennyroyal said Anchorage went down, but there was nothing there. So I was placed aboard Cloud 9 to spy on him, in case he knew what had really become of it. I could hardly believe my luck when I heard that you had brought the Tin Book itself aboard! I sent a message to the Jade Pagoda at once, and orders came back telling me to leave it safe in Pennyroyal's office until help arrived. It is important. It may be the key to a final victory. My mistress does not want it copied, or sent by the usual channels. She is coming to fetch it in person. That is *her* ship out there on the lawn." She looked down fondly at the Tin Book. "She will reward me well when I give it to her."

The gunfire from the gardens had ceased. Wren could hear voices out on the sun-decks, shouting orders in a language she didn't recognize. She stepped towards Cynthia, wary of the gun in the other girl's hand. "Please," she said, "you've got the Tin Book. Can't you let us go? If the Storm catch Theo. . ."

"They will kill him like the coward he is," said Cynthia calmly. "I'd do it myself, but I'm sure my mistress will want to question you both first, and find out how much you know about the Book."

"We don't know anything about it!" cried Theo.

"That's your story, African. You may decide to change

it, once the inquiry engines get to work on you."

"But Cynthia. . ." Wren shook her head, still numb with the shock of Cynthia's betrayal. "I don't suppose Cynthia's even your real name, is it?"

The other girl looked surprised. "Of course it is. Why shouldn't it be?"

"Well, it's not very spy-ish," said Wren.

"Oh? What's wrong with it?"

"Nothing, nothing. . . Just—"

A bulging suitcase, dropped from the gallery above, hit Cynthia on the head and burst open, scattering gold coins, jewellery and valuable-looking bits of Old-Tech. "Oh—" said the girl, crumpling. Her gun went off, and punched a hole in the ceiling somewhere above Wren's head. Theo grabbed Wren and tugged her backwards, afraid that there might be more luggage to follow, but when they looked up they saw only the round, pale face of Nimrod Pennyroyal peering down over the bannisters.

"Is she out?" he asked nervously.

Wren went to stoop over Cynthia. There was blood in the girl's hair, and when Wren touched her neck she could feel no pulse, but she didn't know if she was feeling in the right place. She said, "I think she might be dead."

Pennyroyal hurried down the stairs. "Nonsense, it was only a playful little tap. Anyway, she's an enemy agent, isn't she? Probably have killed the pair of you if it weren't for my quick thinking. I was just upstairs gathering a few valuables, and I heard you talking." He chuckled as he prised the book from Cynthia's fingers. "What a stroke of luck! I thought I'd lost this. Now come along, help me gather up the rest."

Numbly, Wren and Theo began to do as he asked. Pennyroyal, perhaps afraid that they would try and rob him, picked up Cynthia's gun and held it ready while he stuffed coins and statuettes and ancient artefacts back inside the case and sat on the lid to force it shut. The shouting outside drew nearer as Green Storm soldiers, attracted by the sound of the gunshot, converged on the ballroom. "There!" said Pennyroyal. "Now, ho for the boathouse. I tell you what, if you help me carry this lot, you can both come with me. But hurry up!"

"You can't just leave," protested Wren, trailing after him through the listing corridors while Theo stuggled along with the suitcase. "What about your people?"

"Oh, *them*," said Pennyroyal dismissively.

"What about your wife? She's probably a prisoner by now. . ."

"Yes, poor Boo-Boo. . ." Pennyroyal pushed open a door and led them out into the gardens at the rear of the Pavilion. "I shall miss her, of course – terrible loss – but time is a great healer. Anyway, I can't risk my neck trying to rescue her. I owe it to the reading public to save myself, so that the world can hear my account of the Battle of Brighton and my heroic stand against the Storm. . ."

They hurried through the gardens, Pennyroyal in the lead, Wren and Theo taking turns with the suitcase. The Storm's troops had not reached this part of Cloud 9 yet; nothing moved among the cypress groves and pergola-covered walks. Smoke drifted from the wreckage of the Flying Ferrets' aërodrome, but the Green Storm must have thought Pennyroyal's boathouse an unworthy target, for it still stood unharmed among the trees, bulbous and comical, specks of firelight glinting on its daft copper spines.

"I can hear engines," said Theo, as they made their way through the trees on to the landing apron in front of the boathouse. "Someone's opened the doors. . ."

"Great Poskitt Almighty!" shouted Pennyroyal.

The *Peewit* sat poised in the open doorway, her engines purring as they warmed up for take-off. The lights were on in her gondola, and Wren could see Nabisco Shkin at the controls. He must have given up waiting for her to bring him the Tin Book and decided to cut his losses and save his own skin. She hung back, scared of him, but Pennyroyal put on a last spurt of speed, charging towards the yacht. "Shkin! It's me! Your old friend Pennyroyal!"

Shkin swung himself out through the hatch in the side of the Peewit's sleek gondola and shot Pennyroyal twice with a pistol he pulled from inside his robes. Wren saw an exclamation mark of blood fly upwards into the glare of the yacht's lights. Pennyroyal did an ungainly somersault and crashed against a heap of hawsers and was still.

"Oh gods," whispered Wren. Pennyroyal was so much a part of her life, from all the stories she had heard in Anchorage, that she had imagined he was indestructible.

Shkin stepped down from the gondola and strode towards them with his gun held ready. "Do you have my book?" he asked.

"No," said Theo, before Wren could answer. "The Storm took it."

"Then what's in the suitcase?" asked Shkin, and Theo opened it so that he could see. The slaver smiled his cold, grey smile. "Well, that's something, isn't it?" he said. "Close the case and hand it to me."

Theo did as he was told. Shkin's chilly eyes slid towards Wren again.

"Now what?" she asked. "You'll shoot us, I suppose?"

"Good gods, no!" Shkin looked genuinely shocked. "I am not a murderer, child. I am a businessman. What profit would I make by killing you? It's true you managed to annoy me, but it sounds as if our friends from the Green Storm will soon be arriving to teach you some manners."

Wren listened, and heard harsh foreign voices drifting across the garden. Lights were moving among the trees behind the boathouse. She wanted to ask Shkin about her father, but he had already heaved Pennyroyal's case aboard the *Peewit* and was climbing in after it. The engines roared.

"No!" screamed Wren. She couldn't believe that the gods were really going to let that villain Shkin fly away unscathed. But the *Peewit*'s docking clamps released and she rose from the boathouse floor, engine pods swinging neatly into take-off position. "It's not fair!" howled Wren, and then, "The Book! We've got the Book! Theo lied! Take us with you, and I'll give you the Book!"

Shkin heard her voice, but not her words. He glanced down at her and smiled his faint smile, then turned his attention to the controls again. The yacht sped across its landing-apron, passed between two clumps of trees which bowed aside to let it through, and rose gracefully into the sky.

"It's not fair!" Wren said again. She was sick of Shkin, and sick of being afraid. She understood why Mum and Dad had never wanted to talk about the adventures they had had. If she survived, she would never even want to think about this awful night.

"Why did you lie about the Book?" she asked Theo.

"He might have taken us with him if we'd given him the Book."

"He wouldn't," said Theo. "Anyway, if everybody wants it so badly, it must be something dangerous. We can't let a man like Shkin get his hands on it."

Wren sniffed. "*Nobody* should have it," she said. She walked to where Pennyroyal lay and gingerly fetched the Tin Book out from inside the mayor's torn robes. One of Shkin's bullets had made a deep dent in the cover, but it looked otherwise unharmed. The touch of it disgusted her. All the trouble it had caused! All the deaths! "I'm going to throw it into the sea," she said, and ran with it across the smouldering, cratered airstrip towards the edge of the gardens.

But it was not the sea that she saw when she looked down over the handrail. Cloud 9 had drifted further and faster than she had thought. The white wriggle of surf which marked the coast lay several miles away towards the north, with the lights and fires of the other cities strung out along it like pearls on a necklace. Below her, the hills of Africa lay stark beneath the moon.

And as she stood there, staring at them, clutching the Tin Book in both hands, she heard running feet behind her, and turned to meet the torches and the upraised guns of a squad of soldiers. There were Stalkers too, one of whom seized hold of Theo, and a man who seemed almost a Stalker himself, a hawk-faced man in mechanized armour with a sword in his iron hand, who stepped in front of the others and said, "Don't move! You are prisoners of the Green Storm!"

*

As the Peewit slid out through Cloud 9's rigging into open sky, Nabisco Shkin permitted himself a thin smile of satisfaction. Most of the Green Storm's ships were miles away, still engaged above Benghazi and Kom Ombo, and the troops they had landed in Pennyroyal's garden had better things to worry about than the odd absconding slave-trader.

He settled into the yacht's comfortable seats, and patted the case which lay on the deck beside him. Far ahead he could see the lights of the smaller cities twinkling in the desert night. He would set down on one of those until he was sure the Storm had finished with Brighton; then he would go and see what damage had been done to his business there. The Pepperpot would have been battered, no doubt. Servants and merchandise killed, probably. No matter; they were all insured. He hoped the boy Fishcake was still alive. But even without him, it should be possible to find Anchorage-in-Vineland, and fill the holds of a slave-ship or two. . .

He was still dreaming of Vineland when the raptors found him. They were part of a patrol-flock set to guard the skies around Cloud 9. Shkin thought they were just a cloud as they came sweeping down on him, dimming the moonlight. Then he saw the flap and flutter of their wings, and an instant later the birds started slamming into the *Peewit*'s glastic windows, tearing at her pod-cowlings, slashing her delicate envelope with talons and beaks. Torn-off steering vanes whirled away on the wind. The propellers sliced dozens of birds to scrap, but dozens more kept taking their place until the *Peewit*'s engines choked on feathers and slime. Shkin reached for the radio-set, opening all channels and shouting, "Call off your attack! I am a legitimate businessman! I am strictly neutral!" But the Green Storm warships which picked up his signal did not know where it was coming from, and the birds themselves did not understand. They tore and rent and clutched and worried, stripping the envelope-fabric from its metal skeleton, until Nabisco Shkin, looking up through the bare ribs, saw nothing but a kaleidoscope-churning of bird-shapes circling black and splay-winged against the sacred moon. And as the wreck began to fall, they ripped the roof off the gondola and got inside with him.

Nabisco Shkin was not usually a man who let his emotions show, but there were a great many birds, and it seemed a terribly long way to the ground. He screamed all the way down.

30
CAPTIVES OF THE STORM

The man in the mechanical armour was called Naga. Wren heard his men call him that as they took the Tin Book from her and started marching her back towards the Pavilion. It was a scary sort of name, and he looked pretty scary too, stomping along inside that hissing, grating exoskeleton, but he seemed civilized enough, and told his men off when they prodded Wren with their guns to make her walk faster. She was surprised, and relieved; she'd heard stories about the Storm shooting prisoners on sight. She thought about asking Naga what he meant to do with her, but she wasn't quite brave enough. She glanced at Theo, hoping he'd explain what the Green Storm soldiers were saying to each other in their strange language, but Theo was walking with his head down, and would not look at her.

They climbed one of the Pavilion's outside stairways, past a walled garden where a crowd of captured slaves and party guests had been penned by a company of Stalkers. Boo-Boo Pennyroyal was there, trying to keep everybody's spirits up with a rousing sing-song, but it didn't look to Wren as though it was working.

She assumed at first that she and Theo were being taken to join those other captives; but the soldiers kept them moving, past Pennyroyal's swimming-pool, which had emptied itself across the tilting deck in a broad wet stain. Outside the ballroom windows stood a Stalker far more frightening than the mindless, faceless brutes Wren had seen so far. He was big, and gleaming, and his armoured skull-piece did not extend down to hide his face the way those of the others did, but left it partly bare; a dead, white face, with a long gash of a mouth that twitched slightly as his green eyes lighted on Wren. She looked away quickly, horrified at catching the thing's attention. Was he going to speak to her? Attack her? But he just returned Naga's salute and stepped aside, letting the Stalkers and their captives past him into the ballroom.

Someone had got the lights working again. Medical orderlies were taking Cynthia out on a stretcher. Wren heard her groan as they carried her past, and felt glad that her friend was still alive, then remembered that she had only been a fake friend, and wasn't sure if she should be glad or not.

Up on the podium where the musicians should have been playing, a group of officers had gathered. Naga marched over to them and saluted smartly, making his report. The tallest of them turned to stare at the captives. Her face was a bronze death-mask, pierced by two glowing emerald eyes.

"Oh!" cried Theo.

Wren knew at once that this was the Stalker Fang. Who else could it be? She seemed to exude power; it crackled in the air about her like static electricity, making the small hairs on the back of Wren's neck stand up on end. At her side she could feel Theo shaking as if he were in the presence of a goddess.

Naga said something else, and the Stalker stepped gracefully down from the podium, her eyes glowing more brightly as he drew the Tin Book from a hatch in his armour. Snatching it, she studied the symbols scratched into its cover, and gave a long, shivery sigh of satisfaction. Naga pointed at Wren and Theo and asked something, but the Stalker waved his question away. Settling herself cross-legged in the rubble, she opened the Tin Book and began to read.

"What now?" muttered Theo. "I thought she'd want to question us. . ."

"I think Naga thought so too," said Wren. But it seemed they had been forgotten by the Stalker Fang. The Green Storm troops were watching her, as if waiting for more orders, but she was engrossed in the Tin Book. Naga muttered something to one of his companions. Then a woman – young and pretty, in a black version of the white uniforms the others wore – spoke to him, bowed, and jumped down from the podium, making her way to where the three prisoners waited. "You will please come with me," she said in Anglish.

Wren felt relieved. This person looked less stern than the rest of the Green Storm landing party. *Dr Zero* said the printed name-tag on her uniform, under a pair of squiggly characters which Wren guessed would say the same in Shan Guonese. She looked far too young to be a doctor. Her tilted eyes and broad cheekbones reminded Wren of Inuit friends at home in Anchorage, and that cropped green hair suited her elfin face surprisingly. But there was no kindness in her voice. She took a gun from one of the troopers and levelled it at the two captives. "Outside, please. Now!"

They did as she said. As she herded them out on to the sun-deck Wren glanced up and saw the big Stalker watching her again. What had she done to interest him so? She looked away quickly, but she could still feel that green gaze following her.

Dr Zero motioned with her gun for the prisoners to

cross the sun-deck and go down the stairs, as if she were taking them to join the others in the walled garden. But at the stairs' foot, on a half-moon-shaped terrace out of sight and earshot of the ballroom, she suddenly stopped them and said in her soft, accented Anglish, "What is that thing the Stalker took from you?"

Wren said, "The Tin Book. The Tin Book of Anchorage. . ."

Dr Zero frowned, as if the name were one she had not heard before.

"Isn't it what you came here for?" asked Theo.

"Apparently. Who knows?" Dr Zero shrugged, and glanced back in the direction of the ballroom, lowering her voice as if she feared that her mistress might overhear her. "Her Excellency did not see fit to share with anyone her reasons for attacking your city. What is this Tin Book? What makes it so important that she had to come here with warships to get it?"

"Cynthia said that whoever had the Tin Book could win the war," said Wren.

She was trying to be helpful, but Dr Zero just stared at her. Was it only the moonlight that drained her face of colour? Her eyes were wide, looking through Wren towards some terrible vision of things to come. "Ai!" she breathed. "Of course. Of *course*! The book must be a clue to some kind of Old-Tech weapon. Maybe something like MEDUSA, powerful enough to destroy whole cities. And you have given it to the Stalker Fang! You fools!"

"That's not fair!" protested Wren. "It wasn't our fault. . ."

Dr Zero let out a little laugh, but there was no trace of

humour in it, only fear. "It's up to me now, isn't it?" she asked. "It's up to me to stop her!"

She turned and started to run, back up the stairs towards the ballroom, flinging her gun aside as she went.

31

THE MOMENT OF THE ROSE

General Naga, still angry at being denied a chance to tackle Benghazi and the rest of the cluster, had led his shock-troops off to scour the lower levels of the pavilion, hoping to find some lurking nest of townie warriors who might put up a decent fight. In the ballroom, a few battle-Stalkers stood guard while the Stalker Fang sat reading. The metal pages of the book glowed softly green in the light from her eyes; her steel fingertips, tracing the ancient scratch-marks, made faint clicking sounds.

Shrike waited at the window, watching his mistress, but not really seeing her. He focused instead on the face in his mind; the face of the young girl prisoner whom Oenone Zero had just led away. He was sure, or almost sure, that he had seen that face before – those sea-grey eyes, that long jaw, that coppery hair, had all sent sparks of recognition darting through his mind. And yet, when he tried to match the girl's features to the other faces in his memory, he found none that fitted.

Running feet on the sun-deck. Shrike turned, and sensed behind him in the ballroom the other Stalkers all reacting too, baring their claws in readiness. But it was only Dr Zero.

"Mr Shrike!"

She picked her way towards him between the bodies on the sun-deck. She was trying to smile, but the smile had gone wrong somehow, and turned into a kind of grimace. Shrike sensed her ragged breathing, the quick drumbeat of her heart, the sharp, warning odour of her sweat, and knew that something was about to happen.

For whatever reason, Oenone Zero had decided that this was the moment to unleash her mysterious weapon against the Stalker Fang.

But where was it? Her hands were empty; her trim black uniform left nowhere to hide anything powerful enough to harm a Stalker. He switched his eyes quickly up and down the spectrum, searching in vain for a concealed gun or the chemical tang of explosives.

"Mr Shrike," said Dr Zero, stopping at his side and looking up into his face. "There is something important that I must tell you." Beads of perspiration were pushing their way out through the pores of her face. Shrike turned his head and scanned the ballroom, wondering if she had brought something with her from the *Requiem Vortex* when they first landed. He checked the sun-deck too, looking for hidden devices behind the statues on the balustrades. Nothing. Nothing.

A touch on his hand. He looked down. Dr Zero's fingers were resting lightly on his armoured fist. She was smiling properly now. Behind the thick lenses of her spectacles her eyes were filling with tears.

She said, *"The moment of the rose and the moment of the yew tree are of equal duration."*

And Shrike understood.

He turned and walked quickly away from her into the ballroom. He didn't mean to go; he had not told his legs to move, but they moved anyway. He was Dr Zero's weapon; that was all he had been all along.

"STOP ME!" he managed to shout as he neared the Stalker Fang. Two of the battle-Stalkers leaped forward to bar his path, and with two blows he disabled them both, knocking their heads off and leaving their blind, stupid bodies to stumble about jetting sparks and fluids.

But at least he had warned Fang of what was happening. She turned, and rose to meet him. The Tin Book shimmered in her long hands.

"What are you doing, Mr Shrike?"

Shrike could not explain. He was a prisoner in his own body, with no power to control its sudden, deliberate movements. His arms raised themselves, his hands flexed. Out from his finger-ends sprang shining blades, longer and heavier than his old claws. Like a passenger in a runaway tank, he watched himself charge at the other Stalker.

The Stalker Fang unsheathed her own claws and swung to meet him. They crashed together, armour grating, sparks flashing. From behind the Stalker Fang's bronze death-mask came a furious hiss. The Tin Book fell, snapping its rusty bindings, metal pages bounding across the floor. *This is why I couldn't see the danger,* thought Shrike, remembering Oenone Zero's clever fingers busy in his brain through all those lonely night-shifts in the Stalker Works. Why had he never guessed what she was doing to him? He had looked everywhere for the assassination weapon, but he had never suspected himself. And all this time the urge to kill his new mistress had been embedded in his mind, waiting for Oenone Zero to speak the words that would awaken it. . .

He could hear her behind him, scrambling through the wreckage of the ballroom, shouting out as if to encourage him, *"The moment of the rose and the moment of the yew-tree. . ."*

Breaking free, he drove the blades of his right hand through Fang's chest in a spray of sparks and lubricants. The new claws were good; harder than Stalker-skin. Fang hissed again, her grey robes in tatters, her armour ripped open and running with thick rivulets of the stuff that served her for blood. Oenone Zero was behind her, shouting, "You can't harm him! I built him to kill you, and I gave him the weapons to do it! Reinforced armour! Tungsten alloy claws! Strength you can only dream of!"

Irritated, the Stalker Fang lashed backwards and caught Dr Zero a glancing blow which flung her across the dance-floor. Shrike broke into a run and hit the other Stalker hard, the impact driving her away from the fallen woman, out into the moonlight on the sun-deck. More battle-Stalkers grabbed at him, but he kicked their legs from under them and drove his claws through the couplings in their necks. Necks seemed to be the weak point of Popjoy's Stalkers; their severed heads clattered on the paving like dropped skillets, green eyes going dark. Shrike smashed the flailing bodies out of his way. One of them tangled itself in the rags of curtain hanging inside the shattered windows, and the sparks spraying from its neck set the fabric alight. Flames spilled up the curtain and spread quickly across the ballroom ceiling, their light filling Fang's armour as she scrambled away across the sun-deck, one leg trailing, one arm hanging by a tangle of flexes, dented and leaking like a half-squashed bug.

Shrike wanted to give up this fight. He wanted to go back into the blazing ballroom and help Dr Zero. But his rebel body had other ideas. He strode towards the Stalker Fang, and when she lunged at him he was ready for her, caught her by the head and drove the blades of his thumbs in through her eyes so that the green light died and he felt his claws grate against the machine inside her skull.

She hissed and shrieked and kicked at him, tearing the

armour of his torso – she had blades on her toes, too; he had not forseen that – and he slammed her hard against the balustrade at the deck's edge. Stonework splintered, fragments of pillar and architrave exploding whitely in the moonlight and Fang tumbling through it. Shrike, all his nerves buzzing with the fierce joy of a fighting Stalker, leaped after her.

And Wren? And Theo? Abandoned by their captors, they stood gawping at each other on the crescent terrace, not quite daring to believe that they had been forgotten, and too alarmed by the terrible noises coming from above them to risk a break for freedom. Now fragments of balustrade came showering down around them, and the Stalker Fang and her attacker dropped like spiky comets from the deck above. Huddled against Theo, Wren watched wide-eyed. The clash of Stalker against Stalker was something nobody had seen for centuries; not since the Nomad Empires of the north sent their undead armies against each other back in the lost years before the dawn of Traction, when men were men and cities stayed where you put them.

"But I thought that he was on *her* side," complained Wren.

"Shhh!" hissed Theo urgently, afraid that her words would reveal their presence to the Stalkers.

But the Stalkers had other things on their minds. Fang sent Shrike reeling backwards with a kick, but lacked the strength to follow through; instead, she looked about for an escape route, calling out in her whispery voice for help. She gripped the handrail at the terrace edge, and, as Shrike recovered and struck viciously at her back, heaved herself over and dropped down into the gardens.

Shrike jumped after her. He could hear the shouting of alarmed once-born behind him and, looking back, saw Naga and his men running to the broken balcony, staring down. He ran on, following the trail of oil and ichor that the injured Stalker had left. She seemed at first to be heading towards the *Requiem Vortex*, but she was blind now, and perhaps her other senses were damaged too. Shrike followed the sick machine smell of her, through thick shrubberies, through the green corridors of an ornamental maze, down the steep slope of the park. Against the railings at the brim she turned at bay. The trailing arm hung uselessly, and she barely had strength to raise the other. Her claws slipped and grated like broken scissors.

Filled with pity, Shrike blurted out, "I'M SORRY."

"The Zero woman!" hissed the Stalker Fang. "She is a traitor, and you are her creature. I should have been wiser than to put my faith in the once-born. . ."

With a savage blow Shrike smashed the bronze mask from her face. Her head lolled backwards on damaged neck-joints, and moonlight fell across the face of the dead aviatrix; a gaunt grey face, black lips drawn back from olive-stone teeth, smashed green lamps where eyes should have been. She raised her maimed steel hand to hide herself, and the familiar gesture startled Shrike. Where had he seen it before?

She turned suddenly away from him, awkward and broken, her blind eyes staring up at the stars. "Do you see it?" she asked. "The bright one in the east? That is ODIN; the last of the great orbital weapons which the Ancients set in heaven. It has been waiting up there, sleeping, since the Sixty Minute War. It is powerful. Powerful enough to destroy countless cities. And the Tin Book of Anchorage holds the code that will awaken it. Help me, Mr Shrike. Help me to awaken ODIN and make the world green again."

Shrike severed her neck with three fierce blows, her long scream dying as the head came free.

He pitched her body over the handrail, then picked up the head and the fallen mask and flung them after it. The mask flashed in the moonlight as it fell, and Shrike's rage and his new strength seemed to drain out of him. Jaggedy interference patterns crackled across his mind as the secret instincts Oenone Zero had installed there shut down. Memories came flying at him like bats. He raised his hands to ward them off, but still they came. They were not the calm, sad, human memories that had filled his mind while he lay dying on the Black Island, but just the memories of every terrible thing he had done since he became a Stalker; the battles and the murders, the once-born outlaws butchered for a bounty, the beggar-boy he'd broken once in Airhaven for no better reason than the simple joy of killing. How had he done such things? How had he not felt then the guilt and shame which overwhelmed him now?

And then a scarred face rose in his memory like something surfacing from deep water, so clear that he could almost put a name to it; "H. . . HES. . ."

"There it is!" shouted voices close behind him; once-born soldiers blundering out of the shrubbery. "Stop it! Stop, Stalker, in the name of the Green Storm!" Led by Naga in his clanking battle-armour, the once-born approached cautiously, levelling huge hand-cannon and steam-powered machine-guns.

"Where is she?" Naga demanded. "What have you done with the Stalker Fang?"

"SHE IS DEAD," said Shrike. He could barely see the soldiers; the scarred face filled his mind. "THE STALKER FANG IS DEAD. SHE IS TWICE-DEAD. I HAVE DESTROYED HER."

Naga said something more, but Shrike did not hear. He had a feeling that he was flying apart, dissolving into rust, and all that held him together was that memory, that face. She was the child whom he had saved, the only good thing that he had ever done. "HES. . . HEST. . ."

Forgetting the soldiers, he started to run. Stalkers came at him and he smashed them aside. Bullets danced on his armour, but he barely noticed. Damage warnings flashed inside his eyes, but he did not see them. "HESTER!" he howled, and the gardens swallowed him.

32

THE FLIGHT OF *THE ARCTIC ROLL*

On Ocean Boulevard, beneath a lid of smoke, streamers and paper hats lay in drifts on the tilting pavements, the debris of street-parties that had ended suddenly when the air-attack began.

Tom, Hester and Fishcake crept along in the shadows, trying to avoid the gangs of looters and rebellious slaves who roamed the smashed arcades. Troupes of flames were dancing on the stage of the open-air theatre, and every few minutes the deckplates shook as one of the gas-tanks at the air-harbour exploded, sending wreckage sleeting across the rooftops and prickling the Sea Pool into a thousand white splashes. The elaborate, tattered costumes of dead carnival-goers stirred gently in the night air like the plumage of slaughtered birds.

"They're still rioting on the under-decks," said Tom, listening to the noises that came echoing up the stairwells. "How are we going to get back to the *Screw Worm*?"

Hester laughed. She was still feeling happy and proud at the way she had been able to free Tom from Shkin's lock-ups, and even his insistence on bringing Fishcake with him had not dented her good mood for long. "I forgot!" she said. "Can you believe it? In all the excitement it went clean out of my head. Tom, we don't need the *Screw Worm* any more. After all, we can't fly up to Cloud 9 in a limpet, can we?"

"You mean an airship?' asked Tom doubtfully. "How can we hope to get hold of an airship? They've been pouring out of the air-harbour ever since the battle, and all overloaded by the sound of them."

Hester stopped walking and stood and beamed at Tom, while Fishcake cowered behind him. "The *Jenny Haniver* is here," she said. "In Pennyroyal's stupid museum. She's been waiting for us, Tom. We'll steal her. We used to be good at that."

She explained quickly, and then they hurried on towards the Old Steine. Shouting and the sound of smashing glass came through the smoke, and sometimes shots rang out. The bodies of minor council officials and promising performance artists dangled from the lamp-posts. Hester walked with her gun ready, and Fishcake watched her, and remembered the promise he had made to kill her. He wished he had the nerve to do it, but she scared him too much. And there was something about the way she looked at Tom, a tenderness, that unsettled him and made him think she might not be entirely evil, and that it might be lovely to live with the Natsworthys. Shyly, he took Tom's hand.

"Did you mean it, what you said?" he asked. "About me coming with you? You'll really take me home with you to Vineland?"

Tom nodded, and tried to smile encouragingly. "We just have to make a stop at Cloud 9 on the way. . ."

But when they reached Old Steine, he saw the severed hawsers strewn around the cable-car station. Cloud 9 had gone.

"Oh, Quirke!" he shouted. "Where is it?"

It had never occurred to him that it would not still be hanging there; damaged like the rest of Brighton, but airborne, and with Wren somewhere aboard it waiting to be rescued. Now he saw how foolish he had been. That flying palace with its cloud of gasbags must have been a sitting duck for the Storm's air destroyers.

"Wren. . ." he whispered. He could not believe that the gods had brought her so close to him, only to snatch her away.

Hester took his hand and gripped it hard. "Come on, Tom," she said. "If we can get off this dump we might still find the stupid place, ditched in the sea or adrift. It's Pennyroyal who runs it, remember: he won't have put up much of a fight."

She pointed to the stained white frontage of the *Nimrod Pennyroyal Experience*. The front wall had a few nasty cracks in it and was sagging out over the pavement. The doors had been blown off their hinges, too, and as Hester led Fishcake and Tom inside she began to feel a terrible fear that she was too late, that some other desperate refugee would have come here before her and taken the *Jenny* away. But when she ran up the stairs she found the old airship sitting where she had left her. The glass roof had shattered, scattering shards across the floor and the *Jenny*'s envelope, but she looked completely undamaged. She had actually been cleaned up a bit since Hester last saw her, and a large number *1* had been pasted to her flank ready for the regatta. There were even a couple of small rockets in her rocket-racks.

Behind her, Tom reached the top of the steps and stopped. "Het," he said. "Oh, Het –" Tears ran down his face, and he laughed at himself as he wiped them away. "It's our ship!"

"What a pile of junk!" exclaimed Fishcake, pulling on a coat that he'd taken from one of the waxworks down below.

"Fishcake, see if you can turn the lights on," Tom said, and climbed up into the gondola. The old ship smelled like a museum. He ducked under dangling flexes and ran his hands over the control panels, recognizing the familiar instrument-arrays. Lights came on in the room outside, shining in through the *Jenny*'s freshly squeegeed windows.

"Remember how it works?" asked Hester, behind him. She spoke in the sort of whisper you would use in a temple.

"Oh yes," Tom whispered back. "You don't ever forget. . ." He reached out reverently and pulled a lever. An inflatable dinghy dropped from a compartment in the ceiling and knocked him over. He shovelled it under the chart table and tried another lever. This time the *Jenny* shivered and shifted, and the museum was filled with the rising thunder of her twin Jeunet-Carot engines.

Outside, hands clamped over his ears, Fishcake was coughing in the exhaust smoke and shouting, "How do you get it out?"

"The roof opens," Hester yelled back, pointing upwards.

Fishcake shook his head. "I don't think so. . ."

Tom killed the engines. Leaning out of the *Jenny*'s hatch he looked up at the ceiling. With the lights switched on it was easy to see why no one else had bothered coming in here to steal the *Jenny*. A huge hawser, one of the cables which had once linked Brighton to Cloud 9, had crashed down across the *Nimrod Pennyroyal Experience*, smashing the glass above the *Jenny Haniver* and buckling the delicate struts and girders of the roof.

"Oh, Quirke almighty!" cried Tom. He was starting to get the feeling that his god was playing games with him. If he survived this, he was going to think seriously about finding himself a different deity.

He ran back to the flight-deck, and Hester. "The roof's smashed. We'll never get her out!"

"Someone's coming!" yelled Fishcake, peering from one of the museum windows. "A big gang of them. Lost Boys, I bet, come to see what the noise was about!"

Hester stared through the *Jenny's* nose windows at the roof. "Reckon we could shift that debris?"

Tom shook his head. "That hawser is fatter than the two of us put together. We're trapped in here!"

"Don't worry," Hester said. "We'll think of something." She closed her eye, concentrating, while Fishcake ran from window to window outside, hollering something else about Lost Boys. Then she looked up at Tom, and grinned.

"Thought of something," she said.

She started flipping switches on the long, dusty control desks. The *Jenny Haniver* lurched, throwing Tom backwards. Amid all the racket of engines starting up and docking clamps releasing he didn't realize at first all of what Hester had done. Then, as the shock wave of the twin explosions bowed the windows, as the *Jenny* lifted and surged forward, he saw that she had emptied the rocket projectors into the damaged front wall, blasting it into the street and leaving a hole large enough to let the little airship out into the sky.

"You've forgotten Fishcake!" he yelled, over the long screech of an engine pod grazing the museum wall.

"Oh dear!" Hester shouted back.

"Go back!"

"We don't need him, Tom. Not Wanted On Voyage."

Tom scrambled back to the open hatch and reached out, shouting Fishcake's name. The boy was running towards the lifting gondola, hands outstretched, face white and horrified beneath a clown-mask of powdered plaster. Over the roar of the engines and the dull hiss of the explosion still echoing in his ears Tom could not hear the words, but he didn't need to. "Come back!" Fishcake was shouting, as the *Jenny Haniver* rose through the smoke and dust and swung across an Old Steine full of the startled, up-turned faces of Lost Boys and looters, up into the sky where she belonged. "Don't leave me! Mr Natsworthy! Please! Come back! Come back! *Come back!*"

The *Jenny Haniver* flew on, weaving unsteadily this way and that, because Tom and Hester were struggling with each other at the controls.

"For Quirke's sake!" Tom shouted. "We've got to turn back! We can't just leave him behind!"

Hester pulled his hands free of the steering-levers and flung him aside. He crashed against the chart table and fell heavily, shouting out with pain. "Forget him, Tom!" she screamed. "We can't trust him. And he said the *Jenny* was a piece of junk! He's lucky I didn't knife him!"

"But he's a child! You can't just leave him! What will happen to him?"

"Who cares? He's a Lost Boy! Have you forgotten what he did to Wren?"

The *Jenny* came up suddenly into clear air and moonlight. The smoke lay like a field of dirty snow fifty feet beneath the gondola, with the fire-flecked upper-works of Kom Ombo and Benghazi poking out of it a few miles to larboard. Airships were buzzing about, but none showed an interest in the *Jenny Haniver*.

Hester scanned the sky ahead, and far away towards the south saw the tattered envelopes of Cloud 9. She pointed the *Jenny*'s nose at it, locked the controls and knelt beside Tom. He looked up with an odd expression, and she suddenly realized that he was afraid of her. That made her laugh. She took his face between her hands and kissed him, and licked away the salt tears that had gathered at the corners of his mouth, but he turned his head away. She started to feel afraid herself. Had she gone too far this time?

"I'm sorry," she told him, though she wasn't. "Look, Tom, I'm sorry, I made a mistake. I panicked. We'll turn back if you like."

Tom pulled away from her and scrambled up. He kept remembering the strange smile which had flickered on her face as she led him from the Pepperpot. "You enjoy it," he said. "Don't you? Like when you killed all those people at Shkin's place, you were *enjoying* it. . ."

Hester said, "They were slavers, Tom. They were villains. They were the ones who sold Wren. They *sold* our little girl. The world's a better place without them in it."

"But. . ."

She shook her head and gave a cry of frustration. Why could he not understand? "Look," she said, "we're just little people, aren't we? We always have been. Little small people, trying to live our lives, but always at the mercy of men like Uncle and Shkin and Masgard and Pennyroyal and . . . and Valentine. So yes. It feels good to be as strong as them; it feels good to fight back, and even things up a bit."

Tom said nothing. By the light of the instrument panels she could see a fresh bruise forming on his head where it had struck the chart table. "Poor Tom," she said, leaning over to kiss it, but he twitched away again, staring at the fuel gauges.

"The tanks are only half full," he said. "You knew that when we took off. If we go back we might never reach Wren. Anyway, those slaves will have got poor Fishcake by now."

Hester shrugged awkwardly and wished he'd let her hold him. His obsession with the Lost Boy angered her. Why did Tom have to be so concerned about other people all the time? She controlled herself. "Fishcake will be able to look after himself," she promised.

Tom looked hopefully at her, wanting to believe her. "You think so? He's so young. . ."

"He must be twelve if he's a day. I lived alone in the Out-Country when I wasn't much older than that, and I did all right. And I didn't have his Burglarium training." She touched Tom's face. "We'll find Wren," she promised. "Then we'll find fuel, and go back to Brighton and get Fishcake, when things have calmed down a bit."

She put her arms around him, and this time he did not pull away, although he did not exactly hug her back. She kissed him, and ran her fingers through his thinning hair. She hated fighting with him. And she hated Fishcake, for making them argue like this. She hoped the other Lost Boys were already using his nitty little head for a football.

33
DEPARTURES

Theo and Wren had not waited for the Storm to recapture them. They were running away through the gardens when they heard the Stalker Fang's death-cry echoing between the trees.

"What was that?" Wren wondered, stopping, shocked by the awful, lonely sound.

"I don't know," said Theo. "Something bad, I think."

They ducked into the shrubbery as another Green Storm squad went running past. The soldiers' helmets blinked with orange light. Peeking behind her, Wren saw that the Pavilion was starting to burn.

"Theo! It's on fire!"

"I know," he said. He was standing near to her; near enough that, in the firelight, she could make out the goose pimples on his bare chest, and see that he was shivering slightly in the chilly air. Suddenly he put his arms around her. "You should let the Storm take you, Wren. Cloud 9 is going down. You might be safer as a prisoner. I can't let them take me, but you could. They seemed all right, Naga and that Zero woman. You should go back."

"What about you?" she asked. "I can't just leave you here."

"I'll be all right," he said, and then said it again, trying to sound more certain about it. "I will be all right. This place is sinking slowly. It'll come down in the desert and I'll try and make my way south; there's a static settlement in the Tibesti mountains, south of the sand-sea. Maybe I could make it on foot."

"No," said Wren. She pulled herself away from him,

because when he was holding her her brain stopped working and she found herself wanting to agree with everything he said, but she knew deep down that he was talking rubbish. Even if he survived Cloud 9's fall, setting out across the desert on foot would be suicide. "I'm staying with you," she said, "We're going to find a way off, and that's final. Come on. We'll head back to the aërodrome. Maybe there's a flying machine that's still usable. . ."

She set off through the smoky gardens, feeling unaccountably hopeful and rather pleased with herself, but when they reached the aërodrome again she saw that it had been destroyed more completely than she'd realized. The Ferrets' prefab hangars and barracks had been ripped open and scattered, and of the machines that had been caught on the ground only scorched shards remained. But among the ruins of the summerhouse where she had spoken to Orla Twombley the previous night she found a couple of fleece-lined leather tunics hanging incongrously from a coat-stand which still stood upright and undamaged amid the rubble. That seemed some sort of consolation. She threw one to Theo, who pulled it on gratefully, hanging up his silver wings like an angel banished from heaven.

Snuggling into the other jacket, Wren tried to think of a new plan. "All right," she said. "Maybe we *will* end up in the desert. We'll need water, and food. And a compass would be useful. . ."

Theo wasn't listening. A rustling in the foliage beyond the ruins had caught his attention. He gestured for Wren to be quiet.

"Oh, gods!" she whispered. "Not the Storm again?"

But it was only Nimrod Pennyroyal. Shkin's first shot had slammed against the Tin Book in his robe pocket, breaking several ribs, and the second had grazed his temple, knocking him out and covering one side of his face with blood, but he had regained his senses, and dragged himself down to the aërodrome with the same idea as Wren and Theo, of finding some way off Cloud 9. Looking up plaintively at them from the shrubbery he whispered, "Help!"

"Leave him," said Theo, as Wren went towards him.

"I can't," said Wren. She wished she could. After all the things he'd done, Pennyroyal didn't deserve her help; but not helping him would make her as bad as he was. She knelt down beside him and tore a strip from the bottom of her tunic to bandage his head.

"Good girl," Pennyroyal whimpered, as she worked. "I think my leg's broke, too, from when I fell. . . That devil Shkin! The beast! He shot me! Shot me and flew off!"

"Well, now you know how poor Tom Natsworthy felt," said Wren. Blood soaked through her makeshift bandage as soon as it was in place. She wished she'd paid more attention to Mrs Scabious's first-aid lessons back in Vineland.

"That was entirely different," Pennyroyal said. "It was – Great Poskitt! How do you know about Tom Natsworthy?"

"Because I'm his daughter," said Wren. "What Shkin told you about me was true. Tom's my dad. Hester's my mother."

Pennyroyal made gurgly noises, his eyes bulging with terror and pain. He watched Wren tear another strip of fabric from her clothes, looking as if he expected her to strangle him with it. "Isn't there anybody on this flaming deckplate who is who they say they are?" he asked weakly, and went heavy and limp in Wren's arms.

"Is he dead?" asked Theo, coming up behind her.

Wren shook her head. "It's just a flesh wound, I think. He's fainted. We have to help him, Theo. He saved us from Cynthia."

"Yes, but only so he could get his hands on the Tin Book again," said Theo. "Leave him. Maybe the Storm will find him, and take him with them when they leave. . ."

But behind him, with a roar of aëro-engines, Hawkmoths and Fox Spirits were beginning to rise from behind the trees, casting long shadows on the smoke as they threaded their way out through Cloud 9's rigging. The Storm were leaving already.

Oenone Zero had been dragged out of her dreams by the stink of burning curtains. There was a pain in her head, and when she tried to breathe sharp smoke caught at the back of her throat and made her choke and gasp and roll over on to her back.

Above her, flames were washing across the ornate ceiling of the ballroom in rippling waves, like some bright liquid. She pushed herself up, groping for her glasses, but her glasses were smashed, and the flames were rising all around her. Among them she saw the scattered pages of the Tin Book beginning to blacken.

She plunged through a swaying curtain of fire and out on to the terrace. It was a blur of smoke and firelight and running bodies, and as she reeled through it, looking for the stairs, General Naga barred her way. She backed away from him, tripped over a fallen Stalker and sat down, helpless, in the path of the armoured man.

"Dr Zero?" he said. "This. . . This attack. . . It was your doing?"

Oenone knew that he was going to kill her. She was so full of fear that it came seeping out of her mouth in thin, high-pitched noises. She squeezed her eyes shut and whispered a prayer to the god of the ruined chapel in Tienjing, because although she'd never had much time for gods she thought that He must know what it meant to be frightened, and to suffer, and to die. And the fear left her, and she opened her eyes, and beyond the smoke the moon was flying, full and white, and she thought it the most beautiful thing she had ever seen.

She smiled at General Naga and said, "Yes. It was me. I installed secret instructions in the Stalker Shrike's brain. I made him destroy her. It had to be done."

Naga knelt, and his big metal hands gripped her head. He leaned forward and placed a clumsy kiss between her eyebrows. "Magnificent!" he said, as he helped her to stand. "Magnificent! Set a Stalker to kill a Stalker, eh?"

He led her away from the fire, through staring, flame-lit groups of shocked troops and aviators, out across the lawn towards the *Requiem Vortex*. He took a cloak from someone and wrapped it around her trembling shoulders. "You can't imagine how long I've waited for this day!" he said. "Oh, she was a good leader in those first few years, but the war's dragged on, and she keeps wasting men and ships as if they're counters in a game. How long I've tried to think of a way. . . And you've done it! You've rid us of her! Your friend Mr Shrike has run off somewhere, by the way. Is he dangerous?"

Oenone shook her head, imagining what Shrike must

be going through. "It's hard to know. I suppressed some of his memories to make room for my secret programs. Now that he has fulfilled his duties, those memories will be starting to resurface. He'll be confused. . . Perhaps insane. . . Poor Mr Shrike."

"He's just a machine, Doctor."

"No, he's more than that. You must tell your men to search for him."

Naga waved a couple of sentries aside and climbed the gangplank of the *Requiem Vortex*. Inside the gondola he guided Oenone to a chair. She felt terribly tired. Her own face stared back at her from his burnished breast-plate, smeared with blood and ash and looking naked without her spectacles. Naga patted her shoulder and muttered gruffly, "There, girl, there," as if he were calming a spooked animal. He had a soldier's touch, awkward and unused to gentleness. "You're a very brave young woman."

"I'm not. I was afraid. So afraid. . ."

"But that's what bravery is, my dear. The overcoming of fear. If you're not afraid, it doesn't count." He fetched a flask out of a hatch in his armour. "Here, try some brandy; it will help to steady you. Of course, we won't let anyone know that you were responsible. Officially, at least, we must mourn the Stalker Fang's passing. We'll blame the townies. It'll fire up our warriors like nothing since this war began! We'll launch attacks on all fronts; avenge our leader's fall. . ."

Oenone spluttered at the sharp taste of the brandy and pushed the flask away. She said, "No! The war must stop. . ."

Naga laughed, misunderstanding. "The Storm can still win battles without that iron witch telling us what to do!

310

Don't worry, Dr Zero. We'll do better without her. Blast those barbarian cities to a standstill! And when I take my place as leader you'll be rewarded – palaces, money, any job you like. . ."

Dazed, Oenone shook her head. Watching this armoured man stride about the cramped, battle-damaged gondola, she saw that she had underestimated the Green Storm. War had made them, and they would make sure that the war went on and on.

"No," she said. "That's not why I –"

But General Naga had forgotten her for the moment and was issuing orders to his sub-officers. "Put out a message on all frequencies; the Stalker Fang has fallen in battle. Need for calm and stability at this tragic time, etc etc. In order to continue our glorious struggle against Tractionist barbarism I am assuming supreme command. And prepare the *Requiem Vortex* for departure; I want to be back in Tienjing before one of our comrades tries to seize power for themselves."

"And the prisoners, General?"

Naga hesitated, glanced at Dr Zero and said, "I won't start my reign with a massacre. Bring them aboard. But please tell that Pennyroyal woman to stop singing."

The Stalker Shrike watched from a hiding place among the bushes as the Storm's boarding parties hurried back aboard the *Requiem Vortex*. Someone with a loud-hailer was shouting, "Mr Shrike! Mr Shrike! Come aboard! We are leaving!"

Shrike knew that Dr Zero must have ordered them to find him, and felt grateful to the surgeon-mechanic, but he did not show himself. He had to stay on Cloud 9. The girl he had seen outside the ballroom was not among the prisoners who were being shepherded into the air-destroyer. If she was staying, Shrike would stay. In some way that he did not yet understand that girl was connected with Hester. Perhaps by staying near her he would find Hester again.

34

FINDERS KEEPERS

Fishcake lay in the dunes behind the beach. Numb with cold and betrayal, he watched as Brighton fired up its battered engines and paddled lopsidedly away, the voices of the victorious Lost Boys drifting raucously across the water with the smoke.

He had barely escaped with his life. As the Lost Boys stormed the museum he had run like a hare from the hunt, out of a back entrance and away through the burning streets, sobbing hopelessly, "Mr Natsworthy, come back, come back. . ." until at last he reached the city's stern, and flung himself blindly off an observation platform there, seeking safety in the sea.

The swim to the shore had exhausted him, and he had almost drowned in the surf. Now, tired and frozen as he was, it was time for him to move again. For hungry desert towns were rolling past him through the dunes, and fierce amphibious suburbs were steaming towards him, drawn by the wrecked airships and flying machines that littered the sand and washed in and out on the surf. Fishcake, who had never been near a traction town before, could barely believe how high their wheels towered over him in the smoky air, or how the ground shook and shifted as they went lumbering by. Choking on exhaust smoke and upflung sand, he scrambled away from them and ran into the desert.

He really was a Lost Boy now. He had no idea where he was, nor where he was going. He ran on and on, hour after hour, slithering over dunes, stumbling across dry expanses of gravel and piles of barren rocks. He was scared of the dark and the deep shadows, which were growing deeper still as the moon sank towards the western horizon. At last, on the bank of an empty creek, he collapsed, hugging his damp knees against his chest for warmth and whining aloud, "What's to become of poor little Fishcake?"

Nobody answered, and that was what scared him most of all. Gargle and Remora and Wren had let him down, and the fake Mummies and Daddies had tricked him; Mr Shkin had failed him, and Tom Natsworthy had abandoned him, but he would have rather been with any of them than out here on his own.

The moon gleamed on something that lay nearby. Fishcake, who had been trained to hunt for gleaming things, crept closer without thinking.

A face gazed up at him from the sand. He picked it up. It was made of bronze, and had been quite badly dented. There were holes for the eyes. The lips were slightly parted in a smile that Fishcake found reassuring. It was beautiful. Fishcake held it to his own face and peered through the eyeholes at the westering moon. Then he stuffed the mask inside his coat and moved on, feeling braver, wondering what other treasures this desert held.

A few dozen yards further on his sharp eyes caught a movement down on the floor of a dry watercourse. Nervous as an animal, he edged closer. A severed hand was creeping across the gravel. It appeared to be made of metal. It moved like a broken crab, dragging itself along by its fingers. Flexes and machinery and something that looked like a bone poked out of the wrist. Fishcake watched it, and then, because it seemed to have a sense of purpose about it, he began to follow.

Soon he began to pass other, less lively body-parts; a torn-off metal leg bent the wrong way and draped across a boulder, then a gashed and dented torso. The hand spidered over that for a while, then crept on its way. A few hundred yards further on he found the other hand, still attached to most of an arm, feeling its way towards a slope of gravel and small boulders where stunted acacia trees grew.

And there he found the head; a skeletal grey face cupped in a metal skull, surrounded by a tangle of cables and flexes and ducts. It looked dead, but as Fishcake crouched over it he knew that it had sensed him. The lenses of the glass eyes were shattered but the spidery machinery inside twitched and clicked, still struggling to see. The dead mouth moved. So faintly that Fishcake could barely hear, the head whispered to him.

"I am damaged."

"Just a bit," Fishcake agreed. He felt sorry for it, poor old head. He said, "What's your name?"

"*I am Anna,*" the head whispered. Then it said, "No, no. Anna is dead. I am the Stalker Fang." It seemed to have two voices; one harsh and commanding, the other hesitant, astonished. "*We were taken by Arkangel,*" said the second voice. "*I am seventeen years old. I am a slave of the 4th type, in the shipyards of Stilton Kael, but I am building my own ship and. . .*" Then the first voice hissed, "No! That was long ago, in Anna's time, and Anna is dead. *Sathya, my dear? Is that you? I'm so confused. . .*"

"My name's Fishcake," said Fishcake, a bit confused himself.

"I think I am damaged," said the head. *"Valentine tricked me – the sword in my heart – I'm so cold. . . So cold. . .* No. Yes. I remember now. *I remember.* The Zero woman's machine. . . And General Naga stood by and let it happen. . . I was betrayed."

"Me too," said Fishcake. He could see the twisted fittings around the edges of the skull where the bronze mask had been torn off. He took the mask out of his coat and fixed it back into place as best he could.

"Please help her," the head whispered, and then, "You will repair me."

"I don't know how."

"She – I will tell you."

Fishcake looked around. Bits of the Stalker's body were edging towards him through the sand, homing in on the head. The clutching movements of the fingers made him think of crab-cams he'd repaired for Gargle. "I might be able to," he said. "Not here. I'd need tools and stuff. If we could gather up all your bits and find a city or something. . ."

"Do it," commanded the head. "Then I will travel east. *To Shan Guo. To my house at Erdene Tezh.* I will have my revenge upon the once-born. *Yes, yes. . ."*

"I'll come with you," said Fishcake, eager not to be deserted again. "I can help you. You'll need me."

"I know the secrets of the Tin Book," the head said, whispering to itself. "The codes are safe inside my memory. I will return to Erdene Tezh, and awaken ODIN."

Fishcake did not know what that meant, but he was glad to have someone telling him what to do, even if she was only a head. He stood up. A little way off a torn grey robe flapped from the branches of a bush. Fishcake pulled it free and knotted it into a sort of bag. Then, while the Stalker Fang's head whispered to itself about the world made green again, he began collecting up the scattered pieces of her body.

35

MAROONED IN THE SKY

It seemed very quiet on Cloud 9 once the Storm were gone. The wind still sang through the drooping rigging, the remaining gasbags jostled against each other, and the crash of collapsing floors came sometimes from inside the burning Pavilion, but none of them were human sounds, so they did not seem to matter.

Theo and Wren carried the unconscious Pennyroyal into the shelter of a grove of cypress trees between his boathouse and the ornamental maze. There was a fountain at the heart of the grove, and they laid Pennyroyal down and did their best to make him comfortable. Then Theo sat down and rested his head on his arms and went to sleep too. That surprised Wren. Tired as she was, she knew she was far too scared and anxious to sleep. It was different for Theo, she supposed. He'd been in battles before; he was probably used to this sort of desperate uncertainty.

"Boo-Boo, my dove, I can explain everything!" muttered Pennyroyal, stirring and half opening his eyes. He saw Wren sitting beside him and mumbled, "Oh, it's you."

"Go back to sleep," said Wren.

"You don't like me," said Pennyroyal grumpily. "Look, I'm sorry about your father, I really am. Poor young Tom. I never meant to hurt him. It was an accident, I swear."

Wren checked his bandages. "It's not just that," she said. "It's that book of yours. It's so full of lies! About Miss Freya, and Anchorage, and about my mum cutting a deal with the Huntsmen. . ."

"Oh, but that bit's true," said Pennyroyal. "I admit I

may have spiced up the facts a little here and there, purely for reasons of pacing, but it really was Hester Shaw who brought Arkangel down on us. She told me so herself. 'I'm the one who sent the Huntsmen here,' she said. 'I wanted Tom for myself again. He's my predator's gold.' And, a few months later, among a bunch of refugees from Arkangel, I ran into a charming young person called Julianna. She'd been a slave-girl in the household of that lout Piotr Masgard, and she told me she'd seen the deal done; an aviatrix came to her master with word of Anchorage's position. A young aviatrix, barely more than a girl, with her face split in two by a terrible scar. . ."

"I don't believe you," said Wren crossly, and left him there and went out into the gardens. It *couldn't* be true; Pennyroyal was up to his old tricks again, twisting the truth about. *But why does he insist on sticking to that part of his story, when he's admitted the rest was fibs?* she wondered uneasily. Well, maybe he believed it. Maybe Mum *had* told him that, to scare him. And as for Masgard's slave-girl, just because she'd seen Masgard talking to a scarred aviatrix, that didn't mean it was Mum; the air-trade was a dangerous life; there must be lots of aviatrices with messed-up faces. . .

She shook her head to try and drive the disturbing thoughts away. She had better things to worry about than Pennyroyal's silly stories. Cloud 9 was wobbling beneath her feet, and the night air was filled with the groan of stressed rigging. Smoke poured across the tilted lawns, obscuring scattered bodies and overturned buffet tables. Wren gathered up some fallen canapés and stood staring at the Pavilion while she ate them. It was hard to believe the change that had come over the beautiful building. It was stained and sagging, and the only light that came from its broken windows was the reddish glow of spreading fires. The grand central dome gaped like a burst puff-ball. Above it, the gasbags seemed to be holding, but they were smoke-blackened, and some of the fiercer flames jumping up from the roof of the Pennyroyals' guest wing were getting dangerously close to their underbelly.

And as she stood there watching it, Wren became aware of someone standing nearby, watching her. "Theo?" she said, turning.

But it was not Theo.

Startled, she lost her balance on the steep grass and fell, hiccuping with fright. The Stalker did not move, except to brace himself against the tilting of the garden. He was staring at Wren. How could he do anything but stare, with only those round green lamps instead of eyes? The firelight gleamed on his battered armour and his stained claws. His head twitched. Oil and lubricant dripped from his wounds.

"YOU ARE NOT HER," he said.

"No," agreed Wren, in a shrill little mouse-squeak. She had no idea who the horrible old machine was talking about, but she wasn't about to argue. She wriggled on her bottom across the grass, trying to edge away from him.

The Stalker came slowly closer, then stopped again. She thought she could hear weird mechanisms whirring and chattering inside his armoured skull. "YOU ARE LIKE HER," he said, "BUT YOU ARE NOT HER."

"No, I know, a lot of people get us mixed up," said Wren, wondering who he could have mistaken her for. There was no point running, she told herself, but her body, with its eagerness to go on living, wouldn't listen. She pushed herself up and fled, slithering on the wet grass, careering down the sick slope of the gardens.

"COME BACK!" begged Shrike. "HELP ME! I HAVE TO FIND HER!" He started to run after her, then stopped. Chasing the girl would only add to her fear, and he had already been appalled by the terror and loathing of him that he had seen in that strange, familiar face. He watched her fade into the smoke. Behind him, the Pavilion's central dome collapsed into the ballroom in a gush of sparks. Catherine wheels of debris went bowling past him to crash into fountains and flower-beds or bound off the deckplate's edge entirely and plummet down into the desert.

Shrike ignored them, and tilted his head inquisitively. Above the noise his sensitive ears had picked up the drone of aëro-engines.

Whooping for breath, her heart hammering, Wren plunged back into the cypress grove. Pennyroyal was asleep or unconscious again, but Theo leaped up. "Wren, what is it?"

"*Stalker!*" she managed to gasp. "The Green Storm left a Stalker behind. That big ugly one that fought the other one. . ."

Pennyroyal groaned and stirred. Theo drew Wren gently away. "Wren, if this Stalker had wanted to kill us, it would have found us by now, wouldn't it? It would have chased you, and be here by now."

Wren thought about that. "I think it was damaged," she said.

"There you are then."

"I think it was mad," she went on, remembering the strange way the Stalker had spoken to her. She giggled nervously. "I suppose if ordinary Stalkers are meant to go around killing people, maybe a mad one is the best sort to be stuck on a doomed hovery island thing with. Maybe it just wanted to have a nice chat about the weather. Or knit me a cardigan."

Theo laughed. "Anyway," he said, "it's going to be all right. At the rate we're losing gas we should touch down in the desert in another half-hour or so."

"You say that like it's a good thing."

"It is," said Theo. "Come and see."

She went with him through the trees to the far side of the grove. From there, only a short, steeply tilted stretch of lawn separated them from the deckplate's edge. Beyond the handrail they could see the ground, and Cloud 9's shadow slithering over curved dunes and barren outcroppings of stone. All around, clusters of lights and ghostly fans of dust marked the approach of small towns and villages, racing towards the place where they thought Cloud 9 would fall.

"Scavenger towns!" wailed Wren. "We'll be eaten!"

"Cloud 9 will be eaten," said Theo. "We won't. We'll get off into the desert before the towns arrive, and go aboard them as travellers, not prey. We'll take some gold or Old-Tech or something from the Pavilion to pay our way. We'll be all right."

Wren calmed herself. *This is what brought Mum and Dad together,* she thought. *There's a togetherness that comes from sharing adventures like this, and it's strong enough to overcome anything; mistrust, ugliness, anything.* Not that Theo was ugly. Far from it. She turned her head to look at him and their faces were so close that the tip of her nose brushed his cheek.

And it was then – just when Wren knew that they were about to kiss, and half of her really wanted to, and the other half was more scared of kissing than it was of scavenger towns – it was then that the lawn, like the deck of a boat in a stormy sea, dropped suddenly from beneath her feet, throwing her against Theo and Theo against a tree.

"Bother!" she said.

Bad things were happening up among Cloud 9's corona of gasbags. Roasted by the flames leaping from the Pavilion, the central cell had ruptured and the gas was blurting out in a rush of blue fire. A few of the lesser bags still held, but they were not enough to support the weight of Cloud 9 for long. The deckplate tipped even more steeply, and the water from fountains and swimming-pools poured off the brim in brief white cataracts. Debris fell too; statues and summerhouses, potted palms and garden furniture, marquees and musical instruments dropping like manna on the dunes below.

The brindled towns of the desert increased their speed, jostling and squabbling in their haste to be first at the crash-site.

The *Jenny Haniver* flew through smoke and dust into the shadow of Cloud 9. Through her larboard windows the tilted underside resembled a vast, ruined wall, pocked with shell-craters and burned-out wrecks. Hester turned the searchlight on it and watched as some twisted maintenance walkways slid by, then a warning notice in stencilled white letters ten feet high: NO SMOKING. The cable car swung from severed hawsers, blood-stained ball-gowns and evening-robes billowing from the shattered cabin.

"We're too late," said Hester. "There's not going to be anyone alive up there."

"Don't say that!" Tom told her. He spoke sharply, still feeling scratchy and shaky from their argument. He did not want to argue any more, because finding Wren was what mattered now, but things had altered between himself and Hester, and he was not sure they could be put right. The hardness of her, the calm way she had abandoned Fishcake, made his insides curl.

Angrily, he tugged at the *Jenny*'s controls, swinging her up over the top edge of the deckplate and carefully in through the tangle of rigging. He wished suddenly that Freya was with him instead of Hester. *She* would not have left poor Fishcake behind. *She* would have found some way out of Shkin's tower without murdering all those poor men. And she would not have given up hope of finding Wren so easily.

"Remember London?" he said. "Remember the night of MEDUSA, when I came to fetch you from London? That looked hopeless too, but I found you, didn't I? And now we're going to find Wren."

Below them, Cloud 9 swung like a censer. Hester aimed the searchlight at its ruined gardens.

Dragging Pennyroyal between them, Wren and Theo went crabwise across the steep face of the gardens, looking for a place where they could shelter when the deckplate touched down.

"Good work!" Pennyroyal told them, briefly coming to. "Splendid effort! I'll see that you get your freedom for this. . ." Then he passed out again, which made him impossibly heavy. They laid him down, and Wren sat next to him. The ground was five hundred feet below, perhaps less; Wren could make out individual scrubby bushes struggling to grow among the long crescents of rock that dotted the desert, and individual windows and doorways on the upperworks of a town which was bounding along on big, barrel-shaped wheels in Cloud 9's shadow. The air was filled with the sounds of over-strained rigging. Beneath the long-drawn-out metallic moans another noise was rising. Wren looked up. Through the tangles of hawsers which swayed across the garden the beam of a searchlight poked, dazzling her. Then it swung away, a long finger of light tracing aimless paths across the lawns, and behind it she saw a small airship.

"Look!" she shouted.

"Scavengers," groaned Theo. "Or air-pirates!"

The people in the town below seemed to have the same idea, for a rocket came sputtering up to burst in the sky behind the little ship. It veered away, then came edging back, steering vanes flicking like the fins of an inquisitive fish. A face showed at the gondola window. The steering vanes flicked again, the engine pods swivelled, and the ship touched down on a metal patio, not too close to Wren and Theo, but not so far away that Wren could not recognize the people who climbed out of the gondola and came scrambling towards her across the canted lawn.

At first she refused to believe it. It seemed so impossible that Mum and Dad could be here that she closed her eyes and tried to make the hurtful hallucination go away. It couldn't be them, it *couldn't,* no matter what her silly eyes were telling her; clearly the adventures she had lived through had all been too much for her, and she had started imagining things.

And then a voice cried, "Wren!" and someone's arms went round her and held her tight, and it was her father, and he was hugging her, laughing and saying, "Wren!" over and over, while tears made white channels through the ash and dust that smeared his face.

36
STRANGE MEETINGS

"I'm sorry," she said. "I'm so sorry, I've been so stupid –" and after that she couldn't speak; she couldn't think of a single thing more to say.

"It's all right," Dad kept telling her. "It doesn't matter; you're safe; that's all that matters. . ."

Then Dad stepped aside, and it was Mummy hugging her, a harder, tighter hug, pulling Wren's face against a bony shoulder, and Mum's voice in her ear asking "You're all right? You've not been hurt?"

"I'm fine," sniffled Wren.

Hester stepped back and cupped Wren's face in her two hands, surprised at how much love she felt. She was crying with happiness, and she almost never cried. Not wanting Tom and Wren to think she'd gone soft she looked away, and noticed the tall black boy hanging back behind Wren, watching.

"Mum, Dad," said Wren, turning to pull him closer, "This is Theo Ngoni. He saved my life."

"We saved each other," said Theo shyly. He was crying too, imagining how his own mother and father would welcome him if ever he found his way home to Zagwa.

Hester looked suspiciously at the handsome young aviator, but Tom shook his hand, and said, "We'd better get aboard."

He turned away towards the waiting airship, and Theo went with him, but as Hester started to follow them Wren said, "No, wait; Pennyroyal. . ."

Tom and Theo didn't hear her, but her mother did.

Wren hurried through the trees to the fountain. Pennyroyal, revived by the sound of aëro-engines, was struggling to his feet. He grinned as he saw Wren, and said weakly, "What did I tell you, eh? Never say die!" Then, recognizing the figure who loomed behind her he added, "Oh, Great Poskitt!"

The last time Hester had seen Pennyroyal he had been running away into the snow and dark of Anchorage, the night she killed the Huntsmen. The last time she had spoken to him had been shortly before that, in the ransacked kitchen of Mr and Mrs Aakiuq's house, when she had told him how the Huntsmen came to be there.

Pennyroyal backed weakly away, his face a dead, cheesy white beneath the crusted drizzles of blood. Hester caught him with two swift strides, knocked him down, drew her knife as he grovelled and pawed at her feet.

"Please!" he whined. "Spare me! I'll give you anything!"

"Shut up," said Hester, baring his throat to her blade, bending so the blood wouldn't splash her new coat.

Wren hit her from the side, shoving her away. "Mummy, no!" she yelled.

Hester grunted, winded and angry. "You stay out of this. . ."

But Wren would not stay out of it. She had seen the look in her mother's eye when she saw Pennyroyal. Not hate, or anger, or a thirst for revenge, but fear. And why would Mum be frightened of Pennyroyal, unless the thing that Pennyroyal had said about her was true? As Hester started towards him again, Wren leaped between them, spreading her arms to protect him. "I know!" she shouted. "I know what you did! So if you want to silence him, you're too late! If you want to keep it secret now you'll have to kill me too."

"Kill you?" Hester grabbed Wren by the collar of her jacket and pushed her hard against a tree. "I wish you'd never been born!" she shouted. She turned the knife, changing her grip on the worn bone handle. The blade filled with firelight. Reflections slid across Wren's appalled, defiant face, and suddenly it seemed to Hester very like the face of her own half-sister, Katherine Valentine, who had died defending her from their father's sword.

"Mummy?' asked Wren, in a tiny, shocked voice.

Hester lowered the knife.

Tom and Theo came hurrying through the trees, slithering down the steep lawn. "What's happening?" shouted Theo, who was in the lead. "Wren? Are you all right?"

"She's trying to kill him!" Wren had sunk to her knees. She was crying so much that they could hardly make out her words, but she kept repeating them until they understood. "She wants to kill Pennyroyal!"

Tom looked down at Pennyroyal, who raised a trembly hand.

"Tom, my dear fellow, let's not be hasty. . ."

Tom didn't answer for a moment. He was remembering how it had felt to lie on his back in the snow of Anchorage, sure that he was about to die. He could still feel the hole in his chest, and taste the blood. He could still hear the fading throb of the *Jenny*'s engines as Pennyroyal made off with her. For a moment he felt as fierce as Hester, ready to seize the knife himself and finish the old scoundrel. But the feeling passed quickly, and he reached for his wife's hand. "Het, look at him. He's old and helpless and his palace is going down in flames. Isn't that revenge enough? Let's get him aboard the *Jenny* quickly, before this place sinks any lower."

"No!" shouted Hester. "Have you forgotten what happened last time we let him aboard? Have you forgotten what he did to you? He nearly *killed* you! You can't just *forgive* him!"

"Yes I can," said Tom firmly. Kneeling beside Pennyroyal he nodded to Theo to help lift him. "What's the alternative? Murder him? What would that achieve? It wouldn't change anything. . ."

"It would," said Wren, and there was such an odd sound to her voice that Tom looked up at her. She was crying with big, unladylike sobs, her face wet with snot and tears. She scrambled away fearfully when her mother turned towards her, and shouted out, "If she kills him, he won't be able to tell you how she sold Anchorage to the Huntsmen."

Hester jerked her head as if the girl had hit her. "Lies!" she said. She tried to laugh. "Pennyroyal's been filling her up with his lies!"

"No," said Wren. "No, it's true. All these years everybody's been so grateful to her for saving us from the Huntsmen, when all along it was her who brought them down on us in the first place. I wanted it not to be true. I told myself it couldn't be. But it is."

Tom looked at Hester, waiting for her to deny it.

"I did it for you," she said.

"Then it's true?"

Hester took a step backwards, away from him. "Of course it's true! Where do you think I went to, that night

330

I took the *Jenny*? I flew straight to Arkangel, and told Masgard where he'd find Anchorage. It was that or lose you, and I couldn't have – I couldn't have –! Oh, Tom, for the gods' sakes, it was sixteen years ago, it doesn't matter now, does it? Does it? I sorted it out, didn't I? I killed Masgard and his men. And I only did it for you. . ."

But it had been a different Tom Natsworthy whom she had loved enough to betray whole cities for. That Tom had been a brave, handsome, passionate boy who might have forgiven her, but this older Tom, this timid Anchorage historian who stood staring at her with his stupid mouth hanging open in dismay and his stupid daughter snivelling beside him, would never understand what she had done. Neither of them would. She was nothing like them. She had been a fool to believe that she could live in their world.

"All these years," she said, flinging her knife away. "All these years in Vineland," she said, watching it flash as it stuck quivering in Pennyroyal's lawn. "All these years with you both. . . Gods, I've been so *bored*!"

She was shaking, and it made her remember the night of MEDUSA, when she first dared to kiss Tom. She had shaken uncontrollably then, back at the beginning of it all, and here she was shaking again as it all came to an end. She turned and walked quickly away from him across the ruined gardens. Through a gap in the smoke ahead she saw something loom square and low. She thought it was a building, then realized it was some sort of stupid maze. Well, it would do. She strode fast towards the entrance.

"Hester!" shouted Tom, behind her.

"Go!" She glanced back. He was scrambling after her, a frantic silhouette against the blaze of the Pavilion,

Wren hanging back behind him with her African boy. "Go!" she shouted, turning without stopping, walking backwards for a pace or two, pointing at the *Jenny Haniver*. "Just get Wren aboard and go, before Pennyroyal nicks the bloody thing again. . ."

But Tom only shouted again, "Hester!"

"I'm not coming, Tom," she said. She was crying. Smoke blew past her, and burning scraps of envelope fabric, and the hot wind raised the skirts of her coat like black wings, and she looked like some terrible angel. "Go back to Vineland. Be happy. But not with me. I'm staying here."

"Hester, don't be stupid! This place is falling apart!"

"It's just falling," said Hester. "I'll survive. There are towns below; hard desert towns, scav-platforms. My kind of place."

He had almost caught her up. She could see his face shining with tears in the light from the blazing buildings. She wanted very badly to go to him, to kiss him and hold him, but she knew that she could never touch him again, because what she had done would always come between them. "I love you," she said, and turned and ran, plunging into the maze while the deckplates pitched and reared beneath her, and sounds that were half sobs and half laughter came out of her mouth without her meaning them to. Behind her, fainter and fainter, she heard Tom shouting her name. Overhead, Cloud 9's gas-bags were igniting one by one, filling the maze with weird, racing shadows. Hester sobbed and stumbled, the hedges scratching her face as she blundered into them. She was just beginning to realize that this was a bad place to be, that she would need better shelter than this when the deckplate came down, when she reached the

332

heart of the maze. Something crouched there, as if it had been waiting for her all along.

She came to a stop, skidding on the grass. The waiting shape unfolded itself and stood up, towering over her. She thought at first that it was made of fire; but that was just the reflections from the burning gasbags shining in its dented, burnished armour. Its dead face widened into a smile. Hester knew that face; she had shovelled earth over it herself, eighteen years ago on the Black Island, burying the old Stalker deep and piling stones upon his grave. It seemed she'd been wasting her time, though. She could smell the familiar smell of him; formaldehyde and hot metal.

"Hester?" called Tom's voice, faintly, away in the gardens somewhere and lost to her now for ever.

And Shrike reached for her with his dreadful hands and said, "HESTER SHAW."

Another gasbag went up with a roar, a geyser of light escaping into the sky. Tom found himself airborne for a moment as the deckplate dropped. He hit the grass hard, rolled, and came to a stop against a statue of Poskitt. "Hester!" he shouted as he scrambled up, but his voice was cracking with the effort, and then his heart seemed to crack too. He kneaded his chest, but there was no relief; he was on his knees; on his face; pain nailed him to the lawn. He blacked out, and when he woke someone was with him. "Hester?" he mumbled.

"Daddy. . ." It was Wren, her hands on his back and his shoulders, her face looking down at him, tearstained and frightened.

"I'm all right," he told her, and it was true, the pain was passing, though he felt sick and giddy. "It's happened before. . . It's nothing."

He tried to stand, but Wren's friend Theo came and picked him up, lifting him with barely an effort. He must have lost consciousness again as Theo carried him back across the gardens, because he thought that Hester was with him, but when he looked round she wasn't, and they were already at the *Jenny*'s open hatchway, Pennyroyal peering out at them from the flight-deck windows. It was confusing, especially with the whole garden tilting and swaying like this, and the only thing he could be sure of was Wren, who was holding his hand very tightly and trying to smile at him, though she was crying at the same time. "Wren," he said, "we can't go; we have to find your mother. . ."

Wren shook her head, and helped Theo heave him aboard. "We're going to get you away from this awful place before it's too late," she said.

The hatch closed, and as Theo went forward to the flight deck to help Pennyroyal start the engines Wren knelt over her father, holding him the way that he had held her when she was a very little girl, when she was sick, or frightened. "There, there," he used to whisper to her, and so she whispered, "There, there," and stroked his hair, and kissed him, until he was calm again. And she tried not to think about Mum, and the things that Mum had done, and said, and the trembling light that had shone from the blade of Mum's knife. She tried to remember that she did not have a mother any more.

*

How she had aged!

Shrike had thought he understood the once-born and the things time did to them, but it was still a shock to see his poor child's lined and weather-beaten face, her beautiful red hair turning coarse and grey. He reached towards her, sheathing his claws, and she reacted in the way most once-born did when the chase was done and there was no escaping him; that wordless keening, and the sudden hot stink as her bowels emptied. It hurt him that she was afraid of him. He pulled her close as gently as he could and said, "I HAVE MISSED YOU SO MUCH."

And Hester, crushed against his dented armour, could only shudder, and weep, and listen to the saddest sound she'd ever heard; the dwindling roar of twin Jeunet-Carots as the *Jenny Haniver* took off without her.

And Cloud 9 touched down at last, first the dangling cable car ploughing into the sand like a drag anchor, then the edge of the deckplate catching on a reef of rocks. Catwalks torn from the underside went striding end-over-end across the dunes; smashed flying machines and uprooted trees spilled down into the desert. A hawser snapped; a sagging gasbag broke free and fell upward, soaring through smoke and dust. Whole sections of the Pavilion burst, shedding antiques and *objets d'art* like shrapnel. Stairways crumpled; sundecks buckled; swimming-pools imploded. Cloud 9 bounced, slicing the top off a gigantic dune. Candy-coloured domes bowled off across the desert, pursued by greedy townlets. The wreckage crashed down again, belching fire, trailing cables and collapsing gasbags;

crashed and skidded and spun and slewed and shuddered to a stop.

There was a time of silence, broken only by the mineral sigh of a billion grains of up-flung sand sifting gently down. And in that silence, before the scavenger towns came roaring in to gobble up the wreckage, the Stalker Shrike stood up, and lifted Hester in his arms, and walked away with her into the desert, and the dark.

ACKNOWLEDGEMENTS

The lines from *The Four Quartets* from *Collected Poems* by T. S. Eliot are reprinted by permission of Faber and Faber Ltd.

The story is continued in

A DARKLING
PLAIN